CREATING
KATHRYN CROWN

To our mother, our sisters, and friends for their love and support.

Prologue

The odor of death, hot and coppery, melded with the humidity and swept through the room, carried on the dense sea breeze. A last ray of sunlight breached the open French doors and cut a swathe across the beige carpet to illuminate an area in the deep shadows. In the fading light, the woman could see a body on the floor next to the brown sofa, abundant silver curls haloed in a pool of blood, the battered face half hidden by the approaching night. Bile rose in her throat causing her to almost gag.

Car keys clutched tightly in her hand, she hid outside the room's entrance, gripped her purse to her chest, and hugged the door frame praying to remain unseen. Just when she thought escape was within her grasp, a dark form catapulted out of the gloom and charged across the room toward her. She screamed, turned and bolted. Each footstep echoed as she raced down the hall past a wall mirror. The glass briefly captured the image of a shocked white face with a mane of long dark auburn hair.

She fought the front door's brass knob, twisting it violently, and succeeded in jerking the door open to tear down the flagstone steps to the car parked in the curved driveway. Thank God she had forgotten to lock the driver's door. Once behind the wheel, she hit the lock button, rammed the key into the ignition and turned it. The engine roared to life. Rubber tires screamed as she barreled down the quiet street to the highway and toward the bridge.

Eyes wide with fear, she kept glancing in the

rearview mirror to see twin globes of bright light rapidly gaining on her. She rammed her foot down on the accelerator. The Mustang shot forward at eighty, then ninety miles per hour. The speedometer continued to climb. One last time she took her eyes off the road to check the rearview mirror. That was the final act she committed before the scream of metal against metal and her world was devoured by darkness.

Chapter One

Jerked awake, the horror of the nightmare fresh in her mind, Kathryn raised up on one elbow. She took a deep breath and waited for the pounding of her heart to slow and calm the stark fear ripping through her. Shaking and drenched in a cold sweat, with a handful of bedcovers clenched over her mouth to smother an outcry, she glanced around the dark room. With the edge of the cotton sheet, she wiped her face and shivered against the terror gripping her mind.

"Dream, just a dream," she reassured herself, then settled deeper into the mattress and pulled the blanket up over her arms. In vain she tried to keep her eyelids from closing as her mind slid into that realm between sleep and consciousness. The nightmare began to fade, but it left her with an uneasy impression that someone had just left her bedside. The urge to flip on a lamp and plunge from the bed filled her, but she couldn't move. Exhaustion bound her to the mattress. After all, it was only a dream, just another nightmare like the others. She was safe and secure in her condominium.

Absently, she rubbed her chest and licked her dry lips. Pain arced from the back of her head to settle behind her eyes. She clutched her head and moaned as a wave of nausea assaulted her. Taking deep breaths, she fought against the churning of her stomach. Nothing stopped the urge to vomit. Over the bedside she leaned, knowing she would never reach the wastebasket in time. Strong arms gave support to her slight frame, and a deep male voice kept repeating the same soothing phrase.

"It's all right. I'm here. I'll stay with you." A

calloused hand brushed the hair back from her face, and a warm damp cloth wiped her mouth.

"Robert?" she mumbled. Her eyes refused to stay open. "What happened? Why are you here?" No answer came as she drifted back to sleep.

Sometime in the wee hours of the morning, she awakened. Her mind was a little clearer, but her mouth was filled with a bitter taste. The dream and the man forgotten, she lay quietly thinking. Today was D-day, her divorce would be final. The papers were signed and she, at last, would be free of Robert Cantree and could put her life back on track.

The stupid things women did in the name of love would be almost laughable if it weren't so sad. Most women fell for Robert. She had, for a while anyway. She really shouldn't beat herself up about it. Robert could exude more charm and manners than any man she had ever met. Then reality struck.

Marrying Robert was not the worst mistake of her life. No, not the worst, but it ranked near the top. Her entire life was one mistake after another, piled on top of the other, until at times; she couldn't breathe from the memories.

She let her eyes shut and listened. The sounds of a new day soothed her, quieting the demons of nightmares and memories, giving her the courage to face whatever happened. Today she heard nothing. Not the raucous cry of the gulls as they winged their way along the shore, no papery sound of palm fronds swaying in the breeze. No warm salty breeze drifted through the room from the screened balcony door. Instead, a faint, sharp odor permeated the air. She wrinkled her nose. Unease furrowed her brow as she opened her eyes.

A faint light began to flicker through the blinds sending eerie shadows jumping up and down on the walls. The sky continued to brighten from black to pearl gray. Dawn arrived. Sunlight always chased away her mental gloom. She focused. The shadows had disappeared, bringing the room into sharp clarity. Puzzled, she looked around. This definitely was not her apartment.

This was a hospital room. Two chairs were placed before the tall windows. One was a padded metal chair with arms, the other, an upholstered recliner. Grayish blue paper covered the walls, and a wide border of yellow roses wound around the room just below the ceiling. On the bedside table stood a plastic water pitcher, a Styrofoam cup and a vase holding a single red rose.

She sat up and pushed the hair back from her face. Her fingers found a bump on the right side of her scalp. She winced, as her touch sent another shot of pain through her head. It was not a large knot, but big enough to let her know it was there and it was not bandaged, so no skin was broken. She felt a tugging pain, and her eyes dropped to the narrow bed. Held in place by tape, a capped needle protruded from the back of her right hand. She ignored the pain, more concerned as to why she was in a hospital. Had she been in an accident? The knot on her head would indicate so.

Thinking back to the previous evening, she remembered leaving her apartment and driving down

Gulf Boulevard to pick up her grandmother for dinner. The sky was blue, the clouds puffy, and the sun hot. That was it. Her memory stopped at that point. She did not remember turning onto the Bayway or going through the toll booth. Nor could she remember arriving at her grandmother's house on Tierra Verde, or even dropping her off and going home.

What had happened? A faint memory, a shadow, struggled to penetrate the fog in her brain. She rubbed the back of her neck to ease the tightening muscles. A glimmer of a scene came through, a vehicle slamming against some object. That was it. For some reason, that memory made her afraid, and she did not know why.

Her mind raced with questions. How long had she been here? Did her parents know where she was? She could not have been in the hospital long. Someone had been to visit. They had left the rose. Nothing else in the room indicated Grandmother Abby had been to visit. If she had, the place would be filled with flowers and cards. That was Abby's way, always there to cheer her up.

She threw back the blanket and inched past the left side rail to let her feet dangle over the side of the bed. Every muscle protested as she tried to stand. She clung to the railing for support as another wave of dizziness assailed her. Determined, she waited for it to pass.

When her bare feet hit the floor, the cold tile sent a chilly draft swirling about her bare legs. Chill bumps raced up her spine as she reached behind and felt nothing but her own bare backside. Great, she thought a hospital gown, open back and all.

Holding on to the rail, she picked up the phone receiver on the nightstand next to the window and then wedged back to sit on the side of the bed. The instructions for an outside line were simple, so she dialed Abby's phone number. Apprehensive, she waited for the line to ring. A rapid busy signal was all to be heard. Again she tried the number. It was the same. At last, she dialed the operator.

"What city are you calling?" a woman's voice asked.

What a weird question, Kathryn thought, but said, "St Petersburg."

"What state, please?" the woman inquired.

"Florida of course." The call was becoming creepy.

"I'll connect you with a long distance operator."

"But it's a local number." What the hell is going on, Kathryn wondered and frowned? A cold feeling of dread washed over her.

"What is the number, please?" the woman insisted.

Kathryn gave her the phone number. This was ridiculous.

"I'm sorry, that is not a Colorado Springs number," the woman said, and again, "Would you like to be connected to the long distance operator?"

Icy fear gripped Kathryn as vertigo swept over her. "What city did you say?" The woman repeated it. Stunned, Kathryn ended the call and let the receiver drop to the floor. Anxiety knotted her stomach as she raised a trembling hand to open the blinds wider. Nothing could have prepared her for the view outside the window. Instead of the blue waters of the Gulf of Mexico, her eyes were assaulted by a blinding reflection of sunlight on white. Snow!

Her mind fought to comprehend what her eyes were seeing. Where there should have been palm trees, instead stood snow-covered pines, their boughs glistening and bent with the weight. She looked down at the street below. Men and women, bundled in coats and scarves, fought to stay upright as they made their way down slick sidewalks. In the distance, she could see mountains, their peaks also white.

The reality of the scene hit her. She was two thousand miles from home and in a strange city. It was difficult for her mind to accept the indisputable evidence. How long she stood transfixed, she had no idea. Suddenly the sun flashed off a car windshield. She stumbled back to sit on the edge of the bed rocking back and forth.

"I've lost my mind," she cried. "That's it. I've gone flipping nuts!" She clamped a hand over her mouth to stop a hysterical giggle. Although why she felt the need to laugh was beyond her. Cry. Scream. Sure, but giggle?

"It has to be this headache," she muttered to the empty room. "The pain is causing me to hallucinate. Things like this just don't happen," she whispered, peering out the window. "People don't go to bed in one place and wake up in another." In the space of a few minutes, she had gone from one nightmare to another. It was all real.

Kathryn cried out in panic and groped for the bell cord, repeatedly pressing hard on the button. The door to the room burst open; a nurse rushed to her side catching her before she slipped to the floor. The woman helped her back into bed.

"You stay in bed, young lady," she scolded and began adjusting the sheets and fluffing the pillow. "Justin Crown will have my head if anything happens to you."

As the nurse tried to cover her with the blanket, Kathryn cried out, "What am I doing here? What has happened to me?"

Calmly, the nurse answered, "Now, Mrs. Crown, you're going to be fine. Dr. Otis will be here shortly," she said, ignoring Kathryn's questions.

Hands shaking, she fought to control the panic. Kathryn insisted, "How can everything be fine? I'm not supposed to be here. What am I doing in Colorado Springs?"

The nurse stared at her. "Why, Mrs. Crown, you're at the Colorado Springs Medical Center. You were brought here after your accident last night." The nurse paused, watching Kathryn's face. Trying to reassure her, she continued. "Your husband should be arriving any moment. I'm sure he can tell you more about the accident than I."

Kathryn could not believe her ears. Husband! Robert? "I'm divorced. I don't have a husband," she stormed.

"But, Mrs. Crown," she never finished.

"Stop calling me Mrs. Crown!" Kathryn

exploded. "That is not my name." The nurse looked confused and backed away. Kathryn rubbed her forehead in an attempt to ease the pounding. She had to think. Nothing made sense, not this strange city, not the nurse, not even the name of the hospital. If she had wrecked her car, how did she get here from St. Petersburg?

"Good morning, Kathryn," a pleasant male voice interrupted. She looked up. A tall, slender man, with a white lab coat over a dark suit, stood beside the bed. His silver hair contrasted with the weathered tan of his face.

"Who are you?" she demanded and gestured toward the nurse. "Would you please tell this woman I am not this Mrs. Crown she keeps referring to? I am not married. Please tell me why I am in Colorado."

"Dr. Otis," the nurse began.

Seeing the fear on his patient's face, he shook his head as a caution to the other woman. "What do you mean, Kathryn? Why do you say you're not Kathryn Crown?" He watched in surprise as Kathryn bent her knees and huddled on the bed.

The doctor and nurse were staring at her as if she had lost her mind. Maybe she really had gone crazy and had been committed to a nut house. If she were in an asylum, it would make her father happy. But, this was worse than any nightmare she could imagine. As the doctor moved toward the bed, Kathryn ordered, "Stop. I don't know you."

Stunned, he frowned and stopped. "Kathryn, I'm not going to hurt you," he said, backing away. "What's wrong?"

"I want to know how I got here." Her insides were quivering. What was wrong with these people? Why couldn't they just answer a simple question?

The man moved to stand at the foot of the bed. Her outburst was a definite shock. He considered his next words carefully. Before he could begin to explain, a deep masculine voice sounded from the doorway.

"How's she doing this morning, Dan?" A tall man entered the room with an effortless stride.

Kathryn looked at him, puzzled. Who was this addition to her nightmare? His rugged face was handsome in a sharp-edged way. Deep blue eyes regarded her with concern, and when he smiled the corners of his eyes crinkled with fine laugh lines. His nose appeared to have been broken at one time. Though it was slender, a crook below the bridge gave him a hawkish appearance. A neatly trimmed mustache grew above well-defined lips but, his thick, unruly mass of black hair, peppered with gray at the temples, managed to soften his features.

A dark blue flannel shirt and faded jeans accented his muscular body. Western boots added to his over-six-foot height. In one hand, he carried a Stetson by the brim, and a heavy sheepskin coat draped over his arm. Casually, he tossed it in one of the chairs and placed the hat on top. He gazed at Kathryn and leaned forward, his hands gripping the bed's footboard for support.

As Dr. Otis hesitated, the stranger turned then sat down in the vacant chair to study the doctor's face.

"Okay, Dan, what's going on?" He folded his arms across his chest and waited for the bad news.

"Justin, Kathryn is physically fine, but there

appears to be a different problem." Dr. Otis arched an eyebrow, but before he could explain, Kathryn exploded.

"Who are you people?" She looked from one to the other, ignoring the nurse who remained nearby. "Would one of you tell me how and why I'm in Colorado?" Her control almost gone, her voice rose. "What do I have to do to get an answer?" Kathryn's self-control exhausted, rage took its place. "I wake up in a strange hospital, in a city I've never visited in my life, and I can't find out why." She scooted off the bed on the side closest to the door. A death-grip on the bed rail for support, she let anger help combat her fear. "Damn you! What happened to me?"

Shock registered on Justin's face. He turned to Dan. "What is she talking about?"

The two men and the nurse stared at her confounded and concerned. "Kathryn, please calm down. I'll try to answer your questions," Dan said. He moved toward her only to watch as she sidestepped out of his reach.

"Don't touch me!" she ordered and moved farther away.

Justin started to stand but was stopped by the fear he saw in her eyes. The doctor retreated to stand by the chair to give her time to regain her composure.

Eyes filled with mistrust, Kathryn sat on the edge of the bed and glared at them. "I'm calm, but I want answers," she said, but her breathing was still rapid, and in truth, she was anything but calm. But where was there to run. She was physically unsteady, and her head continued to pound.

"Since you don't appear to recognize me, I'll introduce myself. I'm Dan Otis, your doctor, and your friend. I'm also a longtime friend of your husband," he pointed to Justin, "Justin Crown. So you have nothing to be afraid of."

"He is not my husband." Where did these people get the idea she was married to this man? "He is not my husband," she repeated, daring them to disprove it.

Dan placed a hand on Justin's shoulder and pushed him back into the chair. "Relax," he told him. "Kathryn, can you tell me your name?"

Her control began to slip. Even with Dr. Otis' assurance that she had nothing to fear, she did not like his questions. She dreaded his answers even more. Taking a deep breath, she exhaled slowly and said, "Kathryn Fowler Blanding."

"You said you're not married."

"I'm divorced, or any way I think I am."

Justin sat in stunned silence as Dan continued. Would you tell me what month and day this is?" This morning was filled with surprises, and this was the biggest one of all.

"It's supposed to be my birthday, October twenty-fifth. But, with the snow outside the window, I don't believe it's October. I remember a car accident. Have I been in a coma?" Had she even made it to her birthday dinner with Abby, she wondered?

"No, not a coma," he said. So far, Kathryn's answers were what Dan was expecting. "You say your last name is Blanding? Is that your maiden name?"

"Yes. Why are you asking these questions? I

don't have amnesia. I know who I am." Kathryn didn't like the way the two men kept glancing at each other as if they shared a secret. She also disliked the placating tone the doctor was using to ask his questions.

"Bear with me for a moment. What is the year?" Dan was not surprised by her answer.

"For heaven sakes, the year is 2014. I told you, I don't have amnesia. Why do you keep questioning me as if I do? And why do you think I'm married to that man?" her anger still evident as she pointed to the cowboy.

"Oh, good Lord," escaped from Justin. He refused to remain silent and let that statement pass. "Because that's my ring on your finger, Kathryn," he shouted. "I bought it. You know damn well, I'm your husband. And who the hell is this Robert you were muttering about during the night?"

Kathryn's eyes widened. "No!" she yelled back. "You're not my husband! I have never seen you before in my life." She stared at the diamond wedding band on her left hand. It couldn't be true. She started to shake. This was all such madness.

Seeing her shocked expression, Dr. Otis admonished Justin. "If you want to stay in this room, keep quiet and let me handle this." Calmly, he tried to defuse the statement blurted out by Justin. "Ignore what he said."

Ignore what he said, how could she? His words kept reverberating in her brain. She could not have made another mistake and gotten remarried? Was this madness something her father had cooked up? Or, had she really lost her mind.

"Did my father put you up to this? Did he pay you to kidnap me and perpetrate this insanity? I know he wanted to be rid of me, but even he couldn't be this cruel." Dear Daddy had to be behind this charade. That was the only thing that made any sense. But why Kathryn wondered? Lately, she had made a point of staying away from him and her mother just to avoid any trouble.

Dan watched as her eyes darted back and forth between him and Justin. "We don't know your father, Kathryn. No one has kidnapped you. For now, focus on me, not Justin, or anything else," he said and was relieved when she turned her gaze back to him. "I want you to tell me where you live." If he was able to get her to talk, maybe he could understand what had happened to her.

Her voice faltered as she forced herself to keep her eyes glued to the doctor's face. "I have a condo on St. Pete Beach in Florida." Kathryn shuddered. She thought of her parents and Grandmother. Abby must be out of her mind with worry.

Dan noted how her skin had paled and she was holding her body rigid.

"I don't feel well." Her voice was barely audible. A wave of nausea rose in her throat. She pushed the doctor aside and rushed into the bathroom. The violent retching sent searing pain through her head until she thought she would pass out. Relief was a cold damp cloth pressed against the back of her neck, while a warm hand held her hair away from her face. The heaving stopped. She pulled the washcloth away from her neck and wiped her face, but continued to lean over the basin holding onto the sink for support.

"Thank you, she muttered, not attempting to look up.

"Feeling better?" he asked.

She was surprised it was Justin Crown who had followed her into the bathroom. "Yes, thanks." She let the water flow for a moment, then rinsed her mouth and splashed water on her face while he continued to hold her hair out of the way. A towel was placed in her hands. She dried her face, lowered it and stared at her reflection in the mirror.

Her own mirrored image was more terrifying than the nightmare; more horrifying than waking in a strange city. She did not want to believe what she was seeing, but her reflection did not lie. The face of a stranger stared back at her.

A blood-curdling scream boiled up and exploded from her throat. Her knees buckled. Strong arms lifted and carried her to the bed. Striking out wildly at the offered comfort, she screamed, "What have you done to my face?" She dissolved into tears and buried her head in the pillow.

Kathryn rolled onto her back and returned the baffled gaze of the two men staring at her. She brushed away the tears and sat up. When the doctor started toward her, she drew away. "Don't touch me," snarling, she scooted back against the head of the bed. He moved to sit back down in the chair. "What in the hell have you done to my face?" Her voice trembled. "Why are you doing this to me?" Her words tumbled one over the other as she threw questions at them. "Don't act as if you don't know what I'm talking about!"

Bewildered, Dan was the first to respond, his expression filled with shock. "No one has changed your face."

Kathryn raised her knees and hugged them to her chest, hands balled into fists, knuckles white. "Don't you think my mother is wondering where I am? No doubt she has the police looking for me. Is that why my face was changed? So no one will recognize me?" Oh God, oh God, raced through her mind, could this nightmare get any worse? Both men were staring at her like she was crazy. "Say something," she yelled at them.

Justin was mystified. Did she really think he was going to believe this far out story? For nearly four weeks, she had been withdrawn, acting strangely, and now this. Her claim of being someone else was too wild. A new name, new city, and now, a new face were too hard for him to believe. It was all too elaborate. Why she had created this fabrication, he didn't know. But, he refused to let her continue the farce any longer. Even his patience had limits. "Damn it, Dan! You can't honestly believe her ridiculous story?"

Dan glared at him. "Justin, wait for me in the hall. After I finish talking with Kathryn, I have a few things to explain to you."

From the expression on Dan's face, Justin knew if he didn't leave as requested, his friend would be pissed and possibly have him escorted from the room. He retrieved his coat and hat from the chair and stormed out without glancing at Kathryn.

She half expected an argument from the cowboy,

but his tight-lipped expression told her he was only cooperating out of respect for the older man. Justin Crown appeared more accustomed to giving orders than taking them. A sigh of relief escaped her, as he let the door slam behind him.

"I'm sorry." The doctor's eyes expressed genuine concern. His voice was gentle as he spoke. "No one, to my knowledge, has altered your face in any way. You have the same beautiful features you had the first day I met you. That was on your wedding day when you married Justin."

"But, I'm not married to that man!" she yelled, pointing to the closed door Justin had walked out.

"Yes you are," Dan spoke as calm as possible. This was disturbing even for him. "You said you want answers. I'm trying to give you the only answers I have." He paced back and forth as he continued. "Last night, you were brought to the Emergency Room with a head injury. You were unconscious. The CAT scan revealed no serious damage. Justin told me you all had argued. You ran from the house and drove off. He followed on foot in time to see the Jeep spin and slide into a snow bank. The impact threw you from the vehicle." He turned and looked at her. "I won't attempt to explain what you're doing two thousand miles from where you claim you live."

"St. Petersburg, Florida is my home!" she insisted.

"That may well be. But, you have to realize that Justin and I don't have the answers you want. We know nothing about how you came to the Springs or anything you claim. But, we're willing to help you find out what happened if you'll let us." God, Dan wondered, how in hell were they going to find out what had happened to this girl?

Kathryn wasn't sure why, but she believed him. The idea she might really be married to Justin Crown was hard to accept. She couldn't have been that stupid to get remarried, could she? She wondered as doubts of her sanity crept into her mind. When had Dr. Otis said they were married? She remembered. He had not mentioned a date. It must have been recently. Her birthday was in October, and this must be? "What month is this?"

"March," was all he said.

Good. No more than a few months had elapsed. That marriage thing could be rectified and quickly. "How are you going to find out why I'm in Colorado?"

"We can start with an examination of your face. If someone performed plastic surgery, there would be scars." If an operation had been performed, they could try and locate the doctor. At least it was a place to start.

"All right. First, would you take this damn needle out of my hand? It hurts like hell." If it proved her story, she would submit to anything.

He quickly removed the HepLock and dropped it in the Sharps bin. His hands were soft as he brushed the thick hair back from her face. He examined each side, parting the silky strands until he located the faint pencil thin lines, and then let the shiny locks slide through his fingers.

He frowned, puzzled. This was unexpected. It changed everything. Lord, he wondered how Justin was going to take the news. "You do have scars."

"I told you." A win for her, she thought. She wasn't crazy. Well, maybe a little. She'd had to be nuts to live at home.

"Yes, you did. Now, would you stay here while I go talk to Justin? I need to explain this to him, and you need rest. You have several bumps and bruises, and a slight concussion. That's why you may experience bouts of dizziness. Sleep if you can. I'll have the nurse check on you." He nodded to the nurse, who had stood silent and unobtrusive near the door. "Promise you won't try to leave?" he said.

"Since I don't have much choice in the matter, I guess I'll have to stay." To sleep for a while would be a blessing. She watched Dr. Otis walk to the door, and then turned back.

"Trust me, Kathryn. Everything is going to be all right," he said and left.

Promises, promises, she thought as the nurse and Dan left the room. Nothing had ever been all right in her life. Settling back under the blanket, Kathryn closed her eyes, hoping for sleep to take her away from this nightmare.

Chapter Two

As soon as Dan appeared, Justin whirled to face him. "Damn it, Dan. I don't like being sent out of the room like some snot-nosed kid," he roared.

"You heard what she said. Her name is Blanding, not Crown. As far as she's concerned, she should be in Florida," Dan stated firmly, looking as bewildered as Justin.

"That's absurd. Kathryn doesn't appear to be injured that seriously. I can see her losing her memory, Dan, but not waking up as someone else." He stood with his legs braced, feet slightly apart, studying the doctor. This was the man who had delivered him and fixed his broken bones as a child. This was his father's best friend. The man he had called Uncle Dan for most of his life. And this was the man he had run to when Allison betrayed him two weeks before their wedding.

Only Kathryn had been able to help him realize that all women were not like Allison. He winced from the memory of some of the terrible things he had said to her last night.

"Justin," Dan said, "Kathryn really doesn't remember being married to you."

"It doesn't hold up, Dan. I don't know what she's up to, but I'm not buying this amnesia tale."

"Well, in my opinion, it's true, and I'm going to need your help. What can you tell me that might shed some light on your wife's problem?" He rubbed his eyes. Coffee would help combat the fatigue he was feeling. Too many late nights, he supposed. He leaned back against the wall, hoping to give his back a rest. "I'm worried about her state of mind. I think we should call in a specialist. Someone trained to deal with this sort of situation."

Justin stared at him. "This is ridiculous," he said, then gave a defeated sigh. "You know almost as much as I do. She was my secretary for nearly two years. Look, we had an argument last night before the accident, all right? I can't help but think that's why she's doing this."

"I'm convinced it's no act, Justin. She doesn't recognize either of us. Hell, you're her husband, and I've been her doctor for the past year." Dan shifted to a more comfortable position against the wall.

"Well, no matter what you say, I doubt you can explain away the facts I know about her." Justin did not like what he was hearing. Dan had to be wrong. It was bad enough he had to admit to their fighting but to admit his jealousy was difficult.

"Well, tell me." The doctor gave an audible sigh of relief as Justin hesitated, then spoke in a resigned tone.

"I can give you a big chunk of her past. When she came to work for me, she called herself, Kathryn Clark. She told me she had just moved here from California. When she was seven, her parents were killed in a plane crash, and she was raised by an aunt and uncle. The uncle is dead." He took a deep breath, then exhaled slowly, "As far as I know, outside of her aunt, she has no living relatives. I don't know if the aunt is still living. Kathryn has never contacted the woman since we've been married. Nor did her aunt attend the wedding. Kathryn refused to invite her. There's bad blood between them for some reason."

His body was stiff with controlled emotion, so he eased back against the wall and tried to relax somewhat. "Kathryn doesn't like to talk about the past. She told me that her childhood was not a happy one. All she wanted was to bury the bad memories and get on with her life," he held up one hand, "and before you ask, no, she's never told me what the bad memories were."

Justin's voice was filled with regret. "I said we had a fight. That's not quite true. I did all the fighting. Kathryn never said a word. Actually," he was embarrassed to admit it, "I made an ass of myself.

"Look," he went on, "it's my fault she got hurt. If I hadn't been so damn jealous, there never would have been an accident and Kathryn wouldn't be lying in that bed claiming that I'm not her husband. She has to be pissed off at me, or she wouldn't be doing this. I know what I'm talking about.

"I have photographs of her parents, shots of her with her aunt and uncle, and pictures of Kathryn with friends in California." He straightened and slapped the Stetson against his leg to emphasize his words. "Now can you understand why I don't believe her story? She hasn't lost her memory."

Dan shook his head, "Justin, I agree. Kathryn hasn't lost her memory. I believe she's regained it. I can't explain the photos, but I feel she's telling the truth. I think she had amnesia when you met her." He shifted again trying to ease his backache.

"Well, I can't accept it," Justin said, frustrated. He was losing the argument. "That's my wife in there," he pointed toward the door, "not some stranger." Pacing back and forth, he kept shaking his head, refusing to this madness was true.

"I know it's your wife, Justin." Dan was annoyed and too concerned with his patient to tolerate Justin's unbending attitude. He returned his friend's angry glare.

Justin forced a smile and tried to relaxed, "I'm sorry, Dan. But, I like to see what I'm fighting. Lay it out for me. What makes you believe her story?"

"First, your wife has suffered severe mental trauma. One reason I believe her story is the fact I found scars in her hairline. Someone has performed plastic surgery on her face. It's the best job I've ever seen. So good, it's hardly noticeable." It amazed Dan how almost invisible the scars were he had at last found. Only a top plastic surgeon could accomplish that type of surgery.

"My God, Dan, a lot of women have nips and tucks here and there these days," Justin continued exhibit disbelief.

Dan gave an exasperated sigh, "I'm well aware of how much needless plastic surgery is performed, but I'm convinced that's not the case here."

Justin raised an eyebrow but said nothing.

Relieved, Dan continued, "Secondly, she is genuinely terrified. Since waking this morning, she has experienced one shock after another. One fact that hasn't hit her yet is that she has lost over four years of her life."

"What do you mean?"

"Do you remember when I asked her what the date is?"

"Yes."

"She answered October 25, 2014. Before I came out into the hall, she asked me what month it is. I told her March. I didn't mention the year. She's in for another shock."

"How can you be so sure she's not lying?" Justin hated to sound like an old record, yet he knew how Kathryn guarded her privacy. She always avoided any questions related to her past. Maybe it was all connected to the problems she was having now.

Dan's tone softened. "On occasions, we had lunch together. We would talk about different things, never anything personal. Just talk. She loves you very much, she did tell me that. Once she said a strange thing to me. She said that most people go through life taking everything for granted, friends, family, even the place where they live. They don't learn to appreciate what they have until they lose it. Then it's too late.

"I asked her if she had lost anyone. She smiled at me and said the strangest thing. She had lost everything, only she didn't remember when." There was a lump in Dan's throat as he remembered how sad Kathryn had looked.

"That makes you believe her story?"

"Partly." Dan placed a hand on Justin's shoulder, thought for a second, choosing his words with care. "The important thing to remember is that Kathryn has had a blow to the head, and she could crack under all the stress. Until we are able to determine who she is for certain, it's vital we exercise patience. The last thing she needs is to be constantly agitated."

"All right," Justin growled.

With anger he seldom felt, Dan snapped, "Well,

what do you want, Kathryn in some institution or your wife healthy and happy? Stop being so selfish!"

Justin wanted to hit something, anything, even Dan, for the stinging remark. His emotions under a tight rein, he defended himself. "I've never been selfish where Kathryn is concerned, and you know it, "he said in a miserable tone.

Dan blew out a tired breath. He had been at the hospital since midnight. He was too old for these long hours. The few hours' sleep on the couch in the doctors' lounge had not eased his fatigue. Now he felt as if he was dealing with a powder keg and Justin Crown was the fuse. He had to make this stubborn man realize how dangerous Kathryn's condition could be if they didn't handle the situation correctly.

Dan pushed away from the wall and turned to look toward Kathryn's room, then back at her husband. "Justin, I know you're a powerful man, but this time, you can't control this situation. So I'm telling you, back off." He shoved his hands into his lab coat pockets. "Now is not the time to iron out any problems between you and your wife."

Sounding as tired as he felt, Justin said, "I love her, Dan. But damn it, how much am I supposed to take?" His voice began to lose some of its hostility as worry lines creased his brow. "You have no idea what our life has been like for the past couple of months. I'm afraid I'm losing her, and I don't know how to stop it." He took a deep breath before admitting, "In fact, I think she was getting ready to leave me."

"What makes you say that?"

"The police found her purse in the jeep. They gave it to me. I went through it. Ordinarily, I would never do such a thing. But, her strange behavior made me curious. She has over two thousand dollars in her wallet."

"I'm sorry, Justin. I hate to hear that."

"Nothing we can't work out. Or so I thought." He paused for a moment then continued. "You know Kathryn. She's the easiest person in the world to get along with. We've never had a serious argument. I know when she's mad, she gets quiet and refuses to discuss the problem until she's cooled off. Then we resolve the situation in a calm and compromising manner."

Dan could see the worry on Justin's face and the confusion in his eyes. "What's been the cause of your problems?"

"We haven't been fighting exactly. We're just not getting along as well since that damn party," Justin said.

"No one paid attention to that man's drunken remarks about Kathryn. You shouldn't have either. Did you know him?" Dan asked.

"No." Justin had invited twenty-five of his business associates and their wives to dinner. One couple had a guest from out of state, so he had been included.

From the moment the man had walked through the door, he only had eyes for Kathryn. As the night progressed, she became nervous and jumpy. Justin had tried to find out what was wrong, but she refused to discuss it.

Later, the same guest cornered Kathryn in the study. When Justin entered the room, her dress was ripped, and she was trying to fight the man off. He released her and made a smutty remark to explain his behavior. Without hesitation, Justin punched the man and sent him flying across the coffee table onto the sofa.

The party became a shambles with all the guests quickly departing. Kathryn refused to comment on the incident. Their relationship had deteriorated from that night. Now, this?

He was not good at waiting for things to happen. A large plaque hung on his office wall expressing his philosophy. It read simply, LEAD, FOLLOW, OR GET THE HELL OUT OF MY WAY! Now he was being forced to take part in a waiting game, and he didn't like it one bit. "Okay," Justin said, "What can I do to help?"

Dan smiled. He seldom won a tugging contest with Justin. But, this time he was glad to win. "Right now," he said, "we need to think of Kathryn. I'd like to keep her in the hospital for another night for observation. I doubt she will agree to it. So take her home and let her rest there." He clapped Justin on the shoulder, "Go have a cup of coffee. I'll join you after I check on Kathryn." He gladly walked away from the toughest man he'd ever known who had just yielded to another's judgment instead of his own.

After Dan entered Kathryn's room, Justin leaned against the wall and stared at the door, trying to make sense of it. That damn party was the start of it all. Kathryn's refusal to discuss what happened inflamed a jealous streak he didn't realize he possessed.

Jealousy caused their arguments, and it was also

the reason he was waiting in this hallway. For now, that's all he could do. He pushed away from the wall and ambled down the hall to the elevator in search of the coffee shop.

Chapter Three

Kathryn felt relieved when the doctor returned, alone, and actually greeted him with a smile. "Did you get rid of that cowboy?"

He nodded in understanding and said, "I suggested he go to the coffee shop." Taking the chair previously occupied by Justin, he leaned toward her. "Kathryn, that cowboy is your husband. Like I told you, I was at your wedding."

"Doctor, there is no way that man could legally be my husband," she said wondering if her divorce from Robert had been finalized. If it wasn't, she could actually be a bigamist. She thought back to the earlier confrontation with the Justin. When he'd accused her of putting on an act, the entire time his eyes were as cold and impenetrable as the view from the hospital window. Just as hard as her father were when he looked at her. What kind of man was this Justin Crown, she wondered? Then chided herself. Her plans didn't include being around long enough to find out.

Dan rose and walked to the window where he stood staring out at the snow. He hesitated a second, anticipating her reaction, "I think we should call in a specialist."

"You mean a psychiatrist?" Granted, Kathryn thought, she admitted to being a little nuts, but who wouldn't be with the family she had. The only one she considered sane in the family was her grandmother. Her brother, Henry, would be included in that category if he were still alive. But, he was long gone. The heartache for him never lessened.

"Yes. That's exactly what I mean," the doctor said without looking at her. "A psychiatrist could help you. I could recommend one I know." Dan got the reaction he was expecting.

"No. Absolutely not! I don't need nor want a shrink." Kathryn's insides were boiling at the mere suggestion of a shrink. Just like always, she'd deal with her own craziness.

"That's what I thought. But I would be remiss if I didn't try." He turned and faced Kathryn. He'd thought she would be ready to give him a fight from the tone of her voice. Instead, she looked confused. "What's wrong, Kathryn. We're going to help in any way we can."

She stared at him and voiced her confusion. "Where do we start? If you don't have the answers, what do I do now?" As he opened his mouth to speak, she said, "No shrink, Doctor Otis. I mean it. I'm willing to work to find answers, but no head doctor."

"All right then. I won't mention it again, but don't be surprised if Justin brings it up." Dan informed her.

Defiantly she lifted her chin. "He can go to hell with that idea. Anyway, the first chance I get I'm out of here. I'm going home." Home to where the sun was hot and the faint scent of orange blossoms filled the air and Abby. Dear sweet, lovable Abby. God, how she missed her.

Dan smiled, thinking how different she was from the woman he'd known. Justin was in for a rough ride with this new Kathryn.

"You know we'll do what we can, but you have to

cooperate with us." He sat beside her on the bed. "Justin is worried about you." When she started to interrupt, he stopped her. "I know, I know, you don't want to think of him as your husband. But, he is, until you find out otherwise. You have to let him help you. Besides," he said with a slight grin, "how are you going to get to Florida without money?"

"I'll call my grandmother of course. She'll wire me the money I need." Kathryn was positive Abby would send her whatever amount she wanted even if dear old dad wouldn't.

"Do you think your family knows you're here in Colorado?" Dan doubted her family had a clue of her whereabouts.

She studied him. "I don't know." For the first time, uncertainty wrinkles her brow. What if her mother and Abby didn't know? Maybe her father did but was so glad to be rid of her he claimed he knew nothing of her whereabouts. It would be just like the cruel bastard not to tell anyone she was safe. "Don't you think I should let them know that I'm all right?"

"Kathryn, what if they don't know what happened to you? It might be a shock to suddenly hear from you. I suggest you let me or Justin contact them." Dan needed to keep her from any family calls for now. That was the worse thing she could do. They'd reveal the missing years, and the shock could only intensify her stressful situation.

She considered his suggestion. "You may be right." She gave a deep sigh, "I've been in some tough spots before, but never anything like this. I really don't want anything to do with Justin Crown. I really don't. He may be your friend, but he seems a bit cold to me."

Dan patted her shoulder, "Kathryn, all he wants is for you to be well and happy."

"I find that hard to believe," she started disputed his claim.

"Oh, I know he can be bull-headed. Stubborn to the point of being obnoxious at times, but that does not alleviate the fact he does love you. Until you woke up this morning, you loved him. Now as I see it," he said, "you have only one choice at the moment. Accept your husband's help. As far as calling your family, I suggest you wait."

"I've got to go home, Doctor Otis. I have to see my family as soon as possible." Her voice rose as she fought the urge to grab her clothes and run as fast and as far as she could. Kathryn was frightened. Of what, she wasn't sure. So far everything had been shocking, but not threatening. She didn't feel in danger from the doctor or the cowboy. So what was the threat?

"Calm down. You're in no shape to go anywhere. How is your headache by the way? Is it better?" Even though her head injury was mild, he wanted to keep a watchful eye on her.

"Yes. It's down to a dull throb. I do insist on phoning my grandmother. She's very old, and she worries."

"I'll make a deal with you, give me her phone number for our records," he said realizing it would be futile to argue with her. "You try to relax while I go see Justin about discharging you."

"All right," she said and frowned, not really wanting to compromise, then rattled off the phone number. The doctor jotted the number down on a prescription pad and stood. "After that, whether you like it or not, I'm talking to my mother and grandmother." She'd give the doctor a few hours, then she was calling Abby or her mother.

After Dan left the room, Kathryn rose and slowly walked to the window to peer out at the mountains. A robe would have been great to ward off the chill. Even though the room was warm, she felt as frozen as the winter scenes outside the window. After several minutes, she returned to bed and pulled the blanket over her shoulders, wondering what future surprises were still waiting to assault her?

Downstairs Dan entered the coffee shop and spotted Justin sitting in the back booth.

As soon as he saw the doctor, he asked, "Well?"

"Give me a minute, Justin. Let me get a cup of coffee." Dan replied gruffly.

He stopped at the coffee machine and filled his cup, then joined Justin in the booth. "Before you say anything, I want you to understand something." He rested his arms on the table and leaned forward. "That woman in the room upstairs is not the Kathryn we know." He ran a hand through his hair. "We're not talking about a simple case of amnesia. This girl's entire identity has been eliminated. She has no memory of ever having had plastic surgery. She doesn't know whether or not her family even knows she's here. She's frightened, confused, and mad at the world over what's happened to her. She sure as hell doesn't want to have anything to do with you."

"Did she say that?" Justin asked.

"That's exactly what she said." Dan turned in the booth to lean back against the wall. Stretching his legs the length of the seat, he continued. "I want you to talk to her. And," he said with emphasis, "you're going to have to be patient. Don't come across like the tough cowboy we both know you are. I'm a medical doctor. I'm not equipped to handle this type of problem. What we need here is a psychiatrist. I suggested she see Dr. Alexander, but she refused."

"Well I'm still not so sure part of this isn't an act. That's why my wife doesn't want a specialist lurking around. She knows she'll be found out in time." Justin clung to that belief. Otherwise, he'd have to accept the situation as the truth, and he couldn't.

"What purpose would Kathryn have to pretend to be someone else?" Dan scoffed, tired of Justin's refusal to accept Kathryn's condition.

"I don't know why. Maybe it's my way of holding on, trying not to lose her. Call it gut instinct or anything you want. I refuse to believe she's someone else other than my wife." He was being forced to confront facts he didn't want to face.

Dan stirred a spoonful of sugar in his coffee to cut the bitter taste and then laid the spoon on the table. "Good Lord, you're hardheaded. I don't know how your parents put up with you all these years."

"They love me. And so do you," Justin said, smiling at Dan's remark.

"Yeah, I know. But, you sure can rile a person at times. How about this," Dan said. "Convince her to return home with you. Make it sound like a haven until she can recover."

Justin sat hunched forward, his large hands wrapped around his cup. "Hell, Dan, what else can she do? I have her purse. She can't get any money. She doesn't have any charge cards or her checkbook. I suppose she might contact her so-called family in Florida," he said thoughtfully. "I don't suppose we can keep her from calling them, can we?"

"No, there's no way we can stop her," Dan answered. "But I think I've convinced her it would be the wrong thing to do."

"Well, I'll do it your way for now," Justin said, getting to his feet. He pulled on his coat and placed the Stetson on his head. "I have to stop by the office this morning, but I'll return this afternoon and talk with her. I only hope she agrees to your idea," Justin said, looking serious and a little sad.

"It's just going to take time and a lot of patience. I don't see why she can't be discharged. The quicker she's back in her own environment, the sooner her memory will return." I hope, he thought to himself.

"Yeah," Justin said, sounding unconvinced. "I just hope I don't lose her while I'm waiting for her to remember."

After Justin left, Dan sat staring into his cup feeling rotten. It was going to be difficult to explain to his friend the woman he knew as his wife may be gone forever. He sighed; thankful he wasn't walking in Justin's shoes.

On the way out of the hospital, Justin stopped and removed his cell phone from his coat pocket. He had agreed to do what Dan asked, but that didn't mean he had to believe Kathryn's entire story. A call to Harv Anderson, his company's Chief of Security was in order. After a quick conversation, the call ended with a feeling of satisfaction for Justin. A necessary trip to the office was next. Within a week, he would have all the information he needed on both Kathryn Clark and Kathryn Blanding. The truth would be revealed, and he'd be able to confront her with it.

My God, he thought, as he walked through the snow to his car, how is it that I've shared my life and bed with this woman for over a year, and I know so little about her?

Chapter Four

Kathryn was surprised that with all that had happened, she had actually dozed off. She threw off the blanket and sat up. Her earlier dizziness seemed to have vanished, and but her headache was still a dull throb.

She hesitated. The window drew her attention, and she pushed aside the curtains to open the blind wider. The yellow-gray clouds hugging the mountains threatened to dump more snow on the packed and icy streets. The wind whipped the branches of the tall pines next to the building and sent a snow shower down on the pedestrians below. They appeared half-frozen trudging down the sidewalk, yet seemed entirely oblivious to the lacy crystals falling on their heads.

Palm open, she placed her hand against the cold glass and stared at the gold band on the ring finger of her left hand. When Justin ranted about his money paying for the ring, she had not paid it much attention. Now it stood out like a flashing beacon, drawing her eyes to the ornate design. It was not a cheap one like the ring Robert had given her. The band was encircled with carved hearts, each pierced by a small diamond. One sizeable brilliant stone was mounted in a solitaire.

She removed her hand from the window and tried to pull the ring from her finger. It would not budge. Irritated, she twisted it hard several times. No matter how hard she pulled, the damn thing refused to come off. Somehow that seemed appropriate at the moment. Like the ring on her finger, she was inexplicably tied to Justin

Crown.

Disgusted with her now swollen finger, she turned her attention back to the frigid climate. As she watched the people struggle against the wind, thoughts of Florida filled her head.

Her decision was made. By hell, she was going home! Home to her Grandmother Abby who never doubted her. As for her father, too many fights and one giant mistake had put more distance between them than could be crossed. No, Randolph Blanding couldn't care less if something happened to her. In his eyes, it would be fitting justice.

The thought of her mother weighed on her heart. Beautiful, composed and weak, those three words described Sara Blanding. Her mother was so embedded under her father's thumb, and too beaten down to care anymore, especially after Henry's death.

Henry, her dear sweet, gentle brother had been the calming force between them all, loving her, their mother and even their father. Once he was gone, hell had no fury to compare with her father's hatred for her. No, Daddy would not be the one to call. Anyway, that was part of the past and what was it Henry preached? The past can't be changed; you can only go forward to make things better. Well, before she could go forward or call anyone, she needed clothes to wear. She had to have been wearing something when she was brought into the ER.

She glanced at the small closet door and then turned toward the bathroom. First, she had to confront that strange image in the mirror again. It had been horrifying to see a stranger staring back. As difficult as it was to accept, she knew she had to come to terms with her new face. Still, she hesitated before entering the bathroom to stand in front of the mirror.

Her reflection was still a shock. Only her eyes seemed the same, yet they too were somehow different. She was not sure how exactly, just different, maybe a little more almond shaped. She knew she had been considered attractive, but not glamorous or beautiful. Her long auburn hair had been her best feature, not her face. Abby's old saying 'Pretty is as pretty does, pretty ways make pretty people' flashed through her mind. A smile curved her lips at the memory of Abby. What will you think when you see me now, Gran? She thought.

With the tip of a finger, she traced the shape of her nose. It was more slender and slightly tipped at the end. Her face was thinner, the hollow under each cheek more pronounced, and her delicate jawline more emphasized. Of course, her eyes were still a deep shade of green, outlined with thick black lashes. Her lips had always been full. What Robert called kissable. As she continued to stare into the mirror, she could not help but think that now, she just might be considered beautiful.

Gone was the long mass of hair. The shortened shoulder length was still a shock, yet Kathryn had to admit this style was more becoming. Wispy bangs covered her forehead, where before, she had worn her hair brushed back away from her face. The thick curly mass formed a dark auburn backdrop for her smooth, creamy, complexion.

"It will definitely take time to get used to you," she addressed the stranger in the mirror. When she was no longer able to look at her reflection, she brushed her teeth, dropped the gown on the floor and stepped into the shower. Afterward, she wrapped her hair in a towel, and one around her wet body then went in search of clothes. When she opened the closet door, another surprise jumped at her. One hand on the door, the other on her hip, she let her gaze roam over the expensive clothes.

A deep burgundy cowl-neck sweater hung beside a full-length mink coat, soft gray slacks were draped over another hanger. On the floor sat matching gray leather boots. She touched a sleeve of the sweater. So soft, like cashmere. Out of curiosity, she checked the label. Indeed the pullover was one hundred percent cashmere. She picked up one of the buttery soft boots and fingered the fur lining. Even owning her own business, she never could afford clothes such as these.

One by one, she removed the clothes and tossed the coat across a chair. In the nightstand, she found underwear and quickly slipped on the lacy panties and bra while keeping an alert eye on the door. A sudden wave of dizziness forced her to sit on the bed. When it passed, she finished dressing and pulled on the boots. She realized any purse she'd had must have been given to Justin. Without identification or money, she was stuck, forced to depend on him.

Contrary to what the doctor believed, her parents had to know about the plastic surgery, and why she was in Colorado. Her mouth curved in a smile as she picked up the receiver. Dialing the operator, she gave the area code and number at her parents' home. A nagging thought kept running through her mind. What if they really didn't know what happened? Or, what if her mother had come to her senses and left dear old dad? Kathryn hung up the phone, afraid.

She picked up the receiver again, yet could not stop her heart from racing as the phone rang over and over. She was on the verge of hanging up when she heard her mother's anxious voice saying softly, "Hello."

"Hi, Mom, how's it going?" The stunned silence on the other end clearly indicated her mother didn't know. "Mama," she used the childhood expression. "Mama, it's me, Kathryn." There was still only silence. Her heart beat faster, her stomach churned with dread. "Mother," she spoke louder, "can't you hear me? It's me, Kathryn." The harsh and bitter reply nearly drove her to her knees.

"How dare you! I recognize your voice, Kate. You know Kathryn is dead!"

In a choked voice, she cried out. "Mother! What are you saying? I'm not dead. Please listen to me. I can explain."

Her mother's voice was filled with bitterness. "No! My daughter is dead. She died more than four years ago. You of all people should know that. Only a sick mind would play such a cruel joke, Kate. After all we did for you. Do not call here again!" The phone went dead.

Kathryn threw the receiver aside, and sat with her pounding head in her hands, her mind recoiling from her mother's accusations. Hot tears ran down her cheeks. No matter how bad things had gotten in the past, she never let herself cry. Now, she was unable to stop the flood. Something snapped, and she found herself sobbing uncontrollably. Her last hope of sanity in this nightmare of madness died. She lay on the bed, her body curled into a ball, trying to absorb the mind-shattering news her mother had dispatched so harshly.

How could her mother believe she was dead? Why did her mother say that she, of all people, should know about it? And who was this Kate? The words rang in her head. It made no sense. How could this happen? She buried her head in the pillow and let the tears flow, unaware that Justin had returned and stood just inside the door.

From where Justin stood, her gut-wrenching sobs tore at him. At any other time, he would have rushed to her side, gathered her in his arms and comforted her. Now supposedly, he was a stranger. No matter what her past might hold, this was the woman he loved and had promised to honor and protect.

She lay fully dressed, curled on her side, her hair covering her face. He knew she was unaware of his presence. Otherwise, she never would have let him see how vulnerable she was. Still, the sound of her agony ripped him apart. Hell, even a stranger can offer comfort, he thought. In three long strides, he crossed the room, sat on the bed and took her in his arms.

"Come on now, don't cry," he held her close to his chest and rubbed her back. "I know you're scared and confused. Listen, everything's going to be all right. I promise." He sounded more determined than he actually felt, but didn't know what else to say. He was not at all sure he could make things right. He buried his face in the silky mass of her hair, breathing in the fresh, clean scent.

Their passion for each other was as if they were

one mind in separate bodies, each aware of the other's needs without words. Justin couldn't bear to think their relationship might be over. After what Dan had said, he was not surprised when she struggled against his tight embrace. He gave a sigh and released her.

Kathryn sat back and looked at him, her eyes full of pain and frustration. She unconsciously slipped back into the comfort of his arms. Her words faltered as she said between sobs, "I called my mother." Then her words rushed out. "She says I'm dead! She doesn't know me, and she called me Kate. My mother has never called me Kate."

He continued to hold her close and wish he had the answers. Since he didn't, he prayed he would be able to find them. When at last she was calm enough to finish telling him of the conversation with her mother, the only thing he could say was, "Are you sure you gave the operator the correct number?"

"Yes," she said, irritation taking the place of her tears. She sat back, aware of how comfortable his arms had felt. "I know my mother's phone number," she assured him.

"I know, but it's been over four years."

"What!" she stared at him as her mother's harsh words again echoed through her mind? "That's what she said. I've been dead for over four years? It can't be. I can't have lost four years of my life." Stunned, she stared into space. Then his words registered. "You knew! You and the doctor knew and never said a word to me. You let me make that call and have my mother inform me that

I'm dead!" She lashed out at him, missing his face by inches. "Damn you, all to hell."

He grabbed her wrists before she could strike again. "Dan only told me minutes ago. I didn't know beforehand. You informed Dan when you said the year was 2014.

She jerked free, moved off the bed and faced him. "I don't care when or how Dr. Otis found out, one of you should have told me. I would never have placed that call."

With as much tact as he could muster, Justin suggested, "Would you like me to call your mother and explain what's happened?"

"No! Once is enough being told I'm dead."

"I'd like to hear what she has to say for myself." It was not that he doubted her story. Well, it was that, but maybe she really had given the operator the wrong number.

Kathryn watched him place the call. She was still furious and yet apprehensive as he dialed the operator and repeated the number she gave him.

After a few seconds, Justin said, "Mrs. Blanding, my name is Justin Crown. I'm married to a young woman who says she is your daughter and I. . ." He listened to the scream of outrage from the woman on the other end. Sara Blanding's anguished cry could be heard even by Kathryn. He could almost feel Kathryn's despair as he replaced the receiver.

"She told me the same thing. Do you know anyone named Kate?" He did not consider it wise to tell her that she had introduced herself as Kate when they first met. There was no reason to upset her any more than she was now.

"No," she raised her eyes to meet his gaze, "I don't know. It was never my nickname." She began to pace. "I've got to get out of here. I have to get to Florida and make my mother understand I'm not dead."

Justin didn't want to sound cruel, but if this was some elaborate scheme she had cooked up, she was going to cause a lot of pain for a lot of people, including him. "Do you think your mother will recognize you?"

"Yes, as someone named Kate." Frustrated with his constant probing, anger over her situation choking her, she stopped pacing and stood staring at him from the foot of the bed.

He threw another dart in her bubble of hope. "Do you have any proof that you really are this Kathryn Blanding?"

"Not this!" she pointed to herself, "I am Kathryn Blanding!" then in a calmer voice said, "And no, I can't prove it. I have no moles, no scars. No distinguishing marks! I have no way of proving who I am. I don't even have the face I was born with. No. I can't prove I'm me." Kathryn gave him a cold and defiant glare, "There is one thing you're going to have to face, Justin. I am Kathryn Blanding."

He studied the woman who stood before him, hostility raging from every ounce of her one hundred and fifteen pounds. Even as vulnerable as she was, the spirit of fight blazed in her green eyes. Dan had said not to upset her; well, he had managed to do exactly that, so he threw out a peace offering. "How about something only your mother or father might know about you?"

For a few moments, she stood deep in thought chewing her lower lip. Then she brightened. "Possibly my journals. I've kept a daily journal since I was fourteen. I never told anyone about them. Not even Abby. I don't think there's anything about me that Abby doesn't know, except some of the things in those diaries. My God, I wrote things in there that no living soul should ever see. Surely they should be proof of who I am."

"Well now, we have a place to start," Justin said.

It was Kathryn's turn to study him. Was she being fair to him? His day clearly had been as shocking as hers. Maybe she was too harsh. She walked over and sat beside him on the bed, all traces of her earlier anger gone. "I'm sorry. This has to be as bad for you."

"I'm not used to seeing you like this," he said.

"I'm not used to being like this. I don't know who to blame, and I'm scared."

Justin smoothed back the hair hanging across her cheek. "I'll keep you safe. You don't have to be frightened of me."

After a few seconds, Kathryn looked at him with a puzzled expression.

"There's something I don't understand. Mother and I were close in many ways. Yet when I called, she recognized my voice, but as this Kate?" She didn't wait for his reply. "Tell me something. Has my voice always sounded this husky, or have I had a cold recently?"

"It's the same as always."

"It's different to me. Everything about me is different, not only my face but my body. I've never been so physically fit." She stretched her legs in front of her and looked down at them.

"We have an exercise room at home. You work out every morning," he said with a grin. "You've always said you didn't want to be fat."

She stared at her hand lying in her lap, examining the long enameled nails. "Well, at least I don't bite my fingernails now."

"You've always had beautiful nails," he told her softly.

"This is all so unbelievable," she sighed. "No matter how much I wish it, this is no dream."

"No, it's not. But remember, I'm here for you. I'll do whatever it takes to straighten this out."

She supposed she should be thankful to have someone offer to help. Justin believed he was her husband. She had a place to go, and from the quality of the clothes she was wearing, she probably had a bank account. And, she thought, where there is a bank account, there is money.

"Could your father be of help?"

"No," she said and gave a harsh laugh. "My father is the last person I would call. In fact," she continued in a subdued tone, "my father and I do not have much to say to each other." She rose and walked to the window and stared out at the brilliant snow and ice. "There's always been a lot of friction between us. I could never understand why he hated me, yet worshiped my brother." Why was she telling him things she had never told anyone? She had always kept her unpleasant childhood to herself.

She looked back at him, finding it hard not to respond to the compassion she saw in his eyes. Not hard and cold now, but full of warmth and concern. The planes of his face were softer, making him appear younger than he had earlier. She suddenly remembered the problem of the four missing years. "How long have we been married?"

Even though he was beginning to accept that perhaps she did have amnesia, her question still surprised him. "Just over a year."

"I know you, and the doctor, say we're married, but I'd like to see some proof. After all," she added quickly when she saw the warmth leave his eyes, "how can you expect me to just accept your word?"

Justin knew it was a logical thing to ask, yet it seemed to render him speechless. He sat, unmoving, staring at Kathryn, trying not to let her request frustrate him. He didn't know which emotion was stronger, the anger or hurt. How could she? At the same time, his brain told him she had every right. Proof! She wanted evidence of their life together.

Kathryn felt the chill throughout the room. She could see the stiffness in his spine and the implacable coldness in his eyes. His mouth had become a hard, grim line on his handsome face. The seconds ticked by as he continued to stare at her. When he finally spoke, his anger was apparent.

"You want proof?" He abruptly rose to his feet, jerked a worn brown wallet from the back pocket of his jeans, flipped it open and thrust it toward her. "Here's it is, Kathryn."

She stood directly in front of him, never taking

her eyes from his. She knew her request had hurt him. She lowered her gaze and gave a small gasp of surprise. With a trembling hand, she took the wallet from his calloused fingers and stared at the small photograph. The bride was dressed in a fairy tale gown of white satin and lace. The groom, even more handsome, wore a tuxedo that molded his muscular body and emphasized the power of the man inside the clothes.

"It's a wedding picture!"

"Yes, it certainly is. Ours!" His voice was steel grinding on stone.

"Please try and understand. I needed to see something to show me this isn't all a big mistake, some type of mix-up. The woman in that picture has this face, but. . ." her inner sense told her the picture was of her. "Oh damn!" She returned the wallet.

His anger vanished as fast as it had appeared. He refolded the wallet and stuck it back in his pocket. A smile curled the corners of his mouth, "You're right. Why should you just accept what you've been told?"

Kathryn closed her eyes. A brief, vivid memory flashed through her mind of the two of them entwined, making love. She turned away, hoping he had not seen the blush cross her face. The realization that she was indeed married to this man caused an intense fluttering throughout her stomach. She would need time to get used to that idea.

"Were we, are we, happy together?" she asked.

There was a hint of amusement in his voice as though he knew precisely how he affected her. "I'd say we've been happy," he hesitated as if considering the question. "I'd rather not discuss that right now. We have more important matters to take care of first, like getting you out of here."

Kathryn walked to the chair where she had thrown the mink. The sexual attraction she had felt just seconds ago diminished. Good looks do not make a good man. It was another of Abby's quotes that flitted through her mind. Robert had been proof of that statement. Justin was avoiding her question. She didn't like that. Determined to find out what he was hiding, she said, "I would like to know about our life together." She stared at him waiting for his answer.

There wasn't a trace of warmth in his voice, "Yes, we were happy."

"But?"

"But what?"

"There was a definite but in your voice when you said we were happy." she insisted.

"Why do you think there's a but?"

"Oh, perhaps the look on your face, the stiffness of your shoulders." She never took her eyes off him as she draped the mink over the arm of the chair and sat down. She crossed her legs and clasped her hands around her knees. "From the moment I opened my eyes and met you, I've felt you were angry with me for some reason. I have no idea why. But I do know you're mad about something. Now tell me, what?"

Her intuitiveness surprised him. He sat on the bed and leaned against the headboard. He stretched one leg out on the edge of the bed, crossed his arms over his chest. "You're right, I have been angry and bitter lately.

Isn't it enough to know that for the most part, our marriage has been a good one?"

"No, and I'll tell you why. For the most part, my life was terrible." She paused a moment. "It's the bad times that will make you stronger or break you. No matter how hard I try to bury images, they will not go away. They remind me never to let the bad happen again." Her emotions were getting the better of her, so she glanced away. When she spoke again, her voice was lower. "I have a terrible feeling about being your wife. I think there's a lot you haven't told me."

For a brief second his mouth twisted in a cynical smile. "Dan gave me orders not to upset you," he said.

Kathryn drew in an exasperated breath. "I don't care what the doctor said. I need to know."

This woman looked and sounded the same, but there was a new toughness about her. A determination he had never seen before. This version of Kathryn was a fighter and would not give up, no matter how much he wanted her to. His voice held new respect, as he said with a wry grin, "You're not going to let this go, are you?"

"Nope."

"Well," he realized the futility of further argument. "A few weeks ago we had a dinner party, and one of the men made a pass at you."

The look on his face told her it had been more than just a pass. She might not remember but felt embarrassed anyway.

Justin rose and leaned against the window ledge,

his hands shoved into his pockets. He uttered a sigh of disgust. "Kathryn, I don't know what the hell you've been doing the last few weeks."

"Since the dinner party?"

"Yeah."

"Tell me about that party. Please," Kathryn added.

When he spoke, there was an edge to his voice. He recounted the events exactly as he had told Dan, leaving out the details of the man's physical attack on her. "I'm sure Charles Martin introduced the man to me, but I don't remember his name. Anyway, the minute he entered our house and saw you, his eyes lit up."

"Did I know him?" Kathryn frowned sensing there was more.

"You said you didn't." He was silent for a minute as the tension in the room grew.

When Kathryn could no longer stand the silence, "Then what?"

Justin turned and gave her a long look, "He made a pass at you. It was not a simple pass, Kathryn."

Kathryn's eyes studied him. "Just what exactly did he do?" Her eyes widened in surprise as he recited the details of the attack.

He ran a hand through his hair, "I've never seen you so upset. I don't think I've ever felt such rage as when I saw you in that condition."

Kathryn sat in stunned silence. My God, what had she done to provoke such a man? She tried to recall anything from that night. There was nothing, not even a glimmer of memory could she dredge up. "Then what happened?" She had to know.

"I grabbed him, punched him in the nose, and physically threw him out of our house," Justin remembered how the rage had coursed through him and the urge to pulverize the man was overwhelming. He had controlled that impulse, just barely.

"Did he say anything? Apologize? Something?" Kathryn asked.

"Yeah, he called you a filthy name as he went out the door. He also made some reference to an old friend of yours." Justin shook his head. "I didn't know who he was talking about. Neither did you. Or at least that's what you said. Anyway, the party broke up, and everyone went home. End of story." He stood, stretching his arms over his head. "That's it. Now you know as much as I do."

She rose and walked around the room, then stopped to lean against the foot of the bed. "I don't understand why that changed things between us?"

Justin rotated his shoulders trying to ease the tension that had settled there. He let his gaze roam over her before fixing on her face. "I don't have the answer to that. Only you can tell me why you changed. Like I said earlier, it's over and done with. The important thing now is to get you back on your feet."

That icy withdrawn look was back in his eyes, and not knowing why, she felt guilty for it being there. She picked up the coat and slipped it on, then started for the door.

In two strides he was beside her and grabbed her by the arm. "Where do you think you're going?"

She tried to free herself, but he held her in a vice grip. "I haven't any idea, but I'm leaving." Her voice shook with uncertainty as long-buried memories surfaced.

Justin released her arm. He saw the fear in her eyes and felt sick. "If you plan on going to Florida, how are you going to get there?"

"I'll drive."

"How? In what? You don't have any money. I will not give you a vehicle. You've already been in one accident this week because of the snow. I will not help you kill yourself in another car accident," he said. He had to make her see that she had no choice.

Kathryn wanted to run as far away from this man as possible. But, she was trapped. He was right. There was no place for her to go, nor anyone but him to help her. She was stuck and knew it.

"Kathryn, please," he said desperate to keep her focused on him. "Listen for a minute." Justin sat back down on the edge of the bed, not sure how to convince her she needed him. He would not just let her walk out of his life. He rubbed his palms on his jeans and leaned forward not touching her. "Let me help you," he said. "Dan said you can rest much better at home, our home, than here in this hospital."

"I don't even understand why you'd want to help me."

"Damn it, Kathryn, you're my wife!"

She visibly stiffened and returned his glare. "Don't yell at me. Not now. Not ever," she informed him icily. Her insides coiled into a tight knot.

"I'm sorry," he said, "but do you have any idea

how I feel? Last night you were my wife. Now this morning, you say you don't know me." Justin ran a hand through his hair, "This isn't easy for me either. I don't know what I'm supposed to think or feel. Hell, I don't even know what I'm supposed to say to you." He paused. "Anyway, right now, the important thing is to take care of you. Dan doesn't see any reason why you can't go home today. That would give us time to get reacquainted. That is if you want to," he added.

Kathryn's pounding heart slowed as the tension eased. She was forced to acknowledge that two lives had been turned inside out and upside down this morning. As much as she wanted to get back to Florida and forget what had transpired, she owed him some consideration. There was valid evidence that she was his wife. For now, he was the only chance she had of getting out of this hospital and on her way home.

Justin watched Kathryn's expression change from hostility to concern, then acceptance. He knew he had won when she sat twisting her wedding ring back and forth. She always did that when she was unsure of herself. He did not give her the opportunity to refuse his offer.

"I know your immediate goal is to go to Florida. But, this is going to sound cruel, and I don't mean to be, but don't forget what your mother said on the phone. Everyone there thinks you're dead." Before she could respond, he quickly added, "Also, you have to give yourself time to adjust. Then you can start putting your life back together. And," he emphasized, "I'll be there to help." When he could no longer stand her silence, he felt compelled to say, "Well, how about it, Kathryn? Will you come home with me?"

Part of her wanted to accept and go with him. "I'm not sure," she still twisted the ring.

When he looked into those large green eyes, he saw anxiety. "I want to solve this puzzle as much as you do. You're my wife, and I do love you." He rose to stand towering over her. She was a beautiful mystery, this exquisite woman. "I'm not going to lose you," he said softly. "I'll do everything in my power to save our marriage."

Kathryn's face felt stiff as she tried to smile. He had such a serious expression. She wanted to believe him, and she had no choice but to accept his offer.

"What do you say? Shall we go home?" He walked to the door and stood with one hand on the knob. "Don't worry," he told her with a smile. "You won't be alone in the house. Etta will be there when I can't."

Her lack of recognition of Etta's name made him explain. "Etta Graham is our housekeeper. She's been visiting her sister for a few days. I called her. She'll be back in the morning."

"All right," she said, glad she wouldn't be in the house alone with him. "What papers do I have to sign to be discharged?"

"I'll go see Dan about your release." He opened the door, then stopped, turning back to her, "You will be here when I get back, won't you?"

She looked at him a sad little smile curling the corners of her mouth. "As you so aptly pointed out, I have no other place to go."

Her hands were trembling. It pained Justin to see the fear and distrust in her eyes. No matter what, somehow, he would find the answers to what had happened, even if it meant he could lose her in the process.

He desperately wanted to take her in his arms and kiss away her fears, but, that would frighten her more. Instead, he gave her an encouraging smile and left the room.

Chapter Five

The icy wind stung Kathryn's cheeks as soon as they exited the warmth of the hospital. Even though most of the snow had been cleared from the parking lot, and despite the brilliant sun, a small amount of frozen slush remained beside the sidewalk. Four to five inches of snow covered the surrounding lawns, and the walkway looked slippery. She clung to Justin's arm to keep from falling. It was impossible to understand how someone managed to stay upright in high heeled boots in this icy weather. Any sensible person should be inside.

Cautiously, Justin led her to the passenger side of an old blue Ford Bronco. "Don't let the looks of this old bomb fool you," he said unlocking the door of the beat-up vehicle, then helped her climb into the passenger seat. "I only use it at the ranch and in bad weather."

She was startled when he reached across and fastened her seat belt, then quickly shut the door before she could react. He brushed snow off the windows, climbed in and started the engine. "I'll turn the heater on, and you'll warm up in no time." His smile faded as he regarded her tensely huddled form.

"I'm not really that cold," she lied. No, she was not cold; she was freezing even inside the fur coat. "Just nervous I guess." Then to change the subject, she asked. "Do you live on a ranch?"

"No. We live in town." It was such a simple question any stranger might ask, but, damn it, this was his wife, not some stranger. Still, he could not manage to keep the barb out of his reply.

She ignored him, letting the sharp remark slide. It

seemed they had done nothing but argue since he had announced he was her husband. As cordially as possible, she said, "I don't see you as a city man. You look like you'd be more at home on a horse."

"You're right," he admitted. "I hate the city, but it's more practical to have an office in town." He was serious as he continued, "I don't get out to the ranch as often as I would like, and I miss it, the vast sweep of the prairie, the peace and quiet. Everything moves at a slower pace on the ranch. Sure the work is hard. But, manual labor makes me feel good. Also, there's none of the hustle of the city that I hate."

"That's too bad," was all she could think of to say. After that, she fixed her gaze on the front window. They rode in uncomfortable silence, two strangers cautiously working through a minefield of awkwardness and distrust fueled by pain.

Kathryn tried to concentrate on the view. The stark contrast of the dark green spruce and pines against the pristine white snow on the mountains was breathtaking. She thought of the hot summer sun blazing on the warm sand of Florida's beaches, and how good it would feel.

The snow covered any ugliness and made everything appear pure and clean. The homes they passed were large two and three-story dwellings mostly constructed of natural stone and wood. Each large front yard was graced with tall evergreens, their branches outstretched as if in welcome.

It was a relief to focus on something other than

her problems. And Justin's silence was a blessing. What was she supposed to say to him? Oh, by the way, I remember having great sex with you, but nothing else. That would solidify his belief that her amnesia was a lie. No, it was better to keep that bit of information to herself.

So she remained silent savoring the crisp smell of the air and the view, determined to enjoy the moment. Over the years she had learned to hold onto any brief instance that gave her pleasure. This was one of those times to file away regardless of whatever else happened.

A group of children played in a front yard, throwing snowballs at one another. The idea had not crossed her mind that there might be a child. Did she dare ask or would the question cause another backlash? Any inquiry she had expressed so far had irritated him.

"You're too quiet," Justin said.

He caught her off guard. "Do we have a child?" she blurted the question before she could stop herself.

"No!" he said a little too sharply, then frowned knowing he had upset her again. Her resentment surfaced immediately.

She whipped her head toward him. "Look," she blazed. "If you're going to snap every time I ask a question, you can just turn this rust bucket around and take me back to the hospital." She was furious, tired of having to be on the defensive to some jerk she didn't know. She turned away. So much for restraining her temper.

The tension was apparent by the white-knuckle grip Justin had on the steering wheel. Another apology was due. He tried to relax his shoulder as he said, "I'm sorry. I don't mean to snap. Hell, how am I supposed to feel? I take my wife to the ER, and end up bringing you home." Another goof. He regretted the words as soon as they were out of his mouth.

"Oh, thanks a lot. I'm not too happy being stuck with you either." She took a deep breath nervously tapping the armrest. She shifted to look at Justin, waited for her temper to cool then said, "Look, we can't continue barking at each other. Maybe if we try, we can be civil. I'll make an effort if you will." She hoped she would be able to live up to the bargain.

"All right," he agreed. They rode in silence, lost in their own thoughts. Justin missed his gentle wife. This woman was strong-willed and difficult to get along with. Even so, he would continue fighting to keep her.

While Kathryn found the bitter cold exhilarating and the pristine scenery breathtaking, she longed for the balmy breeze of home. Why did her family think she was dead? Her mother had not said what caused her death. These thoughts brought a gut-wrenching pain for the years she had lost. What in the world have I been doing, she wondered.

She jumped when Justin asked, "Are you homesick?"

The man was a mind reader. "I would love to see my mother and grandmother and make sure they're all right."

He didn't miss the quiver in her voice or the way she kept her head turned away. Also, he noted she did not mention her father. That relationship was one he would have to explore. Right now all he wanted was to get her home. He was sure once she was back in their house her memory of their life together would come flooding back. If it had ever left in the first place. He admonished himself. Dan believes her, why didn't he? Maybe because it was all too incredible. His misgivings bit at him. He gave her a quick glance. She was still staring out the window.

A tall mountain in the distance caught Kathryn's attention. "Is that Pike's Peak?" She was awed by its height and majestic beauty.

"All fourteen-thousand, one-hundred and ten feet of it."

"It's beautiful."

"Yes, it is. To the south," he said, pointing to a much smaller mountain "is Cheyenne Mountain. That's where we live."

She stared at the mountain with its snow-covered slopes and dark green pines and wondered how anyone could build a house on such an incline. All she had ever known was flat land. The highest elevation in St. Petersburg was thirteen feet above sea level. The bumps they called hills were nothing compared to the majesty of these peaks. She wasn't prepared for a slippery drive up a steep winding road.

"Don't worry, it's a gradual climb. You won't even notice it. There's nothing to fear."

Kathryn rolled her eyes in bewilderment. He had done it again. It was positively uncanny. The man was definitely a mind reader. Just the same, his reassurance that the road was a gradual climb did not make her feel any safer.

She leaned back and let her mind wander. This

city and its mountains, she tried to remember something, anything about her time here. The only memory to spring to mind was the one she had had at the hospital. One that even made her want to blush. The intimate knowledge of the man sitting next to her was deeply imprinted in her brain. She felt her face grow warm and forced herself to think of something else. There was nothing familiar about the avenue they traveled. The shroud over her memory was still firmly in place.

Justin missed the blush on Kathryn's face noting instead how tired and pale she appeared. This had been a stressful morning for all of them. But Dan was right. Rest was what she needed. Still, she was determined to get to Florida as soon as possible. How was he going to keep her in Colorado Springs until he could take the time to fly her there? Thank God for the snowstorm last night. That would buy him a few days. But as soon as the airport reopened, she would want to leave. What if she never came back to him?

This was different from his affair with Allison. He had never felt this all-consuming love for Allison that he did for Kathryn. But, this was not his Kathryn, the quiet, gentle, sophisticated woman he had married, the one who instinctively knew his needs and how to fulfill them. His Kathryn filled his hectic days by soothing his nights with warmth, love and peace of mind only she could give.

No, this new Kathryn was argumentative and stubborn to a fault, who said what she thought and claimed to be a nail-biter. He was sure there were more differences between the two, and, in the days ahead, he was bound to discover each one.

When he gazed in the mirror, all thoughts of his problems vanished. A green Blazer barreled up the slick roadway behind him. Thankful that the traffic was light, he quickly pulled into the right lane, leaving plenty of room for the other vehicle to pass. But, the Blazer didn't move on. Instead, the driver pulled in behind the Bronco within inches of the back bumper.

Justin pressed on the accelerator in spite of the hazardous road conditions. The man in the Blazer sped up and rammed the Bronco. The truck's back end fish-tailed then began to slide on the slick pavement.

"Hang on!" he yelled, turning the steering wheel into the slide. The truck barely missed slamming into a sedan before coming to a stop on the shoulder of the road.

The Blazer shot past spraying ice and snow on the Bronco, the license plate concealed by mud. Justin did see the driver laugh and wave as he flew past. He started to reach for his cell phone to call the police. What good would it do, the other vehicle was already out of sight. Besides, his first concern was Kathryn. She sat motionless, one white-knuckled hand gripping the center console, the other braced against the dash.

"Are you all right?" He pulled her to him in a fierce grip. "That fool almost killed us."

She was stunned, unable to think clearly. She looked around wildly. Blood. There should be blood. A lot of it. Someone was calling her name, yet when she opened her mouth, nothing came out.

"Kathryn, damn it. Talk to me. Are you all right?"

She shook her head to clear the painful memory, and then looked into Justin's frightened eyes.

"What happened?" she asked, shaking.

"Some idiot rammed the back bumper." The hairs on the back of his neck told him it was not an accidental bump. Had the other guy meant to frighten them, or did he really mean harm? That was the question.

"Why would someone do something so stupid and dangerous?" She pushed away from him.

"Probably trying to scare us." Checking traffic, he pulled back onto the road. "We'll be home in about ten minutes."

Kathryn sat quietly trying to calm her ragged nerves until Justin pulled into a paved, circular driveway.

"This is it," he shut off the engine.

She stared at the two-story dwelling with a large moss-covered rock arch leading to the entrance. This wasn't just a house. It had been built with loving care, every detail exemplifying grace and elegance.

He opened the carved wooden double doors into a spacious foyer with a curved stairway leading to the upper floors. To the right of the stairs, was a room with an immense natural stone fireplace taking up the entire wall. The furnishings were in quiet neutrals with accents of bright blues and deep rose. Beautiful Aubusson rugs were scattered over a gleaming oak floor. My Lord, she thought, as Justin led her through a door into what had to be his study, ranching had to be a lucrative business. At the other end, the floor was raised to create an office area, complete with an old battered table, computer, and bookshelves.

"I'll start a fire," he said, took her coat and draped it across a chair, then turned to focus on the fireplace while Kathryn wandered around the room.

Idly, she touched a vase on a table, a carving of a Remington Western horse and rider, anything that might jog her memory. She moved to stand beside the massive old table being used as a desk and ran a finger over the dark wood, scratched and nicked from use. Then she turned to study the bookshelves lining the walls on either side of the desk. The shelves were filled from top to bottom with leather-bound works by Michener and L'Amour were crowded beside publications on the breeding of cattle and horses.

She had decorated several large homes in St. Petersburg, but always to the taste of the owner. This house was decorated with loving care. Even though the outside was deep in snow and ice, inside was warm, and safe. She walked behind the desk to stare out the tall windows overlooking a large patio. A terrace extended almost a hundred feet beyond the house. Tall pines and spruce formed a wall around the property, giving it a sense of isolation as the afternoon sun sent blue shadows rippling over the snow. She shivered with apprehension, sensing that now was the easy part. Soon things would change. And perhaps, she thought, not for the better.

She forced the morbid thoughts from her mind and turned to watch Justin. My husband! God, how did this happen? She had asked that question too often and still had no answer. As far as her other husband, Robert? She shook her head. He was just one more puzzle to solve.

A long match flared in Justin's hand. He touched the flame to a pile of crumpled newspapers. Soon the stacked logs in the grate were crackling. The odor of pine, more pungent than that coming from the fire, reached her nostrils. She looked around to discover the source.

A tall, sturdy woven basket filled with fresh pine boughs, as well as silk flowers, stood by French doors leading to the terrace. Kathryn took a deep breath and let the fragrance fill her senses as she moved to the sofa in front of the fireplace, leaned back against the pillows to relax. As she ran her hand over the soft velvet fabric, it was like caressing the mink coat. Nothing in the room was familiar to her. She sighed.

She closed her eyes and surrendered to the peaceful mood. Her lids became heavy, and she was almost asleep when she heard the tinkle of crystal. Opening her eyes, she saw Justin standing at a cabinet in the corner, the doors open to reveal a store of liquor and a wet bar. He splashed a generous amount of Scotch over ice and then added a small amount of water. He took a large tumbler from the cupboard and filled it with ice and orange juice.

Her eyes were riveted to his broad muscular back. He indeed was a man she could be attracted to, she thought, as a warm, sensual feeling snaked its way through her. Now was not the time for such thoughts. What she needed was food. She sat up and took the tumbler from him with a trembling hand. She knew she would have to eat soon or she would be in trouble.

He sat opposite her on the sturdy wooden coffee table. "I didn't think you should have wine just yet, with your concussion and all," he said.

"Thank you," she said. The juice would hold her until she was able to eat.

"Kathryn, tell me about Robert," he asked softly. "How long were you married?" He hadn't been able to get the man out of his mind since he heard the name. He had to know whether or not she was still married. She's married to me now, by God, he thought, and that's the way it's going to stay. Another call to Harv was in order.

Her face hardened. "Robert Cantree is pond scum."

"You don't pull any punches, do you? Didn't you love him?"

She stared into the fire. "At one time I thought the man was wonderful," she gave a contemptuous chuckle, "then, I found out the only thing Robert loved was money. My family's money. When he discovered I didn't have any of my own, other than what I earned, that's when his true personality came out. Anyway, I don't want to discuss him. I especially don't want to think that I might still be married to him."

"I thought you said you were divorced."

"I filed, but the hearing was in 2014. I don't even know whether or not I was there." Bitterness edged her voice. She gave up trying to remember. It just made her head hurt. "You know, Justin, you might be married to a bigamist."

"I'm not concerned," he said. "That can be straightened out with a few phone calls."

"Well it may not bother you, but it bothers me a

great deal." A flush of anger stained her cheeks.

"I'm sure the authorities won't send you to jail. After all, if you missed your hearing, the court probably figured you had changed your mind. Don't forget, you have a reasonable excuse. You developed amnesia, didn't you?"

His words were more an accusation than a question. Kathryn was so livid she wanted to slap that smug expression off his face. Why do I even care what he thinks? Because you're attracted to him, a little voice whispered.

Justin's voice startled her. "What's going through that head of yours now?"

"How I'd like to slap your face, but won't. I'm too tired to fight," she said meeting his gaze. "Let's talk about something else, okay?"

He had been out of line with that low remark and knew it. "I'm sorry," he said and added, "God, I seemed to be saying that a lot with you. Look, there are a thousand things we could discuss. Pick one."

"Your house," she said, coming up with the first thing she could think of. "It's absolutely beautiful. I especially like the way this room is done."

"Thanks, but I certainly can't take the credit. You completely refurbished every room yourself. My grandfather built this house," he said. "It was a wedding present for my parents. That was over sixty years ago. As far as I know, nothing was changed after they moved in, except a coat of paint every now and then."

"It's a lovely old home, Justin." Kathryn admired

older elegant homes. The buildings had a history to them. Her parent's house was just such a place.

"I wanted to hire a decorator, but you said you wanted to do it yourself, so I went along with it. Now," he said and smiled, "I'm glad I did. You did a great job."

"That's because I am or was an interior designer. I have my own shop in St. Pete. Or at least I did. God knows what's happened to it since I left." She forced the memory of her shop, and all that it represented from her mind. She could not face the fact that it probably did not exist anymore. "Surely, I didn't get rid of your mother's furniture and things, did I?"

"No, you kept most of it. Actually, this is the only room that was totally redone. Except for that old desk, of course. You loved it and refused to part with it."

"Isn't that strange," she said. "I was thinking earlier that this is exactly the way I would have decorated this room."

"When we married, you said you wanted to redo the house. You wanted a warm, loving home. You also told me you wanted a large family." His voice held a derisive note as he continued, "Somehow I think you changed your mind about the children." He rose abruptly and walked to stand with his back to her as if his only interest lay beyond the French doors.

Resentment reared its ugly head as she stared at his stiff back. She didn't want to think about problems. Not Justin's. Not hers. All she wanted to do was let her mind go blank. Even though it was early afternoon, she felt exhausted. She drained the last of the orange juice, grateful that it had appeased her hunger for a while. She leaned back and closed her eyes. It felt good to let her mind relax for the first time since early morning.

Justin watched the heavy white snowflakes drift down past the window, trying to unravel all that had happened since the morning. Somehow, between the hours of their argument last night, and his walking into her hospital room this morning, the Kathryn he knew had disappeared. Her welfare had kept his mind off the stupidity of that fight, but now it came rushing back to flood him with guilt.

The entire scene was his fault. His eyes burned with jealousy as he remembered what sparked the quarrel. He silently scoffed at himself. It had been neither a fight nor an argument. That took input from both parties. And Kathryn had never opened her mouth.

She had received another mysterious phone call. The calls had come almost every day since the disastrous party. They arrived at different times of the day. Even on the weekends. At first, he didn't give them much thought, thinking perhaps it was a teenager playing a prank. But the more edgy and withdrawn Kathryn became, the more concerned he grew. Especially when he would answer the phone and the other party would immediately hang up.

It was only when Kathryn answered that there seemed to be any conversation. She had refused to tell him who called. Each time he questioned her, she shrugged it off as a wrong number. Then she began disappearing for hours at a time. Never telling him where she had gone, refusing to answer any questions about her mysterious shopping trips.

He had never been the jealous type, but her refusal to discuss the matter had nearly driven him crazy. Their relationship had been one of trust as well as love. His trust had disintegrated with his jealousy. Picturing her with another man, he knew he was capable of murder. The one thing in this world that would force him to kill would be to protect his wife.

Then came their terrible argument. God, it seemed as though it had happened years ago. Yet it had happened in this same room only last night.

He would never forget the shock on her face as he stood over her with clenched fists. His words still echoed in his ears. "Who is he, Kathryn?" he'd yelled at her, then grabbed her by the shoulders and shook her. "Is he your lover? Tell me damn you!" Kathryn hadn't said a word, merely looked at him while tears spilled down her cheeks.

Looking back, he supposed if his ego had not been so injured, he would have realized his mistake. After all, he had no proof his wife was involved with someone else. Instead, he had pushed her back on the sofa and stalked out of the room. So engrossed in the horror of how close he had come to striking her, he didn't hear her leave. He had never touched a woman in anger before and was shocked by his action. Filled with shame and remorse at what he had done, he dimly heard the engine of the jeep start.

He returned to the study, found her gone and rushed to the front door in time to see her speed down the driveway. He followed on foot and watched in terror as the vehicle began to skid and went into a hard spin several times, throwing Kathryn from the Jeep into a snow bank. He had dialed 911 from his cell phone while running, slipping and sliding to where her limp form lay in the snow. He knelt next to her, clutching her icy hand crying over and over, "I'm sorry, babe, I'm so sorry," while he waited for the ambulance. All the way to the hospital he cursed himself for being stupid and vowed never to touch her in anger again.

Justin's thoughts were broken by the glimpse of a green Blazer driving slowly past, pausing briefly. When he opened the door and stepped out onto the terrace, the Blazer drove on down the street. The snow was falling heavier, obscuring a clear view, but he knew it was the same car

Only after the Blazer disappeared from view did he close the door. He walked to where Kathryn dozed on the sofa and sat in one of the large chairs, watching her sleep. He enjoyed how the firelight danced across her hair like an auburn wave rippling across the water. Her eyelashes were thick dark smudges on her cheeks, so long they were often mistaken as false.

She looked vulnerable and helpless. Justin knew better. There were times when she had seemed distant. Then almost in the same moment, she would be caring and warm. The thought hit him suddenly that there were times when she seemed almost like two different people. That would explain why he had always felt she was holding back, never fully committed to their relationship. It had made him wary at times.

He reached out and took her warm hand in his. At his touch, she opened her eyes and gazed at him in confusion. She sat up, a fixed stare of fright in her eyes, then slowly reality broke through, and the fear ebbed.

"You were going to ask me who I am," he said with a slight smile.

"Yes, I suppose I was," she replied softly. "I'm sorry I fell asleep on you. What time is it?"

Justin looked down at his watch, "It's almost six p.m."

He stood and walked to the tall bookshelves. "I want to show you something." He pulled a large leather-bound volume and returned to sit beside her on the sofa. He flipped open the hard brown cover of a photograph album. On the first page was a picture of the two of them.

Her new face stared back at her. They both were smiling into the camera. Justin sat on a bench, while she encircled his neck with her arms from behind. They were dressed in ski clothes, and in the distance, she could see the snow-covered mountains and a ski lift. Written in the lower right-hand corner was an inscription in her handwriting, "To Justin, my husband, may our love increase through the years, Kathryn."

"I find it difficult to associate that face with me," she said. On the opposite page were other photographs, shot at different times. Taped in the middle of the page was a silky strand of dark auburn hair. She touched it and then shook her head in dismay.

"When we met," he said, "you said you were an orphan, that you had been raised by an aunt and uncle in California, Ray and Mary Clark. Ray was your father's brother. They took you in after your parents were killed in a plane crash." He pointed toward the album. "There are pictures of them in here. That's about all I know about you. I believe your aunt is still living." He leaned back and watched her flip back and forth from one page to another.

She read each inscription as she went, feeling nothing, recognizing no one. Finally, she closed the album and handed it back to Justin. "I don't know any of those people, yet they're supposed to be my relatives." A deep sigh of confusion escaped her, "Justin, in spite of what you think, I know who I am. I know who my relatives are. I know where I live. Or did live," she amended. "What I don't know, and apparently you don't either, is what happened. This is all a nightmare, and it scares the hell out of me."

Justin patted her hand, "I know, babe, but I promise we won't stop until we get it all straightened out."

She turned her head to look at him, "I wish I could remember. I know you must feel a great sense of loss, and I'm sorry about that."

"Well then," he said with a sensuous gleam in his eye, I guess I'll just have to win you all over again, won't I?" Then his voice took on a determined tone, "I never give up on something I want, Kathryn. And I want you."

No man had ever looked at her with such apparent desire. Not even Robert had been so ardent in his feelings for her. Their relationship had been a casual one. With Justin, it would be profound, possibly even stormy, but never indifferent. Even his light touch had brought a tingle to her arm. Hoping to dispel her reaction to him, she said the first thing that came to mind, "What time is dinner? I'm starving."

"Good Lord, I forgot to give you food." He rose to his feet. "Why in the world didn't you say something sooner?"

"I didn't want to be a complaining guest. But, all I've had today is that juice you gave me. I don't think I can go on much longer without food."

He wrapped an arm around her shoulders, tilted her chin with his free hand and said in no uncertain terms, "You are not a guest in this house, Kathryn. This house is our home. You're my wife."

When she opened her mouth to argue the point, he put one finger over her lips. "We're not going to discuss it, especially when you're shaking like a leaf from hunger. Now come on," he said, "let's see what we can find in the kitchen."

He led her down a hallway into the large kitchen. The room was a cook's dream of rustic wood and copper. The breakfast nook was an enclosed portion of a large patio giving the impression of being outdoors. Protected from the elements by thick panes of glass, the room had a long ledge that ran the length of the windows. Baskets of potted herbs, spices, and flowering African violets, lined the shelf. It was the first kitchen she had ever seen with its own fireplace.

In short order Justin had the coffee brewing and a fire blazing. Kathryn took a seat at the large oak table and watched him pull a covered bowl and a dish of butter from the refrigerator. He loosened the lid on the container and placed it in the microwave, then took a loaf of homemade bread from a large drawer and put it and the butter on the table.

He joined her at the table with a cup of steaming coffee in each hand. She added plenty of cream to her cup then took a delicious sip. They both sat in silence as though they had run out of things to say.

To break the silence, she said, "I have never seen a fireplace in the kitchen," she smiled, "It's a neat idea."

"The fireplace was another of your ideas."

"Oh." Another item fell prey to her lost memory. He reached across the table and laid a hand on her arm, but before she could react, a scratching noise sounded at the back door.

"Good grief," he said rising and going to the door. "I forgot about Chopper. Hold it!" he ordered as he opened the door a crack. "You're covered with snow!" But before he could wipe the dog down with a towel, the animal pushed the door open. The biggest, woolliest black dog she had ever seen came bounding into the room.

"Chopper! Come here, you're filthy!" Justin yelled and made a grab for the dog's collar. He missed. The dog ran to Kathryn, licked her hand, and then sat down next to her, placing his head on her knee.

Kathryn gave him a hug and scratched his ears. "He's beautiful." The dog put his front paws on her lap and tried to lick her face. "I've always loved dogs, but we were never allowed to have one." Her eyes sparkled with delight as she stroked the dog's wet fur.

"He's actually more your dog than mine," Justin told her. "He decided that the first time he saw you." He took the large animal by the collar and made him lie on an old blanket by the fire, then walked to the sink to wash his hands.

Kathryn followed and did the same. "Why did you name him Chopper?"

Justin dried his hands and took two soup bowls from the cupboard, loaded them with a delicious smelling beef stew, and carried them to the table. He waited for her to be seated before answering.

"I named him after a friend of mine who flew helicopters in Iraq. He died over there."

She could see the faraway look in his eyes, and hear the pain in his voice. She knew how difficult, painful memories were, and her heart went out to him. "You must have been very close.

"We were best friends."

"My brother, Henry, died several years ago. I know what it's like to lose someone you're close to."

He gave her a curious look, "I never knew you had a brother."

"Justin, I suspect there are a lot of things you don't know about me. And," she added, "my brother is only one of many things." She could feel his eyes on her but refused to look at him.

The nagging ache for her brother never went away. At times she wondered when the pain would fade. Her own guilt had only served to double her grief. "I sympathize with the loss of your friend," she said. "No matter how you lose a friend or brother, it's never easy." She tried to smile at Justin. "Anyway, I don't want to talk about Henry, I want to talk about us."

"All right." He pushed his bowl away.

She carried their bowls to the sink and then poured herself another cup of coffee. As an afterthought, she retrieved Justin's cup and refilled it too. She would keep him up all night if need be, but somehow, before she went to sleep, they would make some sense of this mess. "Now," she said and set his cup in front of him, "you said you've known me for almost two years. And I've looked like this? You didn't know me before someone performed plastic surgery on me?"

"You were my secretary. We dated for about six months. We got married on New Year's Eve." He leaned back in his chair, stretching his long legs in front of him.

"In all that time you never wondered about my past? Weren't you interested in what kind of person you were in love with?" Had he tried to investigate her past, she wondered?

"I know what you're thinking, and you're dead wrong," he said. "I fell in love with you. Not your face. Besides, you made it clear from the start that you didn't want to dwell on the past. So, I never pried."

Kathryn couldn't believe her ears. "Didn't I tell you anything?"

"Only what I've told you. You showed me the photographs and said you were alone in the world. I let it go at that. I knew if you wanted me to know more, you would tell me." His voice reflected his growing irritation. "Does that explanation satisfy you?"

"I suppose it will have to do." Her muscles tensed, but she had to keep probing. "Look, I have to adjust to the idea that you and I are married. This isn't easy for me either. That man you said ripped my dress at the party, the one who started the problems between the two of us, are you sure you don't know who he is?"

Justin wearily rubbed the back of his neck. "Give it a rest, Kathryn. Please."

"I can't! This didn't happen to you. I can't let it rest. I have to know!" Then in a calmer voice, "Justin, my whole life has changed. Can't you see that? Please, did you know him?"

He drew in a deep breath. "No, I can't say that I recognized him. He was the guest of another couple. We never saw him after that night."

"You said he was the beginning of our problems? Can you call those people and find out the man's name? That might help."

As if he hadn't already tried.

"Well, you said he started our problems," Kathryn insisted. "I just thought that if we knew his name, it might ring a bell with me. Besides," she continued, "why would an out-of-state visitor go to a stranger's home and cause that kind of scene? It doesn't make sense." She rubbed her forehead, realizing her headache had returned.

He frowned. Calling Charles Martin again was the last thing he wanted to do, but would do it. "I'll give Martin another call in the morning. I tried to find out the man's name before, but Charles never returned my call. I haven't heard from or seen him since the party. I found it odd, but it's his choice." He stood. "Enough about that. We need to get you settled. You're looking very tired. And I'll bet the ranch your head still hurts."

Together they cleared the table and loaded the dishwasher. Kathryn was beyond tired but wanted to delay the bedroom situation as long as possible. She wiped the table, the countertops, the sink and anything else she could think of. All the time, Justin watched her.

Finally, he said, "Kathryn, I won't bite. Besides, I know you aren't ready to share my bed. Now come on, let's get you settled. You can have Holly's room."

She stared at him for just a moment. Another empty slot in my memory bank, she thought. "Who is Holly?"

"My little sister," he told her softly. "The two of you are great friends. Now come on," he insisted. "It's bedtime for you."

Kathryn followed him from the kitchen. At the top of the stairs, he turned left down a short hall and ushered her into a large spacious bedroom. The room was decorated in pastel shades of blue. A full bay window created a lounge area with a small draped table and a chair covered in the same print. A queen-size four-poster bed stood against one wall. A Lone Star quilt in the same shades of blue covered the inviting bed, and Kathryn could hardly wait to snuggle under it.

She turned to Justin, "Won't your sister mind giving up her room?"

He frowned at her then said patiently, "She's away at college, Kathryn. Besides, she lives with my parents in Washington, D. C. And no," he continued, walking toward the door, "Holly won't mind at all. She's crazy about you. I'll be right down the hall if you need anything."

"Uh, Justin," she said to his retreating back.

"Where could I find a nightgown?"

He turned to face her, and then grinned wickedly. "Well, I don't know about Kathryn Blanding, but my wife never uses them."

She could feel her face redden, and gave him an evil stare. Before she could deliver a nasty retort, he walked out the door. She heard him chuckle as he sauntered down the hall and felt like slamming the door but instead closed it softly.

She had just brushed her teeth and was turning down the bed when a soft knock sounded at the door. She turned to find Justin standing in the doorway with a long blue gown and robe draped over one arm.

"Actually," he told her with a grin, "you have several gowns. This one will do for tonight. In the morning, you can get what you want from our, I mean my room."

She took the silky garments from him and laid them on the bed. One part of her hoped he would just turn and leave. The other half, the half she couldn't understand, wished he would stay and talk. For some reason she couldn't explain, she felt safe with him around.

She did not hear him follow her into the room, and when he grasped her by the shoulder, she cried out.

"Hey, take it easy," he told her. "I'm not going to hurt you, Kathryn. I would never hurt you."

She could see the longing in his eyes and knew he was going to kiss her. He pulled her close and gently lowered his lips to hers. She placed both hands on his broad chest with intentions of pushing against him. As he deepened the kiss, she had no control over the response of her body. Just as she thought her bones would melt, he broke off the kiss and gently pushed her away.

Justin was surprised by her reaction to the kiss. He felt reassured. His wife was in there after all, locked in the mind of this woman who claimed she didn't know him. "Darlin'," he drawled, "your mind may not recognize me, but your body sure as hell does." At the door, he turned and grinned at her. "See you in the morning, Kathryn."

This time she did slam the door, but could still hear his laughter as he went to his own room. She quickly donned the gown and angrily climbed into the bed, knowing if she were asked, she could not possibly explain who she was angrier with herself or Justin Crown.

Chapter Six

The next morning the sky was filled with the same yellow, gray clouds that had churned across the mountains the day before. For a brief second, a ray of sun bounced off the snow, forcing Kathryn to step back from the bedroom window.

Today the sun could not elevate her mood. Inside she felt only shades of profound loneliness and a great longing for her brother. Henry would have made everything all right. Seldom did a day pass that Kathryn didn't think of him or feel the guilt for his death.

Even after all these years it still hurt too much to think about it. She knew Henry would tell her that the past can't be changed. Don't dwell on yesterday. Point yourself in the direction of tomorrow and get on with it. He had always tried to teach her to let go of her bitterness, had warned her it would make her old before her time.

"Oh stop it!" she admonished. "Self-pity never gets you anywhere." Filled with disgust for her maudlin thoughts, she dashed to the bathroom, stripped off the gown and showered, letting the hot spray clear her mind and cleanse her skin until it glowed. She stayed in the shower until the water began to cool, then dried and slipped on the blue robe. If Justin were not in his room, she would get something to wear and move the rest of her clothes later.

She opened the door and peered into the hallway. Chopper lay just outside, waiting for her. The dog stood up, wagged his tail and nudged her hand. She patted him on the head, and he followed her down the hall to the master bedroom. It was the last room at the end of the hallway. She knocked and when there was no answer she quietly entered. Chopper immediately went to a large oval rug and lay down, watching her as she looked around the room.

The room was much larger than Holly's. Thick fur rugs covered the carpet in front of yet another fireplace. Erotic visions raced through her head at the sight of those fur pelts, sure they had not been placed there for show. She hurried to a door which led to the large walk-in closet, and as soon as she switched on the light her mouth dropped open.

There were evening dresses of every imaginable design and color encased in clear plastic. Suits, dresses, slacks, sweaters, blouses, and skirts occupied every inch of space. Matching shoes and boots filled racks on one wall, and next to each lay a matching purse. There wasn't a pair of jeans or a sweatshirt in sight. Not one single pair of sneakers could be seen anywhere.

Feeling overwhelmed, she fingered the sleeves of a few silk blouses. It was apparent the Crown woman was a clothes horse. Kathryn just couldn't bring herself to think that she and Justin's wife were one and the same. Besides, his Kathryn had very expensive tastes. Some of the designer labels cost more than she earned in an entire month.

"My goodness, Chopper, I can't believe this. How many outfits could one woman possibly wear?"

The big dog lay on the plush carpet, his eyes never leaving her. She actually felt like a thief, and almost expected him to growl as she selected a pale yellow cashmere sweater and a pair of dark brown wool slacks. She grabbed short brown boots from the shoe rack then hurriedly left the closet.

She found lacy underwear in a bureau drawer, gathered what she needed and returned to her room, followed closely by the dog. After dressing, she applied a little lipstick from the tray of cosmetics on the dressing table and hurried downstairs.

She found Justin in the study shoving papers into an already full briefcase.

"Good morning," he said cheerfully. "You look as if you had a good night."

"Yes, I feel better, thank you." She hesitated a second. "Do you mind if I make some fresh coffee?"

"Actually I was just about to do that very thing. Are you hungry?"

"Starved."

"Well, come on. Let's see what we can do about breakfast. I can't cook as well as Etta, but I can whip up some eggs and toast," he said.

"Justin, I can fix my own breakfast and yours as well. Please don't feel like you have to cook for me." Kathryn felt awkward doing nothing.

He closed the briefcase and set it on the floor beside the desk. "I don't have to, but I want to," he said. "Besides, you're still recuperating." He walked past her into the hallway. "Come on let's get some food into you. You've gotten too thin lately. You're beginning to look like a boy." This last statement was said with a chuckle as he walked toward the kitchen, leaving Kathryn to stare after him, a look of consternation on her face.

When she entered the room, he was pushing Chopper out the back door, then went to the sink, washed his hands, and started breaking eggs into a bowl. "I put your coffee on the table," he said and placed a skillet on the burner.

Kathryn took her seat and sipped her coffee. She wasn't used to being around a man with a sense of humor and wasn't sure how to respond. She glanced at him when she thought his attention was centered on whipping the bowl of eggs. His gray slacks and crisp white shirt molded his body, the powerful muscles rippling under the smooth material. His solid frame seemed more suited for jeans and boots, but, she supposed, he was probably going to his office.

She ran a fingertip over her bottom lip and thought about last night's kiss. Perhaps he had believed it was a way to jog her memory. Her lips certainly remembered the tingling heat he generated. If she remembered correctly, she hadn't tried to resist either.

He seemed willing to give her time to adjust. She needed it. They both did. Justin didn't know Kathryn Blanding any better than she knew him.

Rising from the table, she went to stand beside Justin. "Can I help? I do know how to cook."

"I know you do." He gave her a big smile as he briskly stirred the eggs in the pan. "You fix great meals on Etta's day off. Especially chocolate cake. I love your chocolate cake." Suddenly the stirring stopped, and he stood very still gazing down at her.

"Here, let me," she said, trying to avoid his touch

as she took the spatula from his hand. Kathryn had to do something. Her insides were a quivering mass of nerves. The intense way he stared at her was not helping her nerves. In fact, she wished he'd treat her as anyone other than the woman he was used to sleeping with. Used to being the key words here, she thought. When Justin's hand closed over hers as he retrieved the spatula, she quickly moved away from his touch. She walked to the back door and looked out at the patio.

The sunshine had vanished and the day was wrapped in a blanket of gray. It was snowing again, the flakes were a white lace veil floating from the sky. She watched as Chopper raced around the yard jumping and snapping in an attempt to catch the snowflakes. Right now she envied him his life. She leaned her head against the cold glass and sighed. So many questions, and so far, not one had been answered.

"Come eat, babe," he said.

The eggs were light and fluffy, the bacon crisp, and the hash browned potatoes golden and the whole wheat toast buttered. She ate every bite, and then refilled both their coffee cups.

"Justin," she said and resumed her seat, "I need to leave. I can't sit around here doing nothing." She looked at him. "Can you understand why I have to get back home as soon as possible?"

Justin held his cup of coffee in one hand and rested his chin in the other, "I am trying to understand," he said. He leaned back in his chair and stretched his long legs in front of him, never taking his eyes off her. "This is your home, Kathryn. Don't ever forget that."

"Justin, please."

"No. Let me finish what I have to say," he told her, putting one hand up in front of her. "When we got married, it was for better or worse. Just like the vow says. Up until now, we've had nothing but the best part. Sometimes I thought I was dreaming it was so good." He sighed, and then continued, "Now I guess we're going to have a taste of the worse part. We can get through this, Kathryn, and I know we can if we're both have patience. Now about going to Florida. Just as soon as the weather clears, and I can wrap up a few things at the office, we'll go. That's about all I can promise due to the snowstorm." The second he stopped for a breath, Kathryn jumped in.

"I don't need you to go to St. Pete with me. In fact, I won't allow it! I don't need a keeper, Justin," she said a little breathless.

"Is that why you divorced your first husband because he tried to tell you what to do?" It was a statement more than a question.

His tone told her she had gone too far. She could see the angry glint in his eyes, the stiffness in his shoulders. Well, it didn't matter. She would go home when she wanted. Anyway, as soon as she could get the money. God, he was infuriating.

"The reason for my divorce is none of your business."

"Like hell, it isn't," he snapped. He got to his feet and slammed both hands on the table in front of her. "Until yesterday, I didn't even know you'd ever been married. I most assuredly do think it's my business!"

He realized he had been shouting when he saw the

fear in her eyes. "Why do you look so frightened, Kathryn. You make me feel like a monster."

With a shaky breath, she sat up straight in her chair, her heart pounding. She was not sure if it was fear or anger that drove her. She knew she could not remain seated and be treated like a child. Her hands trembled as she stood and began to clear the table.

His voice broke in on her thoughts, and when she looked at him, his eyes revealed his pain. "I've never given you cause to fear me," he told her gently. "I would never hurt you. You have to believe that."

She managed a slight smile as she turned to stack the few dishes in the sink, then wiped the counter. She kept her back turned as she said, "You would have to be a woman to understand the fear of abuse. Even verbal abuse. When you shout at me, it brings back memories I would rather not recall." She didn't want to have to explain her past fears to a man she barely knew.

She sneaked a glance at him. He was back in his chair, one elbow on the table, his chin resting in his hand. She didn't want to argue anymore. Casually she asked, "Did I have a purse when I went to the hospital last night?"

"Yes, yes you did. It's locked in the safe."

"Why would you lock up my purse? Can I have it back?" she asked.

"I locked it up because there are over two thousand dollars in cash in that purse."

She met his penetrating stare. She tried to keep her voice steady as she asked, "Where did I get that kind of money?"

Justin grinned at her look of surprise. "You have

a substantial bank account, my dear. Two thousand dollars is a minuscule amount."

Well, that solved the problem of a plane ticket. Relieved, Kathryn took a breath. "I'm not accustomed to having a lot of money, Justin. Oh sure, my father is a doctor, and he certainly made lots of money over the years. But he's also always been very tight-fisted. My grandmother, Abby, is worth a fortune. But it's not my money. I would never carry that much cash on me." She folded the dish towel and laid it on the counter, "Do you know why I had that much money in my purse?"

Justin leaned against the counter, both arms folded across his chest, his feet crossed at the ankles. He didn't want to get into this conversation, yet supposed she deserved to know part of what had been going on. "I think you were getting ready to leave me," he said.

That was the last thing she expected. "But why?"

He raked a hand through his hair. "I don't know, Kathryn. I can only think that it must have something to do with the man at the party." He clenched his jaw, suppressing the anger he felt every time he thought of that little weasel.

Kathryn stood next to him, the top of her head barely reaching his shoulder. "But you said neither of us knew him."

His gaze held hers for a moment, then he looked away. "You never really said one way or the other."

Again, she noted the hint of anger in his tone and wondered if he ever really lost his temper. It would surely be a sight to see but from a very long distance.

After all, she didn't know if he was the jealous type. Was he prone to violence? Studies had shown that children who grew up in abusive homes had a tendency to marry abusive men.

That had been true with Robert. At least verbally. He had only hit her once. Each time he yelled and called her names, it reminded her of her father. Had she done it again? Had she married another man who treated women as a personal possession? She hoped not.

She returned to her seat at the table. "Like I told you earlier, I don't like shouting, especially at me."

"Would you like to talk about it?" He desperately wanted to know more. After all, she had done her share of shouting at him since yesterday.

"No. I'd rather talk about what's going on here and now." At his quizzical look, she went on, "Since yesterday, I've listened to you infer that your wife was possibly unfaithful. That you think she lied to you. Now, that she was planning on leaving you."

Justin stood by the window, his hands shoved in his pockets. "I guess that about sums it up, doesn't it? I can't explain any of this. I wish you could."

His statement hurt for some reason she didn't understand. "You know what makes me really angry, Justin?" Before he could say anything, she continued, "Being here in your home, the home you say we shared. I have actually felt guilty for not remembering our life together. If I was unfaithful, there had to be a reason. What did you do?"

He stood still as stone. Not a muscle moved except the one in his jaw. His teeth were clenched tightly, and Kathryn knew he was going to explode. Yet he didn't. When he spoke, his voice was frigid. "Why, do you think I did something to make you sleep around, Kathryn? I gave you everything you wanted. And you wanted it all, babe. The fancy house in the best part of town, the designer clothes, the furs, the expensive shoes. And you got it. You married the boss."

She looked up at him, her eyes filled with hurt and anger. "Are you saying I deliberately set out to make you fall in love with me? That you think I was after your money?"

Justin let out a tired breath. "No, of course not. I sure as hell wouldn't have married you if I thought that. I've been there, thank you. You didn't have to do a thing. I fell for you the minute I saw you in my office." He wished he could change things. To turn back time to two nights before. God, he would have handled everything so differently.

He sat down, rested his arms on the table and looked at her, "I'm sorry. I shouldn't have said those things. I've never thought that you were after my money." He took her hands in his, his voice like velvet. "Things have been turned upside down lately, and I have no idea what's been going on. I love you. I want more than anything for us to put this nightmare behind us.

"Justin, I never cheated on Robert. I could have. There were plenty of opportunities. But I take my marriage vows very seriously." She paused, trying to get her thoughts in order. "Look," she said, "I look at you and see a very nice man. I appreciate the fact that you have taken me into your home and offer to help me solve my problems. I know technically I'm your wife, and yes, there is chemistry between us. I admit it. But until all the questions are answered, I can't consider a relationship with you."

His anger returned full force, and he couldn't keep it from showing. "You are my wife, Kathryn. As for a relationship with me, you already one. We've been sleeping together for over a year," he said getting to his feet, "you certainly never complained about the arrangement before!" He turned abruptly and stalked out of the room.

Kathryn gripped the edge of the table, her knuckles white against the dark wood. Her statement was not meant to insult him. Slowly she rose and started to load the dishwasher. So far her day was not going any better than yesterday.

"To hell with this!" She muttered throwing the dish towel on the counter. "Let him do the damn dishes." She was angry at herself. She had only meant to explain her feelings.

She summoned up her courage and walked to the study, determined to straighten out the mess she had created. When she walked in, Justin was on the phone. She stood just inside the door waiting for him to finish his conversation, and mentally tried to form an apology so as not to offend him further.

"Thanks for calling Mom," he said before replacing the receiver. He turned and saw her watching. All traces of his anger had vanished. "I owe you another apology. You don't deserve the way I've been treating you, and I'm sorry."

"It's okay," she told him. "I guess I didn't phrase

things well. I don't like a lot of arguing. And that's all we seem to be doing."

"That was my mother on the phone," he said, changing the subject. He went to the desk to add more papers to the briefcase before closing and locking it. "I called them yesterday and told them about your accident. If I hadn't Mom would have killed me." He gave her an intense look. "I also told them about your amnesia."

"When are you going to get it through your head that I don't have amnesia?" She threw her hands up in anger and stalked to the sofa and plopped down. "You just won't listen, will you? Have you always been this hard-headed?"

As though he hadn't heard a word, he put on his suit jacket and picked up his briefcase. "I have to try and make it to the office for a while. I'll be back as soon as I can. Don't exert yourself. You're still not fully recovered." He glanced at his watch. "I have to be going. I'm late as it is."

Maybe it was just an unconscious habit, but she rose and walked with him to the door. He took a heavy coat from the hall closet and tossed it over his arm.

Before she had time to turn away, he kissed her hard on the mouth and walked out the door, leaving her with a tingling sensation on her lips and a warm feeling in her abdomen. Smiling to herself she went to the kitchen and put the breakfast dishes in the dishwasher, afterward, returned to the study to look for the safe.

If she had her purse, when the time came, she could throw a few things in a bag, call a cab, and be on her way to the airport in a matter of minutes. She had only been in the study for a few minutes when she heard the front door open. So much for wishful thinking, she thought and walked into the hallway. A strange woman stood in the foyer removing a long scarf from her head and neck.

"Hi there, honey. I'm Etta Graham, the housekeeper. Justin called and told me about your amnesia. So I just told my sister, Helen, that I had to get on back home and take care of things." She removed her coat and hung it in the closet, smoothed her blue-flowered dress and then patted her gray hair in place. "Now you just come on out to the kitchen. We'll have ourselves a nice cup of hot tea and get acquainted all over again."

Kathryn followed behind her, amazed that anyone could say so much so fast. But if one more person said she had amnesia, she would scream.

In the kitchen, Etta put the tea kettle on the stove and set about making tea while keeping up a steady stream of conversation. Her small chubby frame gave her the appearance of an old-fashioned grandmother. Her snappy brown eyes sparkled while she talked, gesturing with hands that were never still. She kept her hair piled on top of her head, "out of the way," as she put it, but long, the way her husband had liked it.

Kathryn wondered if Justin had told her not to ask questions, because Etta went on and on, acting as if nothing were different. The housekeeper may not have had any questions, but she certainly had a few.

Etta tied a large apron around her ample waist, then opened the refrigerator and began rummaging through the crisper drawer. She stopped talking for just a second, and Kathryn jumped in.

"Do you mind if I ask you some questions?" She didn't give the older woman a chance to reply. "Is Justin a difficult person to get along with?" She didn't have any idea why that had been her first question. It had just popped out.

Etta finished pulling fresh vegetables from the refrigerator, then stood to stare at Kathryn. "Lord no, honey. There ain't a mean bone in that boy's body. Protective, that's what he is. What belongs to him, he protects." She carried the carrots, celery, and onions to the sink and began washing them. "Right now he's concerned with protecting you. You're the most important thing in his life. Don't think you're not."

She turned from the sink to give Kathryn a penetrating look. "None of us thought he'd ever care for anyone again. Not after what that Allison woman put him through. Then you came along, and it just seemed so right. For Justin, it was love at first sight, as the saying goes."

"Who's Allison?"

Etta gave her a surprised look then, just as quickly, turned it into one of warmth. "I keep forgetting about your memory problem, honey. Anyway, Allison was a girl Justin met in college. He worshiped the ground she walked on and had every intention of marrying her after college graduation. Then Allison told him she was pregnant, and that changed all his plans."

Several seconds passed, and Kathryn wondered if

she was going to hear the whole story. She was dying to know what happened between Justin and Allison. "What happened, Etta?" she prompted.

Etta hesitated, then said, "I don't know if Justin's ever told you about this, but if he hasn't, I'm going to tell you now." She paused for a deep breath then continued, "That darned Allison wasn't pregnant at all. One of Justin's friends overheard her telling her girlfriend how she was going to be rich after she married Justin. She'd just told him she was pregnant to get him to marry her before they graduated. And how she was going to have anything she wanted." She shook her head in disgust, "Lord, I'm glad he found out before the wedding what a conniving little money-grubbing twit she was."

"I certainly can relate to a money-grubbing twit," Kathryn said. "Now, Etta," she continued, "if I'm going to be here for a while, you and I need to get something straight."

"What's that, honey?"

Kathryn gave her an intense look. "Etta, I do not, and I repeat, I do not have amnesia." Just as the older woman opened her mouth in astonishment, Kathryn jumped in, "I know that's what Justin and the doctor think. But it's just not true."

"Then what?"

"I can't explain it to you right now. I don't even know what happened myself," Kathryn told her. "Now tell me more about this man I'm supposed to be married to. You've known him for a long time?"

"Lord, yes!" Etta said as she turned back to peeling the carrots. "Changed his diapers more times than I care to remember," she chuckled softly as memories flashed through her mind.

"What was he like as a child?" Kathryn asked.

The kettle began to whistle, so Etta dried her hands, turned off the burner and poured the hot water into two cups. She added a tea bag to each and carried them to the table. She placed her hands on her hips and remained deep in thought for a minute before answering. "Happy most of the time. Full of mischief he was."

She sat down, added sugar to her tea, and smiled, then continued. "That boy could get into more trouble than four his size. Him and Frank Cody. They were two of the most mischievous kids I ever saw." She brushed away a wisp of hair with the back of one hand, placing the other hand on Kathryn's arm. "You don't remember me telling you all this before, do you?"

"No," Kathryn replied. "Until yesterday morning I had never heard of Justin Crown."

"Well, I don't pretend to understand any of this," Etta stated. "I just know that Justin will fix it somehow." She got to her feet and returned to the sink. She finished cleaning and cutting the vegetables before placing them around a roast she had put in a large pot.

Kathryn sat thinking that perhaps she didn't want Justin trying to fix anything. It wasn't his problem. Then again, maybe it was.

Etta placed the roasting pan in the oven and returned to the table picking up her story. "Those two boys were always racing their horses around the ranch, one trying to out-do the other. Or they'd be fighting over Mary Ann Caldwell. Actually, the fights were never serious. They were a threesome. Wherever the boys went, Mary Ann wasn't far behind."

"Sounds like they had a happy childhood," Kathryn said. "Didn't Justin ever do anything wrong? Didn't he ever get into trouble with his parents?"

"Lord yes, he got into trouble. But he always took his punishment like a man. Oh, it was never anything serious. Just growing pains, but those growing pains were sometimes hell on his parents."

From the warmth of her voice and the twinkle in her eyes, it was clear Etta loved Justin as if he were her own. Kathryn envied him for the love he'd had growing up.

"Sounds like they were all very close."

"They were. Frank's dad was the ranch foreman. Both boys had chores every day, but they worked together to get things done. They were always protecting each other just like brothers."

"When Mary Ann picked Frank for her husband, that didn't upset Justin too much. Both boys were crazy about her. Justin just said that if he had to lose her, he was glad it was to Frank and not someone else. That way she was still a member of the family."

Etta paused in thought, her blue eyes filling with tears. Her voice took on a sad tone as she continued, "Then Frank died. He left to join the Army and was killed in a helicopter crash in Iraq. Justin was a changed man after that. More serious, not happy and full of the devil the way he used to be if you know what I mean."

Kathryn felt a chill. She didn't want to hear any more. It brought back too many of her own memories. Memories she wanted to forget.

"That would be a shock to a young man. Losing a best friend is never easy."

"You got that right," Etta said. "I never thought he'd ever be the same again. Not even when Allison came along. I knew she wasn't right for him. Tried to tell him she was no good. But no, he wouldn't listen. Had to find out the hard way what a gold digger she was."

Well, that would certainly explain his earlier outburst, Kathryn thought.

"What happened to Mary Ann? I would think Justin would have turned to her. After all, you said both he and Frank loved her."

"Yeah, but Mary Ann only had eyes for Frank. After he was killed, she couldn't stand being at the ranch. So she moved back East somewhere, and we haven't heard from her since."

"Oh Etta, that's so sad." She laid a hand on the older woman's arm. "Justin must have felt terrible over losing both his best friends."

"He sure did. But then you came along, and he brightened right up," the housekeeper said and squeezed Kathryn's hand. "You made him happy. Don't ever doubt it. Give him a chance, Kathryn. He loves you more than anything in this world."

Kathryn didn't know how to respond to that. She had never been loved by anyone that much. Except by Abby or her brother. Still, that had been a different kind of love, not the type Etta was talking about.

She changed the subject. "What exactly is

Justin's business?"

"Other than the ranching end of it, I don't rightly know. I do know that Crown Enterprises is scattered all over the United States. Justin even has offices in some foreign countries," she said proudly.

"That's very impressive." Kathryn was wearing down. She glanced at the kitchen wall clock. It was nearing one in the afternoon. The morning had rushed by as they talked, without her noticing. She sat with her chin in one hand, barely able to keep her eyes open. Fatigue etched its way into her face. She was having trouble focusing on the conversation.

"Head hurting?" Etta asked with concern.

Kathryn tried to smile as though she was okay, but Etta didn't buy it. She took a bottle of aspirin from the cupboard, shook two pills into Kathryn's outstretched hand, handed her a glass of water and said, "Now get yourself upstairs and lay down for a while. I'll wake you when Justin gets home."

"Thanks, I think I'll do just that," she said rising. She dragged herself up to her room, where she turned back the spread. She closed the drapes, and then removed her boots. Within seconds of stretching out on the bed, she was sound asleep, lost in a dream.

Chapter Seven

The ringing of the phone brought Kathryn upright. Groggy, she fumbled for the receiver, only to knock it off the nightstand in her haste to quiet the loud noise. Why didn't someone answer the thing, she thought sleepily and leaned over the edge of the bed to pick it up.

"Hello," she muttered, her voice still heavy with sleep.

A thick, raspy male voice whispered, "Well, well, Kate. How ya' doin' baby? We haven't talked in a while."

Now she was wide awake. "Who is this?"

"It doesn't matter, Katie. I just wanted to be sure you're taking care of yourself."

Her heart throbbed with fear as the man's voice sounded so evil. She thought about slamming the receiver down, yet knew this was somehow a connection to her past, a part of those missing years. Curiosity won out. "What do you mean?"

"Now Katie, you know exactly what I'm talking about. Don't pretend you don't. He knows where you are, Katie."

"Who knows where I am?" she cut in. "What are you talking about?"

"Shut up and listen," the cold voice cut in harshly. "I have a message for you."

"Who told you to call me? What is this about?" Kathryn's heart pounded so hard she felt weak.

The man's voice grated in her ear. "You know

who I'm talking about. There's only one person that would send you a message like this. He said to tell you to stay in Colorado. If you want to live, don't come back to Florida. As long as you stay away, he'll leave you alone. If you come back to cause him grief, he'll kill you. Got it, little girl?"

Kathryn sucked in her breath, slammed the receiver down and stared at it as if it was alive. Trembling from head to toe, her breath coming in quick, short gasps, she forced her legs to carry her across the carpet to the bathroom. After splashing cold water on her face, she stood staring in the mirror. "Just exactly what have you been up to for the last four years?" she asked her strange, unfamiliar reflection. There was no doubt in her mind the caller meant to frighten her. Well, he had succeeded. Those missing years were a shadow behind a dark wall she found impossible to penetrate. Now it seemed that wall was just a scab covering a festering sore.

She straightened the bedspread, then sat on the edge to pull on her boots. Somewhere out there someone was afraid she would remember something. But, what? What did she know that could be dangerous to anyone?

"Damn!" she exploded as she ran a brush through her hair. Should she tell Justin about the call? No, that was a bad idea.

She tried to put the caller out of her mind as she went downstairs to the living room. It would be easier if she had something to do. Idle hands were not for her. She remembered working twelve to fourteen hour days. Now she had nothing, not even any housework to keep her busy. There was Etta. What in the world had

Kathryn Crown done with her days, she wondered. The other woman seemed passive, willing to be taken care of like a house pet. Then she laughed to herself, well, at least his Kathryn had what it took to make him fall in love with her. That's how she thought of Justin's wife. A different woman entirely, yet knew they both shared the same body, if not the spirit.

She wandered around the large elegant living room, still searching for the safe or one small piece of anything that was familiar, and at the same time thinking about Justin. Her footsteps were whispers on the plush carpet. The room was a perfect place for entertaining, but cold. Not like the study where a person felt the warm, cozy heart of the house. In this room, she wouldn't dare curl up on the sofa and nap.

Nothing cut into the blank curtain of her memory. Not the statues of the tall black cats, or the beautiful landscape paintings. A portrait of an older couple hung over the fireplace. She stared at their distinguished features for several minutes, yet there was nothing familiar about them.

She crossed the foyer to the study and walked straight to the desk and took a seat. There were no drawers or file cabinets she could search. An idea struck her. She picked up the phone receiver and dialed a number. After two rings came a voice over the line, "I'm sorry, the number you have dialed is no longer in service."

Kathryn had expected no less. She dialed the number of long-distance information. When the call was answered, she asked for the phone listing for Blanding & Branson Interiors. The response was no different. "I'm sorry, no listing is found."

She tried several variations of the name and still no phone number could be found. As she feared, her partner, Ted Branson, had put her out of business.

What had made her think to contact Ted would help? He probably believed she was dead. But she did exist for someone, someone who wanted her to stay out of Florida. Kathryn Blanding no longer existed.

In defeat, she eyed the bookshelf, then removed a slim volume of Shakespeare's Sonnets. The book was worn and opened automatically to pages which were smudged and well read. At least she and someone, perhaps the other Kathryn, had one thing in common. They both liked Shakespeare. It was just another coincidence to nag at her.

The roar of the fire drew her attention. She replaced the book then went to stand in front of the fireplace. There were several photographs on the mantel she had not noticed before. One was of a young girl about sixteen or seventeen. Her long wavy hair, the same shade as Justin's, yet her eyes were a warm gray. Holly, surely. Kathryn knew she would like this young woman with the friendly smile. At least his family was complete and close. She envied him.

Voices from the kitchen drew her attention, and she headed in that direction. Just as she entered the room, she heard Etta say, "How come you're using the back door?"

"I was following footprints around the house," Justin replied. "Have you or Kathryn seen or heard anything?"

"There's never been a peeping Tom in this neighborhood, Justin." Etta's voice held a nervous edge as she continued, "I sure don't like the idea of one now. I can't imagine someone sneaking around here."

Justin's eyes locked on Kathryn as she helped herself to a cup of tea, and carried it to the table. Did that phone call have anything to do with the footprints? Was someone watching her? She wondered. The very idea sent chills up her spine.

"You're right, Etta," Justin said in a somber tone. "This is a quiet area, but someone was here. There are footprints from the front to the back, and they stop just outside the kitchen window."

"Well, Kathryn's been lying down, and I've been working around the house." She turned toward the fireplace, "Where's Chopper? I put him out a long time ago. Come to think of it, he hasn't scratched to come in, and I haven't even heard him bark."

"I'll find him. He wouldn't let anyone on the property unless something were wrong." He opened the door to step outside, stopped turning toward Kathryn. "It looks as if someone's been spying on you," and with that terse statement, he pulled the door closed behind him.

A tight knot formed in the pit of Kathryn's stomach. They could hear Justin calling the dog's name, yet did not hear an answering bark. Chopper had to be all right.

Etta and Kathryn stood watching out the window. Both women kept silent, their ears tuned for any indication the dog had been found. A few minutes later, they could see Justin hurrying around the side of the house, the unconscious dog in his arms. Kathryn rushed to open the door as Justin carried the limp animal and laid him on the oval rug in front of the fire.

"Oh, my gracious!" Etta exclaimed.

"He's out cold, Etta. Someone drugged him. I think he's going to be okay though." Justin wiped snow from the dog's face and head. "His breathing is normal."

"I'll get a blanket," Etta rushed toward the hallway and quickly returned with a large wool blanket and spread it over the sleeping animal.

After drying the dog's face and head with a towel, Justin covered him with the blanket. Kathryn felt helpless. All she could do was stand and watch. One eyelid flickered, and Chopper thumped his tail in gratitude. They all gave a sigh of relief.

"Is he going to be all right, Justin?" Kathryn asked.

"I think so. I'll call the vet to make sure." He hurried to the phone and placed the call.

"The vet said to keep him warm for now. I also called the police and asked for added patrols in this area." He returned to stoop beside the dog. "I don't think they meant to kill him, just put him out of commission for a time." He rose and walked to the sink. "From now on I want the two of you to keep the doors locked until I get home. Keep Chopper in the house as much as possible," he added, plucking paper towels from a wooden rack to dry his hands.

Etta busily placed the roast on a platter and filled bowls with steamed vegetables. The aroma of freshly baked wheat rolls filled the room. Kathryn's mouth watered as she and Etta took their seats and filled their plates.

After dinner, Kathryn and Justin adjourned to the study. Justin rekindled the fire before pulling her down beside him on the sofa. She could not bring herself to object as he put an arm around her shoulders pulling her close. They sat quietly staring into the fire. She no longer felt nervous in his presence. He was so different from any man she had ever dated. And definitely different from the man she had married the first time. Suddenly a disturbing thought entered her head. "Exactly when did I come to Colorado Springs?" she asked.

"As well as I can remember you came here about a month before you started working for me." He removed his arm and sat forward rubbing his jaw. "I know it was in the summer of 2010." He turned his head in her direction, "We could check with personnel."

"I wonder why I chose Colorado. I've never been west of New Orleans."

"All I really know is that I walked into the office one morning and there you were. My regular secretary was on maternity leave, and you were sent up from the secretarial pool."

"I want to try and backtrack, Justin. It might help me remember something."

"I've told you all I know, Kathryn. I wish I could help, but you've never talked much about yourself." It had bothered him somewhat that his wife never talked about her family. He had considered having Harv check into her past once but changed his mind. She had shown him all the pictures of her family and explained who they were and that they were all dead, so he had let it drop. Maybe that was the wrong decision. What was the old saying, love is blind? It seemed his lack of information on his wife was also an irritant to Kathryn.

"That's it?" she said, clearly annoyed. "That's my entire life as you know it?"

He gave her a long lazy smile. "That's it. Except that when I saw you sitting at Sally's desk, my heart nearly stopped. It took me a week to work up the courage to ask you out. From our first date, I knew I wanted to marry you. I gave you your engagement ring on Christmas Eve, and we were married the next week on New Year's Eve."

"Yet I have absolutely no memory of any of it. It's driving me crazy this blank wall in my memory," Kathryn said

"It's baffling to say the least. Etta was telling me about a talk show she saw on television. Some people forget things as they occur. Others can have one or more memory gaps. They'll lose anywhere from a few minutes to a few hours a day, some their entire previous life. According to Etta, amnesia can be caused by several things, even major life stresses, turmoil over guilt-ridden impulses, unresolvable difficulties with other people and numerous other causes."

Kathryn studied him carefully, "Do you think that's what happened to me?"

"No I don't, and I don't think. . ." He stopped suddenly as though he had said too much.

"Go on," she prompted. "You don't think what?"

Justin wasn't sure he should tell her Dan's opinion of her condition. But then why not, he wondered.

"Justin? What were you about to say?"

"Well, for one thing," he said, "you remember people and things I know nothing about. The only thing your amnesia has affected is our life together."

"You think perhaps I don't want to remember you? Or do you still think I'm just pretending to have amnesia?"

"No, I don't think that any longer. I know something happened to you. I just don't know what it was." He looked at her intently, "I do know that whatever it was, it has drastically changed your personality."

"You know," she responded, "I have this mental picture of your wife as a quiet, almost subservient woman if you will. I've never been like that. As a matter of fact, anyone who knows me would tell you I have a volatile nature."

"You were never subservient, as you put it, just reserved, never passive. Until yesterday morning, I didn't know you had a temper." Justin said.

"Yeah, well, if something doesn't happen soon to clear this mess up, you're going to see a lot more of it! I don't think I can take this sitting around!" Kathryn was not good at waiting, not at all.

"I hope it won't be much longer. The snow has to stop sometime. Then we'll go to Florida, and see what we can find out."

"I wonder if there might be something in my

purse, something that might jog my memory. What do you think?" She was praying he would agree. She needed that money in the purse.

"You have a point," Justin said getting to his feet. "I'll go get it for you."

Kathryn removed her boots and tucked her feet under her. She leaned her head back and basked in the warmth of the fire and longed to talk to Abby about her problems. She was positive that if she could hear her grandmother's voice, everything would fall into place. She stood with intentions of doing that very thing when Justin returned with a small gray purse.

"Here you are," he said, handing it to her. He stood silently while she resumed her seat and emptied the contents onto the coffee table.

She picked up a small address book, flipped through it, laid it back on the table, picked up a tube of lipstick and removed the cap. "That's not my color, I've never worn red lipstick in my life," she said, replacing the tube inside the purse. She spent several minutes looking at every item without recognition. Removing everything from the wallet, she stared at each scrap of paper or credit card trying to force her mind to remember.

"Well?" Justin finally asked.

"Nothing," she said looking up at him. "Not one single thing is even vaguely familiar."

He sat down beside her and watched as she shoved everything back into the purse.

When she came to the neatly folded wad of cash, she gave him a questioning look. "What should I do with this?" she asked, hoping she could keep it. She had good reason to hold onto the money.

"I'll keep it locked in the safe for now," Justin said.

"You don't trust me?" There went her hope of having money for an airplane ticket.

"I want to make sure you don't take off to Florida before I'm able to get away for a few days." He knew she wasn't going to like that response. He was right.

"Then I'm your prisoner."

"No. Etta or I will take you any place you want to go. I'm just not going to take the chance you'll do something foolish." He could see the flash of anger and disappointment in her eyes. "I know how badly you want to get back to Florida. If you give me your word, you'll stay here until I can take you, I'll give you this purse right now." He studied her for any indication she would agree to his suggestion.

"I'll go back to Florida when I want, not when you dictate." She was fuming. How dare he try and hold her prisoner? She placed the money back in the purse, closed it and threw it at him.

He caught it and gave a sigh of resignation. "I was afraid you'd react this way." He tossed it back to her. "Keep it. If you take off, I can't stop you, but it would be a very dangerous idea."

She gave him an endearing smile, lifted her chin and said, "I promise not to run away if you hurry up and finish your business so you can take me to Florida. Otherwise, I will not promise anything."

He raked the hair back off his forehead, "Kathryn, the airport is closed. You have to give me time. I can't just drop everything and leave. I have a corporation to run."

"Why not? Didn't you say you're the boss, and the boss makes the rules?" She wasn't about to give him an inch.

"I have to finalize three contract negotiations. I have to give my approval and personally sign the contracts. Once that's done, we can leave."

Too tired to argue about it any longer, she said, "Oh, all right. I promise I won't take off for Florida for a minimum of a week. After that, don't hold your breath." She laid the purse on the table close by and within reach of her hand in case he changed his mind. Then she relaxed. If he really wanted the handbag, he could easily take it from her. She was no match for his strength.

"I still wonder why I felt it necessary to have so much money with me. I must have been planning on taking a trip." She brushed the hair from her face, "You know," she told him, "I think I should give Abby a call after all. I know what my mother told me, but I'd feel better if I heard it from Abby. My grandmother has never lied to me."

"What makes you think your mother was lying?"

"I'm not saying she doesn't believe the things she said." She gave him a cynical smirk. "My mother does as she's told." She crossed her arms over her chest defensively. "Justin, you would have had to grow up in my home to understand. I love my mother, but she's not a strong woman. My father dominates her. He always has. She does whatever he tells her. She never questions, never stands up for her beliefs. Not like me. My father and I fought daily. I didn't always win, but I stood up for myself as much as I could." And had the bruises to prove it, she wanted to add but didn't.

She sighed, "I'd just feel better if I could talk to Abby. She's the only person I've ever been able to count on to be one hundred percent honest with me."

He couldn't suppress the hurt he felt that she didn't remember he had always been there for her. "Don't you think I've been honest with you, that I've been there for you, no matter what?"

"How would I know if you have or not?" She frowned at him. "Abby, I remember," she retorted. "You and our life together, I don't. I want to call Abby."

"I thought you said she was very old and not well," he said. "Do you think it's wise to contact her just yet? Shouldn't you wait until you've proven your claims?" If looks could kill, at that moment he would have turned to smoldering ashes.

"It's not a claim, Justin. It's a fact. Apparently, contrary to what you said, you still have doubts."

"I just meant that your family believes you died four years ago. How are you going to prove to them you are who you say you are?"

"At the moment I have no idea," she stated hotly as her temper flared. "Absolutely no idea at all." She sat up straight and declared. "But you can bet I'll come up with something. Now if you don't mind," she said jumping to her feet, "I'm going to call Abby."

"Kathryn," he said gently, grabbing her arm as she walked passed him, "why would Mrs. Blanding say her daughter is dead? Why would she just make up a story like that?"

Kathryn stared down at him, her eyes stinging with unshed tears. "You don't believe a word I've said, do you?" Before he could answer, she pulled her hand away and strode toward the desk.

Justin stood and stared after her. "Don't be obstinate, Kathryn. There's no need to rush into this." He followed her. "You're making a mistake, you know," he said. She was heading for tragedy, and there was no way for him to stop her except to be cruel.

"I've made mistakes before, Justin. I'm going to call Abby."

"Fine!" he yelled, exasperated. "Turn an old lady's world upside down just as you have everyone else's!" He lowered his voice, "God in Heaven, Kathryn, how are you going to explain to your grandmother you're not dead. How is she going to react to you being alive? Think. If she's as old and ill as you say, this could bring on a stroke or heart attack. Do you want that?" When she hesitated, he rushed on, "Well, do you?"

His words made too much sense. How could she not have considered the effect the call would have on her grandmother? Kathryn couldn't believe she hadn't thought it through. Of course, she couldn't call Abby. She would have to wait until she got to St. Petersburg.

She stood with a shocked expression on her face. Justin thought she looked like a lost little girl.

She turned her head and pretended to look out the window, ashamed for the stupid mistake she had almost made. "You're right. On both counts. Abby has had a couple of mild strokes. My call could easily cause her to have another one. I suppose I'm just so desperate to hear a familiar voice. To talk to someone who really knows me, you know. I just wasn't thinking clearly." Her large green eyes were bright with tears.

"I'm sorry," he said and pulled her into his arms. Holding her close, he planted small kisses on her temple. He rubbed her back with one hand, talking in a low, gentle tone, "I know you miss your family. My God, I can't even imagine how you must feel."

She was content to let him hold her for as long as he wanted. She felt cherished. It was not the same feeling as knowing that Abby loved her. This was a new feeling, and it was strange to her. Oh, her mother loved her in her way. Her grandmother had always adored her, yet none of them had ever made her feel the way this man did. Certainly, no other man had ever come close.

She knew the exact moment things changed between them. One second Justin was holding her just to comfort her, next his arms tightened around her. His slow, steady heartbeat of a moment ago now thundered in his chest. When she tilted her head and raised her eyes to his, her own heart began to gallop in response to his intense gaze. She knew he was going to kiss her, and if she let him, the night would not end with just a kiss. Her mind warred with the heat coursing through her body. For the moment, her mind won. She pushed against his chest and stepped out of his arms. "I.. uh, I don't. . . ."

"I know, I know," he said with a ragged breath. "You're not ready for this, are you?"

"No," she told him, taking deep breaths to slow her own breathing.

Justin cleared his throat, "Well then. . . uh," he said glancing down at his watch, "it's late, so I suppose we should call it a night don't you?" He didn't want to call it a night. How could he watch her walk down the hall to Holly's room, while he was left to climb between cold sheets? Alone. What he wanted was to carry her upstairs and slowly remove her clothes and make love to her over and over. What he would get instead was a long cold shower.

It wasn't just the sex. That was a major part of any marriage, but with Kathryn, it was more. He loved her. She was a gut-wrenching need that he could not live without. Day or night, he wanted her, to touch her, to hear her laughter, to know she was his to love and protect. Now his need was a painful knot filled with the fear of losing her.

It was not all that late, but Kathryn was eager to leave the room, to put distance between them. "Yes," she replied, "It's definitely time to call it a night." She started for the door when he called her back.

He pulled her back into his arms, "By the way," he told her softly, "in spite of how bad things seem at the moment, shortly everything will be resolved. I promise."

Justin had a great deal more faith in the future than she did. But then, he wasn't the one who had lost four years of his life. He wasn't the one receiving threatening phone calls, with no idea what they meant. She rested her head against his rock hard chest, wishing she could tell him about the call. Yet, her intuition told her it would just bring on more problems between them.

She stepped out of his comfortable embrace, convinced it would not be a good idea to mention the threats. She raised her eyes to his. "Don't make a promise you can't keep, Justin. Life doesn't always turn out like we plan. But, like you said, maybe things will work out."

"Try and get a good night's sleep. You'll see, things will look different in the morning," he told her.

Shrugging her shoulders, she said with a tentative smile, "I'll see you in the morning." She left the room and climbed the stairs, knowing that in the morning things would more than likely be just as they had been.

Chapter Eight

It was now Saturday. She thought of the dramatic events of the past few days in that order, a new name, new face, and a new life.

Where was her old self hidden away? The fighter who could stand toe to toe with her father? The few facts she had gleaned about her persona, Kathryn Crown, made her wonder how Justin could have loved such a woman. It was as if she had a superficial existence, present in body, but without fire or depth. She, herself, was not that agreeable.

She plopped in a chair, exhausted from nervous energy. Justin had provided her with back issues of all the major newspapers and magazines. They were now strewn across the coffee table and on the floor. Too many events had happened to absorb it all. The whole world had changed, and she had missed it.

Too jittery to sit still, she jumped up and went to the window, forcing aside the depression that threatened to overtake her. She stared out at the mounds of snow still on the ground. A beautiful place, she thought. So different from Florida.

Her thoughts turned to Justin. She smiled. No matter how she fought against it, she found she liked him. Really liked him. He was kind and willing to help her. She had never experienced kindness in a man. He seemed to understand her need to go to Florida as soon as possible, yet flatly refused to let her go alone.

She needed to tell him about the threatening phone calls and the nightmares. She returned to her chair and closed her eyes, letting the images of the complicated dreams filter through her mind. They terrified her. Still, if she could identify who the people were, she might be able to connect them to her past.

There was one recurring dream. In it, Kathryn was always in the same house. The room was surrounded in a red haze. Lying in the center of the floor was a body, the head covered with blood. A menacing shadow on the wall terrified her. She never clearly saw a face, yet everything was familiar. The shadow would reach for her, and she would turn to run, too terrified to scream.

Then the desperate running would begin, the shadowy figure would chase her until she sat upright in bed. At this point, she always awoke drenched with perspiration and gasping for breath.

She shivered from recalling the vivid dream. Several times she had tried to force an additional memory from her brain. But the memories were never clear. They were shadows and vague thoughts dancing at the edge of her mind. The harder she tried, the further away they retreated. Yet she was sure the dream was part of her missing past.

Each time she began losing her grip on her emotions; Justin had been there with a word or touch to steady her. Now, much to her surprise, she found herself clinging to his strength.

She was doing better, she had to admit it. She felt at ease in this house and had even started thinking of it as home. In some ways, she had accepted Justin as her husband. He had gone to great lengths to make her feel comfortable around him. They were both always conscious of the sexual chemistry between them. He had promised not to push her, and he had kept his word.

The ringing of the phone startled her out of her reverie. Thinking it might be Justin calling to tell her he would be late, she hurried to the desk and picked up the receiver.

"Hello," she said cautiously.

The man only said, "Don't forget my warning, Kate."

"I don't know what you want, or even what you're talking about. You listen to me. I'll go to Florida or anywhere else I damn well please!" she shouted and slammed the receiver down. She stood shaking with anger.

If Justin found out about the phone calls, he would try to stop her from going back to Florida. She returned to her chair, a worried frown creasing her brow.

"Who was on the phone?" Etta asked as she entered the room.

"Just a wrong number," Kathryn said, trying to keep her voice nonchalant.

"Damn! You'd think these people would be sure of the number before they dial," the older woman said. But, as if testing, she continued, her watchful eye never leaving Kathryn. "You know what's strange?"

Her insides churning, Kathryn was almost afraid to ask. "No, Etta, what's so strange about a wrong number?"

"This isn't the first so-called wrong number we've had lately. I caught this man's call the other day," she said, planting herself in front of Kathryn. "When are you going to tell Justin how this guy is scaring the hell out of you?"

Kathryn looked up at the concern on Etta's face. "I will tell him. Only not right now."

"And why not? This man is damn frightening. He's nuts. If you don't tell Justin, I will. Maybe he can find out who he is."

Kathryn jumped to her feet and spoke more sharply than she intended, "Etta, I don't want you saying anything to Justin about this!" Seeing the hurt expression on the other woman's face, she softened her harsh tone. "Please, let me tell him in my own good time." She took Etta's hand in hers. "Suppose he does find out who's making the calls, Etta. He might get hurt. Neither of us wants that to happen

"No we don't," Etta said, knitting her brow. "But be sure you do. He's going to be mad if you don't. You know he worries about you. And this man sounds dangerous." She gave Kathryn a sad smile, then whipped around and headed toward the kitchen, calling over her shoulder, "Now I've got to get back to my dinner." She hurried out of the room before Kathryn could say a word.

As she followed Etta out to the kitchen, Kathryn knew she had to tell Justin about the calls soon, or the housekeeper would. For right now, she had to do something to distract herself. "Etta, let me help with dinner," she pleaded.

"No indeedy," Etta told her while pulling pots and pans from the cupboard. "You can't help. You sit yourself down and keep me company. You're not to lift a finger. You need your rest."

"I am so tired of resting I could scream," Kathryn said. "That's all I do. Rest and read." She filled a cup with piping hot coffee and took her seat at the table. "What are we having for dinner tonight?"

"Why just plain cooking, honey." Etta opened the refrigerator and removed a package of chicken breasts.

Kathryn's curiosity was piqued by something Justin had said her first night here. "Why do Justin's parents live in Washington?"

Etta stopped her busy preparation and turned to look at Kathryn for a second. "Adam is a United States Senator. He's on his second term. He's a darn good one too if you ask me," she stated in no uncertain terms.

"A Senator. I had no idea. That's impressive, Etta."

"We're very proud of him. He's done a lot of good for this state. He keeps hell-hacking at Justin to go into politics, but he ain't had no luck. Besides, that boy is happy doing what he's doing."

After that revelation, Etta concentrated on preparing the meal. Kathryn looked around the room, and couldn't help but compare her childhood home to this one. In her parent's house, with all its tall windows, elaborately furnished rooms, Moroccan columns, and arches, there was never that feeling of warmth surrounding her that she felt here. In just a few days, Kathryn felt more at home here than she ever had in St. Petersburg. Except at Abby's house, she reminded herself. She had always loved being with Abby.

"What are you thinking about?" Etta's voice broke in on her thoughts.

Kathryn sat with her elbows propped on the table,

her chin in one hand. "Oh I was just thinking about my parents," she said a little wistfully.

"Well, I know you've always said you were an orphan. That's before you got that bump on your head the other night," Etta added hastily. She poured herself a cup of coffee and joined Kathryn at the table. "I don't have a lot more to do just yet, so tell me about your folks."

Kathryn thought about it. She had never discussed her family with anyone, except her best friend from school, Shiloh Martindale. Her grandmother had always told her that family problems were not to be exposed for all to see. Especially, if the cause of those problems was an upstanding member of the community, highly revered by his peers. Not even her friend knew all the gory details.

Etta wouldn't judge her or her family. Kathryn wished that her own mother could be more like this woman.

Etta's soft voice broke in on her thoughts. "If you don't want to talk about your parents, it's okay."

Kathryn jumped a little, "What? Uh no. Sorry, I guess my mind wandered."

The older woman laid a hand on Kathryn's arm, and said, "You know, Kathryn, we've all thought you were an orphan. Now we find out you really do have folks. Don't you think that would make us all just a little curious?"

"Yes, I suppose it does," Kathryn replied, her brow creased in a frown.

"Well, are you going to tell me or not," Etta asked with a steady gaze.

"They're nothing out of the ordinary. My father's a doctor, and my mother stays at home. That's about it. My grandmother is hard as nails. She and my father do not get along and never will. Abby's a Democrat, and my father is a Republican. Oil and water do not mix."

"Any sisters or brothers?"

"My older brother, Henry, died when I was sixteen."

"Oh, my goodness, so young. What happened to the poor boy?"

"A car accident." Kathryn didn't bother to add she was driving. Henry died. She survived. Each day, she lived with the knowledge that the accident was her fault. It was not a fact she was willing to share.

Seeing the distressed expression on Kathryn's face, Etta glanced at the clock over the mantel and hurriedly changed the subject. "There's not much time left. Justin will be here soon."

Kathryn glanced at the wall clock and rose from the table. "I think I'll get a quick shower before dinner," she said hugging Etta, then hurried out of the room.

Kathryn sat in front of the dressing table brushing her hair. Each time she had seen her reflection this past week, she had been startled to see a stranger staring back at her. "But I have to admit, I'm beginning to like it," she said aloud.

"So do I."

She whirled around to find Justin standing in the doorway. "How long have you been there? I'm not accustomed to being spied on, Justin," she said.

"I wasn't spying," he told her, his eyes full of mischief. "I was merely watching you brush your hair. That is a husband's privilege you know."

Pulling her robe tightly around her, she rose and marched over to stand in front of him, knowing the danger of being too close with nothing on beneath her robe. Forced to tilt her head back to look at him, she said, "Look, Justin."

She never finished the sentence. Before she knew it, Justin pulled her against him in one swift move, close enough, so his breath a hot whisper on her lips. "Get mad if you want to, babe. But, I can't endure denying my need for you a minute longer." Then he lowered his mouth to hers. It was an urgent hungry kiss.

Her pulse surged, and her head whirled with the shock of desire that assaulted her body. She wanted to devour his mouth. She wanted this as much as he did and had wanted this to happen for days.

Nothing else existed for Justin, only Kathryn, responding as he had dreamed of for so many nights. Not the problems they were facing, not even the expected background report from Harv. Just Kathryn. Like this, here in his arms. He swept her up and gently placed her on the bed.

His desire for her was almost uncontrollable as he opened her robe exposing her silky, damp skin. He stood and tore off his own clothes, then ever so slowly lowered his body over hers, his muscles trembling from the effort of controlling his needs.

Kathryn moaned. Her sensitive skin heating with

pleasure as Justin rained kisses down the column of her neck to her breasts. Heat boiled her blood as it rushed through her veins, and she nearly screamed as his tongue caressed each hard nipple. Then when he took one in his mouth and suckled, it was almost more than she could bear. Her world spun out of control, and she bit her lip to keep from crying out her need for him. But to no avail. "Now, Justin. Now," she pleaded.

"Not yet, babe, not yet."

She didn't think she could go on much longer as his hands roamed her body, the touch of his lips on her flesh added to her agonizing need. Just when she felt she could stand no more, he entered her. She arched against him as wave after wave of pleasure pulsated through her. Their bodies in harmony with one another, bathed with sweat, Justin cried out her name as they climaxed at the same moment.

Afterward, they lay facing one another, their legs intertwined. Both sated, yet awed by what had just happened.

"I won't say I'm sorry, Kathryn."

"No need," she answered. "I wanted it as much as you." She turned her face to his chest, still feeling the shock of their lovemaking. It was a new experience for her to respond with such fire. With Robert, it had always been his satisfaction. He had never once been interested in bringing her pleasure. And she had never made love with a man like she had now. No, she thought, no other man had ever aroused her as Justin had.

His arms tightened around her, "I've missed you."

She raised her eyes to his and drew his mouth down on hers and felt the stirring of desire once again.

Justin broke off the kiss and raised himself on one elbow. He gazed down at her, a serious expression on his face. "I would love to continue this, but it's been a long day and dinner is ready. Etta will have a fit if we don't eat while the food is hot." With a mischievous grin, he added, "We can pick this up later."

Kathryn pushed him aside and scrambled off the bed. "I'd better get dressed!"

Justin, amused by the look of concern on her lovely face, rose and handed her the discarded robe. He gathered his clothes from the floor and smiled at her disheveled appearance. "You have never looked more beautiful than you do at this moment," he said as he brushed the hair from her face.

Her face grew warm from his compliment and the memory of their lovemaking. "I don't think Etta would agree with you right now," she hastily added. She pulled the robe on and looked toward the closet. "I have to hurry and dress, Justin."

"Okay, don't worry, I'll shower in my room and meet you downstairs," he called over his shoulder. With his clothes in his hands, he left the room.

Twenty minutes later Kathryn walked into the study. Justin stood by the window, his hands shoved into the pockets of his jeans. His white shirt and blue corduroy jacket stretched across his muscular back. She wore gray slacks and a hot pink cashmere sweater. Her feet were encased in black ankle boots. Justin thought she was startlingly beautiful.

Etta called from the kitchen. "If you two are

going to eat, you better come on. The food's getting cold."

"Come on," Justin said. "Let's have dinner, I'm starved."

Dinner was as delicious as Etta had promised. Kathryn remained silent during the meal. A question from Etta drew her attention back to the conversation.

"Do you have any idea which doctor did the surgery on your face?"

"No, but Dr. Otis says it's the best he has ever seen. I only have faint hairline scars. My father's a plastic surgeon, but it couldn't have been him. Doctors aren't allowed to operate on family members." Unless he deliberately did this to her, she thought. "If it were done in Florida, he would know who performed the surgery."

"Why would anyone want to change a person's features?" Etta said. To have your face altered without knowing anything about what was happening was a terrifying thought.

"That's why we're going to St. Petersburg, to find out who and why," Justin said.

After dinner, they retired to sit before the fire in the study. "When are we going to St. Pete, Justin?"

"As soon as the airport opens. I'm sure they're working on clearing the runways. Hopefully by tomorrow, if it doesn't snow anymore. I can't control the weather, Kathryn."

"I know. Just keep your promise that it will be as soon as possible."

"I don't break my promises, Kathryn," he said seriously. He looked at his watch. It was almost nine-thirty. Where had the evening gone? "We'd better call it a night," arching an eyebrow.

"I am tired," she said and smiled.

As they climbed the stairs, her heart beat in anticipation. She glanced at Justin as though trying to make a decision. When they reached the door of her room, he placed both hands on her shoulders.

"What's on your mind, Kathryn?"

"I was thinking."

He leaned over and kissed her on the forehead. As though reading her mind he said, "The decision is yours, babe."

When Kathryn turned her head toward the closed door, Justin said, "Well good night. Sleep well."

He was almost to his own room when she called out to him.

"Justin."

"Yes," he said turning slowly toward her.

"Uh, I don't want to be alone tonight." She went to him placed her hands on his chest. Her voice faltered, "I'm scared. I can't explain it, but I feel something bad is about to happen, and it scares the hell out of me. Please stay with me tonight."

His arms closed around her and she could feel his breath on her hair as he whispered. "You don't ever have to be alone. Rest assured I'll always be here whenever you need me."

As the bedroom door closed behind them, Kathryn felt a niggling guilt in the pit of her stomach. Here she was about to make love with this man for the second time in one day. Yet she knew in her heart, the first chance she got, she would be on a plane to Florida.

She wondered what it was about this particular man that affected her in this way. No other man had ever caused her to behave so recklessly. When he laid her on the bed and kissed her, she knew, in her heart, this would be the only man she would ever truly love.

Chapter Nine

Justin sat in his office at the Crown Building, a tall, circular configuration of steel and glass. His high-backed leather chair faced the windows over-looking the city. To the southeast, the dome of the old courthouse reflected the golden rays of the afternoon sun. The courthouse halls had long ago ceased to ring with the voices of justice. Now the Pioneer Museum was housed there. To the west, Pike's Peak stood like a gleaming beacon against the azure sky.

His thoughts turned to his phone conversation with his past dinner guest, Charles Stanton. It seemed Charles had conveniently forgotten the name of the obnoxious man he had brought to the party. The man left town the day after the party incident and had not been heard from since.

After fending off several more questions, Charles ended the conversation quickly and coldly. Strange, Justin thought. Perhaps Charles was too embarrassed by the actions of his guest, yet he had acted as though he were the injured party and not Kathryn. It was not the reaction he had expected.

He thought of Kathryn. She had issued an ultimatum now that the airport was reopened. Either they leave by midweek, or she was going alone. She had the money that was in her purse and her credit cards. He couldn't stop her if she decided to leave.

When, on occasion, he had caught her staring at him with an odd expression on her face, she would just smile and resume reading the newspaper. He often wondered if their relationship might be returning to what it was before the accident. He dismissed the idea as impossible. Kathryn continued to sleep in his bed, yet she was far different than the woman he was familiar with. Always in the back of his mind was the question, what happened to my Kathryn? He'd loved the old one, but this new version of his wife kept him guessing. This woman would never be boring.

Every day when he arrived home, he expected Etta to say Kathryn had packed her suitcase and left. Each day he was surprised to find her still there. Now, he regretted giving her back the purse. That much cash could be a temptation for her to leave.

The waiting was beginning to wear on him also. He wanted answers just as much as Kathryn. He could not understand what was taking Harv so long to come up with the information he had requested. Not quite two hours ago, he had placed a call to Los Angeles only to be told that Harv was out of the office for a couple of days. Well, Justin thought angrily, he had damn well better be working on that background check.

For several minutes he just sat staring out the window at the grandeur of the Rockies, impatiently drumming his fingers on the arm of the chair. The buzzing of the intercom jerked his mind back to the running of his business, and he whirled his chair around to face the desk.

"Yes, Betty," he said, after pressing the button.

"Mr. Crown, Harv Anderson is here to see you."

"Here in the office? Not on the phone?" he asked surprised.

"Yes, sir."

"Send him in, and if you don't mind, please bring in a pot of coffee."

Surely Harv didn't find something so serious it warranted a personal visit? He rose and smiled as his Chief of Security entered.

Harv Anderson was six-feet-four, big, broad-shouldered, with powerful hands and the body of an athlete. His close-cropped hair indicated he either spent a lot of time outdoors or was turning gray. His deep California tan made his blue eyes bluer and his teeth whiter. His genuine smile didn't match his craggy face, stubborn square jaw or the laugh creases at the corners of his eyes. He looked older than his forty-two years. He always reminded Justin of an actor he'd seen somewhere, but he never entirely placed the name. Today Harv looked out of place in the stiff white shirt, dark blue suit and overcoat. A former Marine, his rough looks hid a sharp mind skilled at ferreting out information.

After a brief handshake, Harv took a seat in front of the desk. He retrieved a manila folder from his briefcase, and then placed the case on the floor beside him. The man looked uncomfortable making Justin wonder what damaging information could make Harv uneasy.

Justin resumed his seat behind the desk and picked up a pen to keep his hands busy and hide his own apprehension. "You must have found something important. Otherwise, you would have just phoned me or faxed your report. What did you find that made you leave sunny California?"

Before the man could reply, a matronly woman in a navy suit entered with a tray holding cups and a carafe of coffee. He waited until she left the room, and then said, "Well, the sun doesn't always shine in LA, but it is a bit warmer than the Springs right now." The expression on his face intensified as he opened the folder. He raised his eyes and met Justin's gaze.

Dread slammed a fist into Justin's gut. "What did you find out?"

"It's not good." Harv leaned back in his chair. "There's no need to go into detail about how we found out the things we did. I know you don't care about that."

A steely expression entered Justin's eyes, "You're damn right, I don't."

Harv took another deep breath then said, "Well the photos you sent are definitely Kathryn Clark. The only thing we could determine was an age difference, snapshots being untouched as opposed to professional photographs being retouched to eliminate flaws in a person's face. That was the only difference we found. We haven't located the aunt yet, but we did talk to several friends.

"Well, this Kathryn Clark was a busy little lady. More than anything, she wanted to be in show business. Particularly the movies. She also did some stage work now and then. It seems Miss Clark would do anything to get into films. She was quite familiar with several producers."

"Are you saying what I think you are?" Justin asked, the knot in his stomach growing by the minute.

"She wasn't into porno flicks. Far from it." Harv

said. "From the various people we found who did remember her, and most did, she left a vivid impression. She had quite an entourage of admirers who were willing to support her. After all, she was beautiful."

Justin held up one hand to stop the monologue. "You've used the word was several times. Where is this woman now?"

Harv shifted positions in the chair, leaning forward to rest his hands on his knees. "Her friends in California didn't have a clue. They haven't heard from her in several years."

"She just disappeared? How could that happen?" He gripped the pen with both hands, a vapor of apprehension curling in his stomach. "Come on Harv, there's not a person on the planet that you can't find."

Harv proceeded cautiously. "You're right. There is more, much more. I don't think you've told me the whole story about this report you wanted." He shifted uncomfortably in his chair, trying to find just the right words. His mind made up, he looked straight at Justin. "Look, Justin, it might help if I knew why you wanted this background check on these two women?"

For several long minutes, Justin sat staring at Harv. Finally, he said the only thing that made sense to him. "I'm not sure. She is supposed to be my wife."

"Your wife?" Harv croaked. "My God!"

"A lot is going on here. I didn't tell you everything, because I didn't believe what's happened." Justin explained. "I was hoping your report would give me the answers."

"Okay. Now, why don't you tell me what's been going on? Perhaps it will help me in my investigation."

As he listened to Justin relay the events of the past week, the pieces of the puzzle began to fall into place. He flipped through the papers in the folder several times, and when Justin finished, he looked up and said, "Maybe I'd better start at the beginning. I was just giving you bits and pieces before, thinking you could read the entire report at a later date." He rubbed his chin thoughtfully, "Now though, I think we both should go over this together."

"I agree," Justin replied. "Exactly what have you got?"

Harv shuffled through his papers, stacking them in a neat pile on top of the manila folder. "Okay, this is what I have, starting with the Clark woman."

"What do you mean by that?"

"Let me finish, then you'll see what I'm talking about. Okay?"

"Sure," Justin said. He leaned back in the chair and tried to ease some of the tension he was feeling. "Go ahead, I'm listening."

"Well in the spring of 2006, Kate Clark left California for a theater job in Florida. She was never heard from again. But, according to her friends we were able to locate, that wasn't unusual."

"You mean she would disappear from time to time?"

"Well, sort of. I talked with six people who seemed to really know her. A couple went to high school with her. Every one of them told me that when she was into a part, no matter where she was working, she actually tried to live that part. And, they said that she felt that to do it, she had to cut her ties with her friends for a while. After she finished a job, she would turn up and hang out until she got another part. Then they wouldn't hear from her until that job was finished. They didn't see anything unusual about it. It was just the way she was."

"Did any of them know how long she would be gone on this last job?"

"Three of them said she told them she would be back in about six weeks. But she never returned. It's been over six years, and they haven't heard from her."

"That seems strange. No one looked for the woman?"

"Well, you'd think one of her friends would try to find her. But that's not the half of it."

"Go on."

"That's all I have on her from California. Except, all her personal belongings were put in storage by her landlord and later claimed by a boyfriend. The name he gave the landlord was," Harv chuckled at the pun, "Brad Hammer from Florida. No such person exists in L.A. or that I can trace to Florida."

"Is that all?" Justin demanded. "The woman just disappeared from the face of the earth?"

"Not exactly. There's more. I don't think you're going to like it." Harv uttered a tired sigh.

Justin filled both cups with steaming coffee, then handed his friend a cup with a napkin. "Tell me the rest, even if I don't like what you've got to say."

"The hard part is yet to come, I'm afraid."

"Now, I won't know that until you tell me, will I?" Justin retorted.

"I understand now why you sounded so upset when you asked for a background check," Harv stated, picking up the stack of papers from his lap. "This is a bizarre set of circumstances, Justin. It seems that Kate Clark, your alleged wife, and this other woman you asked about crossed paths a little over four years ago."

"Where?" Justin's jaw muscles kept clenching and unclenching. Instinct told him he knew the answer.

"They sort of ran into each other down in Florida."

"Start at the beginning," Justin said. "And start with where in Florida."

"Okay. A little over four years ago, a woman named Abigail Pennington was murdered."

"So."

"She was murdered by her granddaughter." Harv paused to take a deep breath. "Kathryn Blanding. Her name was Kathryn Blanding."

The color drained from Justin's face as he managed to choke out, "Was?"

"She's dead, Justin."

"Dead? When? How?" Releasing his grip on the pen, Justin took a deep breath and asked. "When did she die, Harv?"

"October 25, 2014. In fact, it was the same night she killed her grandmother."

"Were you able to find out how she died?"

"It seems she was in a car crash not three miles from the Pennington residence. According to the police and ambulance reports, there wasn't much left of her when the ambulance got there. She wiped out two cars plus her own. I obtained a copy of Kathryn Blanding's obituary photo." He dug around in his briefcase again and pulled out a black and white copy of a newspaper photograph.

"And my wife? What's all that got to do with her?"

"She was involved in the same accident. In fact, she was severely injured. If Kathryn Blanding's father, a doctor, hadn't come on the scene immediately, she'd have died too. He kept her alive until the paramedics arrived. She had several surgeries and an entire year of recuperation."

"Finish it," Justin said, his voice devoid of feeling.

"Well, it seems that the Blanding woman was the cause of the accident. The police report said she must have been doing over a hundred when she went through a light and slammed into Kathryn Clark's car."

He waited for some comment. When none came, he continued. "According to the accident report, both women were thrown from their vehicles. Kathryn Blanding was thrown into a concrete light pole. If she had landed in the grass, she might have lived, but the force of her head and face connecting with that pole was what actually killed her. Kate Clark did land in a grassy area, but she was thrown through the windshield, and her face was all but destroyed."

"How was Kathryn Clark identified if both women were thrown from their cars?"

"When the fire rescue arrived on the scene, she was unconscious, but her purse was lying under her hand. She had several broken bones and massive facial injuries. Not to mention what all that shattered glass did to her face. Randolph Blanding identified his daughter." He looked up from the file, "Kathryn Clark is lucky to be alive, Justin."

"But is she, Harv? Alive, I mean?"

Harv frowned, "You mean you think there might have been a mix-up."

"Here you have two women involved in the same accident, both thrown from their vehicles close to each other. It is possible, isn't it? "

"I don't think so, Justin. Not in the case of Kathryn Clark."

"What makes you so sure?"

"Well, for one thing, I talked with the fire rescue people who arrived on the scene shortly after the accident. They told me that when they tried to remove the purse from beneath her hand, she gripped it so hard, they had to pry her fingers loose. It seems unlikely the other woman had time to clutch onto anything before she died." He sat with his eyes closed for a few seconds, "No. There's just too much other evidence here to disprove a mix-up."

"How so?"

"Well, for one thing, Kathryn Blanding's father is a well-respected plastic surgeon in St. Petersburg. An outstanding member of the community, he belongs to every civic organization in town. My sources tell me, he even repaired Kathryn Clark's face. Free of charge. He was following his daughter from her grandmother's house. That's why he arrived on the scene so quickly and was able to save Kate Clark and identify his daughter's body.

"But that's not the half of it, Justin. Naturally, the doctor and his wife were devastated over the murder of Mrs. Blanding's mother. Then when they were told that their daughter had not only murdered the old woman, she had also caused a horrendous accident, well, it just compounded their devastation. Yet with all they had to deal with at the time, they insisted on taking the Clark woman into their home while she recuperated. She had to have massive facial reconstruction and was there for over a year."

He laid the file on the edge of the desk and crossed his legs. "No, I'm sure if there had been a mix-up, the Blanding's would have seen it right away. Besides, they didn't look anything alike." He handed the obituary photograph across the desk to Justin.

Well, that took care of the mix-up idea, Justin mused and studied the photo. The picture of Kathryn Blanding showed a woman with thick, dark hair and large, expressive eyes. She was attractive, above average looks, but far from the beautiful woman he had fallen in love with. There was a resemblance around the eyes, but other than that, they were as opposite in looks as the sun and stars. He had no doubts which one shone the brightest.

He stood abruptly and began to pace around the room. My God, what kind of woman had he married? He had to find out. He was boiling inside with so many unanswered questions and felt like he was shadow boxing at the answers. He stopped his pacing and stood at the window, his back to Harv.

"They don't look alike at all."

It was evident Justin was upset by the continuous working of his jaw muscles, and Harv knew why. "Justin, there was no mix-up. Kathryn Blanding is dead. Believe me. The only resemblance between the two women was the fact they both had long dark auburn hair and green eyes. Kathryn Blanding's hair was long and hung almost to her waist, and so did Kate Clark's."

Justin returned to his chair, his face lined with worry and frustration. "Are you telling me that the woman I married is actually Kate Clark? And that now she is pretending to be this Kathryn Blanding. Why? Why would she do that? Doesn't she realize she's pretending to be a murderer?"

Harv shook his head, "Apparently not. Maybe she doesn't know about the murder."

"Did you talk with the Blanding's? Could they explain why their daughter killed her own grandmother?

"No," Harv replied. "God knows I tried, but they refused to talk to me. I got most of my information from the newspaper. And I managed to talk to a couple of the hospital personnel. I also spoke with Kathryn Blanding's partner. She owned fifty-one percent of an interior design firm. This Ted is one asshole, a boozer, and from the financial records I could find, ran the business into bankruptcy. Kathryn Blanding had all the talent. All he possessed was a smile and the charm that convinced people to hire the firm. He had a lot to say. Claims his partner was a royal bitch. Also claims she had the hot's for him." Harv shook his head. "He expounded on their relationship like a man who has been rejected one too many times. Also, he firmly believes Ms. Blanding killed her grandmother for money. The elderly woman was found in her home bludgeoned to death. It seems Mrs. Pennington was a very wealthy lady. Her granddaughter was the sole beneficiary of her will."

"What about her own daughter, Kathryn's mother? Wasn't she in the will?"

"On a hunch, I went to the courthouse. The will is a public record. Kathryn Blanding was to inherit everything. Unless she died, then about one third would go to charity, and the other two thirds would go Sara Blanding."

"So this Ted thinks she killed the old woman so she could inherit her grandmother's money?"

"Well, according to him the business was in trouble financially. They could barely meet payroll. He feels Kathryn did it strictly for the money. He told me she was a pretty cold, calculating bitch. In his opinion, money was all she ever cared about. In fact, she was in the process of divorcing her husband because he didn't have any. It seems she had to work and support them both."

Justin heaved a disgusted sigh and said, "What about the husband?" Was Kathryn still married?

"No one seems to know where he went. Robert Cantree was there one day and gone the next. The people I talked with said he was an aspiring musician and left town to pursue a job in Nashville." Harv hadn't been able to find any trace of the man in Tennessee.

"Who else knows about this report? How many people worked on this?" Justin didn't want any of this information being leaked to anyone.

"You have nothing to worry about, Justin. As far as this report goes, I used two operatives, one in California and one in Florida. Neither knew about the other. So there's no way they could connect the two. You have the only copy of the report. I typed it myself, as you'll see by the typos. No one else has seen it. I kept it with me from the time I finished typing it until I laid it on your desk today."

"I appreciate your discretion," Justin said as he escorted him to the door. "I guess I have some thinking to do. Are you settled in a good hotel?"

"I'm staying overnight at the Antlers Hilton. My flight leaves first thing in the morning."

"If you need anything, just call me at home."

"Okay, buddy." Harv stopped at the open door.

Justin forced a friendly smile, "Keep digging on my wife. Find out about the aunt and uncle who took her when she was seven. Find out all about her entire family, go back to the day she was born if you have to. Find out everything you can.

"Also see what you can find out about Kathryn Blanding's family. I want to know everything about them. You know what to look for. For now, I have a lot to work out for myself. Keep me posted on any new developments. Otherwise, I'll see you soon."

Justin closed the door and returned to his desk. He sat down and rested his head in his hands. Lord God, what a mess, he thought, straightening his shoulders, then began shoving the report into his briefcase glancing quickly at each item as he picked it up. There was a list of names and addresses for several people. He didn't recognize any of them. There was an old newspaper clipping concerning the tragic death of Kathryn Clark's parents, along with the photographs he had sent to Harv in Los Angeles.

He closed the briefcase, left it on the corner of his desk, then leaned back in the chair and rubbed his eyes with the tips of his fingers. After a few seconds, he wearily let his hands fall in his lap.

The information related to him was a mass of contradictions. The woman Harv described did not sound like the woman he had married.

It was as though there were three different women. One was the quiet, reserved woman he had fallen in love with and wed. Kathryn Clark, the woman who seemingly had no scruples or morals, and then, Kathryn Blanding, the woman who had murdered her own grandmother. Three women, and yet they were all wearing the same face. How did he find out which was the real one? How could he find out which one was his wife? He tried to convince himself that his wife, could not, would not, kill anyone. Yet that was the same woman she was now claiming to be. In all their talks this past week, she always insisted she was Kathryn Blanding.

Could it be possible that Kate Clark didn't know about the murder? She must since she lived with the Blanding's for over a year. Plainly they talked about it. Then again, if she did, why would she now want to be that Kathryn? Did she think that by posing as the daughter, she would be welcomed back into the family? That perhaps she could become heir to the Blanding fortune? My God, which woman did he bring home? Well, there was only one way to find out. All trails led to Florida. That was Kathryn Clark's last known destination. That was where Kathryn Blanding had lived.

As for his wife, hell, he just didn't know anymore. The answers had to be in Florida. The sooner they went there, the sooner he would find out who the hell was living in his house. God, I love her so much, he thought. Could I have been blinded by that love? Could I have been so lovesick I never saw the real woman underneath that sweet loving nature?

He stretched his arms over his head and then clasped his hands behind his neck. Several vital meetings were coming up. Well damn, he thought, that's what I've got a vice-president for. He had always had trouble delegating authority. In this instance, he felt he had no choice. Right now, his personal life had to come first. His decision made, he buzzed his secretary and called a meeting for the first thing the next morning. After glancing at his watch and noticing the time, he picked up his briefcase and left the office for the day.

Chapter Ten

The next morning Kathryn woke to the shrill ringing of the phone. She waited for either Justin or Etta to answer, and when neither did, she gave a sigh, picked up the receiver and muttered a groggy "Hello."

"You're takin' a chance lady, talkin' to me like you did. But it don't change nothin'. Like I warned you, you don't want to come to Florida!"

The voice brought her awake with a start. She sat up in bed, the blanket falling away to expose her bare breasts. She was almost afraid to breathe. The man's threat raised the hair on the back of her neck, making her tremble with fear.

She was alone in the room, and desperately wished Justin was there. But, for some unexplained reason, he had slept in his study last night.

"You have the wrong number," she stated, starting to replace the receiver.

"Hold it, you bitch," the man yelled.

She stopped and held the receiver away from her ear as the man's voice grew louder with each word.

"I hear you're plannin' on leaving for Florida real soon. There ain't nothin' here for you but a cold piece of ground. Listen real good, little girl, stay out of Florida."

Stunned, Kathryn could not think. She wished she hadn't lost her temper the last time he called. She sat shaking wanting to slam the receiver back in its cradle, but couldn't move. His raspy breathing came through the line as if he was in the room with her. Finally, she managed to croak out the words, "I told you that you have the wrong number."

"I won't call again," he said. "You've had your warning."

The line went dead, and Kathryn dropped the receiver. She was shaking so she could barely get out of bed. His voice had carried such venom.

She stumbled to the bathroom and turned on the shower, welcoming the hot spray that pounded her back and shoulders. The steam filled the stall, surrounding her like a warm blanket. She stood letting the water beat on her head and run down her face, washing away her tears.

Justin had arrived home last night in time for dinner. Although he was pleasant enough, he had been withdrawn. Several times throughout the evening, she had caught him staring at her as though he'd never seen her before. When she finally asked him if there was something on his mind, he had said a curt "good night" without answering her question.

She turned off the shower and wrapped a large towel around her damp body and blow dried her wet hair. Justin was lounging in the bedroom doorway when she walked out of the bathroom, a look of consternation on his face.

He was dressed in a crisp white shirt and brown wool slacks. He wasn't wearing his usual coat and tie making her wonder if perhaps he wasn't going in to work. She sincerely hoped he was staying home. The last thing she wanted this morning was to be alone.

She wanted to rush into his arms but was too aware of the distance growing between them. Instead, she pulled on a heavy terry cloth robe.

"You look upset," he commented.

"I'm just glad you're here," she said, and clutched the robe more tightly, unable to hide the trembling of her hands.

He had lain awake most of the night contemplating Harv's report and what it said about Kathryn. At the moment he was concerned because he could see she was upset. "What's wrong? What's happened? Kathryn, tell me what's wrong."

She knew he deserved to know the truth, so in a quavering voice, she told him about the phone calls.

"Why in the hell didn't you tell me? Why didn't Etta say something about these calls?" he raged. "What in the world were you thinking? That you could possibly handle this by yourself?"

He paced the room, his hands raking through his hair in frustration. Finally, he stopped and looked at his wife huddled on the edge of the bed. "A crazy man has threatened you, and you don't say a word? What is wrong with you? How can I protect you if you don't let me know what's going on?"

"Etta didn't say anything because I made her promise not to. I wanted to find out myself who was behind the threats," she countered, staring at him. "How could I tell you about this? You doubt everything I've been telling you. Besides, I've always told him he had the wrong number and hung up on him."

She did have a point, and those doubts had doubled since Harv's visit. When he left the office late yesterday afternoon, he'd had every intention of confronting her with the things he now knew.

At first, he wanted to wait until after dinner when Etta would be in her room. He definitely wanted privacy when he showed Kathryn the report. But, she had seemed her old self last night, and that had changed his mind. He decided he would wait until they got to Florida until he had answers of his own. Then he would reveal everything about the report. Thank God, he thought, I'm glad I waited. Things have changed. Again.

Kathryn continued to stare at him. He stood so still, acted so distant, what was he thinking, she wondered? Would this be one of the times Justin believed her? Or would he just give her that look which said, I know you're making this up? She had to solve the mystery of her missing years. No matter how hard she tried, she couldn't think of one single person who would have cause to threaten her.

Her hands were still shaking when Justin sat on the bed next to her. He covered her cold hands with his warm ones.

His steely blue eyes softened as he looked at her. "You can't keep things from me. You hear? I can't help you if you don't tell me what's going on." He released her and reached for the phone and dialed a number. As he listened to the ringing on the other end, he said, "I know how to be sure you're safe when I can't be here with you."

"What are you doing? Who are you calling?" she asked.

He ignored her questions, turning away when the phone was answered. "Jon, Justin here," he said in a clipped voice, "I need you to come ASAP and move into the house until I can clear up some business. Then we're taking a trip to Florida. I'll explain when you get here." He paused for a reply, then said, "See you shortly."

As soon as he had replaced the receiver, Kathryn asked, "Who's Jon?"

He turned to her, glad to see that she was no longer shivering. "Jonathan Campbell is my pilot and our best friend," he told her. "The two of you hit it off the first time you met. We've been buddies since college. He's worked for the family for several years, and although he has a degree in engineering, he prefers to fly. Now, I won't have to worry about you when I'm not here." He pulled her to him and held her in a warm embrace, wanting nothing more than to make love to her. Not now. Not after yesterday. That damn report had changed things.

Kathryn felt his heartbeat increase as she lay in his arms, but when she would have pulled his head down for a passionate kiss, he moved his hands to her shoulders and gently pushed her away from him.

"Jon will be here soon, so perhaps you should get dressed." Even though his mouth was curved in a smile, his eyes held a glint of that same cold, blue steel she had seen at the hospital.

It surprised her that within a few short days, she had fallen in love with a man she barely knew. She wanted nothing more than to show him that love. But something had changed between them. Even though he showed great concern for her safety, aloofness emanated from him now. She knew he wanted to make love as much as she, but something stopped him.

She had to say something. So she said the only thing that came to mind, "Thank you for thinking of my welfare, Justin."

Justin took her face in his hands, "I love you, Kathryn. Don't ever forget that fact. Please don't keep things from me again."

She looked up at him. There was a hint of wariness behind the emotion in his eyes. What, she wondered, would she have to do to erase it?

She meant every word. "I won't keep anything from you again. But, you have to do the same," she said, her voice husky but serious, hoping Justin would tell her what was bothering him.

"You bet," he said and stood. "Now you'd better get dressed before Jon arrives. I'll go on down and make sure there's plenty of coffee."

Kathryn hurried to the closet and pulled on a pair of rust wool slacks and a pale yellow sweater, then pushed her feet into a pair of soft brown leather boots. She ran a comb through her still damp hair and applied a pale lipstick. "I'm as ready as I'll ever be," she commented to her reflection and hurried downstairs.

She followed the sound of laughter into the large family style kitchen. Justin, Etta and a man she assumed to be Jon sat around the table drinking coffee.

Jon's lanky frame was sprawled in the chair, his coppery hair unruly, and his bright blue eyes filled with amusement. He stood when he saw her. She could see he was as tall as Justin but wirier. Freckles sprinkled his nose, giving him a boyish look, even though she knew

Justin and he must be around the same age. A wide grin split his mouth at the sight of her, and he picked her up, swinging her off her feet.

"God, Kathryn, you get better looking every time I see you." He noticed her astonished expression, and set her down, resuming his seat at the table.

Justin said with a grin. "You're not making a good impression. Why don't you wait to be introduced before you force your attentions on her?"

"Hell, buddy, I don't need an intro where this pretty lady is concerned," he said in a western drawl. He patted the chair next to his, "Come on over here and sit by me."

Justin pulled out the chair beside him, "Sit here, Kathryn. I can see you need protecting from this guy. He fancies himself a lady's man. However, I know better."

She took her seat, while Etta poured her a cup of steaming coffee and whispered to her, "Don't worry about him, honey. He's as harmless as a baby. He just likes to joke around."

"Sorry. Justin told me about your memory problem." Justin had also cautioned him that she refused to admit she had amnesia, and that she blew a gasket when that particular word was used. "I guess I just thought you still might remember me."

"That's all right, Jon," she said. "Justin told me you're a close friend."

"That I am," he responded. "Now what is this about someone threatening this sweet thing?" he directed his question to Justin.

Justin explained the situation to him

"My God!" he said. He gave Kathryn a compassionate glance then turned his attention back to Justin. "We can leave tomorrow as far as I'm concerned. I've got nothing going on for a few weeks."

"I have a meeting this morning I can't get out of and one in the morning, then we can pack and leave tomorrow afternoon."

"Okay then," Jon turned to Kathryn. "Consider me your watchdog while Justin is at his meeting. I'll be right beside you at all times."

"You don't have to stick that close," she said. "It's not like we're going to be running around." She picked up her cup. The coffee was still hot, and she took a long swallow.

"You watch her," Justin directed. "Don't let her leave the house. She's safer here than anywhere else." Then he placed a quick kiss on Kathryn's cheek and left the room.

"Look at it this way, Kathryn. We'll have some time to get to know each other again."

She knew it wasn't his fault, but at the moment she was irritated with everyone, herself included. "I am just a little tired of having to get reacquainted with people, Jon."

"Well, it won't do you any good to be nasty to me. I'll still stick to you, no matter what you say. So you might just as well smile and make the best of the situation. After all, I do work for Justin. What he tells me to do, I do." After a few minutes he tried to break the stony silence, "Hey look, maybe I'll say something witty that will spark a memory for you."

She could not help but smile at his boyish charm, "Okay, I suppose you have a point. Maybe I'm overreacting."

"There you go," he said. "You do as I say just until we leave, and I'll try not to say anything to make you mad. Okay?" He held out his hand.

His blue eyes gleamed with sincerity. Kathryn liked this man.

There was no pretense to Jon. He was what he was. An intelligent man with a great sense of humor whose passion was flying. Yet he could recite poetry if prompted, and could recall every poem Robert Frost had written. He loved history, especially anything concerning the Civil War, Rock, and Roll or Country music, while she and Justin preferred light classical.

That evening they had finished eating dinner, and Jon insisted on teaching her to play chess.

"Go on, babe. Jon's an excellent teacher," Justin said.

"Oh, all right. I suppose it won't hurt to give it a try."

"That's the spirit, Kathryn," Jon said and gave Justin a wicked grin. "If Justin can get the hang of it, I know you can."

"Hey, watch it, pal," Justin said.

Kathryn sat down at the small table and began setting up the chess board according to Jon's instructions. She had never had the patience for playing board games and always found herself slightly nervous at the prospect of learning a new one. She had just finished setting the pieces on her side of the board when her hand accidentally brushed against the king sending it falling to the floor.

Just as she and Jon both leaned over to pick up the chess piece, one of the panes in the French door exploded. Kathryn screamed as Jon threw himself on top of her.

"Stay down! Don't anybody move!" Justin shouted and looked around and saw a hole in the opposite wall.

"What's going on in here?" Etta shouted as she ran down the hallway.

"Get back, Etta! Don't come in here!" Jon ordered.

"Jon, is Kathryn okay?"

"Yeah, he missed her."

"Everyone stay put. I'll call the police," Justin instructed. He grabbed the phone and dialed 911. "Don't get up yet. He may still be out there, and none of us have weapons."

Kathryn's heart thundered in her chest. She tried to breathe, but the weight of Jon's body was crushing her. "Please, Jon, you're killing me," she told him as she gasped for air.

"Sorry," he mumbled and rolled off her. "You stay put. That shot couldn't have been aimed at anyone but you."

The initial shock slowly wore off as she lay on the floor where she had landed. She was on her stomach but raised her head slightly. "Are you okay Justin?"

"Fine, babe," came his reply. Then he yelled to

Etta, "You're not standing near any windows are you?"

"Lord, have mercy, no. I'm sitting on the floor here in the hallway."

"Stay there, Etta," Jon told her. "We can't be sure he's gone yet."

Soon sirens could be heard in the distance. In case the gunman was still outside, they remained on the floor. Justin crawled to the door and switched off the lights, plunging the room into semi-darkness. The only light came from the fireplace. Etta had already turned off the light in the hallway.

Within minutes of being called the police were pounding on the front door. Jon helped Kathryn to the sofa, and Etta joined her. The men met the two officers outside. After they inspected the grounds and found nothing, they questioned Jon and Kathryn as to possible enemies. Kathryn wondered why they didn't ask Justin the same questions. After all, Justin Crown was a prominent businessman.

Justin pointed out the bullet hole in the wall above the fireplace. One of the policemen dug it out with a knife, slipped it into a plastic bag, tagged it, and then put the bag in his coat pocket. After speaking quietly with Justin, the officers left with assurance a patrol car would be parked on the street in front of the house for the rest of the night.

When Justin returned to the study, he looked directly at Kathryn. "Are you sure you've told me everything about those phone calls?"

When she hesitated, he asked, "Well?"

"There is one thing I. . . ."

"What?" he cut her off.

She took a deep breath to calm herself against the anger in his eyes. "Well," she said hesitantly, "the other day I did tell him I would go wherever I damn well please." She gave a feeble smile. Before Justin could respond, she continued, "He just made me so damn mad. Telling me to stay out of Florida. Who does he think he is anyway?"

"A killer, Kathryn. He's a killer. That should be obvious now, don't you think?" Who was it he wanted to kill, Justin wondered, Kathryn Clark or Kathryn Blanding?

"Justin, honestly. As usual, I spoke before I thought. Abby has always said my mouth is my worst enemy."

"Abby's right." Justin announced, "Let's pack. We're leaving bright and early tomorrow morning."

Jon had brought clothes for the trip when he had moved in to protect Kathryn. "Justin, I'll go check out the plane and make sure it's ready for tomorrow's flight. Shouldn't take me more than a couple of hours. I'll be back to stay here tonight."

After Jon left, Kathryn was both elated and frightened over the trip. One moment she couldn't wait to get back home; the next, she would remember the phone calls and her insides would churn. Still, she wanted to get to Florida as fast as possible.

The next morning as they boarded the sleek Lear Jet, Kathryn vacillated between eagerness and terror.

"Make yourself comfortable," Justin said. "I'm going to sit with Jon." and he hurried to the cockpit.

"Make sure you fasten your seatbelt," he called over his shoulder.

She fastened her seatbelt and looked around the cabin. The interior of the plane was spacious. Besides the two dark-blue leather seats facing each other, two double rows faced the front of the aircraft. Justin had insisted on leaving before Etta fixed breakfast or even coffee. Caffeine was a staple for Kathryn, and she was dying for a cup.

He had been as anxious to make this trip as she. It made her wonder about that as the small plane lifted off. Lost in thought, she was unaware of the noise or aroma of coffee coming from the galley until Justin handed her a steaming cup.

"Here," he ordered, "I know you must be craving a cup."

Kathryn looked down at the cup. "Why is it," she asked, "that every time you want me to do something you make it sound like an order? I swear there are times you remind me so much of my father."

She didn't wait for him to respond before taking several sips from the cup.

He sat in the seat across from hers, watching. Justin ignored the remark, but now he was curious. When she lowered her cup, he said, "Tell me about your father. You've hardly mentioned him."

She stared at him for several seconds. "In some ways, you're a lot like him."

"How so?"

"He's a pompous ass," she said.

Justin roared with laughter. "Am I that bad?"

Forced to smile, she replied, "Sometimes. In fact, most of the time," she added.

"Well, damn." He rubbed his chin thoughtfully. "I never would have thought of myself as a pompous ass."

"Well you do have some good points too," she added.

He sat with one elbow propped on the arm of the seat, his chin in his hand. "We'll discuss those later," he said, his eyes crinkling with amusement. "Right now I want to hear about your family."

"My father's a difficult man. He's a control freak. No one's opinion counts but his."

"You don't like him much, do you?"

She averted her eyes and glanced out the window, wondering just how much she should tell him. When she faced him again, her eyes were filled with the anguish of past memories. "Justin, my father is the world's greatest son of a bitch. Actually, I despise the man."

"That's pretty drastic, Kathryn. Was he really that bad when you were growing up?" Justin thought of his own father, whom he loved dearly. He couldn't imagine what had caused her to feel the way she did. It was such a contradiction to Harv's report of a man who was a leader in his community, a kind man who repaired the face of a woman, destroyed by his daughter. Kathryn's version of the man puzzled him.

"Your house is truly a home, Justin," she continued. "It's full of love and warmth. I feel more at home with you than I ever did in my father's house." The more she talked, the more animated she became. Her eyes flashed with suppressed anger and resentment. Her hands sliced the air as she drove home her point.

"Do you realize that until I was in your house, I had never eaten in the kitchen? No," she emphasized with a shaking finger, "the kitchen was for the cook. The family ate in the formal dining room. I don't think my father ever entered that room. Whenever he had orders for Sally, our cook, he summoned her to his study."

"You make him sound like an ogre, Kathryn."

"Believe me, he is. My father is an overbearing, arrogant bastard. He has this idea that only low-class individuals come to the dinner table improperly dressed. Dining was an occasion in our house. He always told us, it was his way of separating the classes. We had to maintain our status. Status and public opinion mean everything to him. He ruled the house with an iron fist. I mean that literally."

"You mean he was abusive?" Justin was appalled by the image of any man striking his wife.

The memory of what she was about to tell him brought tears to her eyes. "Yes. Once, when I was sixteen" she said, pausing for a moment. There was a tremor in her voice when she continued. "I was determined to defy him. I came to the dinner table in jeans and an old sweatshirt. That was the first time he had hit me in years. That night as soon as I walked into the dining room, he stood up and slapped me across the face and ordered me from the room."

She tried to smile through her tears, "I was a very determined young lady. When I stood my ground, he slapped me, picked me up and carried me up to my room kicking and screaming all the way. He locked me in that bedroom for three days. Without food, I might add."

"Dear Lord," Justin whispered. "Didn't your mother try to stop him?"

When Kathryn spoke, her voice was filled with shame. "I never once saw her stand up to my father."

"Did he abuse her?"

"God, yes," she replied. "When I was small, I didn't realize the real reason for her bruises. Then one night when I was six, I woke up and wanted a glass of water. I went down the hall to their bedroom door. That's when I learned why my mother cried most of the time. I could hear him beating her, and her begging him to stop. But he wouldn't. The sound of his fists hitting her terrified me. From that night on, I stayed as far away from him as possible. Not that it was a chore, mind you. My father never loved me like he did my brother. That night I swore, when I grew up, I would take my mother far away so he couldn't find her."

Justin found it hard to associate the picture she was presenting of her father as the same man in Harv's report. If Randolph was as abusive as she claimed, why would Sara stay with him?

"But you didn't, did you? Take your mother away that is."

"No. After the blue jean incident, I moved in with my grandmother. I never spent another night in my father's house. Not that he wanted me there," she said, with a heavy-laden sigh. She sat back in her seat, relieved to have finally gotten some of her bitterness off her chest. "After three days, my father gave my mother permission to unlock my bedroom door. I went straight to the kitchen and got the largest knife Sally had. I marched to his study and kicked open the door. You should have seen his face," she said chuckling at the memory. "He turned white as a sheet when I told him that if he ever laid a hand on my mother or me again, I would cut his throat while he was sleeping. Then my mother and I had a terrible argument. I packed my things and moved in with Abby. I couldn't stay and watch it any longer. Besides, I knew that one of us would kill the other if I didn't get out of the house."

"What about your mom? Why would she stay and take that kind of treatment?" He unconsciously shook his head. "I don't understand it."

She leaned against the back of the seat, listening to the drone of the plane's engines. "I don't know why she stayed. I begged her to leave, Justin. Every time he beat her, I would cry and beg her to leave. She refused. She would tell me he didn't mean it, that it was all her fault. If she hadn't made him so mad, he wouldn't have hurt her."

She shook her head. "That man is such a hypocrite," she bit off each word. "Do you know that he does volunteer work for the battered women's shelter! Oh, they think he's wonderful. The great plastic surgeon, Randolph Blanding, repairing the battered faces of the women who come to the shelter to get away from their abusers. Then he goes straight home and beats his own wife. My God! It makes me sick to even think about it!"

Wary, Justin watched her. She sounded so

convincing. How does she do it? He wondered. How did Kathryn Clark learn about all this going on in the Blanding family? Did she just make up the things she told me? No, she's not that good an actress. No one is. And yet she hadn't mentioned the dead grandmother. Surely if she knew about the abuse, if there were abuse, she would know that the real Kathryn Blanding murdered her grandmother.

He wanted to confront her at that moment. More than anything, he needed to get to the bottom of the puzzle, yet knew he couldn't. He had to wait and see what would come next. What would she do once they got to Florida?

There was more to it than that. Justin had a big problem. He loved his wife. He wanted her to be just who she said she was. Kathryn Blanding with a case of amnesia. That would also mean she would have to stand trial for murder. He had to stop thinking about it or go crazy trying to figure it out.

Kathryn saw a change come over him. She could see beads of sweat on his upper lip and forehead. "Justin, are you all right?"

"I'm fine," he said, knowing otherwise. "Didn't your grandmother do anything to help your mother?"

"She tried. Though I don't believe she was ever aware of the extent of Randolph's abuse. Mom always had a rational explanation for her bruises. Or if she had been beaten really badly, she would just stay away from Abby until she healed. Abby tried to talk mom into leaving, but she got the same excuses I did."

"That's too bad. It really is," Justin stated. "What about your brother? Did he just stand by and let it all happen?"

Kathryn paled at the mention of her brother. She almost choked as she said, "Henry did everything he could to keep us safe. The only peace we had was when Henry was home, and that was only during school breaks. Dear Daddy kept him at a military prep school most of the time. It was after that dinner scene. Henry had come home from school for some reason. He came over to Abby's to pick me up. I insisted we go to a party at one of my so-called friend's house." She didn't want to remember, but the images swirled around in her head. It had been all noise, flashing lights, booze and marijuana clouding her brain that night. How quickly a person can sober up when something terrifying happens, then it was pain, fear, and grief beyond comprehension.

"I drank too much," she confessed, "smoked some pot, got thoroughly sick. Henry found me in one of the bedrooms and insisted on taking me home. In the car, I got it in my head he was taking me back to my father's house." She couldn't stop the tears rolling down her cheeks. "I grabbed the steering wheel. We flipped two or three times, I don't remember exactly. I was wearing my seat belt, Henry wasn't. You know the old saying; God takes care of drunks and fools. That was me, drunk and a fool. Henry died at the scene. I walked away with minor bruises. It was my fault. I've had to live with that ever since."

Stunned into silence, Justin sat staring at Kathryn. What could he say to ease a pain of that magnitude? He was saved from trying to find the words by Jon's voice coming over the intercom to break the mood.

"We'll be landing in about thirty minutes, Justin."

Justin leaned over and placed a kiss on her forehead. "I'm sorry for all you've been through. Try not to worry. I'll see you in a few minutes."

Kathryn watched him walk through the door of the cockpit after securing the galley. After her confession about her family, she realized he was nothing like her father. She fastened her seatbelt and prepared for the landing in St. Petersburg.

Chapter Eleven

As soon as they stepped onto the tarmac at Albert Whitted Airport, both Kathryn and Justin realized their mistake. The sun beat down on the asphalt with a ferocious intensity.

Kathryn's gray wool slacks and cashmere sweater were already clinging to her body, and her upper lip beaded with perspiration. "Lord, I've lived here all of my life. I should have remembered how hot it can be this time of year."

"Well, we'll change as soon as we get to the hotel," Justin took off his wool jacket and draped it over one arm.

Jon secured the plane and made arrangements to leave it in a hanger during their stay. He loaded the luggage in the rented Lexus and climbed behind the wheel. Justin and Kathryn climbed into the back seat, welcoming the icy blast of the air conditioner.

It was a short drive from downtown, across the Bayway to St Pete Beach. The moment Kathryn saw the large building, she sucked in a breath. There in the distance was the Don CeSar. She had always loved this view of the hotel. As they drove onto the bridge, the water was greener than she remembered, and the grand hotel stood pink and palatial in the distance. It was a picture postcard scene.

The Don, as it had always been called, wasn't exactly pink. It was more a blend of pink and coral. She remembered reading that the color had been specially blended for this hotel. It was called Don CeSar Pink. The windows were trimmed in white and stood out against the backdrop of a cloudless blue sky and the turquoise horizon of the Gulf of Mexico.

She had wanted to spend a weekend at the Don's Resort and Spa. The beautiful people, the top celebrities in the country stayed there when in town. The rooms were pricey, but for her, it was the Penthouse or nothing.

As Jon drove over the bridge leading to the beach, Kathryn couldn't drink in the sights fast enough. She hadn't realized how much she loved this place until now. She had always taken it for granted.

Kathryn felt Justin staring at her and glanced over at him. He had a morose expression on his face. Feeling her eyes return appraisal, he turned his head to stare out the window, giving her cause to believe he had something on his mind. Something he didn't want to talk about.

For a brief second, she wondered if perhaps she should have come alone. She knew she would have more success in finding out what had happened if she were by herself. Then again, she thought, maybe I should have stayed in Colorado longer until I felt ready to take on the past.

When Jon turned the car toward the beach, and the sun bathed everything in a golden haze, she knew she had been right to come. Quickly, she rolled her window down just enough to breathe in the scent of the salt water. God, it felt good to be home.

To her surprise, Jon pulled the car into the parking lot and up the ramp to the entrance of The Don. How could Justin have known, she wondered? I don't remember saying anything about it to him. Then again, she reminded herself, he has a habit of reading my mind.

She turned to Justin and smiled, but before she had a chance to thank him for being so thoughtful, Jon turned off the engine and turned toward them. "Just as you ordered, boss. The best hotel in the area. The Don CeSar," he proclaimed.

Justin helped Kathryn out of the car, and keeping his hand at the small of her back, he said, "I, for one, am dying of thirst in this heat." He turned to Jon, "Why don't we get checked in, freshen up, and then meet in the restaurant later." He took Kathryn's arm and propelled her toward the front desk, then dropped back to speak quietly to Jon.

Kathryn was pleasantly surprised by the two-bedroom suite with a clear view of the Gulf. The room was designed for the needs of the active business man or woman which included a complete workspace and a well-stocked mini-bar.

Justin immediately called room service for ice and a pitcher of tea, then quickly showered and changed into a pair of lightweight tan slacks and a blue polo shirt. "Why don't you take a shower and rest," he said. When he saw the frown on her face, he added, "I need to see Jon for a few minutes, then you and I can have a leisurely lunch."

"I think I'll take a shower," she told him. "But then I want to get started. I'm anxious to see my mother and Abby."

"I know you are, but I think we should wait at least a day. I'd rather we relax until tomorrow. That way we can get a fresh start before trying to unravel your past." He stood with his hands in his pockets, his expression revealing he fully expected her to abide by his decisions. This angered her in the way nothing else could have.

"I'm not here for a vacation, Justin. I want to get started on my search for the truth as soon as possible," she said, her voice conveying her irritation.

"Look, Kathryn," Justin said, running a hand through his hair in frustration, "I already have Harv working on some things. When I hear what he's discovered, then we'll have a better handle on how to proceed."

"Am I to understand that we'll proceed at your direction? Is that the way it's going to be?" Her anger was getting the better of her, and she knew it. She grabbed a lime green sun-dress from the pile of clothes she had unpacked, rummaged through her suitcase for underwear then said stiffly, "I'm going to shower."

Before she got halfway to the bathroom, Justin grabbed her from behind and wrapped an arm around her waist. "Hey, wait a minute." He caressed one side of her face. "It was only a suggestion," he said. He drew her stiff frame to him, wrapping her in his arms. They stood in that position for several minutes until Kathryn's breathing slowed and she regained her composure.

Kathryn stepped out of his arms, "Why wait, Justin. I really want to get started." Her tone was more controlled, but at the same time, her anger was still smoldering.

"I know you do, Sweetheart, but," he took a deep breath and continued, "look, Kathryn, I didn't really want you to know this, but Jon thinks we were followed from the airport."

"What!" she exclaimed. "Is Jon sure about this?"

"Well, he thought he saw a car behind us most of the way here. He's downstairs now watching to see who comes and goes for a while. We just want to be sure, Kathryn. That's all." He went to the small wet bar and poured himself a drink, then came back to stand in front of her, "You know," he said smiling down at her, "we don't even have a plan yet."

"A plan?" she stammered. When Justin looked at her like that, all rational thought fled.

He knew he had won by the expression in her eyes. He also knew he could take her to bed this minute, but now was not the time. First, he had to make sure she was safe. Then he would satisfy both their desires, he told himself.

"Yes, a plan," he said after a long moment. "We can't go storming into your father's office, or your grandmother's house." He wasn't about to bring up the fact that her grandmother, if indeed the old woman had been her grandmother, was dead. There would be plenty of time for that later. Yet as he stood there looking into those huge green eyes, he knew in his heart that this woman had never killed anyone in her life. She may not be as innocent as she claimed, but she was not a killer. Of that he was sure. The rest could be dealt with at a later time.

"No, I don't want to see my father just yet. But I am going to see my mother. Don't try and stop me, because no matter what you say, I'm going," she said, throwing the clothes onto the bed.

Damn! His plan wasn't going to work. He knew it wouldn't do any good to forbid her. She would go whether he wanted her to or not. He sure as hell wasn't about to let her go alone.

Trying to get her to see reason, he suggested, "I'll go talk with Jon, you get your shower," he glanced at his watch, "then join us downstairs in about an hour. After we've eaten, we'll do some sightseeing, then visit your mother first thing in the morning. How about that?"

"No, that is definitely not okay with me." She wasn't about to budge from her decision to see her mother today. "I've been gone a long time, Justin. I've seen the sights around here. I'm not a tourist. This is my home, and I'm not waiting another day to see my family."

Voice little more than a growl, he bit out, "Apparently you've forgotten one crucial point, Kathryn. Your family thinks you died almost four years ago. How do you plan to explain the fact that it wasn't you they buried? And," he added a little too viciously, "exactly who did they bury?"

He knew he had gone too far, and wished he could take back his words. He caught the stony glare Kathryn shot his way. The way she was gritting her teeth revealed how close she was to losing her temper.

Kathryn turned her back on him. She had to, or she would have thrown something at him. God, I hate it when he's right, she thought. She managed to smother her anger, then turned to face him. "I'll go along with your idea of a shower and lunch. You and Jon feel free to go sightseeing, but I'm still going to visit my mother. I'll make her understand it's really me, Justin, I know I can."

Justin knew he was beaten. It would do him no good to argue with her further. "All right," he told her with a defeated sigh. "We'll do it your way. Just meet us downstairs in the lounge whenever you're ready."

He walked to the door, then slowly turned back to face her, "Don't even think of taking off on your own," he said, before closing the door behind him, leaving Kathryn standing in the middle of the floor ready to do further battle.

She picked up the clothes she had thrown on the bed and stormed off to the shower. She dried herself with one of the hotel's large fluffy towels and slipped into her underwear and sundress. After applying a pale pink lip gloss, she brushed her hair until it gleamed with red highlights. She stood staring at her reflection in the mirror. She now had the sort of complexion that Abby often referred to as "That damn Yankee look, all pale and washed out."

She turned and looked longingly at the telephone sitting on the bedside table. Abby! God how she wanted to talk with Abby. She took two steps toward it and stopped herself. No matter how much she wanted to, it would be wrong to call her. Justin had been right when he said it might be too much for a woman her age. She shook off the despair that clung to her and stepped out onto the balcony. She had to maintain control and be logical.

The waves lapped the shore like soft kisses, and she let the peaceful sound wash over her. No matter what had happened in the past, this was home, and it felt good to be back. For a few minutes longer, she enjoyed the caress of the sea breeze on her skin. The sun felt good after the chill of the room's air conditioner. She stepped back inside and checked her watch. Nearly an hour had elapsed since her fight with Justin. Her anger over his obstinacy still lay just below the surface.

She picked up her purse, left the room, and took the elevator to the first floor. She found Justin and Jon at a table in the back corner of the restaurant. They appeared to be deep in a serious conversation. When she approached, they stopped talking. "Don't let me interrupt you, gentlemen," she said, sitting across from Justin.

"You didn't," he responded.

They ordered a light lunch and ate in silence. As soon as the meal was finished, Kathryn stood. "Ready?" she asked as though there had never been a heated argument just two hours ago.

Jon went for the car while Justin paid the bill. Kathryn waited at the front door of the hotel, now uncertain of her plan. Perhaps Justin was right; maybe she should wait until morning. No, there was no backing out now.

"Where to?" Jon asked the moment they climbed into the back seat.

"My parents live on Snell Isle. Once we get across the Bayway, I'll give you directions."

"Oh, I know where that is," he said, grinning at her in the rearview mirror.

She gave him the street address and then sat back in the corner of her seat.

They rode in silence for a time. Whey the car

entered St. Petersburg city limits Justin leaned across the seat and put a finger under Kathryn's chin, forcing her to look at him. He wanted to kick himself for fighting with her. "If you want, we can forget about all of this, and go back home tonight. It's entirely up to you."

Her irritation faded just as quickly as it had come when she saw the sincerity in his eyes. "There's nothing I'd like better, Justin," she told him. "But I have to see this through. I can't spend the rest of my life wondering what happened to me. The answer is here, and I have to find it."

"That's what I thought," he said gently, giving her a quick kiss, and leaned back in the seat. He knew she was nervous and needed time to prepare herself for the upcoming confrontation. He had no doubts it would be just that. After all, he had heard Sara Blanding's screams of outrage over the phone.

Kathryn sat quietly, her mind absorbed by the dread of being rejected by her mother. Her palms were sweaty, and her stomach was rolling. She fervently wished she hadn't eaten lunch. "Jon," she needed to take her mind off the impending visit, "you've been here before? You seem familiar with this area."

He turned his head briefly, flashing her a bright smile. "Yeah, I was a beach bum for about a year after I got out of the Marines. But the heat and humidity were too much for me. Besides, I missed the mountains too much."

After that exchange, the silence became stifling. Kathryn could feel the tension building within her, yet was powerless to stop it. Even Jon's usually bright smile dimmed as they drew nearer their destination.

Sooner than expected, Jon pulled into the circular driveway in the front of the Blanding residence with its red tile roof just as she remembered. It was a massive two-story Spanish/Mediterranean style house with five bedrooms and five full bathrooms and two half baths. She always wondered why they needed so many. Her bedroom and Henry's had been on the second floor. Her room had been at the back of the house with a balcony on the opposite side from her parents' master suite on the ground floor.

Sandwiched between the master suite and the living room was her father's dreaded study where he had issued his daily commands to her and her mother. She hated that room with its dark furniture and cave-like atmosphere. The rest of the house was different, light and airy with arched-top windows, French doors in each leading to the verandah. Even her father's study had French doors.

It was an impressive house. The main entrance was dramatic with the hint of Moroccan columns and arches leading to stained glass double doors. The stained glass art was protected between two panels of shatterproof glass. She remembered how proud her father had been when the doors were installed. He'd boasted that each window pane had cost him forty thousand dollars.

The waterfall crystal chandelier in the grand foyer hadn't cost nearly that much. On rare moments, the arched windows over the front doors would bounce a ray of sun through the crystals and shoot rainbows around the foyer. Kathryn thought of how those few moments had given her so much joy more than the elaborate doors.

As Justin walked around to open her door, she glanced at the two cabbage palms across from the entrance and on the other side of the driveway. The palms were new. The bed of roses was the same. Taller perhaps, yet other than that, unchanged. He took her hand, and she stood beside him, suddenly trembling from head to toe.

Jon's voice startled her as he said, "Don't be nervous, Kathryn. Justin will be right beside you. And," he added with his jaunty grin back in place, "if you need me, all you have to do is yell."

"Thanks, Jon," she said, her voice full of emotion.

She gripped Justin's hand as they walked to the imposing front doors, wishing with all her heart that she could just open it and step in. She used to stop by to see her mother at least once a week. Things were different now. Now she had to wait for Sally, the housekeeper, to open the door. With this in mind, she reached out and pressed the bell with a shaking hand and racing heart.

Too soon the door opened, and a large black woman in a navy and white uniform smiled a greeting. "Hello, Sally," Kathryn said softly.

The woman just stood there, a surprised expression on her round face, then after a moment, her brown eyes lit up. "Well my goodness. Come in, Miss Kathryn, come in."

The cool foyer was a welcome relief from the hot sun beaming down on the front stoop. Kathryn could feel her tense muscles relaxing a bit. Sally's friendly but polite manner seemed strange. But then again, she had no idea how much time had elapsed since her face was changed. Still, she did seem to know her. She had to make sure, "Do you know who I am, Sally?"

"Sure I know you, honey. Now you all come on in the living room. I'll just go tell Mrs. Blanding you're here. I know she's going to be surprised."

They followed her out of the foyer through the arched doorway into an all too familiar living room. Only the best furniture would suit her father. He had ordered each table and chair crafted to his specification. They sat on the sofa and waited. Matching wingback chairs in gold velvet sat in front of the fireplace, each chair placed for maximum effect. As soon as the housekeeper left the room, Kathryn turned to Justin.

"She recognized me," she whispered with a breathless catch in her voice.

"It certainly seemed like it. But she did seem a little stand-offish, don't you think?"

"My father requires the servants to be friendly, but aloof. Familiarity breeds contempt, per the old saying and my father," she replied, letting her gaze roam around the room, taking in all the familiar things she grew up with. It was as if the missing years had never happened. The room was the same as the day she left. The baby grand piano still sat near the three French doors leading to the outside lanai.

In all the years she had lived in this house, she had never paid the slightest heed to how perfect it all looked. Not a speck of dust dared to touch the tall silver candlesticks sitting on the mantel above the floor to ceiling stone fireplace. The heavy green tied-back drapes at the tall windows could shut out the sun with a quick pull of the gold and red tasseled cord. The latest magazines, arranged in a perfect fan on the gilded wooden coffee table, were new, as was the vase of red roses.

Original paintings by famous Florida artists hung on the walls in perfect alignment. Even the white roses in the crystal vase on the piano were perfectly arranged. Yet for all the radiant colors in the room, the room lacked warmth. There was not a sign that anyone had ever relaxed in one of the chairs, nor sat on the sofa to sip hot chocolate by the fire on a chilly winter's evening. It was a showplace, for appearance only.

Why had she never noticed it before? She had always taken the big old house for granted. It was their home for so long. Hers and Henry's. The memory of her brother flashed across her mind, bringing back the pain of his loss. God, how she wished he was here, but then reminded herself that if Henry were alive, this would never have happened to her. Whatever this is, she thought.

Her nerves tightened. She clutched her stomach as fear rose in one giant knot. She was grateful when Justin put his arm around her shoulder.

"Don't forget, babe. I'm right here. We'll get through this."

Before she had a chance to respond, they heard footsteps coming down the hallway. They both stood and turned to face the room's entrance expectantly.

Sara Blanding walked toward them hesitantly. She wore pale yellow slacks and a crisp white cotton blouse. Not a tall woman, her short dark hair was styled to add more height to her small frame. She had the same large green eyes as Kathryn, but there the resemblance ended. Sara had an elegant and reserved air about her. The perfect companion for a successful doctor.

There was no smile of welcome on her face. Instead, her eyes held a look of wariness; her mouth was set in a grim line of hostility. "After that vicious joke you tried to play on me, Kate, I'm surprised you dared show your face around here. I should have had Sally show you both out, but I'm not completely without manners. I told Sally to bring in some coffee. Or would you rather have iced tea?" she said, turning to Justin.

Kathryn was unable to reply. Yet there was so much she wanted to say. Where was the mild and meek mother she had grown up with? The mother who walked on eggshells, afraid of offending anyone. This woman was full of angry confidence that Kathryn had never seen before.

Realizing they were staring at her, Sara said, "We might as well sit down, although I really don't think we have anything to discuss." Kathryn and Justin returned to the sofa, while Sara took a chair facing them.

Kathryn gripped Justin's hand like a lifeline hardly able to breathe as her mother gave her a cold smile. She had no idea how to proceed and turned to Justin. For once he was no help.

"It's your show, babe," was all he muttered before turning his gaze back to Sara.

She desperately wanted to address this woman as

mother, but Sara's hostile attitude told her it would be a mistake. Instead, she clasped her hands in her lap to keep them from trembling. There's only one way to go about it, so she began, "Mrs. Blanding, do you know who I am?" she asked.

Sara stared at her for a long moment, "Of course I know who you are. You lived here for over a year, or don't you remember that, Kate?"

"No, I don't, that's partly why we're here to see you," Kathryn stammered, for lack of another answer. She couldn't just blurt out the truth. Not yet anyway.

Sara shifted her gaze to Justin, who was sitting quietly watching the two women.

"I'm sorry, this is my husband, Justin Crown," Kathryn said quickly.

Sara sat quietly thinking for a moment, "We spoke on the phone before," she said with a quizzical look. "That name sounds familiar to me for some other reason. Have we met before, Mr. Crown?"

"I don't think so, ma'am," Justin replied stoically. Sara was still watching him, so he added, "Perhaps you've heard of my father, Senator Adam Crown."

"Oh yes," Sara responded, her smile a little warmer, "he's been in the news a lot lately."

"Yes ma'am, he has."

Sara then turned her attention to Kathryn. "Well Kate, you've done pretty well for yourself since you left us so abruptly."

Justin leaned forward, "When was that, Mrs. Blanding?"

"That would have been in the early fall of 2016, I believe." She cast a sad glance on the wall above the fireplace. "Yes," she said, "it was almost two years after the accident."

"You mean the one where I was injured," Kathryn whispered.

"Yes, of course, that one." She sat in silence for a moment, lost in thought. "Such a tragedy," she said, a note of bitterness in her voice. "Such a waste. But then again perhaps it was for the best after the. Well, never mind," she whispered, her eyes sparkling with unshed tears.

"Please finish what you were going to say," Kathryn encouraged. "I really would like to know all about it."

Sara ignored Kathryn's plea and continued staring at the wall, her mind clearly in the past.

"Mrs. Blanding," Justin said a bit forcefully to draw her attention back to the present.

Sara started, "Yes. Yes, it was almost a year after the accident." She could not seem to take her eyes from that one spot above the mantel. "There used to be a portrait of my daughter there, but after her death, Randolph insisted on putting it in the attic. He said he couldn't bear to look at it anymore. Our daughter's death nearly destroyed my husband. He hasn't been the same since." Then just as quickly as she had become heavy-hearted, she turned toward them, a forced bright smile on her face. "Well, enough of that. Life must go on, you know."

Kathryn couldn't believe what her mother had said about the painting. Did her father really love her so much he couldn't bear to look at her portrait? That thought stunned her. She had grown up believing her father never cared for her, thinking that he only loved her brother.

She watched her mother closely for any sign of recognition, but there was none. Her mother honestly believed she was this Kate person. Her heart was nearly breaking. Enough was enough, just a few more questions and she was going to tell her the truth.

"Mo," she caught her mistake quickly, "I mean Mrs. Blanding, would you mind telling us exactly what sort of accident you're talking about?"

"Well honestly, Kate. Surely you know what I'm talking about," Sara stated firmly. "Oh, you may not remember the exact moment of impact, at least you always told us you didn't. But, you can't have forgotten living here in this house? Surely not."

Kathryn was more confused than ever. Her mother did indeed recognize her. But not as she had hoped. She had convinced herself that all she had to do was show up on the doorstep, and she would be welcomed back with open arms. How stupid! Had she forgotten the phone call to this woman? My God, when was she going to get it through her head that her own mother didn't know her?

Justin, his clasped hands resting on his knees, said "Mrs. Blanding, if you don't mind, I would like to hear about the accident. You see," he gave Kathryn a warning look, "my wife has never told me much about it. Actually, she's been having some memory problems lately, and to help her, the doctor said she should try and relive what happened."

He sat back on the sofa and reached for Kathryn's hand. His grip, as well as his stern look, told her he would handle this for now.

She was grateful for his intervention but wished he'd trusted her not to lose control. He was aware that her nerves were strung too tight. She added her own requests to Justin's, her words clipped and strained. "Yes, Mrs. Blanding, do go on. I'd like to hear your account of the accident."

Sara seemed confused by the sudden tension emanating from the young woman she had helped to heal for over a year. Her expression of distrust showed that she thought Kathryn was up to something, yet she couldn't be sure what. When she spoke, her voice held a hint of hostility.

"That's too bad, Kate. I'm sorry you're still having trouble with your memory, but the doctors didn't think you would survive the night. But, you did," she said extending one hand toward Kathryn. "And here you are, just as beautiful as ever." She gave Kathryn a cold smile, "Why you even have a senator's son for a husband. I'd say you got everything you wanted."

Both Justin and Kathryn noticed she had suddenly cast aside her attempt at friendliness.

Kathryn couldn't stand it another minute. "Mrs. Blanding," she said firmly, still unable to call this woman, mother, as she wanted. "When I called you last week, you accused me of playing some sort of practical joke on you."

"That was cruel of you, Kate," Sara interrupted. "You know how devastated we were. We had lost our daughter, and then you leave without a word." She stopped and looked accusingly at Kathryn.

Kathryn jerked her hand free of Justin's grip and jumped to her feet. "No!" she all but shouted, "That's the reason I'm here!"

Justin reached out to take hold of her arm, but she shook him off. "No," she said emphatically, "This can't go on any longer." She looked at Sara, her voice shaking with emotion, "You have to believe me. I have no memory of any accident or why I look the way I do now. But I am not Kate. I am your daughter, and I am not dead."

For a few minutes, the two women stared at one another.

"You're mad. Stark raving mad!" Sara's voice was glacial as she rose to her feet, trembling with fury. She paced the floor, her hands balled into fists. She suddenly turned back to Kathryn, "Why are you doing this? It was bad enough when you played your terrible joke over the phone, but to have the audacity to come into my home with your horrible lies, that's just too much."

Justin feared the older woman was on the verge of a heart attack. She was so overwrought he expected her to collapse at any moment. Kathryn had been convinced that all she had to do was show up, and Sara Blanding would accept her as her daughter. But Sara's reaction told him this had been a giant mistake. Was Mrs. Blanding right? Was the woman he married really just playing a cruel joke on the Blanding family?

It was time to leave. Again Justin tried to take

Kathryn's hand. Again she jerked away from him.
"Kathryn," he grabbed her by the arm. "This isn't the
time for this. Let's go."

"No. I'm not leaving," she responded adamantly.
"She has to believe me, Justin." She turned her head
toward him, her eyes large and luminous in her pale face.
"Don't you see? I have to make her believe me."

She was out of control. Justin put an arm around
her shoulder. Her entire body trembled, and she seemed
unsteady on her feet.

His voice was soft but firm. "Now is not the
time."

"No. I've waited too long as it is. It's now or
never," she stated and shrugged off his arm. She took
several steps toward Sara, "Mother please. . . ."

"Stop it!" Sara screamed. "How dare you call me
that! You are most certainly not my child. My child is
dead. No matter what the police claim. My daughter
wouldn't mur," she hesitated, "For you to pull this, Kate,
you," she said pointing a shaking finger at Kathryn,
"you're capable of anything. Get out of here!"

Justin took a step toward the hysterical woman,
but she backed away as though he were a rabid dog.

"Mrs. Blanding," he said trying to keep his voice
calm and soothing and let the woman regain some
semblance of control. "We're not here to upset you.
We're trying to find the answers to some important
questions."

From the corner of his eyes, he saw Kathryn
weave and put out a hand to steady her. He began to lead
her back to the sofa, when Sara screamed, "NO!
Nooooo!"

She stood frantically wringing her hands. "Out!" she shouted. "Leave this house immediately! Get out now!" She fled through the archway, her hysterical crying fading as she disappeared down the hall.

Kathryn felt tears running down her cheeks, but was powerless to stop them. It was all a disaster.

"Come on, babe," Justin said and led her into the foyer, "it's time we leave."

As they reached the front door, Kathryn stopped. She looked back through the archway. "I'm going to prove it to her, Justin. I won't stop until I do." She walked out the front door and climbed into the car.

Chapter Twelve

Kathryn's emotions lay in tatters as Jon drove back to the hotel. She felt cold and numb. Not until Justin reached across the seat and wrapped his arms around her shoulders, did she realize she was shivering. Leaning against him, she savored the warmth of his broad chest. His arms were like a cocoon keeping her safe.

Desperately she wished she could forget all that had happened and really be a woman named Kate Clark from California. But she wasn't from California, and she was not that person.

Justin's voice brought her out of her gloom pit. "You weren't prepared for her rejection, were you, even though you had to know she wouldn't recognize you?"

"Oh, but my mother did recognize me. It just wasn't in the way I had hoped. I wanted to believe she would throw her arms around me and welcome me home, but it was a disaster instead."

Her chills subsided as she lay in his arms. She leaned into him for a few more minutes, then sat up massaging her neck to relieve the painful tightness in her muscles.

"I have to face the reality of it, Justin. I had convinced myself that all I had to do was waltz into that house and this nightmare would end." She turned to look at him, her eyes large and somber, "Somehow, I think maybe it's just begun."

"What do you mean?"

"I'm not sure. Just a feeling I have. Oh, I don't know, Justin. I'm just too confused right now to think straight." She scooted back to her side of the seat.

Justin, engrossed in his thoughts, was more than a little confused. Although he didn't voice his concerns, he also felt impending doom. And had felt it for several days each time the report in his briefcase came to mind. He shook his head slightly. He didn't want to think about it, especially not after what he had just witnessed between his wife and Sara Blanding.

Each woman had been so intense in their claims. How was he going to make any sense of it? He had an urge to tell Jon to head to the airport. Kathryn would never agree to it, he silently scoffed. No, for some reason he couldn't fathom, she would see this thing through. Justin had no idea just what this thing might be. So he remained silent, wishing like hell they could just go home and put this mess behind them.

The old Kathryn would have agreed immediately, he thought. She would have questioned why but concurred if he made the suggestion. But he was no longer dealing with the old Kathryn. He was now facing a stubborn mule-headed woman who would have no qualms about telling him to go to hell if he even hinted at going back to Colorado.

Not another word was spoken until Jon pulled up in front of the hotel. Kathryn opened her door, and then turned to Justin, "I'll see you upstairs," she said as she hastily climbed out of the car, slamming the door.

Justin wondered what was going through her mind as he got out and followed her. She was through the hotel doors and almost to the elevator when he caught up with her. "What's the matter with you? You nearly broke the car door."

Kathryn stabbed at the up button on the elevator then turned to face him. "I'm sorry, Justin. I'm just thinking about my mother's attitude. I've never seen her so confident. She isn't the same weak woman I remember." She put a hand on his arm, "I don't know what to make of it."

"People change, Kathryn. Maybe she has," he said as they entered the elevator. "Put it out of your mind for now." He smiled down at her as they rode up to their floor.

"Thanks. I appreciate that you understand. It'll make it easier to tell you the plan I've come up with."

"What plan is that?" he asked as he unlocked the door to their room, and ushered her inside.

After throwing her purse on the bed, and kicking off her shoes, she opened the door leading to the small balcony. The afternoon sun streamed into the room, bringing with it a warm tropical breeze. Kathryn stood in the doorway letting the fresh air wash over her. It felt so good to feel the breeze on her face. She stepped onto the balcony and allowed the sun to bathe her in its warmth.

Justin took a bottle of beer and a can of Pepsi from the bar. He opened both drinks and joined her. After handing her the can of soda, he asked, "So what's this plan you've come up with?"

Kathryn took a long drink from the icy can. "It's not much of a plan, really," she said, "more of a conviction that I've been right all along. I can't sit around feeling sorry for myself any longer. I've spent the better part of a week wallowing in self-pity. No more," she stated before turning to face him, a look of pure determination in her green eyes. "And I can't depend on anyone else to solve my problems for me."

Justin did not miss the meaning behind her statement, "You mean you're going to try and go it alone, whether I agree or not. That's what you're really saying?"

She gave him an answering smile, "I suppose you could say that's what I mean."

We'll see about that, he thought but knew better than to say it. He'd play along with Kathryn for a while, just to make sure she didn't get into any trouble. "Well, what do you plan to do first? Try and convince your father of who you really are?"

"Not yet. First I'm going to the cemetery."

"Why? Why do you want to go there?" He had not missed the fact that Sara Blanding had almost said the word murder when speaking of the night her daughter died. He didn't think Kathryn had heard her. She's been too upset to catch the slip. No one had mentioned Abigail Pennington's death to her.

He set his now empty bottle on the small patio table. "Why the cemetery? What do you hope to find?"

"My grave!"

"That's ridiculous," he said firmly.

"What's so ridiculous about it? If everyone thinks I'm dead, then I want to see where I'm buried."

"That will only cause you more pain," he said in a softer tone. "It isn't going to do any good to stand over a grave with your name on it. It's morbid, and I'd rather you didn't do it."

"It may be morbid, but I'm going. Please try to understand, you don't have to go with me."

"I'm not letting you out of my sight. Have you forgotten about the threatening phone calls you received or that someone shot at you?" Justin declared.

"No, of course not," she said, when in fact, she had pushed it out of her mind. "You're right. But," she said, "I'm going where I want to go and see whomever I want to. Got it?"

"In other words, I'm just supposed to follow you around, is that it?"

She saw the anger in his expression and wished she could make him understand. He was used to his wife agreeing with his every wish.

Kathryn heaved a frustrated sigh, "Of course not. I know the people I need to talk to. You don't. That's all." She reached out and laid a hand on his chest, "I know you want to protect me. You want to shield me from being hurt anymore. But don't you see, Justin? I can take care of myself." She gazed out over the water, watching a sailboat in the distance. "It feels strange having someone trying to take care of me all the time." Then she turned back to him with a contrite smile, "I'm having a hard time accepting it."

Justin wrapped her in his arms, hugging her close. "All right," he uttered a deep growl. "You're an independent woman, and I'm not used to that. But I promise not to be so over-protective. We'll do it your way, for now," he added before letting her go. He held onto her for a moment, "Get one thing straight, Kathryn," he told her sternly. "If I think you're getting in over your head, or at the very first inkling you might be putting yourself in danger, I'll throw your butt back on that plane so fast you won't know what hit you. You got that?"

"Got it," she said, smiling up at him, secretly glad he wanted to protect her. Not since Henry's death had anyone cared enough to act as if she needed to be protected. It felt good.

She walked inside and sat on the edge of the bed while Justin remained standing in the balcony doorway. "First thing in the morning I want to go check out the newspaper article on the accident at the public library. Maybe it will give fuller details and list any witnesses. If we could get a copy of the police report, that would help. Could you ask Harv Anderson to obtain a copy?"

"I'll call him," Justin said as he watched a flock of gulls fighting over something a little boy was throwing into the air. He wondered if he should prepare her for what she would find in the paper, but decided against it. He needed to see her reaction to the murder of the Pennington woman. It would be devastating to Kathryn Blanding if that's who she really was. Dear God, he thought, it was difficult to put aside his doubts about her after reading Harv's report.

He walked into the room and pulled another beer from the fridge. "That makes sense." He plopped into a chair by the window, kicked off his shoes, and leaned back. "What else do you have in mind?"

"I have to find Robert, Justin," she said fiercely. "I know you won't like it, but I have this feeling somehow he's involved with what happened."

"All right," he told her, his voice filled with

resignation, "if that's the way you want it, then we'll both go. I'll not have you confront that ex-husband of yours alone."

Kathryn faced him, "I was hoping you'd say that." She gave him a warm smile.

"Did you have any doubts about it?"

"Yeah, I did. I wasn't sure you would go along with me on this."

"Well for your information," he said, getting to his feet, "I'm in for the duration. I may not agree with what you're doing, but whatever lies ahead for you, is ahead for me also."

Kathryn walked into his outstretched arms, welcoming the feeling of security they offered. She knew he had reservations about coming to St. Petersburg, yet he was willing to stay and help. In her estimation, that told her what kind of man she had married.

The next morning Kathryn knew the day would be hot. She thanked God for the low humidity, but still dressed in a lightweight white blouse, dark green slacks and a pair of brown wedge sandals. Both men had traded their wool slacks for tan Dockers, pullover short-sleeved cotton shirts and loafers to combat the rising temperature.

After a leisurely breakfast, Jon drove them to the main public library. A woman in the reference section gave directions to the second floor and the microfiche and viewer. She then explained how to operate the machine.

Kathryn sat on a stool, Justin in a chair beside her. She picked up the film for the last week of October 2014. She stopped and stared at the front page of the old St. Petersburg Times for several moments.

"Here it is," she whispered.

Justin lowered his head, and they read the article together. It was a major story, a full half column, accompanied by a picture of two mangled automobiles:

DAUGHTER OF PROMINENT PHYSICIAN KILLED IN ACCIDENT

Kathryn Fowler Blanding, 27, daughter of Doctor and Mrs. Randolph T. Blanding was killed last night when she lost control of her 2014 Chevrolet Camaro on the Pinellas Bayway. According to the Pinellas County Sheriff's Dept., Ms. Blanding was traveling at a high rate of speed, ran a traffic light and slammed into a Toyota Corolla driven by Kathryn Clark, an actress from Los Angeles, California, performing here at the Abbott Dinner Playhouse.

Ms. Blanding suffered massive head and facial injuries and could only be identified by her father. Ms. Clark also suffered extensive injuries to her head and face and is listed in critical condition at Bayfront Medical Center.

It is believed that Ms. Blanding was leaving the scene of the murder of her maternal grandmother, Abigail Fowler Pennington. (see related story, pg 8A). At this time Ms. Blanding is the only suspect in the murder of her grandmother.

"Abby? No!" she whispered. Dead? Murdered? She wanted to scream. Her grandmother gone? Oh my

God, was all she could think. And I'm the prime suspect. It couldn't be true. But there it was in black and white for the entire population of St. Pete to read and believe. Kathryn wanted to cry but had to wonder why the tears wouldn't come. Perhaps she had already used up her allotment. She hadn't been sure what she would find at the library but had never expected to discover Abby had been murdered.

Kathryn searched for the related story and read how Abby was found bludgeoned to death in her home on Tierra Verde. Nothing was missing from the home to indicate a robbery had gone wrong. A neighbor, Mrs. Grace Goodwin, had witnessed a woman running from the house and driving away. She identified Kathryn by her long auburn hair but admitted to not having seen her face.

"Abby is dead?" she mumbled still trying to come to grips with the news. "She's dead."

Justin quickly turned the machine off and helped her to her feet. He felt the trembling in her body, saw the pale withdrawn expression on her face, and the look of devastation in her eyes, yet she didn't shed a tear. Was she as surprised as she appeared to be?

If she was acting, then she was one hell of an actress. He was more than half convinced it was all real, everything she had told him. Yet still, there was that niggling in the back of his brain that told him not to be too confident of things. It might well turn out that she was actually Kathryn Clark. Hell, he thought, I can't stand much more of this.

Kathryn showed no emotion as she let him guide her lead her to the car.

"Let's get back to the hotel, Jon," he said as soon as they were seated.

She didn't want to believe what she had read. Dear sweet Abby dead. Why? Who would want to hurt an old lady? According to the newspaper, she was responsible for her death, had actually murdered her own grandmother. It was all she could do not to give in to her grief. It wouldn't help anyone to fall apart now. Now, more than ever, she was determined to find out what had happened the night of her birthday party.

She leaned her head against the back of the seat and closed her eyes. Why did the police think I killed Abby, she wondered? What happened to give them that idea? Why was she murdered in the first place? It had happened the night of Kathryn's birthday. That meant she must have gone to her house to pick Abby up for the party. What went wrong? What had happened at that house?

"Justin, regardless of what that article says, I would never hurt my grandmother. I loved her too much. Besides, I wouldn't hurt anyone deliberately. Forget the hotel, there's no time for laying around feeling sorry for myself. I haven't changed my mind. Let's go to the cemetery."

Dear Lord, he thought. "Tell Jon where to go and let's get it over with." Damn, she was hard headed. He relaxed against the seat, hoping to relieve the tension in his own shoulders.

She gave Jon directions and, in less than fifteen minutes, he pulled the car through the gates of Rosewood

Memorial Gardens. It was a sprawling well-maintained cemetery with fresh cut grass between the tombstones and monuments to the dead. Off in the distance rainbows created by the sun's rays and the spray of water from the sprinklers arched above the graves. The car stopped before a large square building with urns of flowers on either side of the doorway.

"I'll find out where it is," Justin said as he opened his door.

Without waiting for Justin, Kathryn quickly climbed out of the car, "Never mind, I know where it is," she said over her shoulder as she walked down the path toward a clump of trees. Right now, all she wanted was to pay her respects to Abby.

Justin heaved a frustrated sigh and ran to catch up with her.

"Slow down," he urged as he reached her.

She stopped and looked up at him. "I'm sorry. I've never been a very patient person. When I want to do something, I want to do it now, not later. My mother always told me I got my impatience from Abby. She was a lot worse than I am."

The impact of her grandmother's death hit her again like a fist in the stomach. White-faced she turned and continued to walk toward the grave. Abby had been the mother she'd never had, there when she needed someone to care, always believing in her, no matter what. Now she was gone. It was almost unbearable.

"I'm sorry too." He wrapped his arms around her, holding her close. "Are you sure you wouldn't rather go back to the hotel?"

"No," she managed to mumble through her tears.

"Please understand, I have to be here."

"I think I understand how you feel, Kathryn. I mean that."

He was a remarkable man, she thought, genuinely kind, and she needed that kindness now. Pain gripped her heart, and she thought she would break from the agony of her loss. Abby had always been there after Henry died. Her grandmother had been her haven during her darkest days, and now that sanctuary was gone.

Looking at Justin, she was thankful to be able to lean on him. She took his hand and led him to the family plot and stood gazing at the headstones. Close behind her, he rested his hands on her shoulders.

Kathryn shivered when she saw her name on the tombstone. Her eyes riveted to the marble, she studied the intricately carved letters. A single white marble rose adorned a towering marker to tell the world this was her final resting place. Only it wasn't. Another poor unfortunate woman rested there. She could almost hear the sound of laughter. But whose? The person who knew she wasn't dead? Or was it the ghosts of a thousand souls entombed in the ground, laughing because the joke was on her? She shivered again.

She looked over at her brother's grave. It was hard to believe fifteen years had gone by since that horrible day, and she was still fighting the guilt. Someday maybe she would forgive herself. She gave a sigh and let her gaze drift to the left.

Abby's stone stood taller than the other two. She knew that had been her mother's doing. It was right though. Abby deserved it. An eerie feeling came over her as she watched a yellow butterfly land on top of the headstone. It beat its gossamer wings several times and then flew in her direction. It circled above her head then landed on the stone once more.

Without warning, she was once again overwhelmed with grief. She turned around and wrapped her arms around her husband's waist and laid her head on his shoulder. She could no longer hold back the hysterical sobs that suddenly overcame her.

Justin held her tight, caressed her hair and kissed the top of her head hoping the sobs racking her slender frame were being shed in real grief.

Kathryn's sobbing ceased, and he felt her straighten in his arms. She raised her head, wiped the tears away and stepped back. Her eyes dark, and Justin knew there was a storm brewing.

"Let's go visit my father," she said.

He was right. He didn't like her suggestion at all. Was she bent on self-torture, he wondered? "Are you sure that's what you want to do? Wouldn't it be better to wait?"

"I think four years is quite long enough! Maybe he can shed a little light on this situation." She walked off leaving him to follow.

As he hurried after her, his thoughts dark and morose, he muttered under his breath, "If there is any light to be shed."

Kathryn overheard his remark and whirled on him. "What do you mean if?" she demanded.

"Nothing," he declared, not sure himself why he had uttered the remark, and admonished himself about recalling thrown stones.

Each hand balled in a tight fist, she stormed at him. "You still think I made this whole thing up, don't you? You still don't believe me!"

Justin felt as if an arctic chill whirled around him as her voice turned cold and calm. No matter how much he wanted, he couldn't get the memory of that damn report in the briefcase out of his mind.

"Justin, I know who I am, and I intend to prove it.' She turned and stomped off in the direction of the car, chin up, hair whipped by the wind. Hot angry tears rolled down her cheeks, but she ignored them. It hurt to think Justin still didn't believe her. Why couldn't he trust she was telling the truth? Her mind whirled with determination. She'd get to her father's office if she had to walk.

The sound of hurried footsteps behind her caused her to stop. She knew it was Justin. Through bitter tears she turned and stared at him, waiting until he was beside the car.

"Go back to Colorado, Justin. There's no need for you to stay here any longer. I'll do this without you." She didn't give him a chance to reply but continued walking away as fast as she could before he could see she was crying.

Justin stopped. "Damn." he exploded. Talk about open mouth, insert foot. Boy, he had done it this time. He climbed into the passenger seat and slammed the car door. "Follow her for a couple of blocks, Jon. Maybe she'll listen to reason by then."

Kathryn walked blindly down the small road leading to the cemetery entrance. Already she could feel the heat from the pavement rising up and making sweat bead up on her face. Why was this March so darn hot? She didn't recall it being this hot this early.

She didn't hear the car, but whipped around, when a hand grabbed her from behind forcing her to stop.

"Get in the car," Justin ordered.

"Leave me alone," she hurled the word at him.

"No. I'm not leaving you out here alone."

"I'll catch a cab," she retorted.

"Kathryn. Get in the car. Now!" When she hesitated, he said, "I'm not playing games with you," and physically lifted and placed her in the back seat. His eyes were hard, cold steel boring into her own, and his mouth was set in a tight hard line, his jaw muscles working feverishly.

"All right, we'll talk," she said meeting his steely glare.

He climbed in and sat in silence for a moment trying to collect his thoughts. "Now," he faced Kathryn, "if you'll listen to me for a minute. I only know one thing for certain, you're my wife, and that gives me the right to agree or disagree with you. It's my choice, because I love you, and do not want to lose you." He paused to see if she was listening. "If it will make you feel better, we'll go see Dr. Blanding, together. I don't like it, but I'm willing to see if he can help. But, Kathryn, if he can't, will you consider going back to Colorado and accepting your situation as it is?"

Ha, she thought, I think not! She sat forward in her seat astonished by his words.

"You're serious, aren't you?"

"Very."

A fire burned in her eyes as she returned his gaze. She was aware she should feel guilty for the outrage she felt. The man had just professed his love for her. But, what about all the unanswered questions eating away at his feelings? Until her identity was proven and her innocence established, she could not settle for less. If she did, her relationship with Justin would be destroyed by the disease called doubt.

Kathryn forced a calmness in her voice which she didn't feel. "You want me to go back to Colorado, forget my life has been wrecked, and knowing I will always be blamed for my grandmother's murder? Also that if by some freak chance I prove my identity, I'll be arrested and tried for that murder. You honestly expect me to give up?"

She leaned back, trembling, afraid to speak and glared at him. She had lost everything, and he wanted her to accept it and pretend it never happened. She forced herself to continue to gaze at him and opened her mouth to speak. Nothing came out. All she could do was turn her head from side to side in dismay.

Aware that what he was asking was hard for her to hear. "I know what I'm asking is a difficult thing to accept, Kathryn. But, will you at least think about it?"

His touch was like a knife on her skin, hot and searing. He had no right to ask her to just walk away and forget all that had happened. "Justin, I want you to leave Florida, tonight. I have enough problems. Your lack of trust will become a problem for me. I have enough to deal with as it is."

She turned to speak to Jon, who was finding it impossible to ignore their fight.

"Please drop me off at the clinic, and take Justin to the hotel for his things. I don't want him to waste his time here any longer," Kathryn ordered.

If she had slapped him, Justin wouldn't have felt the blow any harder. He remained silent for only a second. "I said I would help you." Without taking his eyes off Kathryn, he growled, "Take us to the damned clinic, Jon."

Chapter Thirteen

Attached by an overhead walkway between the hospital and the parking garage, SunBay Medical Clinic was a simple design. Five stories of gleaming white concrete and amber tinted windows. The clinic faced the west entrance to the hospital with a three-tiered fountain centered in the middle of the circular brick drive.

Kathryn and Justin stepped off the elevator on the fifth floor. Without breaking her stride, she walked briskly past all the reception windows to the end office that had a view of the entire city. Desperation made her ignore the pleas of the young receptionist to sign in and wait to be called. She hurried past the nurse opening the door to the examination rooms and marched straight down the hall into the doctor's private office. She faced the man seated behind the large ornate desk. He stood. Broad shouldered, and over six feet tall, his deep bronze tan accented the deep blue of his eyes and white teeth. A dark navy suit was tailored to show off his perfect physical condition. With a hint of nervousness, he watched Kathryn stride toward him.

"So, it's true. You came back. Sara called and told me about your visit. I was shocked, Kate." He gave her a wide smile. "How are you, by the way? You look great, but then you should."

"I'm fine," Kathryn stated, all her old bitterness floating to the surface. "How have you been, Daddy?"

Randolph Blanding's eyes turned cold. His smile changed to a viper's grin. "What game are you playing this time, Kate? I'm not your father. I was a sucker for you once, but it won't happen again."

"What do you mean?" Justin said.

The older man eyed Justin warily and then indicated a long low sofa. "Sara said Kate had married the son of Senator Crown. Have a seat, and I'll explain."

Randolph had a hard glint in his eyes which Kathryn remembered too well. The look that said, you will obey my wishes. She hated it as much as she hated him.

Perched on the edge of the desk, he faced them. "Why didn't you stay in Los Angeles where you belong?" he demanded.

Kathryn stared at him, her face white and still. "I want to find out why my mother thinks I'm dead and refuses to recognize me? And why you deny me now? There has to be something about me that resembles Kathryn Blanding."

"Our daughter is dead!" He was losing his calm facade.

"I'm not dead. Why won't you tell the truth?"

Justin gripped her arm and led her to the sofa, afraid Kathryn was becoming hysterical.

Randolph returned to his chair behind the desk, picked up a pen and toyed with it, doodling on a notepad. "I'm sure your husband is interested in the truth as well. Did you tell him about us?"

"What?" Stunned, Kathryn's face blanched.

Dr. Blanding directed his comment to Justin. "After the accident, I performed the plastic surgery to restore her face. All I had to work from were the promotional photographs from the dinner theater where

Kate had been performing. Mr. Crown, I knew Kate before the accident. She came here to act in a play at the Abbott and decided to stay.

"We met at a time when my wife and I were having marital problems. Kate and I became involved for a brief time." Noting the effect his statement was having, Randolph continued, "Oh, she was good too. I don't mean acting, mind you, but outstanding at the only thing she was good for. Sex!" He waited for the effect to hit full force and then proceeded.

"Kate and I fought over money an hour before the accident. She was livid and stormed out of the condo and drove away. That was the last I saw her until I came upon the accident. I administered aid until the paramedics arrived. The truth is, Mr. Crown, your lovely wife is a user and nothing more than a whore. If you don't believe me, check her past history in California."

"That's a lie!" Kathryn shouted, jumping to her feet. She rushed to stand in front of the desk. "I am not Kate! I am your daughter, Kathryn!"

Randolph's face turned white. He stood abruptly, slamming the chair back against the wall. "I performed surgery on you because my daughter was responsible for the accident. I took you into my home for over a year. When you were well again, what thanks did I get? You took off without a word."

"Wait a minute." Justin was having trouble believing what he was hearing. "You took your mistress into your home with your wife there?"

His composure regained, Randolph's voice

betrayed his suppressed anger. "It was her idea. My wife had no knowledge of the affair. Besides, Kate's memory was gone. Sara had just lost her daughter and wanted to care for Kate because Kathryn had caused the accident. Sara even put her in our daughter's room. I think my wife was trying to make up for what happened. Nothing could make up for Kathryn's mistakes." Venom poured out of his mouth with such hatred when he spoke his daughter's name, Justin turned to look at Kathryn, her white face, and fear filled eyes.

"Can you explain why my wife seems to know a lot about your daughter, Doctor Blanding?"

"I'm not surprised. After Abby was murdered and Kathryn was killed, we emptied out her apartment. We found a stack of daily journals my daughter had written over the years. I believe Sara let Kate read them. I don't know why. Maybe she wanted to believe that Kathryn was basically a decent person. I find that ironic considering what she did to her grandmother."

Randolph leaned on the desk, palms flat against the wooden surface. "Now you show up claiming to be my daughter." He began to laugh, the sound cruel and sinister. "Are you sure you want to do that?" he sneered. "A DNA test will prove if you're really her. If you are, then the police will lock you up for killing Abby. You belong locked away, you bitch. You took everything from me!"

He slammed the desk with his fist so hard his thick salt and pepper hair fell forward across his forehead. He raked it back out of his eyes and stared at Kathryn as if ready to come across the desk and grab her by the throat. The hatred emanating from Randolph

Blanding was a visible thing.

All the old fears rose up and choked Kathryn. Without thinking of anything except escape, she whirled and raced out of the office.

Seething with rage, Randolph stormed at Justin, "Keep your whore away from my wife. I have a reputation to maintain in this town, and I will not have it smeared by the likes of her."

Justin balled his hands into fists, "Don't threaten me Dr. Blanding, and don't ever call my wife a whore."

Randolph sat down and wiped the sweat from his brow, the animosity in his eyes slowly diminishing. He focused on Justin, knowing he was not far from being punched in the face. "Leave my office or I will call security." He picked up the phone receiver.

Without another word, Justin left and followed Kathryn to the car. She was curled up in the back seat, shaking. "It all came rushing back," she clung to him, mumbling into the shoulder of his jacket, "all the fear, the hatred. It was almost as if I had never left home. No matter how I try to stop it, he can still scare the hell out of me."

"It's all right, Kathryn, everything will be all right." He only wished he believed it himself.

Later that evening, Justin sat at the bar and sipped his glass of Dewar's. Kathryn had turned down his invitation to dinner. It was just as well. Maybe they both needed time to think. She still looked pale and withdrawn when he left her in their room.

The trip so far was a bigger disaster than he had anticipated. He needed to be alone, had to sort out the nagging doubts rambling around in his brain. He kept remembering the things Randolph Blanding had said. Kate had lived with them for over a year, had even read their daughter's journals, probably been fed constant information by Sara. Kate knew as much about Kathryn Blanding as her parents did.

Photographs, there had to have been plenty of pictures for Kate to see. How else would she know what the other woman looked like? The doctor had admitted performing the surgery. He knew the difference between his daughter and another woman. Surely, he had not made an error.

"No," Justin muttered, "it wasn't Dr. Blanding who made a mistake." He drained his glass and motioned for another. Too many thoughts kept rushing at him, too much information to sort out. The bartender set a drink on the bar. He drained it in one swallow. As he handed the empty glass back, the bartender arched a brow.

"You're not planning on driving, are you?" he asked, filling the glass once more.

"I have a room here," Justin snapped, "I can get drunk if I want." And drunk he was getting and knew it. Tonight he didn't care. He picked up the scotch, vowing to make it last longer and wondered how one person could be right when the rest of the world kept telling her she was wrong. It didn't make any sense. He shook his head in confusion.

"Boy, you are the lucky one." A voice, slurred by

too much booze, drawled beside him, interrupting his concentration.

"How so?" he asked, giving the man a quick glance.

"Come on fella, every guy on the beach wishes he was lucky enough to spend one night with Kate, and you lucked out." The man was trying to keep his seat on the barstool.

Justin could feel his temper rising as he looked at the short fat man with the pig eyes. "What the hell are you talking about?" he demanded with a dangerous growl.

The stranger looked up at him with watery eyes. Beads of sweat popped out on his forehead as Justin's eyes held his. "Well, uh, you know," he stammered in a thick voice, as he pointed at Justin. "I saw you come in with her earlier."

The combination of scotch and his already dark mood made it difficult for Justin to hold his temper in check. He wanted to put his fist through that pudgy face. Something stopped him. Maybe it was the man's drunken lack of fear, or it was his own need to know what the stranger knew about Kathryn.

"What do you know about her?"

The little man gave a weak smile. "It's mostly just what I've heard."

"Well, that would be more than I know," Justin said, placing an elbow on the bar and cupping his chin in his hand.

The rotund little man drew himself up, pulled a

handkerchief out of his inside pocket and mopped his face. "Well, sir," he said, suddenly feeling important, "this Kate, I don't know her last name."

"Doesn't matter, just tell me what you do know," Justin said, his heart growing colder by the minute.

"Okay. Well, she hit town about, I'd say, close to four years ago. She used to hang out at my buddy's place up the street. She's a lot classier now, but it's the same girl all right. You know," he went on in his high-pitched voice, "for a while, she went out with a few men I knew. She liked to enjoy herself if you know what I mean. She cost plenty to date, too. She only dated," he winked when he said the word dated, "businessmen with money. Then one day she was gone."

"What do you mean, gone?"

"Well, she just disappeared. Then about a year later, she showed up again. Only this time she was different, more sophisticated, you know." the man's eyes were bright now, comfortable with the story he was telling. "Word had it she found some rich guy to keep her. It must've been true. She sure stayed by herself."

"How so?"

He leaned forward and lowered his voice. "I offered Kate a thousand bucks one night to go out with me. She turned me down flat. Said she wasn't that type. Said she had a boyfriend and to stay away from her." He leaned back in his chair and laughed. "I told her I knew her when."

"Did you ever see the man she was with?"

"No. He must've been married or something. I heard he set the little lady up in a fancy condo up the beach. I know I saw her driving a sports car a few times.

Well, anyway, looks like she's back in town again." The man looked around for the bartender, ordered a drink and reached for his wallet.

"No, I'm buying," Justin said, placing a twenty on the bar.

"Thanks," the little man said. "By the way, is she your girlfriend?"

Justin said through clenched teeth, "She's my wife." He stood and towered over the man, then turned and weaving slightly, made his way to a table occupied by Jon and a young blonde girl.

"Sit down, Justin," Jon urged indicating the empty chair. Justin plopped in the seat and waved down a waitress for a drink. Elbows on the table, he propped his chin in his hands and gave the blonde a lazy smile. "You won't mind if he has to work tonight, will you, honey?"

"Well, I was hoping he'd take me to Billie's'." She leered at him and let her gaze hold his for a second, Jon quickly forgotten.

"Billie's'?" Justin asked, his eyes drooping.

"It's a neat place on Tierra Verde where you can drink and have a good time at the piano bar. Want to go?" she asked.

"Nah. I'm married," Justin muttered, a hint of bitterness creeping into his voice. He fumbled in his wallet and handed her a fifty. "This should buy you a few drinks."

She took the money and stood. "Thanks a lot," she turned to Jon and said, "Well, guess I'd better be off and leave you to your work." She walked off toward the door her hips reminding Justin of two ripe melons waiting to be picked.

"Thanks," Jon sighed in relief. "I wasn't sure how to get rid of her."

"You never are." Justin retorted. "Give them money, it'll work every time."

The remark was out of character for Justin, but Jon chose to ignore it. "Now, what is it you want me to do?"

"I need my briefcase from the room."

"You don't have anything relating to business in this town, Justin. Besides, even if you did, you're not sober enough to conduct it."

Justin stared at him, a spark of anger in his eyes. "Just get the briefcase, Jon," he barked. "I'll decide on my business interests, okay?"

Jon knew it wouldn't do any good to argue with him. He left the table and headed for the elevator. Draining his glass, Justin ordered another. When Jon returned and placed the briefcase on the table, it was clear he was not happy about playing fetch. Any other time, he would have told Justin to fetch and carry for himself. The man was not himself, or he'd never have requested Jon to do something he could do.

Jon sat down and eyed Justin, wondering how many additional drinks the man had consumed since he left. From the way Justin fumbled with the latches, there was no doubt he was drunk. When he finally got the case open, he picked up a manila folder and handed it to Jon.

"You want me to read this now?"

"Go ahead, you'll find out about it sooner or later."

Jon pushed the lid shut and glanced at Justin, who had ordered yet another drink, then opened the folder and began to read. When he finished, he tossed the file back on the table and sat shaking his head from side to side.

"You're wrong, Justin," his voice was filled with sadness. "I know what you're thinking and, in my gut, I know you're wrong."

"Maybe."

Jon leaned forward, placing his hand on the report. "The person in this report is not the same girl sleeping peacefully upstairs in your room."

"There's a hell of a lot more than just this report."

Anger formed a knot in the pit of Jon's stomach. His blue eyes snapped as he blurted out, "Well you think what you want to, pal, but your wife is not this broad I just read about."

"Dammit, Jon, look at the pictures, man. They're the same," Justin exploded.

Jon stood up, abruptly knocking over his chair. "You've had too much to drink."

Justin raised his head, "Well, aren't you the one," his words were beginning to slur. "I'll tell you what, old buddy, don't concern yourself with my drinking or my wife."

Justin's temper could flare at any moment. Jon didn't want to fight with him. The best thing he could do was leave. "You're right," he said, "it's none of my business. But, I'm telling you, you're wrong about Kathryn, and you know it. I'm going back to the plane. If you need me, that's where you can find me." He turned and walked out of the bar, feeling a rift growing between them that might never heal.

Justin watched his best friend leave. He was sick inside from the booze. What was happening to him? Was he going crazy from all the data thrown in his face? Or was he just unable to face the truth about Kathryn? Could he pretend Harv's report and all the evidence didn't exist? Nothing made sense anymore.

How could so many people be wrong, and Kathryn be the only one telling the truth? His head began to pound as he stood and tossed the folder back into the briefcase and snapped it shut. His fingers gripped the handle as he weaved his way to the elevator, his mind intent on finding out the truth before the night was over.

Kathryn was caught up in a beautiful dream. Justin was making love to her. It wasn't wild abandoned passion, but slow, gentle, sweet lovemaking that captured her heart and bound her to him with a love she'd didn't think she was capable of feeling. Suddenly her eyes flew open. It wasn't a dream, and it wasn't sweet lovemaking either.

Justin was on top of her, ripping at her nightgown and muttering to himself. She could not understand what he was saying, but she could smell him. He reeked of alcohol and had not even taken the time to undress. She pushed hard against his chest with both hands, repulsed by his actions. He fell to one side on the bed, rolling flat on his back like an empty sack.

"What are you doing?" she screamed, then leaped

from the bed and pulled the front of her gown together.

Justin rose up on one elbow and tried to look provocative at her with his glazed eyes. "I just wanted to love you, honey," he slurred.

She watched him as he sat up on the side of the bed and rubbed his eyes as if to clear his vision, then rested his chin on his chest. His fingers fumbled as he attempted to unbutton his shirt but only succeeded in ripping the button off.

Kathryn stood staring at him, wondering how he even had made it up to their room. He looked pathetic, and for a fraction of a moment, she felt sorry for him. The instant passed quickly as anger began to boil inside her.

"You, madam, are trying to pull the wool over everyone's eyes. But I'm onto you. You can't fool me any longer," he said and rose to his feet.

His words sank in and suddenly, she felt numb. She straightened, her hair falling forward to hide her shocked expression.

"I have proof of your lies," he spat at her. He wanted to reach out and shake her, but his legs trembled. He was aware that he'd had too much to drink, but could not stop the tirade he had started.

His mind was aflame with the indignation at this woman using him for her own purposes. His foggy brain could not figure out why, but used was the right word. He stumbled to the dresser and fumbled with the briefcase latch, somehow managing to get it open. He clutched Harv's report in one fist and shook it at Kathryn.

"Here, take a look at this," he shouted and threw the folder at her feet. In the deep recesses of his brain, a spark of guilt tried to ignite, but he was too consumed with his anger, disgust, and way too much Scotch

"Read it, damn you, then try to tell me how it's all a fabrication of lies."

"No!" Kathryn exploded. "I don't want to read it." Now she was frightened

He grabbed her arm and spun her around to face him. "I went to a lot of effort and expense to find out about you. Damn it, you are going to read all about it," he snarled.

Kathryn tried to pull away, but his fingers dug deeper into her arm. She looked at the papers scattered on the floor and nodded her head. Justin continued holding her in a fierce grip as he reached down to gather up the pages. She could not control the tears or her shaking as he pushed her into a chair and shoved the report into her hands. She straightened the wrinkled papers and read as Justin stood over her with clenched fists.

Kathryn dropped the papers in her lap, not wanting to touch them and could not bear to look at Justin knowing he believed the vile things written about her. "It's not true! Justin, I swear to you, I never did any of those things," she cried, and covered her tear stained face with her hands.

He took the photographs and stuck them under her nose. "Look at these," he growled. "These don't lie."

She took the pictures slowly from him. One was of herself and an older woman. They had their arms around each other and were smiling at the camera. There was one of her by a pool, sitting between the legs of a young man with blonde hair. She wore a string bikini with a Band-Aid style top, and the man had his hands over both her breasts.

There were other photos of her and other men. One was taken outside a nightclub or restaurant, the name of the place partially hidden by the silhouette of the man against the neon sign. The camera angle was shot from a crouching position and from a distance. The man may have been in shadow, but the woman's features were well lighted. Again her new face stared back at her. This was the most innocent of all the pictures.

She threw the pictures and papers as if they were contaminated and they scattered across the floor.

"I don't know these people," she said through her tears.

"Come on, Kate," Justin scoffed. He pointed to the older woman, "This is your Aunt Mary, and this young god in the other picture is your rich, young lover in California. You want to tell me you don't remember him?"

She rubbed at her eyes. Somehow she had to make Justin believe her. How? It was as if she had been proven guilty without knowing why she was on trial. "I know you showed me pictures before, but I've never met these people, Justin."

She stood and wiped at the tears that refused to stop. They were tears of anger now. She no longer feared Justin or his anger. Rage consumed her as she walked to the bed, taking deep breaths, fighting for control, before turning to face him. She stood defiantly with her hands on her hips.

"You believe all this completely, don't you? There is no doubt in your mind that this report is about me. It doesn't matter to you that this is not my face. It doesn't matter to you that Dan Otis confirmed someone had done plastic surgery on me." She was really wound up now. "Oh, no, I'm guilty as far as you're concerned, because you have a few pictures and a damning report of some woman that I happen to look like."

"What would you have me believe after reading and seeing all this?" he said, eyes as hard and cold as a winter mountain.

She met the gaze of the man she had come to love so much in such a short time. "You could try believing me," she stated, the fight in her evaporating like mist in the sun, her shoulders slumped in defeat. Her throat tightened with the effort of her next words. "You said you love me."

"How do you think I feel?" he shouted. "I see my wife in all these photographs with all these men." He paced back and forth, his fury boiling, begging for release. He wanted, needed to hit something, but not Kathryn, never Kathryn.

Kathryn sat down in the chair, as numbness set in. Who was this cold, unfeeling man, who had been so kind, so gentle and was now made of stone?

"How long have you had this report?" She looked down at the papers and photographs on the floor.

"Since before we left Colorado," he said and turned from the balcony door.

"Why did you wait until now to tell me about it?"

Unchecked tears rolled down her face. This time she made no attempt to wipe them away. His icy stare made her shiver.

"I didn't really want to believe it at first. We all have a past, things we're not proud of doing. I thought there had to be some mistake, it couldn't be you."

"What changed your mind?" She had to know. She could not let him go without knowing why, now that he had shown her the damning report.

In an instant, Justin was cold sober. No sign of his drunkenness remained. He stood with his hands in the pockets of his slacks, his face pale and drawn, a five o'clock shadow covering his lower jaw and chin.

"Your so-called father, for one thing. He remembered you a little too well, didn't he? You weren't expecting him to admit to his affair, were you?" He took a deep breath and continued in that same cold, emotionless tone. "For some reason, which escapes me, you expected the man to claim you as his long-dead daughter, and it backfired on you."

"I am his daughter!" She reeled. "You didn't believe him when we were in his office, what changed your mind now?" Her blood chilled as he gave her a icy, calculating smile.

"I met a friend of yours this evening, a guy who knew you when," he said.

"What does that mean?" She was more confused than ever.

"It means," anguish tore his words from him, "that he knew you when you were playing your games in the hotels along the beach."

She was pushing him, but she didn't care anymore. She knew what he meant, but wanted to hear him say it, had to hear him voice the word before she would believe all was lost to her.

He gave a bitter laugh then said, "Why, Kathryn, you know as well as I do what line of work you were in. You went with the highest bidder." His mouth twisted in a cruel sneer and his eyes burned into hers.

She had to remain calm, had to convince him he was wrong. She took a step forward, her arm outstretched pleading.

"Please, Justin," she begged, "listen to me. I don't know who the man was that you talked to earlier, but he doesn't know me. I'm not the woman in that report either. I could never do those things. I don't know who that is in those pictures. I'm not even sure that it is me. Justin, I can't prove what I'm telling you, but I will. I will prove I'm telling the truth, but I need your help to do it."

"My money, you mean. That's all you ever wanted from me or any man, was money!" he spat at her, an expression of pain twisting his face into a man she did not recognize.

A memory flashed through her mind. Another time, another place when she had seen Justin like this. He stood over her than with the same expression seared into his features. She tried to remember the whole ugly scene, but it slipped away and was gone, just as Justin was sliding away from her, soon to be as lost as her missing years.

His voice husky, choking back emotion he said,

"I've had a lot of women; I've loved only one and then swore I'd not love again. When you came into my life, I felt as if even during my worst times, the worst storms I had to weather, you filled me with a rebirth of hope and love. But it's over, Kathryn." He gave a shuddering sigh of sadness. "I don't know what you hoped to get from me, but whatever it was; I hope you got it because that's all you'll get."

Kathryn tried to speak, but no words came from her dry, parched throat. A tightness in her chest made it difficult to breathe. She watched in horror as Justin took his suitcase from the closet and filled it with his clothes. He grabbed all the papers and photographs from the floor and tossed them into the briefcase and snapped the lid shut. He set it next to the suitcase by the door, took out his wallet and threw a wad of bills on the bed.

"Some people might infer that you're a high-class call girl. In my book, you are nothing but a whore. There is two thousand dollars," He pointed to the money. "That should cover the cost of your services. From what I hear, a whore comes cheap." He turned, picked up the suitcase and walked, out leaving the briefcase behind.

Kathryn's control dissolved with the slamming of the door. She stood motionless for a few seconds, stunned by the words he had thrown at her. She stumbled to the bed and collapsed, sobbing, her tears soaking the pillow. She chastised herself for not running after him and forcing him to admit he was wrong. It would have been useless. There was too much damning evidence to convince him otherwise. He would never listen to her or believe her again. Justin was gone, and she was alone. Exhausted, she lay on the bed, unable to sleep. Visions raced through her mind of snow-capped mountains and wild spring flowers just out of reach.

Chapter Fourteen

Kathryn hid away in the motel room, not wanting to see or talk to anyone until late the next afternoon. She even refused entrance to the maid wanting to change her bed and towels and ordered room service only because she had to eat. She had cried until there were no tears left to shed.

If she wasn't on the bed, then she sat staring out the window trying not to think about the report or Justin. He was gone. There was nothing she could do about it, and as much as it hurt to admit, she wasn't sure she wanted him back. She sighed, and a deep sense of loss shot a pain through her heart. There were other matters she had put aside that were now beating at her mental door for attention.

The nightmare about the dead woman had returned to jolt her wide awake at four in the morning. She had been afraid to close her eyes after that. She trembled with the recollection of the dream. There was no reason for it, yet she felt terrified. Somehow it involved her past, and could be related to Abby's murder. If that was the case, she had to have been at the scene. But her last memory was of leaving her condo, but never arriving at her grandmother's house. Plus any related memory was lost, and that made Justin believe she was lying to him.

She had forced herself to eat a sandwich at lunch, but the thought of dinner made her nauseous, but she had to eat. She had to get dressed, pull herself together and get out of this room, even if it was to go down to the restaurant. This was not the time to sit around and feel sorry for herself.

She rose and walked to the bathroom and stood staring at her image in the mirror. Her hair was tangled and her eyes were ringed by dark shadows from lack of sleep. A shower and makeup would do wonders for her disposition, so she grabbed the hairbrush and ran it through her hair, wincing as the bristles encountered the knots.

Justin's leaving wasn't the end of the world, she told herself. All she had to do was decide on her next move. She didn't need him or his money to prove her identity.

The memory of his cold, impassive face frightened her. She felt lost, afraid and indecisive. Had all her bravado with Justin been just that, a front to hide the terror she felt at being alone, without him?

Who was there to turn to or trust? Not her mother, who rejected and now despised her. Henry was long gone, but God, how she missed him. And Abby, dear sweet adorable Abby, was dead. She had never hurt anyone in her life. Why would anyone want to harm an eighty-year-old woman?

At the library, she had read the related story about Abby's death but did not understand why the Sheriff's Department placed her at the scene. Just because a neighbor had seen a woman with the same color hair as hers, didn't mean she was that person.

As the prime suspect, if, and it was a big if, she succeeded in proving her claim, then the police would be after her for Abby's death. She was damned if she did and damned if she didn't clear her name.

It had been a shock to hear dear old Dad freely admit his affair with Kate Clark. The pillar of his church and community openly saying he was flawed like everyone else? Why? Unless it had already been exposed. Yet, her mother didn't appear to know. Was he making up the entire story?

Her head was beginning to ache with too many questions and not enough answers. Where was her partner, Ted? She was curious as to what had happened to their company.

Her ex-husband Robert, on the other hand, would do anything for money. As a musician and part-time photographer, he was privy to local gossip around the beach nightclub scene that most people never heard about. If there was dirt to be found, Robert could dig it up. He'd know any rumors about Abby's murder and possibly had obtained information on the Clark woman that wasn't in that damned report.

But, where was he? He went through money too fast not to be lurking around somewhere. He probably had latched onto some poor, unsuspecting rich widow and was living off her money. At least finding Robert was a place to start.

Feeling better now that she had made a determined decision, she showered and washed her hair, then put on her prettiest dress. Justin had said that the green flowers were the exact shade of her eyes. The delicate blossoms scattered throughout the yellow silk material did set off her eyes. She couldn't let herself think about Justin now. She was on her own.

She was actually hungry for the first time since yesterday. Maybe there was hope yet. She slipped her feet into sling-back pumps, grabbed the wad of bills on the dresser, shoved them into her purse, and walked out the door. She ate in the hotel's small restaurant on the first floor. It was pleasantly cool inside. The dining area, filled with rattan chairs and glass top tables, was sectioned off by a smooth wooden railing. She took a seat at a table near the bar. When the waiter arrived, she ordered a shrimp salad and a tall glass of ice tea.

Several men were openly staring at her, but she tried to ignore them. She finished her salad, paid her check and was about to leave when a short fat man walked up to her table.

"Hi, Kate," he said, his beady eyes roving up and down her body making her skin crawl. Beads of perspiration covered his forehead and upper lip on his flushed round face. His fat hand trembled as he started to sit down.

"My name isn't Kate," Kathryn corrected, her words barbed.

"Well it was a couple of years ago, honey, and my memory is very good." He took a napkin from the table and mopped his face. "Where you been keeping yourself? We've missed seeing you around."

His gaze dropped to her breasts, making Kathryn want to cover herself. She stood, not wanting to make a scene, just wishing pig eyes would go away and leave her in peace. She knew he wouldn't. "I'm sorry, but you've made a mistake. I don't know you."

He reached out and grabbed her wrist. She

stiffened, as anger roared through her at the feel of his hot, sweaty fingers on her skin.

"Come on, Kate, let's you and me go to my apartment. Your husband will never have to know."

"How do you know my husband?" she snapped and jerked her wrist free of his greedy hold. He gave her a sneering smile, reminding her of a fat hog turning on a spit over a roasting fire.

"We had a long chat last night. That man was full of questions about you. Guess you never told him much about yourself, did you? I sort of filled him in, if you know what I mean."

"My name is not Kate. If you know what's good for you, you'll stay far away from my husband and me." She turned and rushed from the restaurant. Only when she was in her room did she feel secure. Immediately she called the desk and told the clerk she would be checking out first thing in the morning. Then she packed her bags and sat on the bed, once more afraid to go to sleep.

The next morning she awoke lying on top of the spread, still in her clothes. She showered and changed into jeans, a short sleeve blue cotton shirt, and loafers. It didn't take long to check out of the hotel and arrange for a rental car to be delivered. When the clerk presented her with the bill, she almost choked. Staying three nights in one of the better suites during the tourist season cost nearly two-thousand dollars. She handed the clerk one of the credit cards and prayed Justin hadn't canceled the card. The clerk ran it, then gave it back with a copy of the hotel bill stamp paid. A smile curved her lips, and she quickly arranged for a rental car using the same card.

As she drove up Gulf Boulevard, she was shocked at the changes. The beach shoreline was hidden from sight. Both sides of the street were crowded by high-rise apartments, shops, restaurants or motels. She settled on a quiet motel, not far from the Don CeSar, called the Dutchman Inn. It looked clean and relatively secure, with a swimming pool, beach area and a large parking lot next to the main entrance which led to the beach. When she checked in and presented the credit card, the charge went through without a hitch. She paid for a week and arranged to stay longer if necessary.

In no way did her room compare to the suite at The Don, but it was clean. Her corner room looked out on the parking lot and also had a partial view of the beach. The linens were clean, the king size bed had a firm mattress, and the room had the usual bolted down flat screen TV. She would survive.

The air was hot and smelled musty from being closed up for hours, so she flipped on the air-conditioner, locked the door and headed for her rental car. Now was as good a time as any to begin looking for Robert.

After four years, how many of his old hangouts would still be in existence? She didn't know, but would soon find out. At first, she tried calling different bars where he had worked. Each person who answered was new and had never heard of him. Maybe a personal visit to each place would be better.

Before that, she wanted to see Abby's house on Tierra Verde. It was a beautiful day for a drive. The weather was warm and breezy. Most of the winter tourists were gone, and Kathryn smiled at the few she did see. It wasn't hard to tell a snowbird from a permanent resident. They were either lily white or beet red.

On the outside, nothing had changed except maybe the people living there. The sight of the home only made her heartache. The drive along on Gulf Boulevard was reminiscent of the one to what was supposed to be her birthday dinner four years prior. Now there were more hotels and motels. She still had to turn left at the Don CeSar and pass through the toll booth to pay her seventy-five cents. The drawbridge was down, so traffic flowed smoothly all the way to the Fort DeSoto turnoff that would take her to Tierra Verde and the small bridge over to Sands Point.

The sprawling Spanish style house faced the street with a long curved driveway. Across the back of the house, a covered veranda faced the bay. Abby had never liked nosey neighbors, so had purchased three lots for privacy and immediately installed a six-foot fence dividing the property line. On both sides of the property, from the front edge of the lot to the wooden barrier, tall red, white and pink Oleander bushes acted as barriers.

Kathryn sat in her car and gazed at the house. She started to get out and walk up to the front door. The garage door opened at the right side of the house, and a black Mercedes pulled out. It suddenly hit her. This was no longer Abby's home. Seeing a stranger drive out of the garage was the final knife in her heart. She hurriedly drove away, back toward the Gulf beaches, tears streaming down her face.

Across the bridge to Gulf Boulevard, Kathryn

turned north to Upham Beach where Robert had hung out for a time. Upham Beach was near expensive condominiums and just the sort of place he would frequent.

Within fifteen minutes, she was there. It was still her favorite spot. Only about a mile long and nestled in between tall condominiums at the north and south end, it was still pristine and beautiful, even if a bit crowded with locals and tourists. No longer open access, wooden boardwalks crossed the sand dunes to the beach and protected the seagrasses, planted to prevent erosion.

The Seaside Grill, situated in the middle of the access area, offered cold drinks, food and a place to sit. Shower stands were installed beside the restaurant to rinse off the salt water and sand before returning to the cars parked at meters along the road.

Today, the wind felt good, and the sun was warm on her skin. Kathryn piled her hair on top of her head and watched the sandpipers scurry along the water's edge, running away each time a wave broke across the sand. She walked barefoot along the shore, letting the waves wash over her ankles. In years past she would have seen hundreds of coquinas, tiny, oval clams left after each wave. Their myriad of colors would turn the wet sand into a kaleidoscope until they dug their small bodies beneath the surface, waiting for the next wave to carry them away. The coquinas were gone now, as were the starfish, the sand dollars, and too many others. Now the shore was littered with tourists and seaweed. Only occasionally could you find a seashell.

As she splashed along, Kathryn searched for her favorite shell and felt tears sting her eyes when she found a baby's foot, a small black shell with a perfect imprint of a tiny foot. She had collected them as a child and knew there were jars of them tucked away in a chest at home.

Overhead, she heard the roar of a jet, and her thoughts turned to Justin. She wondered where he was, and if he had given her any thought after he left.

Loneliness gripped her as she walked back to the Seaside Grill and sat down at an empty table to stare out over the Gulf of Mexico. Far out on the horizon, she could see ships that looked like toys. She longed to be on one, sailing away from the emptiness inside her and to laugh and forget the pain filling her life. Even the soothing lap of the waves could not ease the hungry longing she felt. She refused to admit that it was for Justin, her need for his quiet strength and smiling eyes.

She stood and stared at the tall condominium at the north end of the beach. An eerie sense of familiarity touched her. She hurried to her car to sit and stare at the concrete structure.

Her mind was partly in a daze. It was as if she were watching a movie. She could visualize the entrance to the complex, the friendly old guard waving her through the gate. She could even picture the apartment, how the rooms were laid out and even the white furniture and gold accessories. The shadowy figure of a man moved about the rooms, calling her name.

She gripped the steering wheel as terror shot through her with lightning quickness. His blue suit showed off his broad shoulders, but she still couldn't see his face. Breathing hard, she started the car and backed out onto the street. She was shaking inside as she rounded the corner and parked across from the entrance to the condo. To her knowledge, she had never been in the building, but in her mind, she could see the lobby and knew the apartment was on the sixth floor.

Getting out of the car, she slowly walked up to the guard house. The old man inside looked up and smiled, then opened the door. "Well, well, Mrs. Clark, how are you?" he beamed. "We sure have missed you around here!"

"Mrs. Clark?" Kathryn stammered.

"Yeah, well, sorry, at least we thought he was your husband. Even though, he was only here a couple of days a week. You know me and the other guards figured he traveled a lot."

Kathryn stared at the old man. Uncertainty ripped at her insides. How well did he know Kathryn Clark? "I'm not Mrs. Clark."

"You're not? Boy, you could be her twin then! I've never seen two people look more alike. My mistake, Miss," He shook his head in amazement.

"When did she live here?" she asked.

The guard scratched his head for a minute as if pondering the question. "Let me see, I think it must have been two or three years ago."

"Do you know where she went?"

He shook his head, "No. Seems she just up and left one day and never came back. The guy on duty that day did tell me she was in a big hurry. That was the last time any of us saw her. She was such a nice lady."

"Thank you," Kathryn said, turned and walked toward her car.

"Say, Miss," the guard called after her, "was there something you wanted?"

"No, nothing really," she called over her shoulder. "I just wanted a closer look at the building." She got in her car and drove away.

The air conditioner cooled the flush of her heated face, but could not slow the racing of her heart. It was terrifying to be continually mistaken for someone else. The man in the restaurant, the old guard at the gate, her mother and father, all insisted she was Kate. Even Justin no longer believed her story. He'd also had his security man check her out just to prove she was lying. She wasn't Kate Clark, she couldn't be. Her only problem, she had no way to prove it. DNA, sure, if she wanted to face murder charges.

Doubts nagged at her. All those people claiming she was Kate. Was she crazy? Could she be Kathryn Clark? If so, how did she know all those things about Kathryn Blanding? Could she have learned everything, all her memories, from spending a few months in the Blanding home? Was that possible? Her mind raced with questions without answers.

White-faced, she drove into the parking lot of her motel and pulled into a vacant space. She sat with the engine idling and terror gripping her mind. To accept the idea she was not Kathryn Blanding, but a woman with the morals of a prostitute would be the end of her. No! She would not accept such an idea. She was a Blanding, a survivor, a fighter. Abby had taught her that. And there was no way she could have harmed Abby.

For all of Justin's talk of love, how quickly he had been swayed to lose faith in her. How quickly he had made her fall in love with him. Was he trying to trap her in a lie the entire time he was kind and loving?

"God, he must have been laughing at me the whole time," she muttered. She'd had enough heartbreak to last a lifetime. Never again would she let a man get that close to her. Justin was her past, and that was where she was going to keep him.

She hurried to her room, washed her face and changed into white cotton slacks, a deep blue flowered blouse and sandals. She was determined to grab a quick bite and again search for Robert. Some bars Robert frequented would open early for dinner. She had several to visit this evening, and it was already seven o'clock. The dinner hour ended at nine, but the bars stayed open until two a.m.

The first place she checked was Dominic's, a restaurant on the north side of Blind Pass Road near the turnoff to Sunset Beach. Known for the quality of its food and as a meeting place for the hard-partying crowds, it also had been where she first met Robert.

The restaurant had changed little in four years. Kathryn made her way to the second-floor entrance, walked past the doorway leading to the bar, and entered the dining room.

After being seated at a table, she ordered a dish of shrimp pasta. Kathryn wasn't surprised at how fast the lounge area was filling up. Three bartenders were working behind a long circular wooden bar. Tall stools were placed so customers could gaze out at the lights and water across Blind Pass Road. One of the bartenders looked familiar. She wondered if he had known Robert.

Most of the stools were occupied first. Couples and single men and women sat at the numerous tables encircling the dance floor and bandstand. She paid her bill, made her way to the bar and waited to catch the attention of the man she recognized.

In the shadows sat a big man with sharp features and dark hair. His powerful shoulders and muscular arms were emphasized by a dark short sleeve shirt. His gaze stayed riveted on her face. Chills covered her body. It was too dark in the place to see his features clearly, but somehow she knew his eyes would be cold, hard and unforgiving. All she needed was to run into another one of 'Kate's' friends.

Finally, the bartender stopped in front of her. "What'll it be?"

"Glass of White Zinfandel, please." When the glass of wine was placed on the bar, she pulled out a twenty and said, "Do you know Robert Cantree?"

"Robert, the leech, Cantree? "

"Well, that's an apt description of him, yes. Have you seen him lately?" Kathryn had to smile. This man did know Robert quite well.

"What would a classy woman like you want with the likes of him?"

"Just a few questions for him, that's all," she assured him. "Has he been around?"

"He won't come in here anymore."

"Why not?"

"Because he took me for close to five-hundred

bucks and hasn't paid me back. I haven't seen him for over two years. He's either moved out of state or gone underground somewhere, hiding from all the people he owes money to in this town. Take my advice, lady, stay away from garbage like him." He pushed the twenty back toward her. "The drink is on me. Stick around, and I'll buy you breakfast."

She gave him her most charming smile, then said, "Thanks for the offer, but my husband is expecting me home soon."

"Too bad," he said and turned his attention to the woman seated on the next stool.

Leaving her wine untouched, Kathryn hurriedly left, eager to be away from the piercing stare of the stranger. As she pulled out of the restaurant parking lot and turned north toward Gulf Boulevard, she glanced back at the stairs leading to the building's second floor. Coming down the steps was the same man who had been staring at her.

Her neck muscles tightened as she gripped the steering wheel. Was it just chance that the stranger had left so soon after her? She pressed hard on the gas pedal and the car shot into traffic, leaving the man and her uneasy feelings behind.

At the Island Hotel on Treasure Island, no one even knew Robert. The same was true at a bar on Madeira Beach, Redington Beach and back down to the Sea Breeze Resort on St Pete Beach.

The Lagoon Bar hadn't changed much. It was one large room with a baby grand piano in one corner surrounded by tall bar chairs and windows that overlooked the manmade waterfall. A long wooden bar ran the length of the opposite wall, facing the piano. It led to another exit, across from the entrance, next to the bathrooms. Tables and chairs were crowded into the remaining space, and tonight the room was filled to capacity with tourists.

The man playing the piano was belting out an old Nat King Cole song. "Unforgettable" was immediately followed by "What I did for Love." As he began to sing the old song, "Someone to Watch Over Me," Kathryn thought of Justin. She forced the thoughts from her mind and tried to concentrate on the business at hand. It was going on eleven o'clock, her feet hurt, and she was exhausted from lack of sleep.

She stood behind a post near a blonde woman seated in a tall chair next to the singer. While Kathryn waited for the man to finish his song, she glanced out the window directly behind him. Crossing the stone footbridge over the lagoon, leading straight to the bar, was the same man from Dominic's. Without hesitating, she turned, hurried out the other exit and dashed to her car.

It was only a short distance to her motel, and she felt relieved when she was safely locked behind the door of her room. Most likely, the man's appearance at the Lagoon was a coincidence, and she was overreacting. None the less, the man frightened her, and there was no sense in taking chances.

Tomorrow she could continue her search. Tonight all she wanted was a shower and a bed. She glanced at her watch, amazed it was nearing midnight.

She was exhausted. Once she crawled between the fresh, clean sheets, it was not long before her eyes closed, and she was fast asleep.

She dreamed of the room with the body, but this time the body was male. The faceless shadow of a man was still there, standing over the victim, his bloody hands clenched at his sides. This time, the crumpled figure on the floor looked familiar. When she inched her way down the hall, the shadowy figure rolled the body over with his foot. She screamed as Justin's lifeless face was caught in the faint beam of light coming through the French doors. He stared at her, his eyes open and accusing. She tried to run to him but found a door barring her way. It was locked. She beat on it. The pounding of her fists shook the windows as a blaze of light flashed around the room.

Kathryn sat up in bed to the sound of thunder. With a trembling hand, she snapped on the bedside lamp. She shivered and rubbed her arms as the cold air from the air conditioner hit her bare skin.

She padded barefoot across the carpet to the window and peered out. The night was alive with flashes of purple as lightning snaked across the sky. She looked down at the parking lot. Cars filled all but three vacant spaces. Apparently, the hotel's occupancy had increased since she checked in. As a streak of lightning cut the darkness, she caught a glimpse of a dark figure standing beside a green car parked under the orange glow of the light pole. His hat dripped drops of rain on his already wet slicker. He stood facing the building ignoring the downpour. She glanced at the travel clock on the nightstand. The bright red numbers told her it was closing fast on one-thirty

Suddenly she felt cold as he tilted his face up and stared at her window. He was watching her room. She backed away until the back of her legs touched the bed, and she sank down, her knees weak.

She recalled the warning voice on the phone back in Colorado telling her not to return to Florida. She had defied that warning. She reached for her robe at the foot of the bed.

Her hand froze as her eyes caught the slight movement at the door. The doorknob turned ever so slightly. She didn't just imagine it. Someone was there, trying to open her door. Her heart thumped loudly in her ears as she picked up the phone and dialed the desk. The seconds dragged until the desk clerk answered. Her words tumbled over each other. "Someone is trying to get in my room," she whispered. She was afraid to breathe.

The desk clerk cautioned her to stay on the line. A security guard was on the way to her room.

"Please hurry," she urged.

"Stay calm, our man is on the way, Mrs. Crown," the clerk assured her.

Hysteria was building within her. She tried to remain calm, but the fear was in control. She began to shake as the knob continued to turn. The door moved as the unknown attacker pushed hard against it. Then loud voices and the sound of rapidly retreating footsteps beat a rhythm down the hallway. The loud knock on the door made her jump, and she realized it was the security guard.

"Mrs. Crown, this is security, are you all right?" a man shouted.

Overcome with relief, she let the receiver fall to the floor and stumbled to the door. She cracked it and gave a cry of joy when she saw the blue uniform.

"Are you all right, ma'am?" he asked.

She managed a weak "Yes," and dropped into a chair.

"Everything appears to be okay now, Mrs. Crown. Whoever it was is gone. It was probably someone on the wrong floor."

Kathryn looked at his badge which displayed his photograph and the name John Snyder.

"There was a man in the parking lot watching my room, Mr. Snyder. I think he was the one who tried to break in." He was ready to dismiss the whole incident as a misunderstanding. She was not.

"It was probably a beach bum or someone at the wrong door."

She stared up at the man. "I tell you, someone was trying to break in." The harshness in her voice emphasized her stress. She pushed the hair back from her face and glared at him.

"Mrs. Crown, I assure you, you are safe here," Snyder said as he turned to leave.

Frustrated that he refused to believe her, she tried to convince him she wasn't hysterical. Someone was trying to harm her. Only at her insistence did he reluctantly call the police. Within minutes, two officers arrived. When they entered the room, Kathryn noticed one of them gave her a quizzical once-over then smiled at her. It was more of a leer than a smile.

The security guard introduced her. The older policeman kept staring at her. "Don't I know you?" he asked, as recognition settled across his face.

"No, I doubt it," she said, almost positive what he was going to say next.

"I'd swear I know you. Is your name Kate?"

John Snyder looked back and forth between the police officer and Kathryn. "You know each other?"

"Maybe," the cop said.

Kathryn came to her feet like a cat, her green eyes dark with anger. "My name is Kathryn Crown!" She balled her hands into fists as if she were ready to strike him.

"Take it easy, lady. I'm sorry if I've made a mistake, but you look enough like someone to be her twin."

"Please leave," she cried.

"All right, all right," the officer said and motioned the other two men to follow him. "If you have any more problems, don't hesitate to call. We're here to help." He turned and left the room.

After they reached the corridor, Kathryn slammed the door and locked it. The policeman had placed one more nail in her coffin of doubts. Shattered, she slid to the floor in a heap. She whispered over and over, "Please God, don't let me be Kate. I don't want to be that awful woman."

A feeling of longing swept over her. Inside, she felt an emptiness that would never be filled now that Justin had left her. She slowly got up and lay across the bed, her cell phone so close she only had to reach out and grab it if needed.

Kathryn stared at the screen and wanted to pick it up, but fought the urge with every ounce of pride she had. Justin had made his feelings clear. He wanted nothing more to do with her. He was the one who walked out and slammed the door between them and would have to be the one to re-open it.

With an angry cry, she rolled over on her back. Somewhere, someone knew the truth. The most likely person was Robert. Her only hope was to find him. Tomorrow she would begin her search all over again. Anything was possible if she believed enough, and she was a believer.

Chapter Fifteen

Justin hadn't been sleeping well. It had been four days since he'd stormed out of the hotel suite and left Kathryn standing with tears streaming down her face. Jon had been furious with him for leaving her behind. Once the plane was airborne, he had wanted to agree with the pilot, but his stubborn pride wouldn't let him. How many times did a man have to be played for a fool before facts kicked him in the head? The only type of a woman he seemed to meet saw dollar signs. Never again would he let himself be betrayed by some conniving woman. No sir, he didn't need any woman that much.

Once the plane landed in Colorado Springs, he had stayed overnight at the house on Cheyenne Mountain Boulevard. That had been a disaster. He had gotten in a fight with Etta, tried to fire her, then went to the office, but had not been able to work. So he headed straight to the Triple Crown Ranch south of the Springs. He wanted to be as far away from any memory of Kathryn as he could get. The house in town held too many memories.

Traffic on I-25 at that time of night was sparse. Most families were home, settled down for a cold evening before a fire or already in bed. Focused on Kathryn and not on his destination, Justin almost missed exit to the road leading to the ranch. He hit the brakes, swerved onto the ramp, hit the road spinning gravel and a cloud of dust behind him for a quarter of a mile. As he roared up to the white stone cottage, he almost expected to see lights come on at the larger house. The windows remained dark. One of the ranch dogs came out of the barn growling. A quick voice command from Justin and he retreated back inside where it was warm.

The ranch house was small but comfortable. Located closer to the horse barns than the main house, it was built strictly for his convenience when he stayed at the ranch. Besides, he didn't need a lot of room to do what he planned on doing, which was to get wasted. He wanted to numb his brain so he couldn't think, couldn't remember the taste of her lips, or how silky her skin was or the smell of her hair after a shower. He didn't want to recall the tears in her eyes or the shocked expression on her beautiful face after he hurled the foulest, most vile words he could think of at her. He was disgusted with himself for what he had done. At the same time, the information from Harv's report was seared into his brain. Still, guilt over what he had said to Kathryn had twisted him harder than any bronco ever could.

He unlocked the door, dropped his bag, and flipped on the light switch, then headed straight for the liquor cabinet. He downed two shots of scotch before he considered closing the front door. The icy wind howled around the room like a ghost bent on revenge. Grabbing the bottle, he ignored the cold, kicked the door closed and settled himself in an overstuffed chair before the fireplace to do some serious drinking. Not bothering to build a fire in the grate, he slumped back as if defeated by the only woman he really wanted. Glass after glass of the potent liquor burned its way down his throat until his head whirled, and his stomach churned. He staggered to the bedroom and dropped fully clothed onto the unmade bed. Lost in an alcoholic haze, he passed out, oblivious to anything around him.

Sometime during the night, he realized the house was cold, rose from the bed, staggered to the wall and turned the thermostat up to seventy-five. He hadn't eaten since noon the day before, and now his stomach rebelled from the liquor he had consumed. He found himself half crawling to the bathroom to hang over the commode, sickened by scotch and his hasty act of malice toward Kathryn. After brushing his teeth, he washed his face, then stumbled back to the bedroom and collapsed again on the bed.

The next morning his stomach threatened to rebel again, and he was forced to consume something other than booze. He finally changed from his suit to jeans, boots, and a flannel shirt. He didn't bother to shower or shave. As the days passed, one into two, then three, and four, he lost count of the hours and the quantity of liquor he ingested. It wasn't until the pounding on the front door of the cottage roused him from the heavy stupor. He stumbled to the door.

Jon stood with his hands braced against the door frame and an expression of disgust on his face.

"Well aren't we a pretty sight? Hit the bottom of the pity bottle have you?" he snapped as Justin opened the door.

Justin roared back, suddenly sober. "Don't give me any crap. I'm not in the mood to see you or anyone else. What the hell are you doing here anyway? You're supposed to be in Florida keeping an eye on Kathryn. Why aren't you?"

Justin left the door open and returned to the chair to hold his throbbing head in his hands. The world was cockeyed, and he was hanging upside down in it, sicker than a hairy dog, which he deserved. The fresh air whipped around the room and was a blessing as it chased out the odor of booze, smoke, and sweat. When Jon didn't answer, Justin stood and stared at him. "I asked you why you're not in Florida?"

"Because you told me to leave." Jon's face flushed red with anger. Hands balled into fists at his sides, he wanted to hit something, and Justin looked like a good target. So he sent him flying with one punch.

"Mr. high and mighty Justin Crown, too good to believe his wife might be innocent of all that garbage in Harv's report, ordered me to fly him back to Colorado. That's why I'm here, hoping you've come to your senses and you're ready to go and bring Kathryn back home where she belongs."

"If you're so in love with her, you go find her, but leave me out of it." Justin's anger flared as he rose to his feet and faced his longtime friend. Unsteady, he stood rubbing his jaw. "You hit me." No one was going to tell him how to handle his marriage, no matter who they were or how long he had known them.

"You deserved it. I'd leave you right now if Kathryn would have me. But, she's too in love with the likes of you to ever give me a second glance." Jon stopped, embarrassed by the words he had blurted out. He had carefully hidden his feeling about his best friend's wife. Now it was too late to retract his secret.

Stunned, Justin could only stare at Jon. A streak of jealousy, for a brief moment, sent wild images racing through his mind. He tossed them out, knowing Jon would never cross the line and encroach on his relationship with Kathryn. His jealousy was ridiculous. Leaving Jon standing alone, Justin walked to the small L-shaped kitchen and began making coffee. "How long have you been in love with her?" he called over his shoulder.

Jon marched over to lean on the counter and stare at Justin's back. "Since the first time I saw her at your office. I was too tongue-tied to ask her out right away, then you beat me to it. The rest is history. Kathryn loves you and only you. Granted she's different now, stronger, a fighter, but where it counts; she is still the same woman you fell in love with and married. I don't care what Harv's report says. That is not the woman you and I know. As soon as you get your head out of your butt, you'll know it too. The only thing riding you is jealousy. Get over it, or some nut may kill her before we can find out the truth."

A contrite Justin turned, "Call Harv, have him meet us in Florida. I know when I've made an ass out of myself, without you having to tell me." He rubbed his eyes, trying to scrub the sleep from them. "I want every bit of information he can dig up on this supposed husband of Kathryn's and her father. Randolph Blanding is one hard son of a bitch to hate his daughter as much as he does.

"I hate to admit it, especially to you, as you'll never let me forget it, but you're right. I refuse to believe the woman I love is the woman in Harv's report. I lost

my head for a while, but my brain is working now."
Justin poured two cups of coffee and handed one to Jon.
He stood leaning back against the opposite counter as he
took a sip of the black hot brew.

"The plane is gassed and ready. When do we
leave?" Jon asked.

"As soon as I drink this coffee, shave and get this
stink off me." He blew on the hot coffee, took a sip and
carried the cup to the bathroom while Jon dropped into a
chair, grabbed the phone and dialed Harv's number.

Chapter Sixteen

Kathryn checked every bar, nightclub, and restaurant Robert had ever mentioned or visited. Some she checked twice on the chance she might have missed asking the right person the right question. In some places the bartenders had never heard of him, in others, she was told he had not been seen for a couple of years. He had vanished.

Tired of searching without positive results, she stopped at one last place before admitting defeat. Located on Pass A Grille Way and the Intracoastal side of St. Pete Beach, the Sea Spray Tavern and Restaurant was not Robert's regular hangout. It was an old style, family owned, out of the way pub with indoor tables and a bar, as well as outdoor dining. It was down-home Florida cooking served with a smile and plenty of food. Robert had eaten there a lot and swore it was the friendliest pub on the beach. It was twilight when Kathryn walked into the restaurant.

The bartender registered surprise and admiration as she slid onto a barstool. He was used to seeing the beach bunnies in their cutoff jeans, T-shirts or bikinis, and the sunburned tourists. This woman was straight out of Town and Country in her dressy gray slacks and soft pink blouse. She stood out like a Spanish doubloon on black velvet in a museum.

"What'll you have?" he drawled, a big grin spreading across his face, his white teeth sparkling against his dark tanned skin.

"A Coke."

He continued his appraisal without the usual leer. He was different from the others Kathryn had talked with. He did not undress her with his eyes. Not like some who made her feel naked under their leering gaze while lying to her about whether or not they knew Robert. She knew they were not telling the truth. She had been to some of the bars where Robert had played guitar with a band. They might not recognize this face, but she knew theirs.

She had discovered that if she wanted information, she had to be friendlier. She drew in a deep breath, gave the man a warm smile, then asked, "I'm looking for someone, a man, Robert Cantree. Do you know him, and have you seen him lately?"

One eyebrow raised, he pondered her question for a moment before answering. "What do you want with him?"

"We used to be friends. And I desperately need to find him." An honest answer to his question was her best bet.

"I haven't seen him for a while, but Charlie might have." He pointed to a booth at the back alongside the bar.

"Thanks." Coke in hand, she slid from the stool and walked to the booth. The man stood as Kathryn approached.

"I'm Charlie," he said as she stopped at his table. "I saw Al point me out to you. Have a seat."

She slid onto the bench across from him, her back to the entrance and studied his dark curly hair and deep brown eyes. He wasn't handsome, but he had even white teeth that showed a friendly smile that reached his eyes.

There was a scar on his chin giving him the appearance of a street fighter. He wore no shirt, only a denim vest, cutoffs, and sandals that just added to the impression. He was no more than two years older than herself, but his eyes spoke of wars fought, and roads walked far beyond his years. He had seen too much of life's hard side.

"What can I do for you, young lady?" He even treated her as if he was a lot older.

"My name is Kathryn Crown, and I am trying to locate Robert Cantree."

He studied her face for a few moments before replying, shrugged his shoulders as if making an inconsequential decision. "Well, that could take some doing. I haven't seen Robert since May of 2016."

"How can you be so sure of the exact date and year?"

He chuckled, shook his head and said, "Well, Robert had this great plan. We were going to Nashville together."

Kathryn suspected Charlie was another of Robert's creditors. "He always had big plans."

"Yes, he did. Yes, he did," Charlie acknowledged, each word clipped and precise. "Only this time, he had the money to back it up. The trip was a definite go. He even showed me a wad of bills the night before we were to leave. He actually paid me the twenty-five hundred he owed me. "

"Where would Robert get that much money, Charlie? He didn't earn that kind of money playing the clubs around here. And what he did earn, he always blew on booze or women."

Surprise registered on his face as he stared at her. "You really don't know, do you?"

"No. Robert never had money when I knew him." She frowned as memories invaded the day, memories of Robert's tantrums centered on her refusal to support his wild spending. Cruel memories she wanted to forget.

Charlie leaned his forearms on the table and clasped his hands together, his brow wrinkled in thought. "Look, Ms. . ."

"Kathryn. Please call me Kathryn."

"Okay, Kathryn. All I know is that Robert lived high on the hog for about six months before he disappeared. He told me you were his meal ticket to fame and fortune."

Which me, she wondered? She couldn't believe what he was saying. "Why would he say something like that?"

Charlie took a long draw on his beer and wiped his mouth with a paper napkin. It was clear he was becoming uncomfortable with the conversation. Charlie looked away, his eyes searching the room for a reply, before turning back to Kathryn. "He pointed you out to me one night at this lounge where we played. He said you were his good luck piece. I asked him what he meant, and he just laughed. Said it was a big secret, but as long as you were around, he had it made. That's all he ever said about it."

Her heart pounded as she leaned forward and asked, "Charlie, are you sure it was me you saw? Could it have been someone who looked like me?"

He gave her a shy smile, "There isn't another

face like yours in this town. It was you all right."

She frowned.

"Hey, did I say something to upset you?"

"No, I'm okay," she assured him. "Back to what you were saying about Robert disappearing, what did you mean exactly?"

"Just what I said. Robert had bought this new expensive car, and we were supposed to leave on a Saturday night after work. I packed all my stuff and brought it to the club so we could head out when the place closed. Only old Robert never showed. I haven't seen him since. At least I got my money back. That's more than I can say for a lot of folks."

"You never heard from him? Not even a phone call?"

"Nope. I called his sister, but she wasn't any help. They never got along, so she didn't have much to say."

Surprise must have registered on her face because Charlie gave her a strange look. "I never knew Robert had a sister. Do you know where she lives?"

"Yeah, Angel lives in a condo on Tierra Verde." He shook his head and added, "I'm not surprised you didn't know about Angel. She's not a woman Robert would admit was his sister, especially to the rich crowd he wanted to run with. Looks as if Angel's running with the rich and famous now. She found some rich man to keep her, so thinks she's too good to speak to the people who knew her when she hustled on Central Avenue."

Kathryn leaned back in the red vinyl booth,

picked up her glass and took the last sip of the watery Coke. "You've been a big help, Charlie. If you could give me Angel's address, I'd appreciate it."

He picked up the check for her Coke, "Got a pen?"

She fumbled in her purse, found one and handed it to him. He jotted the address on the back of her check and passed it to her. Kathryn carefully placed both in her purse. He had helped her more than he knew. At least she had another lead to Robert. The man couldn't have vanished altogether, could he? She stood and stuck out her hand, "Thanks, Charlie. I have to go, but it's been a pleasure meeting you."

His grip was firm, and his palm and fingers had callouses. He was hard-working and friendly, and continued to hold her hand. "Same here, Kathryn. If you don't have anything to do some night soon, come by the Treasure Cove on Treasure Island. I'll buy you a drink. I'm playing there for the next two weeks."

"Thanks," she pulled her hand free, "maybe I'll do that." She looked out the window noticing for the first time it had grown dark. The street lights brightened the road, but across the Intracoastal Waterway, she could see the black, broken only by bright windows in the night. As she turned to leave, a man at the bar attracted her attention.

When she caught him looking in her direction, he placed money on the bar and quickly walked out. Something about him made her nervous. She didn't recognize his face, but he was familiar.

She hesitated and turned back to Charlie. "Would you mind walking me to my car? I don't like the way that man stared at me, and it's dark outside."

"No problem." He rose and walked beside her toward the front entrance. "I'll be right back to settle up for the beer and Coke, Al," he called as they passed the bartender.

When she tried to pay Charlie for her drink, he protested. "When I can't treat a beautiful lady to a Coke, it'll be a cold day in hell. Keep your money in your purse." He gave her a big smile and guided her out the door.

Safely in her car with the doors locked, she waved goodbye to the big man as he watched her pull into the Pass a Grille traffic. She was thankful to have found him. His tip might lead to Robert.

It still amazed her how little she knew about Robert's family. She hadn't even bothered to find out if Robert's parents were alive. What did that say about their relationship and her? Not much.

From the start, Robert must have known her real reasons for marrying him. Sure, he had his own schemes for marrying her, but she could have tried to make their marriage work, instead of flaunting him in her father's face. Her father had not forgiven her for being born, nor had he forgiven her outrageous marriage to a musician, a damned beach bum as he had so aptly put it. Robert had justified her father's negative attitude towards him.

At least she had Angel's address tucked safely away. She was approaching the Don CeSar on her left when she noticed the headlights behind her. The lights were reflected through the rearview mirror and blinded her. The car was too close to her back bumper. As she passed the Don, the glow of the street lights illuminated the green color of the car behind her. She had seen the car before. It was identical to the one was parked beside hers at the beach, and again when she had gone out to dinner. She'd swear it was the same one she'd seen at bars when she searched for Robert.

A startling memory came rushing back. The night of the thunderstorm, the man in the parking lot had been standing in the rain beside a dark car. Now she was frightened. With a white-knuckled grip on the steering wheel, her foot pressed harder on the accelerator. Damn the traffic, there was no way she could drive faster.

The vehicle continued to stay two car lengths behind. She heaved a sigh of relief, quickly whipped the sedan into the hotel parking lot and drove into the first space she found empty. Any minute she expected to see the green car pull in behind her. It didn't. Feeling foolish and chalking it up to an overactive imagination, she hurriedly locked the car and quickly walked to the elevator. Once in her room, with a chair wedged under the doorknob, she felt more secure, not entirely safe, but at least secure for the night.

She didn't go out to dinner, afraid of encountering the driver of the menacing green car. As nervous as she was, exhaustion claimed her, and she was asleep almost as soon as she leaned back against the stacked pillows

She heard the noise, but it didn't register in the thick fog enveloping her. It was a replayed dream, one of the many fights with her father and Robert. This time Randolph and Robert were arguing, their fingers pointed at each other, placing blame for some imagined impropriety. She covered her ears to block out the brutal accusations as they both turned on her at the same time. She begged them to stop, but they paid no attention to her pleas. Then Justin rushed into the room with a gun and shot them both. As bright red soaked the gray carpet, he turned to her and screamed, "Liar! Liar!"

She woke with a start to the ringing of the phone. Reaching out, she picked up the receiver and gave a groggy, "Hello." A raspy whisper on the other end yanked her wide awake.

"Go back to Colorado. You're stirring trouble into this pot, and it's gonna cost more than you'll want to pay. Go back to Colorado and live."

She threw the phone to the floor and stared at it, watched it coil like a snake ready to strike, afraid to touch it for fear the man would still be on the other end, listening. Huddled in the middle of the bed, the blanket clutched to her chest like a shield against the unknown, she felt as if the room had eyes boring into her, seeing her terror.

She could not bring herself to look at the phone or replace it on the cradle. Her nerves were stretched thin. Another call would be too much to bear. The television droned on and on. Only after she found the remote and turned the TV off did she rise to pace the floor, ignoring the pulsating bleating of the coiled phone in front of the nightstand. She was afraid to go to sleep. Her fear was a tangible thing that enveloped her with chilling dread. She was going to die if she stayed in St. Petersburg.

Several times during the long night she made up

her mind to leave as soon as the sun rose. There was enough money to take her far away from this town. If she packed her bags and caught a taxi to the airport, whoever was watching would know she was leaving and she'd be safe.

Yet something nagged at her not to run away. It was a ghostly whisper across death's void as her grandmother's voice muttered in her ear, "You're close. Stay. The answers are near." Why else was she receiving these calls? Someone was responsible for killing her grandmother and destroying her life. They deserved to pay for it.

As dawn's first rays streaked across the horizon, slow anger began to boil within her. Wrath gnawed at her insides until she was consumed with a fury for vengeance. More determined than ever to find Robert, she was even willing to pay him for information if she had to. She was positive he was the first key to solving the puzzle.

The sun was streaming through the window by the time she had formulated a plan. She was tired, but not sleepy. She replaced the phone, glad the noise and the long night was finally over.

After a quick shower, she dressed in white slacks and a blue pullover shirt and sandals. It was going to be another hot day. She stopped by the front desk long enough to arrange for a room on the gulf side and blocked any incoming calls to her room. There would be no more calls like last night. It never occurred to her to make a call from Justin an exception.

After coffee at a nearby restaurant, she walked to her car. It was barely nine o'clock, but the sun was already high. The heat rose from the pavement in waves, and the breeze from the water brought little relief. She drove south on Gulf Boulevard, then across the Pinellas Bayway turning at the light toward Tierra Verde and Fort De Soto Park.

It took ten minutes from the turnoff to reach the island that used to be nothing but vacant land. She kept glancing from one side of the road to the other. The entire area was one massive land development stretching as far as she could see. Gone was the natural paradise that once teemed with wildlife. Too many mangroves had been cut back, filled in and built up. Packed almost back-to-back, condominiums lined both sides of the four-lane road from one end of the island almost to the fort. Beautiful sharp angled buildings of concrete and wood were surrounded with lush green landscaping created by man instead of nature.

At the sign indicating Cristo's Cove, she pulled into the parking lot, climbed out of the car and looked for the correct building number. The Cove faced Tampa Bay and the Sunshine Skyway Bridge so that the entrance was at the rear of the structure.

The three-story units were constructed of rustic, weathered wood capturing that aged appearance mixed with the sharp lines of the architectural design. All the buildings looked alike, except for the numbers vertically listed on each door frame.

As she walked toward the building, she cautiously glanced over her right shoulder in time to see a dark green sedan drive past, more slowly than the other cars.

The dark-haired man in sunglasses behind the wheel watched her until she was out of his range of vision. She stopped and stared after the car, then turned away only after it continued on toward Fort De Soto. The sight of the car made her nervous. She hurried to Angel's door and rang the bell. Anxious, she waited for the door to be opened.

Angel was not what she imagined Robert's sister to be. Petite, she was shorter than Kathryn's five-foot-six by a good four inches. Where Robert was blonde and blue-eyed, Angel's hair was almost black, and her eyes were such a dark brown, they nearly matched her hair. Her brother may have believed in keeping fit, but his sister appeared to indulge her appetite. Her eyes flashed in surprise and one corner of her mouth curved in a smirk.

"Can I help you?"

"My name is Kathryn Crown, and I would like to speak with Angel if she's home," Kathryn said.

"I'm Angela. What can I do for you?"

"I'm sorry, I was told your name was Angel."

The woman smiled slightly, "That was a long time ago," then she stepped aside to invite Kathryn in.

Kathryn followed her upstairs to the lavish second-floor living room. One wall was sliding glass doors leading to a large balcony of Cyprus planking. A white patio lounger, along with a table and chairs of the same metal, stood out against the dusty gray of the wood.

A sea green, blue and beige velvet sofa, with matching chairs, faced the Gulf view. Heavy brass and glass bookshelves were filled with leather-bound volumes on sculpture and art. Original Florida landscapes covered the walls, and Kathryn stood transfixed. A painting of a great blue heron perched on a tree branch was so realistic she almost expected it to fly away to the small island she could see in the distance.

A long counter divided the kitchen from the living room. A fresh floral arrangement sat next to a gold birdcage. Inside a bright blue parakeet perched on a swing. Every now and then the bird let loose with a brief chirp.

Angel's voice interrupted her appraisal of the creature. Kathryn turned.

"Please sit down," she indicated a chair by the open door. "Would you like a glass of iced tea? It's terribly humid this morning."

"No, thank you," Kathryn said and sat in the proffered chair. Angel sat opposite her and flashed a broad smile in her direction. She wore a white tennis dress, which made her tan look darker. She was pretty, with an innocent face and wise, knowing eyes.

Kathryn felt guilty for her earlier thoughts. This woman did not look the type to hustle for a living. She appeared too refined and educated. "I'm in town for a short time, and I need to find your brother."

"What do you want with Robert?" Her voice held a note of suspicion.

Kathryn decided a half-truth was better than a lie. "I'm hoping he'll be able to supply the answers to a few questions. I've been looking for him, but everyone I've asked hasn't seen him for a long time. I was referred to you by a man named Charlie. Can you help me?"

Angel gave her a piercing stare for a moment, stood, went to the kitchen and returned with two glasses of tea, handed one to Kathryn, then plopped down in the chair, curling one leg under her while the other swung back and forth over the tan carpet. With one manicured nail, she twirled her ice cubes around and around in her glass, then looked at Kathryn.

Kathryn placed her glass on a coaster on the coffee table and waited for Angel to say something, anything. The silence in the room was overwhelming. Finally, she couldn't stand it. "Angel," she began.

"Angela, my name is Angela." The other woman emphasized the words. "I don't like the name Angel."

"Okay, Angela. Do you know where I can find your brother?"

A sly grin crossed Angela's face. "If anyone knows where Robert is, it's you," she mocked.

A hot flush raced up Kathryn's face. "Why do you say that? I haven't seen Robert in over four years."

"Look, you and my brother left this town on the same day. As far as anyone knew, you were together." Angela snapped back, then sipped her tea.

"Exactly when was that?"

The dark-haired girl stared at Kathryn as if she had lost her mind. "You don't know the date you left?"

"Not really."

"Well, this calls for something more than tea." Angel rose, walked to the wooden bar and poured vodka over ice in a tall glass. "All I know is what Robert told me, that as long as you were around, he had it financially made. Of course, he never included me in his windfall." Her voice was filled with bitterness.

Kathryn studied the woman, the way she stood leaning back against the bar like a kitten with a mouse caught in a trap. Her sensuous mouth was turned up in a secretive smile.

"You know who I am, don't you?" Kathryn wondered what secret Robert had confided to his sister.

"Sure. You call yourself Kathryn, but Robert, and that guy you were living with, always called you Kate."

Kathryn gasped, stung by the impact of Angela's words. She was almost afraid to ask the next question, but had to know, "Was the name of this man Randolph Blanding?"

"I don't know. Robert never said his name, but he knew him. According to my brother, he was some rich guy who would pay a lot to keep his secrets from becoming public knowledge." She took a large drink of the vodka and returned to her chair. She had drunk half the glass of straight vodka, and her eyes were showing the consequences. Angela's posture slipped as she draped a leg over the arm of the chair. "My brother was a self-centered bastard. He never missed an opportunity to stick it to someone if he could."

"Did Robert know what the secret was?" Her stomach muscles tightened.

"He must have. He said he would never have to work again if he didn't want to."

The implications were ugly. Kathryn didn't want to think about it. Whoever Robert was blackmailing had to be important. It would take a lot of money to satisfy his greed. "Did this secret have anything to do with me?

Was I the secret Robert was using against this man?"

"No. Robert said you were just in the wrong place at the wrong time, an added benefit. He said he could use you if need be and before you ask, I don't know what he meant by that either."

"Did you ever see me with this man?" Her hands shook as she waited for a response.

Angel's eyes glittered with antagonism. It was clear she did not like Kathryn. "I did see you with him one time."

"Where? When?"

"Late one afternoon when Robert and I went to Tampa on a family matter. We went to lunch at one of those little out of the way places. You know the kind I mean, dark and cozy. Robert pointed you both out to me. He said the man was your lover."

She was close, Kathryn could feel it. "Can you describe him?"

"Not really," Angel frowned in concentration. "I do remember he had thick hair. He had the most beautiful salt and pepper hair I have ever seen on a man. It showed off his tan, and he looked like an actor." She thought for a moment, then added, "He was tall and had broad shoulders. That's about all I can remember."

"Angela, please. This is so important. Try to recall more about him," Kathryn begged. She could feel her heart sink as Angel shook her head.

"That's it. Sorry."

Kathryn was frantic. She reached out to place a hand on Angel's arm, but the girl pushed it away, anger showing in her dark eyes.

"Look," she snapped, "all I know is that my

brother found himself a gravy train. He was riding high. He even planned on going to Nashville, then just like that, he disappeared." Her harsh voice grew calmer as she continued. "I checked with his friends, but they didn't know where he went. One of them told me you left town on the same day. It's been over two years next month since I've seen or heard from my brother. That's all I can tell you." She turned and picked up a tennis racket from beside the sofa. "If you'll excuse me, I have a tennis lesson."

"One more question." Kathryn didn't move. "Who told you I left town?"

Angel let out a disgusted sigh. "Some guy Robert knew. I think his name was Jack. He hung around at times when Robert needed money. He was pissed off because my brother stiffed him out of twelve-hundred dollars."

Kathryn's hope rose. "Where can I find this Jack?"

"You can't. Jack smashed his car up on the Bayway. He was killed instantly. Now if you don't mind," she looked at her watch, "I really have to go. I'm late as it is."

"Of course," Kathryn apologized, picked up her purse from the chair and walked toward the stairs. She turned back and said, "If you remember anything more, would you give me a call?"

"Sure, leave me your number. I don't think I will remember anything else, it was a long time ago."

Kathryn pulled a slip of paper and pen from her

purse and wrote down her motel and room number, then handed it to Angel.

She glanced at it and said, "Don't get your hopes up. I have a terrible memory."

"Maybe something will come to you," Kathryn said as she went down the stairs and out the door. Angel stood staring after her with a sly gleam in her eyes and a secretive smile on her lips.

Chapter Seventeen

Kathryn abandoned her search for Robert. He had driven into the night and vanished. Deep inside she felt he would never be found otherwise he would have gone to Nashville as planned. At least she had located his sister, thanks to Charlie, and she knew more than she was telling. But, Kathryn was also positive Angela would not contact her.

On the drive back, as she tried to decide what her next plan of action would be. Upon arrival at the motel, the green Chevy was parked across the street. Kathryn pulled into the parking lot and got out.

Heart pounding and hands shaking, she hurried toward the automatic glass doors, glancing over her shoulder all the way. The man continued to sit behind the steering wheel staring out the open window. The sun flashed off his reflective sunglasses, obscuring his eyes. His nose appeared immense, but she couldn't be sure. The shape of his head and the way he held his cigarette was the same as the man who had been following her.

Suddenly she froze. He tossed the cigarette to the pavement, and then opened the door, got out, and started in her direction. She desperately wanted to run but felt paralyzed. He was almost across the street. His gaze was fixed on her, his mouth curled in a cruel smile. He kept clenching and unclenching his fists, as if eager to wrap his long fingers around her neck.

The spell was broken by the loud squeal of tires. She lunged for the doors and ran to the elevator. Three people were exiting as she rushed past to push the button for her floor. Just before the elevator doors closed, she saw the man enter the lobby and look around. Her heart was beating so loudly in her ears; she didn't hear the bell ring signaling her floor. The doors slid open and she flew down the corridor, frantically searching her purse for the room key. She almost dropped the key card before she was able to insert it in the slot. Just as she got the door open, she heard the ding of the elevator stopping on her floor.

She locked and chained the door, grabbed her suitcase and threw it on the bed. If she was going to survive, she had to get out of St. Petersburg.

California came to mind. She'd go to Los Angeles and find Kathryn Clark's friends. She had exhausted all leads to Robert. She still had Justin's briefcase with Harv Anderson's report inside. The report listed the names and addresses of Kate's friends. They shouldn't be hard to locate. As she reached for the phone to call a cab, someone pounded on her door. Fumbling, she dropped the receiver and grabbed for it as it hit the floor.

"Kathryn, let me in. Kathryn? Open the door." The doorknob rattled. Without hesitating, she wedged a straight back chair under the knob and backed away. "Who are you? What do you want?"

"It's Jon, honey. Open the door and let me in. Justin sent me to find you."

Instant recognition penetrated the turmoil in her mind. "Thank God!" she cried and unlocked the door, flying into his arms.

"Well," he said, hugging her close, "this is a nice

howdy do." Easing the grip she had around his neck, he gently pushed her away and gave her a serious look. "What the hell is going on? I came in just as you got on the elevator, and you were white as a sheet."

Kathryn closed the door and on wobbly legs made her way to the bed and sat down. "Jon, someone has been following me. Everywhere I go, I keep seeing the same green car." Her eyes wide, she whispered, "When I came in just now, he was parked across the street."

"Why didn't you call me? I would have flown back immediately."

"I don't know anymore. All I know is that I've been warned to get out of St Petersburg or suffer the consequences. God, I hate being this wimpy woman afraid of her own shadow. I've never been like this."

"You're not a wimp, not as long as I've known you anyway." He sat beside her and slipped his arm around her shoulder. "A stalker is something else. Why didn't you call us and let us know what was happening? We could have been here within a couple of hours. In the meantime, you should have called the police."

"Oh yeah, right! Me call the police and tell them what?" She made a wide-eyed, silly face and said, "Excuse me! I'm trying to prove I'm Kathryn Blanding. Duh, I know I'm the prime suspect in my grandmother's murder, but please help me. There's a man following me." She stood and began pacing the floor. "And oh, by the way, I didn't kill her. I just can't prove it because I've lost my mind." She wanted to yell out the last part but didn't. All she could do was stop and stare at him.

"See what I mean?"

Jon had to admit she had a point about the police. "You should have called us. I could have called a friend of mine to keep an eye on you until we got here."

She sat back down on the bed next to him, staring at her hands in her lap. "I did start to call the house one night. I couldn't bring myself to speak to Justin, so I hung up before anyone answered." She suddenly looked up a frown on her face. "What are you doing here?"

"I told you, Justin sent me."

"Why would he send you?"

"To find you, silly! Kathryn, for the last two days, we've been calling every hotel or motel up and down this beach trying to find you. He sent me after you." He turned her to face him. Softly he said, "He loves you, Kathryn, and is sick with worry."

"Oh, he really showed me how much he loved me. If he loved me so much, why didn't he believe me? Why did he leave me here all alone?" Nerves ragged, she began to pace once more as her eyes grew bright with unshed tears.

"Kathryn, try to look at it from his side and understand. All of a sudden, the woman he loves claims to be someone else. Then when he goes digging into her past, well, you know the end result of that." Nervously, he watched her. He wanted to tell her that he would never have left her, but knew it was not what she needed to hear. She still loved Justin. Instead of saying what he felt, he reached out and grabbed her wrist to stop her pacing. "Sit down and listen to me."

She did as he asked, the pain in her eyes shining through tears. "In your present situation, you'll be the first to agree you know very little about Justin."

She shrugged her shoulders, "I'll concede that fact. I thought I was beginning to know him, but I guess I was wrong."

"In his defense, he knows very little about you as Kathryn Blanding. All he has to go on, where it concerns his wife, are those reports. He's hurting Kathryn. When you woke up in the hospital, he not only lost the wife he thought he knew, but found out all these nasty little facts about the woman he loved. How would you have reacted?"

She didn't answer. Maybe Jon was right. But, dammit, if you love someone, you give them the benefit of the doubt. Justin had hidden the report and in a drunken rage thrown it in her face. He should have shown her the report when he was sober and at least given her the chance to deny it.

When she continued to sit in silence, Jon said, "Look, Kathryn, I've known Justin for a long time, and I think I know him pretty well. Anyway, I don't know everything that happened the night we left, but I've never seen Justin so miserable. He was stinking drunk when we flew out of here. When he woke up the next day, he wasn't the same man I've known.

"Kathryn, he was a wild man. Etta told him off, so he tried to fire her. Bless her heart, she refused to leave. Told him he'd change his mind in the morning. He informed her he didn't need any damn women in his life. When she wouldn't leave, he did. Went out to the ranch and shut himself up in the house. He wouldn't answer the phone or let anyone in. He stayed drunk for four days. I finally went out there after the foreman kept calling two, three times a day. I've never seen such a mess. He was unshaven, stinking and still in the same clothes. Anyway, we got into it, and I had to deck him." He gave her a sheepish grin. "It wasn't hard. He was out on his feet. I don't think he'd eaten a bite the whole time."

Kathryn's eyes softened as she asked, "Is he all right? Is he still at the ranch?"

"Hell no. Justin is here. He sent me to fetch you and bring you to The Don. Like I said, we've been searching for you."

"What!" She all but shrieked the word. "If he came back, why isn't he here himself?'

"Because he's afraid you'll slam the door in his face. He just wants to talk to you. Will you come with me and see him?"

It tore at Kathryn that Justin would return to Florida and not come to face her himself. After all the things he'd said, he owed her more than an apology. She sat quietly for a moment and then said, "You don't know the things Justin said to me. He really hurt me. Why should I go rushing to The Don to see him?"

Jon stood. "You seriously need to consider seeing him. Down the beach is the one person who is willing to help you, besides me. He can do whatever it takes to straighten this mess out. I can't." A harsh edge crept into his voice. "You need him as much as he needs you. You can't stay here if someone's after you."

Kathryn's pride would not allow her to rush back to Justin. "If he loves me so much, tell him he has to come to me. He owes me that."

Jon walked to the door. "I'll tell him, but stay in this room until we get back." He nodded to her, opened the door and walked out, shutting the door behind him.

She stared after him, contemplating what he had said. He was right. She'd never be able to prove who her identity, or that she didn't kill her grandmother without Justin's help. He had Harv Anderson, many connections and the money to investigate. All she had to do was call him, but she couldn't wait. Jon was right, she had to face him. Glancing at her watch, she realized that Jon would already be at The Don. She picked up her purse and rushed out of the room.

At The Don, Justin growled and slammed down the receiver. "Damn, she's not answering. You told me you talked to her. Now, where the hell could she be?"

"I just left her; she's got to be there. She said she thought she was being followed. I told her she should have called us. Harv could have had someone keep an eye on her."

"Christ, Jon, I should have gone myself. She has to think I'm a coward for not coming with you. Which I am! I dread having to look Kathryn in the eye after all the disgusting things I said to her. I hope she'll forgive me and chalk it up to my being drunk and stupid."

"I'm sure she knows how stupid you can be at times," Jon said and started to sit down. Before Jon could get seated, Justin grabbed his jacket and headed for the door.

"Hey, where are you going?" Jon followed after him.

"Where in the hell do you think? After Kathryn! What if that man is at the motel and waiting for his chance?"

"Justin, wait up," Jon called.

But Justin wasn't waiting any longer. He had made a big mistake leaving the first time. He wasn't going to do that again. Nothing mattered anymore, only Kathryn. She needed him, and he hadn't been there to make sure she was safe. If anything happened to her, he'd never forgive himself. He didn't wait for the elevator but pushed through the stairway door just as Jon caught up to him. Justin was silent until they reached the car.

"You drive," he growled, his mouth set in a grim line, worry lines furrowing his forehead.

Jon didn't say a word as he pulled out into traffic and headed for Kathryn's motel. He had screwed up by not dragging Kathryn back with him. Hell, Justin knew how stubborn she was. Anytime you pushed her to do something, she dug in her heels and wouldn't budge. If he'd tried to force her to come with him, she'd have screamed bloody murder.

"I'm sorry, Justin. I should have dragged her back with me even if she took my head off."

"Forget it. It's my fault for leaving in the first place. Damn, what a fool I've been," Justin snarled and slammed his hand down on the dash.

"Harv's report cast a lot of doubts on Kathryn. What else were you supposed to think?" Jon tried to offer up a plausible excuse for his friend.

"Don't give me that," Justin glowered, "you never believed that report. How can you excuse me for believing it? I should have had as much faith in her as you did. Why didn't I?"

"I love her, but you married her," Jon stated. "Maybe you're too close. Harv is an honest man. You've trusted his word for too many years to doubt him. The initial shock of that report threw you into a tailspin, and all you could do was feel and not think. You know Kathryn isn't that type of woman, no matter what that damn report says," Jon insisted.

"Maybe, but there are still a lot of questions. With Harv here digging around, maybe he'll unearth some answers." Justin became silent, irritated that it was taking so long to travel the mile to Kathryn's motel. He saw the green Chevy parked near the entrance as Jon turned into the motel driveway. He glanced through the windshield and shouted, "He's got Kathryn!"

Before Justin could get his door open, the car pulled away and merged into traffic. He had seen the terrified expression on his wife's face and prayed she had seen him.

The man grabbed Kathryn just after she walked out the motel doors. He came from nowhere. Suddenly there was an arm around her waist, a gun barrel in her side, and a low warning, "Smile real pretty and keep quiet."

His harsh words convinced her to do as he said. Plastering a matching smile on his face, he led her to the vehicle parked under the entrance canopy with its engine running. He opened the door on the driver's side, forced her across the seat and climbed in next to her.

"Say one word, and I'll kill you right here. Now keep smiling pretty for the onlookers," he snarled and jabbed the gun in her left side again. She gasped from the pain and grabbed her ribs. She nodded her head to indicate she'd remain silent. He placed the gun in his lap, and quickly and merged into traffic.

"Just sit quiet and don't even think of trying to get away. You don't stand a chance. I'll shoot you, shove your body out the door, and no one will realize what happened until I'm long gone. So don't be stupid." He drove south toward the Bayway.

Those were not idle threats he'd made. The man would do exactly as he'd stated Kathryn was positive. Her mind numb, she avoided looking at him. All she could think was that if she had taken the time to call Justin, or had gone with Jon, she'd be with them instead of in this car. She couldn't die now. There was too much to say to Justin. She had to have the chance to say she was sorry. If he loved her as Kate Clark or Kathryn Blanding, she didn't care anymore. All that mattered was he'd come back for her.

She glanced at the gun lying across the man's lap. The sun glinting off the barrel sent a chill of terror through her.

He glanced at her. "I can see you're taking me seriously." He gave a cruel snicker. "You should've left town when you had the chance or stayed in Colorado. I warned you, but you wouldn't listen. You had to come down here and stir the damn pot. You couldn't leave well enough alone, could you? You had it all and blew it." He glanced at her and grinned as if hiding a secret. "The man said you were stubborn. If I couldn't scare you off, I was told to bury your ass. You made your choice, missy, not me."

Her voice was barely a whisper as she said, "Why are you doing this?"

"Money. Why else? Lots and lots of money."

She stared at him as if to memorize each detail of his face and body. His hair was black, cut short and neatly combed. His eyes were an icy shade of blue and just as cold. She had never seen eyelashes that dark or that long on a man. His nose was not large at all, but straight and fit his face. His lips were well-defined lips and skin was flawless. If he was handsome in a terrifying sort of way, but his muscular body, t-shirt, worn jeans, and scruffy brown work boots gave the impression of a physical laborer.

The interior of the vehicle was dirty. The dashboard had never felt the touch of a dust cloth. The floor beneath Kathryn's feet was littered with candy wrappers, Coke cans and other items she didn't want to identify.

He gave her a quick appraisal, his eyes lingering on her breasts for a second. "Don't sit there getting yourself worked up over something you can't do nothing about. I'm only doing what the man ordered. I hire out for a job, I earn my money. That way there's no complaints." He leered at her, "Besides, the man said I could have a little fun with you first."

His words hit her with such force she put a hand over her mouth to keep from getting sick. She had to remain calm, try to escape. But how? He was driving on the inside lane, so if she screamed or tried to jump from the vehicle, she'd be shot or hit by an oncoming car. Death was better than what he had planned for her.

There were only two places where she might have a chance to get away. One was the red light at the Don CeSar. The other was the toll booth. The red light was iffy at best. He'd stay in the middle lane to turn left and cross the Bayway Bridge. She might have a chance if the light was red. If the light was green, forget it. The traffic on the right would mow her down before she had a chance to get to the sidewalk.

A thousand feet from the light was the toll booth. He'd need the exact change because he wouldn't dare go through the attended lane with a gun on his lap. She didn't see any coins in the ashtray or on the dash. Maybe, just maybe she might get her chance at that time.

She tried to make herself relax, to let her fear show, but inside remain calm and alert. It wasn't difficult, because there was no acting involved, she was terrified. Soon, unless she escaped, she was going to be very dead and wouldn't have to worry if Justin believed her or not. "Where are you taking me?" Her voice sounded scared even to her ears.

"I got a perfect spot south of the Skyway Bridge for what I have in mind." He gave another sinister laugh and turned his attention back to driving, mindful of his speed.

She trembled. It wasn't fear of dying that was so abhorrent. God, she didn't want to die, but the thought of what he planned terrified her more than death.

As if reading her mind, his lips curled in a sneer. "Forget it, sweetie. You can't get away. I'd shoot you before you could get the door open. Besides, it isn't often I get a bonus like you if you know what I mean."

Kathryn shrank away as close to the passenger side door as possible, his words hammered repulsively against her ears. The image of his big rough hands touching her shot through her mind. She'd die before she'd let that happen.

The man had to hear the wild pounding of her heart. She leaned against the door and laid her forearm on the armrest, her fingers just inches from the door latch. She kept her gaze focused straight ahead. Just a few more blocks and they'd be at the light. Please God, let it be red, she prayed.

He must have seen her lips move. He grinned and said, "Prayer won't help you now, honey. You're in a fix you can't get out of this time."

Hoping to keep him from becoming suspicious she asked, "What do you mean, this time?"

"When you found yourself in the wrong place at the wrong time, seeing things you shouldn't have seen."

"When was that?"

"Stop pretending. You know what I'm talking about. The man said you'd claim not to know, but not to believe you."

"Who is this man you keep referring to?" She could see the light a block ahead. The traffic picked up speed. Inside, she groaned.

"I don't know." The man stared ahead checking the light.

"What do you mean you don't know? You have to know who's paying you." If she could keep him talking, perhaps he'd not notice her hand inching closer to the door latch as she leaned a little forward. "If you don't know who you work for, how can you be certain you'll get paid?"

"Only one man ever tried that," he scoffed. "He didn't live long. I have my ways of finding out who's behind my jobs if I want to. I have a backup man who makes all the arrangements. He keeps tabs for me." He seemed to enjoy boasting about himself, so she kept probing for other information.

"Have you ever worked for this man before?"

"Yeah, I did a couple of jobs for him a few years ago."

"Do you remember who?"

"Some smart-ass kid who thought he was going to be a big country music star. He went out a star all right. I didn't do the job personally, just dumped the body. Hacked him up good so the wild hogs would eat him. They even eat the bones, and there's no evidence left to find."

She almost vomited, especially when he gave her a sly grin.

"So now you know what's going to happen to you."

Her hands began to shake. This monster had chopped Robert into pieces and fed him to wild hogs! My God! She fought back the bile rising in her throat. Even if he shot her, it was a better death than what he planned. Alone, raped, murdered and then to end up like Robert. She felt cold inside as if she already had accepted her death. It was up to her to determine the when and how.

"I fixed his buddy's car as well. That car went up like a roman candle when it hit that tree," he continued as if proud of his work. He enjoyed seeing the fear in her eyes as he told her what he had done. He thrived on her fear.

Images began flashing through her mind, the apartment near Upham Beach, a white carpet splattered with bright red and the body of a man. She had run that night as fast as she could, gotten into her car and never looked back. Only then, she wasn't Kathryn Blanding or was she? It didn't matter that she had witnessed Robert's murder. She didn't know who the killer was and right now, didn't care. All that mattered at this instant was to escape.

They were nearing the traffic light at The Don, and it was red. The man pressed the accelerator. The Chevy shot forward just as the light changed to green. He turned the corner and was forced to slow down as the cars in front decreased their speed for the toll booth ahead.

She had lost her chance. Her eyes looked glazed, the way a trapped animal waits for death. Fists clenched until her nails bit into her palms, she took in ragged breaths. A scream began to rise in her throat, and she fought to control it. She could barely see the door handle as tears of frustration, and utter terror welled in her eyes.

As the road curved to the right, she saw the square yellow sign announcing a thousand feet to the toll booth. Two lanes of traffic fed into three lanes. The two blue booths on the left were for exact change. The car ahead slowed and entered the center one for exact change, and her kidnapper followed. Her abductor tucked the gun under his right leg, the handle barely visible, as he fumbled in his shirt pocket.

Just as the vehicle slowed, without thinking she jerked the handle and wrenched open the door. Her purse hit the ground as she jumped out the passenger side and ran, dodging around the cars. Blindly, she raced away from the toll booth, not seeing the big sedan sitting with its engine running at an entrance to the side road. All she could focus on was the Don CeSar Hotel and reaching Justin.

She heard tires squeal and expected any second to feel the impact of a bullet. Horns blared, and brakes screamed as cars slid to a halt to avoid hitting her. The pounding of heavy boots on the pavement reached her, as someone shouted her name. The man was chasing her.

She'd die before she'd get back in that car. A hand grabbed her by the shoulder, and powerful arms circled her from behind. She screamed, kicking out as he lifted her off the pavement and held tight. Her arms were pinned to her sides, and no matter how hard she tried, she couldn't break his hold.

He carried her and deposited her into the back seat of the car. She tried to twist free, but he still held her firmly, the tone of his voice soothing now, instead of harsh like before. The car door slammed, and the engine roared as the vehicle shot away. The man voice finally reached her terrorized brain.

"Kathryn, it's all right now. You're safe." It was Justin who held her. She looked up at his worried face, then threw her arms around his neck and sobbed harder.

"He was going to kill me, Justin. He told me so."

Justin's arms tightened.

"Jon, have Harv check us out of the Don, then meet us at the Vinoy. Also, ask him to have someone pick up Kathryn's things at her motel as well, if he doesn't mind. I know the police are going to want answers, so we need to be ready."

Jon cut down the side street and around the parking lot and drove north on Gulf Boulevard toward South Pasadena, before placing the call to Harv Anderson. It was the long way around, but they could avoid the local police who flew past with sirens screaming. It would give Harv time to prepare the other hotel for their arrival.

Kathryn continued clinging to Justin. Finally realizing she was safe, she relaxed in his arms. She sat up, gave a brief smile to Jon in the rearview mirror. "You don't know how glad I am to see you both. I've never been so scared in my life. I really thought I was going to be fed to some hogs somewhere."

"What?" Jon glanced at her in the mirror. "My God, that is one sick dude."

"How'd you know where I was?"

Justin pulled her closer. "I saw you in his car looking terrified, so we followed. We were never more than a car behind you. He won't get away. We'll get him. Don't you worry about that."

Kathryn gazed at Justin. She knew he meant what he said, but she could only pray he was right and her nightmare would soon be over. And hopefully, this time he would not leave her.

Chapter Eighteen

Harv Anderson, having arrived in St. Petersburg the evening before, was waiting for them when they reached the Renaissance Vinoy Hotel. He ushered them past the desk and straight to their room on the seventh floor. It was a large two bedroom suite with a sitting room and a view overlooking Tampa Bay. Their belongings had not yet arrived, but that was the least of their concerns.

Kathryn studied the man who had singlehandedly destroyed her relationship with Justin by his sordid report. She wanted to dislike him but instead found comfort in his presence. Well over six foot tall. His close-cropped hair was turning gray, and his blue eyes were intense. His nose had been broken, from a possible fight which emphasized the stubborn set to his square chin. His appearance had a hard edge that showed he was tough and capable. Harv Anderson was not a man to back down unless it was to his advantage.

He was not dressed like other winter tourists. His gray slacks, white short sleeve pullover shirt, sports jacket, and lace-up shoes were all business. No tie choked him, and his skin was tanner than most for this time of year. If she remembered correctly, he was from California.

With swift efficiency, he checked out the rooms and had them take a seat on the sofa. He surprised Kathryn. She expected his voice to be as rough as his appearance. Instead, he spoke in a deep, gentle voice laced with a raspy growl.

"I've contacted the Beach police and explained that it was an attempt to kidnap you. They want a description of the man, Mrs. Crown. You'll have to give them a statement. But, we can have a doctor say you're too traumatized to give one at the station. I think a police officer coming to the hotel would be your best bet if you'll agree?"

Kathryn and Justin nodded in agreement.

"I'll contact the police department and set up the interview for tomorrow morning," Harv said.

"Fine," Justin responded. "I'd like for you to be present if you don't mind. Have you had any luck with that other information I asked you about?"

"Some. I'm still checking out a few things."

"What additional information are you looking for, Mr. Anderson?" If he was digging up more dirt about her, Kathryn wanted to know. "Is it like that report you gave him about me?"

Harv didn't blush or turn away but gave her a direct stare. "I was doing a job for my client. I'm sorry if the report has caused you problems, but it was an accurate report, and that's what I get paid to do, find out the truth."

"How can you say your report was the truth? You don't know anything about me. Your report was about some woman I've never heard of."

"That woman has your face, Mrs. Crown. And that face has a known history. All I did was present the facts. If you remember, as Kathryn Blanding, you have other complications to deal with in St. Petersburg. When you give your statement to that police officer tomorrow, I would not mention anything about being Kathryn Blanding." He pulled up a chair and sat facing them.

"You don't have to warn me about that. I'm well aware I've been blamed for my grandmother's murder." She straightened her spine and glared at him. "One fact I want you to understand, no way would I have harmed a single hair on my grandmother's head. She gave me love and refuge when I had nothing and no one to turn to other than the streets. So if you want to find out the truth, find out who really murdered her, but don't lay that blame on me. I did not kill her. Now what other dirt are you digging up?" she demanded.

Harv looked at Justin, waiting for the go-ahead to tell her what she wanted to know. The approval was a brief nod.

"To answer your question, Mrs. Crown. . . ."

"Drop the Mrs. Crown, Mr. Anderson. Call me Kathryn. I hate formalities."

"Okay, Kathryn, if you'll call me Harv. First, I don't dig up dirt, I dig up facts. Your husband asked me to look into your father's background."

Kathryn let out a harsh laugh, gave a nervous hiccup, and said, "All you had to do was ask me. I can fill you in with all the facts you could ever need."

"We can't use hearsay, Kathryn. Everything has to be documented." Harv again glanced at Justin.

What was going on between these two men? Kathryn didn't know why or what type of documentation Justin wanted, but she knew all kinds of facts about her dear daddy. "Did you have any luck cracking his polished knightly armor?"

"Not a lot, but it definitely has cracks. Before I tell you what I found out, you tell me what you know about Dr. Blanding." He didn't refer to him as her father.

Kathryn's smile was grim as she studied Harv's face. There was no telltale sign betraying his reason for the request. All she could do was ponder how to respond. How best to describe her father? "He's a bastard under his Mr. Perfect disguise. As I've told Justin, to the community and the medical profession he is the savior of abused women. Not only does he perform miraculous plastic surgery on deformed children, but dear old Dad also fixes the broken faces of women whose husbands have beaten them beyond recognition. He takes the ugly and makes them beautiful again. Isn't that a crock?

"Being a God feeds his ego. Who, in his circle of friends and professional associates, would believe he's an abuser? None! If they were confronted with the truth, found out his secrets, his position in the community would be ruined. They'd still work with him, but never have anything to do with him socially. Kathryn had to pause as all the bitterness she had held in check exploded.

She continued. "My earliest memory of him beating me was when I was about five years old. To the public, he was the best husband, the doting father." Her eyes took on a glazed appearance as if she was looking into the past and writing in her journal.

"Every Christmas Eve, my mother and father gave this party, a big elaborate affair to show off how successful he was. The house was decorated with wreaths, garlands and several Christmas trees, one in the foyer, one in the main living room. We had every conceivable Christmas decoration you can imagine, right down to lights on the outside trees and a full-size Nativity scene near the front entrance. It was like a fairy tale, riding up the driveway with all the lights aglow. My brother, Henry, and I were allowed to attend. It was at that party I learned it was strictly for show, so daddy could reinforce his image as the ideal father to his friends and colleagues."

As the image played out in her mind she smiled wistfully, "Henry always looked so handsome. He was tall for his age and had this thick mass of dark curly hair. For as long as I can remember, his big blue eyes were filled with such sadness. As if he guarded a secret, that he couldn't share with anyone, but it was breaking his heart. God, I loved him. He was always trying to protect me from my father. He didn't always succeed. Until that party, my father had never struck me. He was distant, but never physical." Her voice hardened as the memory rose in her mind.

"Anyway, at the party, my father had been putting on his usual false display of affection for me. I ate it up. At the dinner table, I timidly crawled up into his lap. I can remember my heart beating so fast I was sure all those strangers at the table could hear it. He just laughed and pulled me close and hugged me. I was in Heaven. He kissed the top of my head and sat me down gently on the floor and instructed me to go sit in my seat next to Henry like a big girl. I reached my arms up to him, gave him a kiss on the cheek, and told him I loved him. Then I went back to my own chair. Henry had this strange look on his face when he helped me back into my chair. I didn't think anything about it at the time, I was too happy. My daddy did love me after all.

"Later I realized it was fear I saw in Henry's eyes. Dear daddy came to my room after the party when I was getting ready for bed. He brought my mother with him to watch as he beat me with his belt for that ridiculous display before his noted guests as he put it. I was never to approach him in that way, ever again. And I didn't. Instead, I got his attention in other ways." She fought against the knot rising in her throat.

"I know it's stupid to still hurt after all these years. I keep remembering how I felt at that tender age. Something was horribly wrong with me, or else my father would love me. What had I done that was so terrible to make my father hate me so much? I never knew why. At times that hurt more than his beatings. My poor brother tried hard to make up for the loss of that love. It cost him his life." She stood unable to sit still a minute longer or stop the pent-up feelings and words suppressed for too many years.

"Every time I did something despicable to get back at my father, Henry took the blame. I busted the headlights on the new Mercedes. Henry claimed he did it accidentally." She took a deep breath, looked from Harv to Justin, then dropped her gaze and continued. "That was until Daddy shipped Henry off to a boarding school. He wasn't home from school the day I carved fuck you on my father's antique desk so he couldn't take the blame for that stupid act. Boy, did I get a beating for that. He knew Henry didn't and wouldn't do such a thing. Henry tried hard to love our father in spite of everything.

"Another time I brought a group of my pothead friends to one of his fancy parties and caused a scene. He called the cops on us. When I got home, there was another beating. What made him even angrier was the fact I refused to cry. He'd beat me, and I'd laugh at him. He knew just how hard to hit me and inflict the most pain without doing permanent damage. I went around black and blue for a few days. He locked me in my room until I healed. I know there were times he wanted to kill me. I think he was afraid to go that far. That would certainly destroy his lily-white reputation, and I would have won. He'd die before he'd let that happen. To my father, his image and standing in the community is everything.

"Finally when it became clear to Henry that our father wasn't going to buy his stories that he was responsible for all my wrong-doings, Henry threatened to run away from school. Then, Henry threatened to never speak to him again if my father hit me one more time. He stopped beating me, but he just increased the beatings on my mother. By then, I was headstrong, defiant and out of control. I came close to destroying myself. I smoked pot, did other drugs and did everything I could to ruin his squeaky reputation, to no avail. It made his friends sympathize with him against his outrageous daughter.

"I hated him even more for what he was doing to my mother. In some ways, I hated her for letting it happen. The day I threatened to kill him, my grandmother put a stop to it all. She told my father if he ever touched my mother or me again, she'd destroy him. I don't know what she had on dear old Dad, if she had hired a detective or what, but he stopped beating my mother. I went to live with Abby.

"I still did everything I could to embarrass him. Even went so far as to marry a man who only saw dollar signs when he looked at me." She stopped pacing and stared at Justin.

"So you see when you accused me of marrying you for your money, you were wrong. I'd never do that because I know how it feels. I would never hurt Abby. She saved my mother and me from a life of hell."

Kathryn resumed her seat next to Justin. "What else would you like to know about dear old dad?"

Harv swallowed hard. The image of the little girl vying for her father's love at a Christmas party tore at his heart. Then to be beaten for wanting to be loved made him want to hurt Randolph Blanding severely. Not one flicker of Harv's true feelings showed on his face.

Instead, he studied Kathryn. Knowing the information in his original report that she had been an aspiring actress made him believe two facts, either she was a much better actress than her peers gave her credit for, or she really was Kathryn Blanding. She was convincing with her story. It made him better understand Justin's dilemma, but he was still curious about some things.

"Kathryn, why have you been searching for your ex-husband, Robert Cantree?" Harv asked.

"Because that sleazy rat called me before I went to pick up my grandmother. He wanted me to meet him and give him money. I told him no and that I was through feeding his habits. He knew I was going to pick up Abby, so I'm sure he would have gone there to waylay me and talk one of us into giving him cash.

"Abby had repeatedly told him to stay off her property. He never did. Robert would park his car on the side street and hide in the bushes to catch me as I was leaving her house. I was hoping if he was there the night she was killed, he might know something. But that's a dead end. The man who abducted me told me he disposed of his body," she blanched as she repeated what the man said, "cut him up and fed him to wild hogs." She had to swallow hard to keep from vomiting at the resurgence of that image.

"I've been doing all the talking, Harv, now would you please tell me what you've found out about my father," Kathryn stated and took a seat feeling exhausted by the purge of memories.

"Did you know that your father was the main witness against you in your grandmother's murder?" Harv crossed his legs and cupped his laced fingers around his knee. He studied Kathryn, looking for any sign that would indicate she was lying. What registered on her face was shock.

"You have to be kidding! My father was at Abby's that night?" Why had no one mentioned that fact before?

"Did he visit your grandmother often?" Harv asked, avoiding her question for the moment.

"He'd go over with my mother. Mom was never allowed to go out much by herself, especially to see Abby. Before my grandmother was killed, my mother stole away several times to see her. Abby told me she was talking about filing for divorce. Mrs. Hatcher, the housekeeper, heard us arguing about whether my mother actually would go through with it. That happened several nights before the murder. Divorce was disapproved of in our family, but Abby thought it was best."

"Do you know a woman named Allison Goodwin?" Harv waited to see her reaction.

"No."

"Allison Goodwin was a neighbor of your grandmother's. In fact, she lived next door. The night Abby Pennington was murdered Ms. Goodwin was driving past the house. It was dark, but she saw a young woman with long dark hair run from the house to her car and hurriedly drive away. In her rearview mirror, the woman saw the vehicle squeal out of the driveway and tear off down the street, almost sideswiping another parked car. She was the other witness against you. The other car was your father's. He supposedly had just arrived at Mrs. Pennington's home."

"But I've never met her, so how could she identify me?"

"She didn't. She told the police what she witnessed, and the time it happened."

"I don't understand." Kathryn looked confused.

"Allison Goodwin drove on into her driveway and parked her car in the garage. Randolph called the police from his cell phone while chasing you down the highway trying to stop you. He told them he was calling Abby to let her know he was coming. While on the phone with your grandmother, the doctor heard you and Abby in a heated argument about a loan for your business, which by the way, records show was in financial straits. He heard a scream and then nothing. You were driving away upon his arrival. He hurried inside, found Abby dead and rushed after you. The doctor claims he followed you so the police would know where you were.

"Bloody footprints left a trail down the hallway from the back room. They matched the shoes found near the Blanding girl at the accident scene. Kathryn Blanding was saved from being arrested by that car wreck involving Kate Clark. For the police, it was an open and shut case. The daughter had a history of violent actions against her father; why not her grandmother? Plus two people saw her leave the house at the time of the murder, and one heard her in a heated argument with the dead woman."

Kathryn stared at him. "My father is lying, and Allison Goodwin is mistaken in what she saw. Where was the housekeeper?"

"She had the night off."

She turned to Justin, "Did you know about this?"

"Yes, that's why I asked Harv to keep digging into your father's background."

There was too much loss, too much pain. Would she ever be free from all the guilt? Would she ever be free of this nightmare?

Justin saw the anguish in her eyes. "When we were at his office, his hatred for you was so vicious, that it stuck with me. Why would a man hate his daughter that much? From what you're telling us now, he's hated you from your childhood. I want to know why? All the evidence in Abby Pennington's murder points to her granddaughter. Are you so certain you want to prove you are that person?" he asked.

She stared at him. "You still don't believe me, do you? That's why you didn't mention my father testifying against me."

"It doesn't matter to me. I don't care who you are anymore. I love you, not some image from the past, but the woman I know today."

"Well, it matters to me. Until you believe me, we don't have a future together." It took all her effort to say those words, but Kathryn knew if she was ever to have Justin trust her, he had to believe her. She wouldn't take his love without trust. "I told you, back in Colorado, why my father hates me so much. I was responsible for my brother's death."

"There's more to it than that, Kathryn. Think about it. He beat you from the time you were five years old. Why?"

"I don't know," she yelled. "I can't give you the answer to that question. I don't care about Randolph Blanding." She rubbed her forehead. A throbbing ache was centered between her eyes and threatening to become a raging headache.

"All I want to do is prove who I am and that I did not murder my grandmother." She looked from one to the other, expecting to see disbelief scored across their faces. Instead, she saw genuine concern.

She continued, "One fact I know for sure is that Robert was on the property and saw something. Otherwise, why would his sister, Angela, say that he was blackmailing someone for a lot of money?

"According to the man who abducted me,

whatever evidence Robert had, cost him his life. His sister used to be a prostitute, now she's the proper lady? Where, suddenly, did she get all her money? She lives in an expensive townhouse not far from Sands Point, takes tennis lessons, probably drives an expensive car and who knows what all."

"I know quite a bit," Harv interjected and gave them all a smile. "Computers are grand avenues of information. I have a couple of experts who work for me and have a knack for digging up bits and pieces of info about people. Angela Marie Cantree's fortune appeared shortly after her brother disappeared. From what I've been able to find out, Robert spent a lot of money rather freely for a short time. He was not one to share, but he did buy his mother a cheap trailer in a park on the South side of St. Petersburg.

"He never gave Angela a penny, left her to the streets. Within a month after he disappeared, she left the profession, paid cash for a condo, and acquired a substantial bank account on her own. Twice a month, she makes deposits of five thousand dollars cash. She gives her mother five hundred dollars a month but rarely goes to see her. At the moment, I don't have anything to tie Randolph Blanding to Robert Cantree or his sister, except you, Kathryn." Harv glance at Justin who kept his eyes focused on his wife.

"Well, that leaves me in the same position I was before, the main suspect in Abby's murder or Kate Clark." She frowned, scrunching up her eyebrows as she tried to think of something, any idea to help prove her innocence. "When you did your original report on Kate, did you talk to anyone she knew here in St. Pete? When I talked with Angela a few days ago, she claimed Robert, and I left town together. Of course, that would have been impossible since he was dead. Anyway, do you think some of Kate's or Angela's friends would know anything?"

Harv smiled slightly, "Angela is not a woman to acquire close female friends or even long-term male relationships. The people Kate worked with at the theater didn't have a lot to say about her. She kept to herself, liked rich men and had one or more boyfriends. Randolph Blanding was one of her men." Harv looked Kathryn in the eyes when he said the last.

Kathryn could feel her face growing hot with embarrassment. "That is the same thing he told us when Justin and I went to see him at his office. But it wasn't me he was seeing. One new piece of information you've found out is about Robert's mother, I thought she was dead. He never mentioned her"

"Can you tie Blanding and Angela together?" Justin asked. He had been listening to the exchange between Harv and Kathryn. He was testing her, and Justin wasn't sure if he liked it. It was time to put a stop to the interrogation and take action. He focused on Harv's response to his question.

"If Randolph Blanding is the source of her income, it's not showing up in his financial records, anyway, none that we've been able to access. The research is still going on. He has a lot of real estate investments in town and out. It will take time to track all the information down."

"We don't have time to wait," Justin said. He was tired of sitting around. "Why don't we pay Angela another visit and ask her more directly?"

"When?" Kathryn inquired.

Harv looked at the faces staring at him. "How about right now?" he said. "The sooner we get the answers we need, the faster we can get the hell out of this town. Too many things are going against you here."

All the suspicious questions made her dizzy. She leaned against Justin and closed her eyes for a brief moment. Her body started to tremble as images flashed through her mind. A man stood over a body. Just like her nightmare, except this time, instead of a woman, it was Robert laying on the floor with blood running down his face. For a second, she saw the features of the killer, and then it was gone. She opened her eyes and looked at Justin.

"I saw Robert's murder." She said it so softly, Justin had trouble hearing her.

"What?"

"I saw my father kill Robert. That's why I ran away to Colorado. I have this vague memory of Robert being hit over the head."

"Who were you at the time?" Justin asked.

"I'm not sure. I don't know if the vision is real or something I dreamed. I don't know who I am anymore. I'm sorry! I'm sorry I can't give you what you want, positive proof of who I am."

"You saw Randolph kill Robert?" Harv asked.

"I think it was him." She shook her head in

confusion. "I'm not sure. I saw someone hit him over the head with a poker. Whoever it was kept hitting him until he fell to the floor."

Harv shook his head, "It wouldn't matter if you did witness him killing Cantree. As Kate Clark, with her reputation, your testimony against him would be suspect. Since Kate was Blanding's mistress, you could be under suspicion as an accomplice in the crime. You're screwed any way you look at it, whether as Kathryn Blanding or Kate Clark. If he killed Cantree, why would he be trying to kill you? You're no threat to him."

Kathryn jumped to her feet and glared at him. "Get this through your head once and for all. I was never his mistress. I am not Kate Clark. Regardless of the charges, I am Kathryn Blanding, and I did not kill anyone."

Harv stood and threw up his hands as if to protect himself from the small bundle of fury facing him. "What do you say we stop guessing and go get some answers? First stop, Angel, then Randolph Blanding."

"It's about damn time." Kathryn grabbed her purse and headed toward the door. She stopped and looked back at the three men staring after her. "Are you three coming with me or am I going by myself?"

Hesitating, Harv suggested, "I think you should stay here."

A smile curved Justin's lips and Jon laughed out loud. Harv was in for a surprise.

Kathryn wasted no time in snapping back. "Well, you can forget that idea. From now on, where you three go, I go."

"All right, let's do it." Harv opened the door for

her, and they filed out.

Chapter Nineteen

There were only three cars in the parking lot at Angel's condominium. Kathryn could feel her stomach knotting as they exited. Justin gave a reassuring smile, but it didn't help ease the tension tightening her neck and shoulder muscles. She glanced nervously around, expecting at any minute to see a green Chevy barrel down the driveway in their direction. Nothing happened.

Harv rang the doorbell, and they waited.

Justin rang the bell again. Still, no one came to the door, even though loud music could be heard coming from upstairs.

"Harv, do you know if Angela's car is here?" Justin asked looking at the three parked vehicles.

Kathryn answered instead, "I don't know what she drives. I was only here once."

"Well," Jon said, "either she went off and left the stereo on, or she just doesn't want company this morning."

"She drives a black Mercedes," Harv said, glancing around and easing over to the garage next to the entrance. "And she always parks it in the garage." He peered in a small window in the garage door. "It's here, so she must be home."

Justin leaned closer to the door. "Someone is upstairs. This door isn't completely closed." He pushed, and the door swung inward to reveal plush carpeted stairs leading up to the main living area. Not wanting to startle Angela if she should see him, he called out, "Hello. Angela, are you home?"

No one answered.

Harv moved ahead of Justin and began to work his way cautiously up the steps. He had a foreboding feeling about the loud music and the open door. They were breaking the law entering the condo without permission. That fact was not going to stop Justin or him. There were answers here. He was sure of it, and he intended to find them. He paused at the top of the stairs, then took the last step into the spacious living room. Justin stepped up beside him, Jon and Kathryn followed.

The beige and blue sofa had been cut to shreds exposing the bare wood of the frame. The matching cushions were strewn about the floor, the fiber filling ripped out. The carpet was littered with everything that had been on the bookshelves. The glass shelves were broken, pages were torn from the books, statues smashed, and even the paintings jerked from the walls, the paper backing slashed, cutting through the canvases. Someone had been looking for something.

A gasp came from Kathryn.

"Go back to the car, Kathryn," Justin ordered. "It isn't a good idea for you to be here. It might not be safe."

"No, I'm staying. There's no guarantee I'd be safer in the car."

"She's right, Justin," Harv said. "Jon, keep her here while Justin and I look around. Don't touch anything, not even the wall. And for God's sake, don't move from that spot." Suddenly, a gun was in Harv's hand.

"I know you're trying to protect me, "Kathryn said, "but after this morning, I'm not about to be left alone." Ignoring Harv's warning, she walked over to the bar, being careful not to touch anything. Her breath caught, and she covered her mouth to stop the scream rising in her throat.

The birdcage sat on the counter. The lifeless body of the little parakeet lay on the floor of the cage. Perched on top of the open door was the blue head. Dried blood had dripped down the bars of the door turning the brass to dark red.

She felt a hand on her shoulder and jumped. It was Justin. "This is terrible," she whispered. "I'm afraid, Justin. Find Angela."

"Boss, you had better see this," Jon had followed Harv and now stood in the doorway down the hall off the living room. When Kathryn took a step in that direction, he shook his head, "No, Kathryn, not you, just Justin."

"Stay right here, Kathryn." Justin hurried to the door and looked in. "Oh, my God," he uttered. Kathryn was beginning to get irritated by their constant orders and ignored his warning and moved to stand behind Justin. She leaned around him to peer into the room. She could see Harv standing just inside the doorway. This room had been ransacked as well. But, the real disaster lay on the bed.

In life, Angela had been beautiful. In death, she was grotesque. She lay on the four poster brass bed, eyes open and unseeing, the young face brutally beaten. Her mouth was covered with silver tape, and her throat had been cut leaving her skin a pasty white. She was naked, hands bound together and pulled over her head and anchored to the bed's headboard. Her legs were spread and tied to each bedpost. There were fresh burns on her abdomen and breasts. Blood soaked the sheet beneath her body

Harv was pissed, "You people don't listen," he growled. "You're contaminating a crime scene. Get out of here," he ordered. "Whoever did this was more than angry, he was in a rage. I'll bet he tied her up first, and then tore up the place during his search. When he didn't find what he was looking for, he tried torture. Either he got the information he wanted and killed her, or gave up looking and decided not to leave a witness who could testify against him. Either way, she's dead." He motioned for them to leave the room. "Let's go. The police could be on their way."

Kathryn couldn't seem to move. Jon physically led her back into the living room. She was aware of being led down the stairs and ushered into the car.

She couldn't get the image of Angela's ravaged body out of her mind. It was hard to comprehend that one human could inflict such viciousness on another. This was animal savagery. Whoever had murdered Angel was insane. The man from the green Chevy fit that description. That could have been her if not for Justin and Jon.

She trembled, and Justin pulled her close. She was never to be left alone. A madman was on the loose and Kathryn could be his next target. Whoever had killed Angela had arranged for Kathryn to be kidnaped and eventually murdered. The attempt had failed, and that person had a secret they were afraid Kathryn would tell. Whoever it was would stop at nothing to prevent that from happening.

"Harv, what do you suggest we do?" Justin asked from the back seat.

"Get out of town, today."

"We can fly back to Colorado tonight," Jon suggested.

"We can't," Kathryn reminded them. The Beach police were due to come by for an interview the next day. Harv had arranged it.

"All right," Justin agreed, "but as soon as the police are gone, we're flying out of here."

"That'll give me a chance to see what additional information my team has dug up," Harv said.

Justin wondered what else Harv was searching for besides the connection between Angela and Randolph Blanding. "Are you looking for anything specific?"

"I checked out the original accident report involving Kate Clark and Kathryn Blanding. My men have been in contact with the Reporting Police Officer, the Emergency Medical Team, and the helicopter transport company. Kathryn, I need you to sign an authorization to release information for your medical records. Once they receive the authorization, my man can pick up a copy. I have another angle I'm working on. I won't say what it is until I have all the information, and I'm sure of the facts. If we stay at the hotel for another day, I can follow up on some leads my men have been checking out. Right now, I suggest we check on Angel's mother. If her killer didn't find what he was looking for and knows about the mother, he may go looking there."

"Shouldn't we call the police? If they find out we were here, won't we be arrested?" Worry lines creased

Kathryn's forehead, and she shifted her position uneasily.

Harv shook his head. "I'll call them to make sure they're on the way. You three will not be involved. I'll tell them I came by as part of my investigation into the disappearance of her brother, Robert." He removed his cell phone from his inside jacket pocket and made the call. After a brief conversation, he frowned and hung up.

"I have to stay here. Jon," Harv scribbled a note on a paper from a small notepad he removed from another pocket, "get over to this address as fast as you can. This is where Angela's mother lives. Her name is Agnes Sawyer. If something has happened, get Justin and Kathryn out of there and call me. I hope we're not too late to save the mother."

Jon grabbed the paper and climbed in the driver's side. They drove away, leaving Harv watching after them.

The address Harv had given Jon led them to a questionable part of town. A narrow paved lane split the park in half. Mobile homes, recreational vehicles, and campers lined each side, some in fair condition, and others in desperate need of repair. Weeds grew between one camper-trailer and the next. The trailer they were looking for had been permanently set up on concrete blocks with an additional room built on for extra living space.

A car drove past as Justin knocked on the door. He dreaded the thought of no one answering and the occupant of the passing vehicle remembering them being on the scene.

Relief flooded him as the door was opened by a tiny woman. She was not over five feet in height, in her seventies, with short gray hair and twinkling blue eyes. She wore a fresh pair of green slacks, matching blouse and sturdy shoes. A crisp white apron covered her clothes for protection. A spot of flour graced one cheek, and her face was heavily lined with wrinkles. She spoke in a birdlike chirp as if afraid someone might hear her.

"Mrs. Cantree," Justin said, forgetting the name difference, "my name is Justin Crown," he turned to indicate Kathryn and Jon, "this is my wife Kathryn and my associate, Jon."

Cautiously, the old lady cocked her head to one side, and a tired expression flashed across her face. "It's Sawyer, not Cantree. I remarried," she corrected. "Is this about my daughter?"

"Yes, it is. May we come inside and speak with you?"

She walked deeper into the room addition, allowing them to enter and pointed to a worn leather sofa along one wall. "Have a seat. Is Angela in trouble again?" She sat in a rocker facing the three.

Justin was in a quandary, should he tell her about her daughter or not? If he didn't, how would he get the elderly lady to come with them without scaring her into a heart attack? He chose the easiest route. "Mrs. Sawyer, there isn't a delicate way to say this, but I need you to accompany us back to our hotel for your safety. I have good reason to believe you may be in danger. Someone may come here and threaten you or even harm you. Will you come with us?"

She stared at him a moment and then looked from

one to the other. "Oh God! Angela's dead, isn't she?" Tears began to roll down her cheeks. Hurriedly, she wiped them away with her apron.

Stunned by her insight, all Justin could do was nod.

"I've been expecting it. When did it happen?" Mrs. Sawyer managed to choke out.

"I don't know exactly. The police are at her place right now. How did you guess?"

"Because of your wife," she pointed at Kathryn as she continued to wipe at the corners of her eyes. "First Robert disappears and now Angela." Tears welled again, and this time she couldn't contain the sobbing as she wiped them away. Her voice was hoarse as she continued, "I knew when my daughter started living high, something wasn't right. She didn't have the education to get a job making the kind of money she spent. Did someone kill her?"

"Why do you ask that?" Kathryn said.

"I know what my daughter was," she whispered. "In her profession, if some disease doesn't kill you, then some pimp will. She may have left that profession behind to move up in the world, but whatever she was doing, I doubt it was legal. Angela," a memory flitted across her mind, and she reminisced, sobbing as she said, "I always called her my little angel. She was so tiny and fragile as a child, so angelic. I certainly misnamed her. Anyway, my children always wanted everything, but they didn't want to earn it." She wiped at her eyes again and continued. "I tried to teach them better. What you put into life is what you get back. I worked as a cleaning woman for many of the families on Coffeepot Bayou and Snell Isle to keep a roof over our heads. Never stole a dime from those people, no matter how poor we were. Robert and Angela sometimes would go with me to help out. They saw the easy life the rich had and wanted it, but without the effort it took. Well, it's cost both of them."

"How so?" Justin asked.

"They're both dead. I knew Robert was dead two weeks after he disappeared. He never came by to see me, but he always called me twice a week. Didn't want his wealthy friends to know about me." She looked at Kathryn in sadness. "You didn't know his mother was alive or that he had a sister, did you?" It was a statement, not a question.

"No. I didn't," Kathryn admitted.

"Proves my point. You were married to my son and didn't know. Why would anyone else know I existed if you didn't?"

Kathryn sat back, stunned by Agnes's statement. "You know who I am?"

"Yeah. You're Robert's wife, Kate, but Lord knows the marriage only lasted a month. He found greener pastures. Dr. Blanding's daughter."

"I'm not Kate Clark, Mrs. Sawyer. My name is Kathryn Blanding. I am Dr. Blanding's daughter. When were Robert and Kate married?" That certainly put a twist on things.

"For your sake, I hope you're wrong. It was over four years ago, just before my boy set his sights on Dr. Blanding's daughter. Just you wait right here." She rose and hurried into another room at the back of the trailer. She returned with a flat box wrapped in brown paper and tied with a scarlet ribbon.

"I almost forgot about this." Her hands trembled as she handed the bundle to Kathryn. "Angela gave this to me shortly after Robert disappeared. Said someday it might make me rich, if I wanted to use it, should anything happen to her. If I didn't use it, then I was to give it to you should you come around asking questions. You're here. It's now yours to do with what you will. I started to look at it once but changed my mind. I'm sure you'll understand it all. I never read the letter. It wasn't addressed to me." She paused, sat down and covered her mouth, looking like the frail little woman that she was. "You say I need to get out of here." Her voice cracked as she rose, "Let me pack a bag, drive me to the airport and buy me a ticket to Chicago. I have family there I can stay with."

"We can do that. Would you like for me to handle your daughter's funeral arrangements?" Justin asked.

Shaking her head, she said, "Angela took care of that several years ago. It was as if she knew something might happen to her. I'd like to stay for her service, but you say I might be in danger."

"I have a private plane, Mrs. Sawyer," he said. "I'll see that you're here for her funeral. It won't be for a few days. My concern right now is getting you to safety. If you hurry, we can leave right away."

"Give me ten minutes. I don't own much."

Agnes was fighting to keep from crying. Her chin was quivering as she left the room. Jon followed to give her a hand with the suitcase.

Kathryn could hear the low mutter of their voices from the back room. All she could do was stare at the package on her lap. She could feel it. Here, wrapped like a present, were the answers to all her questions. Did she want to know the answers? What if they were not what she thought they would be? What if everything Harv's report said was true, that she was not Kathryn Blanding, but was instead Kate Clark? Could she face that truth? Could Justin? Would he still love her if she was Kate Clark? Her mind burned with questions.

Justin rose and motioned for Kathryn to follow him. He led the way to the front door just as Agnes and Jon emerged from the back room. Jon carried one small suitcase and an overnight bag. He gave Justin an odd look, then walked out the door, and put the luggage in the trunk of the car. He returned to act as a front guard for the old woman.

"Mrs. Sawyer, I'm sorry, but we have to hurry. I don't want to take a chance with your life," Justin said, slipping an arm around her shoulders and hurrying her to the car. Once she was seated between him and Kathryn and they were on the way, he inquired, "How are your finances, Mrs. Sawyer?" It wouldn't do to send the lady off to a large city like Chicago without sufficient means to live better than she had been.

"Mr. Crown, I never spent a penny of the money Angela gave me. I have enough. It doesn't take much for me to live on. I'll move in with my sister. She's been after me for some time to come live with her." She gave him a weak smile. "I'll be fine, don't you worry about me."

"I'm sure you will, Mrs. Sawyer, but I want to make sure." He leaned forward in the seat. "Jon, I want you to fly Mrs. Sawyer to Chicago and stay with her until she is safely at her sister's. Once she's settled, and you have a bodyguard in place, come back to St. Petersburg. Hopefully, everything will be settled, and Mrs. Sawyer can come back for the funeral. Then, we'll be able to go home to Colorado." He leaned back, patting the old lady's hand. "Jon will take good care of you."

Justin retrieved his cell phone and dialed Harv's number. He didn't answer. Probably still tied up with the police. It was getting late, and he was tired and hungry. Kathryn had to be as well. They hadn't stopped since her attempted abduction at noon. Now it was close to five o'clock. He'd be glad to get back to the hotel and review the contents of the package Mrs. Sawyer had given them. He noticed Kathryn was gripping it like a lifeline. She looked drawn. He was sure the day's events were taking their toll on her nerves. They were on his.

He read about murders every day in the papers or heard on the nightly news about some person killing another. Angela's death was up close and personal, an attempt by someone to silence her. She'd had the foresight to try and protect herself. It hadn't worked because she had been dealing with a madman.

At the airport, Jon drove right to the plane and Justin boarded with Mrs. Sawyer. Once she was securely strapped into her seat, and Jon was warming up the engine, he departed, and Jon closed the plane's door. Justin climbed in behind the wheel of the sedan and headed back to the Vinoy.

All the way to the room, Kathryn clutched the package to her breast. She acted as if she was afraid to let go of it, afraid it might vanish. Once in the room, she sat in a chair staring down at it in her lap.

"You might as well open it, Kathryn."

"I'm terrified of what's in it." Her hands trembled as she played with the ribbon. "Don't you think it's ironic that Angela tied it with this red ribbon? I guess in some ways it's appropriate since the price for it was her life."

Slowly, she untied the bow and knot and dropped the ribbon on the table next to the chair. She opened the plain brown box and stared at a stack of eight by ten photographs. Placed neatly on top of the pile was a long white envelope with two names written in big bold letters on the outside. It was Robert's handwriting. One name on the envelope was Kate, and the other was Kathryn. The envelope flap was not sealed, and she removed several handwritten pages. It was a letter from Robert.

Dear Kathryn or Kate,

Ain't life a bitch. If you're still alive and reading this letter, then I'm dead, and Angel must be too. We had a good run while it lasted, but I'll be damned if I'll let him get away with it all. I won't lie and say I'm sorry. I liked the money too much. Randolph Blanding has lots, more since he killed Abby Pennington. Guess you didn't know that, did you? I was outside the French doors with my camera and saw it all.

I came by the Sands Point house an hour early to wait for Kathryn to pick up Abby. As usual, I needed money. I hid out at the back of the house. The doors were open just enough for my camera lens to fit in the crack. Anyway, Randolph and Abby were having a hell of a fight over a report and photographs taken by some private detective she'd hired. Abby was going to have him thrown out of the Snell Isle house after she convinced his wife to divorce him. I overheard her tell him how she planned on ruining him and his perfect reputation. You know how he is about his public image. She was going to show the world what a perverted bastard he really was.

I started snapping pictures right after the first blow. The bastard hit the old woman with a poker. I couldn't have stopped him. He would have killed me as well. The photographs and negatives should be with this letter. When he charged out of the house, I took off and followed him. I don't know which one of you two he was chasing. You both have the same color hair. I only know one of you witnessed the murder, the same as me. Never saw the vehicle until I drove past the accident and saw both your cars were involved. Randolph was at the scene bent over a body. I don't know if he was trying to help or hinder.

I followed the ambulance to the hospital and hung around for a while. The survivor was put in a trauma room with another person. The cops wouldn't let me in.

Guess the idea of blackmail popped up the next

day when I stopped off at the hospital. You had been put in a private room on Dr. Blanding's orders. I waited around until the private duty nurse took a break, then I entered your room. The woman in the bed was unconscious, and her head and face were covered with bandages. I couldn't tell who it was in bed. The name on the wristband said, Kathryn Clark. I don't know why that bothered me, but it did. I started to raise the blanket to look at the woman's body. That's when Dr. Blanding caught me in the room and went berserk. He ordered me out of the hospital. So I'm not positive who lived or died in that accident.

I waited a week before calling Dr. Blanding for a meeting. He was willing to pay for my silence. Especially after I sent him a copy of the photographs. It cost him more than he wanted to spend, but he paid. I have another item which should get me a big score off him if he doesn't kill me first.

I plan to head up to Nashville once I have the money. I'm leaving this package with Angel in case something happens to me. Dr. Blanding is crazy. I have to be careful how I handle him. He's warned me to stay away from you. Said he'd kill me if I come near you. I feel it's only fair to warn you about him. The few times I've followed you since your recovery, you've acted strange. I don't know what he has done to you, but you're different. You're not like the Kate or Kathryn I knew. I finally figured it out. The answer is right there in those photographs, but you're going to have to find it like I did. Nothing's free. The answer is going to cost you either way. Good luck.

Robert"

The letter ended, and Kathryn almost could hear Robert laughing at the joke he was playing on her. She looked up at Justin. "That bastard! This letter still doesn't prove who I am. Robert does say Randolph killed my grandmother and he took pictures of him committing the act. He witnessed the murder and was blackmailing my father."

She shuffled through the photographs in all their colorful gore. "My God, how many did he take?" Listed on the back of each picture were the date and name of the place where the snapshot was taken. There were shots of her at the beach, taken as she looked before the accident. There were shots of Kate taken outside the dinner theater, plus numerous shots of each woman before the car crash. Then only pictures of the survivor.

There were casual shots, scenes of Randolph and Kate unaware they were being photographed. Others of her at a restaurant, at a gym, a nightclub and many others. When Kathryn picked up the shot showing Randolph with his arm raised, poker in hand, and Abby on the floor covered in blood, she turned away and put the stack down, unable to look at the pictures any longer.

She handed the letter and photos to Justin. "Read this and then look at the pictures. See if you can see what he's talking about. He said the answers are in these photographs. The only thing I can see is my vindication of my grandmother's murder and that we need to notify the police."

Justin studied the top picture of Randolph with the poker in his hand. "You're right about the police, but I want to talk to Harv first."

"Then call him and get him over here," Kathryn stated. "I want my name cleared of all charges. Mostly I want to be there when the cops put handcuffs on the great Dr. Blanding and lead him away. He murdered Abby, and the bastard needs to pay for it."

"Aren't you curious about the other photos and papers?"

"Of course, but I don't want to give my father the chance to run."

"Kathryn, he's not going anywhere. He doesn't know we have the package. Mrs. Sawyer is on her way to Chicago. I seriously doubt he has a clue that anyone is wise to what he did. Let me see what Robert was referring to in these photographs. Maybe if we sort them by date, we'll see something." Justin began to lay each glossy on the table, arranged by date and person, Kate, or Kathryn.

Kathryn couldn't get Robert's letter out of her mind. He'd written the truth about Abby's murder with photographs to back up his statement. She now knew her ex-husband had known Kate before, had even married her prior to their marriage. Why had he followed her and Randolph after the accident? Robert said in the letter, that she was different, not herself.

Accidents change some people, but there was another detail that was bugging her. According to Dan, Justin and her mother, she was missing four years of her life. As Kate Clark, she had spent a year recuperating at the Blanding home. That accounted for one year. Justin said they had been married just over a year. If, as Angel said, Robert had been missing for nearly two years, and they both had disappeared around the same time, then that was four years. What had she been doing from Kate's recovery in 2015 and the move to Colorado in 2016? What had she been doing during that year?

"Justin, are any of those photographs dated 2015?" She held her breath, afraid of his answer.

"Yes, several. Robert was a busy boy. He must have followed you and Dr. Blanding everywhere. There are shots of you walking on a beach, at a restaurant, coming out of a restaurant, on a balcony and several others. Why?"

She dropped into the chair. "Oh my God. How could he? How could he have done such a thing to me?"

"What are you talking about, Kathryn?" Justin stopped and stared at her.

"My father," she cried. "Don't you understand what he did? After my facial reconstruction, I lived here almost a year before moving to Colorado."

It didn't register with Justin what she was referring to.

"I didn't believe him, but he did make me his mistress. His own daughter! What kind of a sick monster is he that he'd do such a thing? What kind of person am I to let it happen? I knew he hated me, but I never realized how much." Her eyes filled with anguish as she gazed up at Justin.

He pulled her into his arms and held her tight. What a terrible blow for Kathryn to find out exactly how vicious her father really was. A dark expression settled on his face. He seethed with rage at the man responsible for all her pain. Randolph Blanding deserved to burn in hell.

"It's not your fault, love," he whispered into her hair. "You didn't know what you were doing. The blame belongs to him, not you. He's a monster. Any man who'd take his amnesiac daughter and do what he did has to be sick or insane."

She clung to him, drawing strength. Then, she began to pace, all the time muttering to herself over and over, "It can't be true, it can't be true." She stopped at the table and looked at the photographs, then resumed her pacing. It was difficult for her mind to grasp the full implications of Robert's letter and the images on the prints. She felt that somehow she should have known better.

Justin tried to reason with her, to absolve her of any blame. It wasn't until he said, "Kathryn, you're going on an assumption from Robert's letter and those damned pictures that you slept with Randolph. What if that never happened? What if all the innuendo made by your ex-husband isn't true? What if he did all this just to get back at you? Remember, you had filed for divorce. He was about to lose his chance at the Pennington fortune. You were going to inherit a lot of money when your grandmother died. Back in Colorado, you told me she was not well, that she had a heart condition."

He paused. He now had Kathryn's attention. It was as if he could see it all. Robert going to the Pennington house to lay in wait for his ex-wife. Then the idea took seed. What if he gave the old woman a heart attack and she died? Kathryn would find the body, call an ambulance and then inherit all that money. Robert would be rolling in the green. Justin presented that idea to Kathryn. He could see her mind working, her expression changing as she began to contemplate the concept.

"Why would Robert lie about everything?" She stood studying the picture of Randolph holding the poker. "He got what he wanted from my father," she said. Had he been lying from the beginning?

"You said he was a good photographer." He pointed to the prints, "These prove it. All I'm saying is that he could have doctored the images to show what he wanted to show."

"Why would he?" Kathryn asked. "In his letter, he knows he's living on borrowed time, that's why Cantree planned the trip to Nashville, one last score and he was off to music city. He went on a trip all right, but not the one he'd planned. Anyway, that's what the man who abducted me implied. Don't forget, I witnessed his murder. That explains our disappearance on the same day. He was killed, and I ran."

"That may all be true, but I don't believe you were Randolph's mistress."

"If I wasn't, then how did I live for those seven months before I ran off to Colorado?"

"Maybe you received a settlement from the auto insurance. Maybe Randolph felt guilty about what he was doing and paid for the apartment, food, and expenses. I don't know. But, I will not believe you willingly had an incestuous relationship with your father. Knowing you the way I do, you told him no, and that's another reason why he hates you as much as he does."

Justin had given her a lifeline of hope. She prayed he was right. Lord, she was tired, so weary of it all she could cry but refused to shed one more tear. The sun had gone down, and they hadn't even noticed. She looked out the window. Looking northeast across the bay, she could see the lights of Tampa cutting the dark purple sky. People were home from work, settling in for a quiet meal and television. Here she was looking out from her train wreck of a life. She wasn't sure what she felt if anything. Her world had gone mad, and she was hanging onto the only stable person in her life, Justin. She turned, and he was behind her. She wrapped her arms around his waist and laid her head on his chest. "Can we survive this together, Justin?"

He pulled her closer. "You know we can. I won't leave you again, Kathryn. Like I told you before, I don't care who you are, Kate Clark or Kathryn Blanding. You're Kathryn Crown now, my wife, no one else. That's all that matters to me. Anything before our wedding day doesn't count. As the old saying goes, that was the first day of the rest of our life. Corny, but true."

"When are we going to confront Randolph?" She couldn't bring herself to refer to him as her father. Never again would she do that. She concealed the rage she felt. Her fury had started as a pinpoint of anger and had steadily grown. She had to face him; but dreaded it, not for herself, but because of what it would do to her mother. The son of a bitch would never admit to what he had done. He'd be forced to when she threw the pictures in his face and demanded to know why. The photographs did not lie. He'd was a murderer. She had to laugh. The great Randolph Blanding being brought to his knees by his daughter. It didn't matter what he had done to her. She couldn't change the past, but she would make him pay.

If Justin knew of her plans, he would try and stop her. He wouldn't want her to see Randolph alone. She had to. Taking off her sandals, she moved to sit on a chair facing him.

"We're not going to confront Dr. Blanding," Justin stated. "We're going to let Harv and the police handle it. I'm going to have him pick up the photos of Randolph killing Abby and take them to the police. The other prints, the letter, and negatives, I want him to have analyzed to see if they've been altered. Maybe he'll see something we don't." He pulled out his cell phone. Harv was still at the police station. As soon as he finished, he'd take a cab back to the hotel.

Kathryn didn't say anything as she listened to him explain what had happened and asked Harv to pick up the box the next day. She looked at her watch. It was almost on 8:30. Feigning a yawn, she was anything but sleepy; but had to make Justin think she was exhausted.

Justin felt drained, overburdened from too many revelations and too few definite answers. The day had been filled with danger and stress. Tomorrow would bring further inquiries from the police about their involvement in Angela's death, the abduction attempt, and the evidence against Randolph. Would the police be willing to re-open the Pennington murder and clear Kathryn Blanding with the evidence in their possession? They'd have to wait and see.

When he saw Kathryn yawn, he was relieved. Maybe they could go to bed and get a decent night's sleep. But first, they needed to eat. They had been running on nervous energy all day.

"Are you hungry?" he asked. "We can ring for room service."

Kathryn hadn't been aware she was hungry until Justin suggested food. All of a sudden she was ravenous.

"I'd better eat something, or I won't make it through to morning. Order us whatever is the fastest."

Justin placed an order for turkey club sandwiches and a pot of hot herbal tea for Kathryn, and a double scotch and water for himself. After his bender in Colorado, he shouldn't be ordering booze, but he wanted a stiff drink to help him relax.

Maybe, within the next two to three days, everything would be over. Then they could all fly home to Colorado and put this nightmare behind them. Kathryn needed a stable home, where she could be happy and never have to worry about who she was other than being his wife.

Their meal came. Kathryn cleared the table, stuffing the photographs back into the slender brown package and placing it on top of her suitcase. Starved, she attacked the sandwich and tea, then sighed, contented. Once her appetite was sated, she brushed her teeth and prepared for bed. Justin followed suit. She lay on her side facing the bathroom door. When Justin joined her in bed, he pulled her against him. She made no attempt to resist and turned to give him a kiss. When he pressed closer against her, she whispered, "Not tonight, Justin. I can't. Give me a few days, please."

He kissed her again and curled his body around hers. "Go to sleep, love. All I want tonight is to hold you."

She sighed with relief. From experience, she knew it wouldn't take Justin long to fall asleep. Then she had an errand to run.

Chapter Twenty

Kathryn hadn't meant to drift off. She awoke with a start and sat up on the side of the bed. Quickly she glanced in Justin's direction, hoping he hadn't awakened. He stirred, and then rolled over, his back to her, his breathing rhythm unchanged. She glanced at her watch. It was 11:40. She had planned to wait until Justin was deep in sleep, then slip out of bed, dress in the other room and sneak out, taking the photos with her. She had wanted to catch Randolph earlier but would have to settle for now.

By the time she got dressed in black slacks, a dark blouse, jacket, and slipped on her sandals, it would be after midnight. In her rush to leave, she forgot and dashed out, leaving the photographs behind.

It was almost twenty after twelve by the time the taxi dropped her off in front of the Blanding house. She waited until the vehicle turned the corner. Two houses down, she noticed another car cruising slowly by, and waited for the other to pass, then continued up the circular driveway.

Randolph would still be up. He kept late hours and rose early, existing on four to five hours of sleep each night. She made her way toward the back of the house and the veranda with the French doors. The light was on in his study. She could see him clearly through the glass pane.

The dark paneled walls, lined with shelves of unread books, shone from their daily polishing. Randolph hated dust. The heavy, dark leather sofa and chairs, and the massive stone fireplace added to the gloom in the room. Sunshine was not allowed in. That's one of the reasons she hated that room.

It was a dungeon above ground where she had stood and faced him while he drilled her on the importance of conduct and a proper public image. Then he doled out his punishment with his fist or belt.

Tonight he was sitting in the brown leather chair behind his antique mahogany desk, reviewing a file. His caseload was heavy from people willing to pay for the kind of perfection only he could give them. She was proof of his ability with a knife; his ability to turn human flesh and bone into clay and remold it to his will.

She had forced herself not to dwell on what she would have looked like if he hadn't restored her face. Even the wrong face was better than the alternative. She refused to feel a grain of sympathy for him. He owed her. Owed her for every lost year, the missed childhood, the struggle she had endured her entire life. Owed her for the crimes he had committed against her mother and her brother. Tonight he was going to pay. She tried the doorknob. Slowly she opened the door and stepped into the room.

He looked up, unsurprised. "I wondered when you'd finally get here. I expected you. His grey suit jacket was tossed in one of the chairs sitting before his desk. His crisp white shirt was pristine.

Kathryn casually moved to stand behind one of the leather chairs in front of his desk, to quell the shaking of her knees. To hide the trembling of her hands, she gripped the chair back. "All I want to do is talk."

"What could you possibly have to say that I would want to hear? I most certainly have nothing to say to you," Randolph sneered.

"Oh, but you'll want to hear what I have to say. Two reasons actually, Robert saw you kill Abby and left the evidence with Angel." She saw him pale a little beneath his tan.

"That's impossible. I didn't kill Abby, my daughter did."

She spat the words at him, "I am your daughter, and I did not kill Abby! You did! Robert took pictures of you, which will prove I'm innocent of my grandmother's murder."

"No matter what you claim, you are not my daughter!" His voice rose, and the veins stood out in his neck. There was an actual pained expression on his face for a second, and then it vanished like smoke. The beast was back.

"You stupid bitch! You were warned not to come back here. Why wouldn't you listen?" He lowered his right hand to open a drawer. "I tried to save you, Kate. I hired that man to warn you off after a friend of mine saw you in Colorado. He even shot at you. Still, you had to come to Florida. I never wanted it to come to this."

He rubbed his eyes as if tired. "Why wouldn't you believe me when I told you I loved you?" He stood. "I did love you, Kate, but I can't let you destroy all I've worked for. Robert could have altered those photographs to try and blackmail me. Now here you come along with the same idea. Angel was just as stupid as her brother trying to rob me of all that was mine. It cost her."

He had been the murderer, not the other man!

The image of his attack disgusted Kathryn. "You beat and tortured that woman, then killed her. For what? A reputation built on quicksand. All your lies eventually would boil to the surface someday anyway."

"No! I thought I had gotten rid of all my obstacles. Abby, I shut her up and destroyed all the documents she had. You and my daughter managed to do each other in, her dead, you with amnesia. Robert had a win-win situation until he got greedy. He came by the condo that night with all his lies about you and to deliver his ultimatum. He wanted a million dollars. I wasn't about to give him that kind of money."

The anger was building in him. Kathryn could see it in the flash of his eyes and the wild gestures of his hands. Why hadn't she admitted to herself that if he'd murder Abby, he'd kill her as well, even if she was his daughter? Cold fear made her shiver as he continued to rant on about Robert.

"He was a stupid man." He stared at her hard. "How could you ever have let him touch you, let alone marry such scum?" He shook his head as if trying to shake off some of the anger. "If I didn't give him the money, he was going to the papers with the story that I had turned my daughter into my mistress." He paused as past images raced through his mind. "Do you know what that would have done to me in this town?"

She knew. Randolph would have lost everything. To prevent that from happening, he'd stop at nothing.

"I killed him. His head cracked so easy, like a soft-boiled egg." He almost smiled as he said it.

The sound and image of the iron, poker striking Robert's head would live on in her nightmares.

He reached into the drawer. When he raised his hand, it held a gun. He rose and started to walk around the desk, his gun hand hanging at his side. Kathryn moved to the next chair to maintain the distance between them but kept her eyes on the gun. He stopped

"You. I saw you standing just outside the door in the hallway. You looked at me as if I was mad, then you grabbed your purse and ran from the apartment. I didn't follow you because I knew it would never be the same. You had heard what Robert said and believed it. I never saw you again." He paused, and an expression of anguish briefly flashed across his face, then it was gone, and the anger was back. "I had that man I hired to take care of the body, and then I packed up all your things and put them in storage. There was no one to report you as missing other than myself. Besides me, who cared where you went? I told everyone you moved back to California. No one could dispute my word." He started toward her again.

"Stop," she said, and he did, remaining near the other chair. "I didn't hear what Robert told you that night. If I heard it, I don't remember it. I'm sure all the information he had on you is in the papers and photographs he left behind. Justin has everything, including the letter from Robert." Her anger was a hot burning knife cutting through her fear and giving her the courage to face him and force him to admit the truth.

"I want you to know exactly what I think of you." Her lip curled in disgust as she dished out her venom her voice growing louder with each word. "You are a perverted, repulsive man who is not fit to live. You're going to be locked away for the rest of your life. Not only for what you did to me, and Abby, but for the murders of Angel and Robert. Justin and I are going to see to it. You remember? They execute murderers in this state."

His face turned white as the image entered his mind.

He looked at her in confusion for a moment, and then his anger took control. His eyes became crazed. He looked around the room, at all his treasures, the paintings, the sculptures, the first edition books. She was going to take it all away from him, his good name, his reputation among his peers, just like Abby had threatened, just like Robert and Angel. She had to be stopped, the same as the others. She was no different than they were. Without hesitation, he raised the gun and fired.

She never heard the loud crash or saw the glass shatter when the French door slammed back into the wall as Justin charged at Randolph. Kathryn's world exploded into a black sky filled with flashing stars and searing pain as she was thrown backward by the force of the bullet. Without a sound, she slipped into a black void.

It was the click of the room's door shutting that brought Justin upright in bed. He called out Kathryn's name. When there was no answer, he threw back the bedspread and jumped out of bed. She wouldn't dare try and face Blanding alone, would she? She couldn't be that crazy. He checked the bathroom on the off chance his suspicions were wrong. Just as he feared, the suite was empty. He quickly threw on the clothes he had worn that day.

As he raced to the hotel lobby, he dialed Harv, with orders to rendezvous at the Blanding home on Snell Isle. Harv was to call the police on his way to the island. Justin exited the hotel lobby in time to see a yellow taxi pull away with Kathryn in the back seat. He jumped in the next cab as it pulled up to take the other's place and felt like a fool when he said, "Follow that cab."

He instructed the driver to hang back far enough so as not to be seen. No sense in letting Kathryn know he was following her. Once on the island, he made the driver drop him off two houses away and waited in the shadows until both vehicles were out of sight. Kathryn was a ghost moving against the darker shadows as she made her way toward the back of the house. Trying to be as quiet as possible, he hurried to follow, but not be seen.

He wondered why she would risk facing Randolph Blanding alone and chance getting herself killed. He could feel his old doubts about his wife creeping back into his head. He had told her none of it mattered to him, and he refused to let it. He banished the doubts. She was Kathryn Crown now, and that was all he cared about. That and saving her life. If he were to do that, he'd have to hurry. Kathryn had vanished around the side of the house.

As he neared the back corner of the house, a hand touched his shoulder. He whirled to face his assailant, arm drawn back and fist clenched. Harv stood almost nose to nose with him, a finger to his lips.

Justin whispered, "You almost got a fist in the nose, pal."

Harv smiled and shook his head. Justin was big, strong and fast, but he wasn't trained to take a man like Harv down.

"Come on," he said and led the way toward the room with the lights on "We have to find Kathryn before everything starts coming apart. Randolph is a man on the edge and can jump over at any minute."

Harv drew his gun, his black clothes blending into the shadows. When they reached the French doors, they saw Randolph and Kathryn facing each other. The rage on the doctor's face was indicative that he had lost control. At the precise instant, Randolph started to raise the gun, Justin charged the door, but was too late to stop him from firing. Before he could get off the second round, Harv fired his weapon. The bullet caught Randolph in the chest. He remained standing long enough to gasp out a raspy whisper.

"Is she dead?" he gasped. His legs gave way as he sank to his knees, blood running down his left shirt pocket toward his belt. Those were his last words. He collapsed on the carpet without an answer, eyes open and fixed.

The sound of sirens filled the night air. Harv stepped through the shattered door into the room and rushed to where Justin was cradling Kathryn.

Justin yelled, "She's still alive! Call an ambulance!" Then chaos ensued. The police rushed into the room at the exact moment Sara Blanding opened the study door and screamed.

Fire Rescue raced in behind the police while Justin tried to stop the bleeding coming from Kathryn's chest. She was unconscious and deathly pale. The EMTs took over; quickly applying a pressure bandage to the wound. They inserted a needle in her arm, started an IV, and immediately transported her to the hospital. Justin rode in back of the ambulance all the way. Once again Harv remained behind to confer with the police and console Mrs. Blanding.

An hour later, he found Justin sitting in the surgery waiting room, his face pale and drawn.

"Any word yet?" He took a seat in the chair next to him.

"None." Worry lines creased Justin's forehead, and stubble shadowed his jaws and chin. He regarded Harv with eyes mirroring exhaustion and fear.

"How was it you got to the Blanding home so fast?" It was an idle question, one to try and keep his mind off the life and death struggle behind the double doors in a room down a hall.

"I was almost to the hotel when I got your call. So I was right behind you all the way to the Blanding house." He changed the subject. "You know she's going to be all right." It was a statement, not a question. "She is a tough lady."

Justin leaned forward, clasped his hands and rested his arms on his knees. "She deserved more than I gave her, dammit." He was carrying a heavy load of guilt, and it showed. "All she wanted was for me to believe in her when no one else would. I let my own stupid doubts cloud my judgment. I wasn't there for her when she needed me. This is my fault."

"No way, man. This mess started long before you ever met your wife."

"That may be, but part of the blame rests on me. At least now we know Kathryn was telling the truth. She really is Randolph's daughter."

"Maybe."

"What do you mean, Harv, maybe?"

"I'm sorry Justin, but there's no proof that she is Kathryn Blanding."

"That's impossible. You heard what Randolph said."

"Yes, he kept denying she was his daughter right up to the end. Keep that in mind, Justin."

"I don't care anymore. It doesn't matter. Kathryn is my wife. Whoever she is, I love her, dammit, and that's all that is important to me now."

"We can solve this riddle once and for all with a DNA test," Harv said. Justin looked at him without saying a word, so he continued. "Mrs. Blanding was not overly grieved by her husband's death and blamed him for the loss of her son and daughter. The woman has lost everyone she loved because of him. Her mother, her son, and lastly her daughter. She wants to know if there is a chance your wife could be her daughter. She's willing to give her blood for testing. She's going to have her daughter's remains exhumed for DNA testing and wants you to authorize the test for your wife. Will you do it?"

"Maybe I don't want to know anymore."

"That's fine for you, but what about Sara Blanding? Would you deny her the joy of getting her daughter back? I can't believe you're that selfish."

"I'm not."

"Didn't think so. You talk with the doctor about the test, and I'll take care of the rest."

"One thing that has bothered me from the start," Justin said. "Kathryn Blanding's fingerprints had to have been all over her apartment. After the accident, didn't the police try to identify the victim by her fingerprints?

"I doubt it. Remember, the great Dr. Blanding was the first person on the scene. He identified both women. No one had reason to doubt him."

"What about now? Does Mrs. Blanding have anything that might have her daughter's prints on it?"

"You won't give up on this. Time has destroyed any chance that her fingerprints would be preserved. The woman we know as Kate Clark lived in that house for a year. Her prints would be all over the place, as well as his daughter's prints. There's no way of telling whose are whose. Give it a rest, Justin. The DNA tests will solve the problem. The results take a good six weeks. We'll have our answer sooner if I can push some buttons."

The double door sprang open, and a tall, slender, gray-haired man in green scrubs walked straight to Justin.

"Mr. Crown, I'm Dr. Wallace. We removed the bullet, but your wife's condition isn't stable. We'll be moving her to ICU after recovery. I suggest you go home. You can come back and see her for a few minutes, but after that, go home and get some rest. It's all up to her now."

Justin had expected the worst, and his shoulders sagged with relief. Kathryn was still alive, and where there was life, there was hope. Like Harv said, she was a tough woman. She'd pull through. He had to hang onto that belief, or he'd never make it. Losing Kathryn would destroy him. He'd realized that the moment Randolph had raised his arm to fire the gun.

"Harv, wait for me?" he said and followed the doctor.

"I'll be right here."

Justin was stunned when he saw Kathryn. Her skin was the color of paste, and she had tubes in every orifice and wires leading from her to monitors. He was afraid to touch her, but bent down and planted a light kiss on her forehead and held her hand. He whispered close to her ear, not sure if she could hear him.

"I'm here Kathryn. The doctors say you're going to be fine. I want you to know that I love you, always have, always will. You have to come back to me, babe. I can't make it without you." His voice broke. "I was stupid for ever doubting you. I'll never do that again. Don't leave me, Kathryn," he pleaded. "Please, I need you so much." A tight knot in his chest was threatening to rise and choke him.

"The doctor won't let me stay any longer. You rest, and I'll be close by." He squeezed her hand. For an instant, he thought she had pressed his hand. When he looked at her face, her eyes were still closed, and there was no sign of consciousness.

He returned to the waiting room where Harv was

still slouched in a chair. He rose when Justin entered the room, and they walked to the elevators.

"I'm taking you back to the hotel. You need to get some sleep," Harv said.

"I will. Tomorrow, I'll call my mom and dad, then Jon and Etta, they'll want to know about Kathryn," Justin said. He tried to stifle the yawn but couldn't. He was exhausted, and it showed.

"Jon already knows. I called him. He'll fly back in the morning. Mrs. Sawyer is safe now that Randolph is dead. She can come back with him if she wants." They had to exit the hospital through the Emergency Room. Harv glanced at his watch. It was 4:35 a.m. They would get to the hotel in time to get four hours of sleep and return to the hospital.

At the hotel, Justin climbed out of the car.

"Justin," Harv called before he could walk away, "I'll come by the hospital later to check on you and Kathryn. I still have a few things to tie up with the police and finalize some paperwork."

"Speaking of paperwork," Justin said, "come up to the room. Mrs. Sawyer gave us a box of evidence against Randolph. You can give it to the police. Robert Cantree took photographs of Randolph killing Abigail Pennington. Give those to the police. That'll clear Kathryn of the murder charge. Keep the letter and the rest of the prints. Have them examined to see if they've been doctored."

Harv parked the car in a loading zone and followed Justin to the room. After Harv had the box in his possession and departed, Justin stripped off his clothes, took a hot shower and dropped into bed. Within seconds after his head hit the pillow, he was in a deep sleep.

Kathryn spent the next three days in ICU before being moved to a private room. Justin, Jon, and Harv stood around her bed waiting expectantly.

Gripping her hand, Justin watched her eyes flutter open and recognition register. She smiled up at him, muttered a soft "Hi," and then closed her eyes once more.

Justin wanted to have her immediately transported back to Colorado, and put under Dan Otis' care. Dr. Wallace would not hear of it. Her condition was still considered guarded, and until she was out of danger, he was not going to chance a setback. So they were stuck in St. Petersburg for the time being.

On his next visit, Kathryn was awake but still weak. She pushed the button to raise the head of the bed.

"Hi, Cowboy. You look like hell."

"Well, you look wonderful to me. How are you feeling?"

"Like someone shot me. My chest hurts like the devil, and the doctor said I'm lucky to be here. Is my father under arrest?"

"No, Kathryn. He was going to shoot you again. Harv was forced to kill him. I'm sorry."

"Don't be. How's my mother?"

"Coping. Sara's been here off and on. Each time, you were sleeping." Maybe it was the wrong time to bring up the subject, but it couldn't wait. "Kathryn, I need to ask you something."

She eyed him with suspicion, "Like what?"

"Harv made the suggestion, I agreed and so does your mother, that to prove beyond a shadow of a doubt, to her, not me," he quickly added. "That if you submit to a DNA test, it will prove who you are once and for all. Mrs. Blanding is having the test done on herself. She also had the body at the cemetery exhumed. We've even requested DNA testing on Randolph. Will you agree to have the test?"

"All right, Justin, once and for all, prove who I am." She glanced out the window. The sky was bright blue, and as she listened, she could hear the whirling thump of a helicopter landing. "How soon can the doctor release me? I want to go home to Colorado."

That was the first bright note in Justin's day. She wanted to go home. "The doctor said another couple of days, and you should be well enough to travel. I'll hire a nurse to accompany us back. I'm going back to the hotel to make all the arrangements." He bent and kissed her lightly on the lips. "I love you Kathryn, and that's all that matters to me."

"I love you too, Justin. I only want us to be happy together." Her eyes were starting to droop, as she fought off the sleep her body required.

"We will, babe. We will, I promise." Her eyes closed and Justin left, shutting the door partway so the noise in the corridor would not disturb her. At the nurse's station, he left a request for Dr. Wallace to contact him regarding the DNA testing and then headed back to the hotel.

He stopped to check messages at the reception desk in the hotel lobby. There was a message from Harv to call him regarding a statement for the police. He returned the call and scheduled a time to go to police headquarters and talk with them. Then he called Jon and made arrangements to fly back to Colorado in two days. He was surprised when Mrs. Blanding requested to come along. Seems her doubts about Kathryn's identity were wavering, and she was accepting the fact her daughter was his wife. Sara wanted to be there to help nurse her back to health. He agreed she could join them as long as she didn't upset Kathryn.

All business with the police was concluded by the end of the week. On Sunday morning, the first week of May, they flew back home to the Rockies. Justin prayed all their nightmares were finally behind them.

Chapter Twenty-one

They had lived through the nightmare of April. Back in Colorado, May's promise of spring had slipped past too quickly. Kathryn's crocus's had bloomed and faded, the flowering crabapple trees had burst into full bloom as had the lilacs. The forecast for snow was gone except for those freak storms that occur once in a while in the Rockies. The weather generally was warm and sunny with an occasional chilly day. Even in June, Pikes Peak was covered with a light layer of snow.

The trees had lost their first fuzzy bright green buds, and the leaves were turning a darker hue. Summer had arrived in all its glory, and the Fourth of July was just around the bend.

Kathryn had recovered, and their lives had resumed as if the past horrors had never happened, with one exception. Sara Blanding had blossomed caring for Kathryn. The circles under her eyes had disappeared, and the sadness in her was gone. She laughed all the time.

The main thing for Justin was that Kathryn was happy and they were a family. The family had grown. Etta and Sara had become the best of friends. Most nights found Etta, Jon, Sara, Kathryn and Justin sitting around the dinner table. Life was good.

Today was different. It had been over eight weeks since the request for the DNA tests were sent off. Harv had called right after breakfast with a request for a ten o'clock meeting. Justin did not tell Kathryn or Sara that he was coming to the house. It was now five after ten in the morning, and a smiling Harv sat on the sofa before the fireplace in Justin's study. Kathryn and Sara were on the back patio enjoying the warm weather.

"You have good news, I hope?" Justin dreaded his answer.

"Depends on how you look at it.

"It won't change anything for me," Justin said, "but it will set Sara's mind at ease. She and Kathryn are as close as any mother and daughter could be. I just don't want to be the one to destroy the relationship."

"You don't have to."

"Then my wife really is Kathryn Blanding?"

"Yes and no." Harv gave Justin a wicked grin, enjoying the prolonging of his agony.

"For Christ's sake Harv quit dragging this out." He hated it when the man refused to get to the point.

"You have to let me explain. Your wife is Kathryn Blanding, but not the one she thinks she is."

"Great, that makes a lot of sense." It was worse than he thought.

"Here's how it goes. Remember Randolph saying something about Abby hiring a private investigator?" He shifted his position trying to get comfortable.

"Yeah," Justin growled.

"I found him," Harv said. He had Justin's complete attention. "Mr. Paul Mason keeps meticulous records and the originals of all his reports to his clients." Harv was enjoying watching Justin squirm with impatience.

"Abigail Pennington had hired Mr. Mason continuously for years to investigate various people. Her main interest, needless to say, was Randolph. She wanted as much dirt on him as Mr. Mason could find. She had Kate Clark, Robert Cantree and his sister Angel all investigated, as well as Mrs. Sawyer. There was another man by the name of Sergei Romanski involved in this affair. He worked as the family chauffeur for a short time."

He paused, considering where to begin. "This mess begins back in late 1968 when Sara Pennington was seventeen years old and considered herself a flower child."

Justin arched an eyebrow at that revelation.

"Oh yes, that mild-mannered, won't raise her voice, woman staying at your house was as wild as you could get in the sixties, and just as defiant. She ran off with a neighbor's son and attended the Woodstock Music Festival. Abby Pennington had a fit. That old woman was a person with a strong hand where her daughter, Sara, was concerned. It took Mrs. Pennington several months to find her. She had her hauled back, using the threat of having her committed to a mental hospital, Abby forced her daughter into marriage with a local up and coming doctor, one Randolph Blanding."

"My God, Abby did that?" Justin was stunned. The way Kathryn talked, she was a sweet, timid, elderly lady.

"Oh yes. It gets better. Abby was aware that Blanding came from an abusive background, but he was the ideal son-in-law. Handsome, well thought of in the community, and a doctor. She felt Sara needed a strong man to control her. They were married in June of 1970. Randolph never laid a hand on her at first. I will give the man credit; he tried to make his marriage work. Sara would have none of it. She didn't want him to touch her, so he forced her. That was the beginning of the abuse. She became pregnant and gave birth to Henry in 1971. The boy took after his mother in personality. He was a gentle soul. After he grew older, he became the peacemaker between his mother and father. Odd as it may sound, Randolph worshiped his son.

"Right before Randolph was scheduled to go to California for a medical seminar in January 1980, he found out Sara had taken a lover, Abby's chauffeur. That's right, Sergei Romanski. He was furious when he found out, but couldn't do anything about it. While in California, he must have decided to pay his wife back. He had a fling with a nurse, one Marsha G. Harris.

"Marsha was beautiful, a duplicate of your wife. I think Randolph might have cared for her, but she didn't have any money. Abby was paying him plenty to stay with Sara. He settled for bucks instead of love.

"While he was playing around with Miss Harris in California, Sara and Sergei were playing house back in Florida. Fate can be a bitch at times. Both women became pregnant around the same time." Harv rose and went to the mini-bar and poured himself a glass of water, taking a long drink before returning to his seat.

Justin was amazed by all the intimate information Harv had about the Blanding family. "How did you find out all this?"

"Paul Mason is a damn good investigator. Some of the info was given to Mason by Abby. Most of it came from his tracking down friends and relatives who knew the people involved. Marsha Harris told a girlfriend, who later moved to Florida and kept her informed about Randolph. Marsha married James Clark two months after she met him. He was listed as the father on her daughter's birth certificate.

"When Randolph came home and found out Sara was pregnant, he knew it wasn't his child. There was nothing he could do about it. If he wanted to be rich and continue the lifestyle to which he'd grown accustomed, he had to stay married to her. Right after Sara gave birth, that's when the actual beatings started.

"Sergei Romanski was involved in a hit and run auto accident and is in a nursing home. His bills are paid by a trust fund set up by Abby. He is paralyzed from the neck down, but his mind is sharp, and he has a long memory. He claims Randolph Blanding was behind his injury. It was never proven. Randolph had a solid alibi; he was at home with his wife and mother-in-law." Harv shook his head. Even he was amazed at the web Abigail Pennington had spun. She was a black widow at the center controlling everyone's life. It cost her.

"And Kathryn Blanding, Sara's daughter, what of her?" Justin said.

"Both women had a hell of a life, both were abused. Your wife has told you a big part of hers. The memories she has are accurate, but they're not her own. I checked with a buddy of mine, a psychiatrist. When Kate Clark woke up without a memory and was taken into the Blanding home to recuperate, she had such an influx of information supplied by Sara, and by Kathryn's journals, it was an overload. You have to consider the whole series of shocks to her, physically and mentally.

"First, those photographs supplied by Robert, I gave all but one to the police. The one I kept, in the dark shadows of the inside doorway to the murder room, with computer enhancement, you can see the faint image of a face. That face belonged to Kate Clark. Whatever was said in that room, she heard it, just as Robert did. We'll never know why she was at Abby's house that day, but she was. The answer to that question is buried in her lost memories and with Randolph.

"Anyway, she witnessed Abby's murder. She ran for her life and was in a major accident which resulted in her amnesia. Then, lucky her, she is a witness to Robert's murder. If I had been her, I'd want to forget who I was too." Harv sat shaking his head in wonder.

"As for the Blanding girl, she should have been a writer. Her journals are so detailed about her life, Kate Clark couldn't help but know everything about her. From the time the girl was around nine or ten, she kept a detailed daily record of what happened in her life. Anything prior to that time, Sara Blanding loaded her daily with all the information.

"My doctor friend told me, he doubts if Kate will ever regain her memory due to the numerous blunt force traumas she's suffered to her head. So when, as your wife, she was in another auto accident, and again struck on the head, she woke up with all of Kathryn Blanding's memories."

"What did the DNA results show?"

"Your wife is Randolph Blanding's daughter. Sara's daughter died in the accident."

Justin rubbed his forehead, a worried frown on his face. "What about Randolph's claim that my wife was not his daughter?"

"He was in denial. It's that simple. As much as he was capable, I think he loved Kate Clark. He couldn't handle the idea of what he had done, so he denied she was his daughter."

"I see," Justin said.

"I don't think you do. For all intent and purposes, Kate Clark essentially died in that accident as well. Her memory of her prior life was erased. She really believes she is Kathryn Blanding, Sara's daughter. By the way, how are they getting along?"

Justin turned to glance out the window at the two women sitting on the patio, heads bent close together as if they were sharing a secret.

"Fantastic," he said and turned back to Harv. "Sara has bloomed. They are ecstatic being with each other. It's been wonderful to see Kathryn laugh and carry on with Sara."

"Then why deprive yourself or them of this newfound happiness? Your wife is legally Kathryn Blanding."

Justin smiled and nodded in agreement. "You're right, Harv, except for one thing. My wife is Kathryn Crown. She might have been created from the lives of two women, but she's my wife now, and I intend to do everything in my power to see she stays happy. You can burn all this information as far as I'm concerned along with the DNA results. In fact, please do. I don't want Sara or Kathryn to ever get wind of its existence."

"Will do. The report will cause nothing but pain.

So now what?"

"The women are cooking me a belated surprise birthday dinner. Would you like to join us?"

"Thanks anyway, but I'm on a flight back to LA in two hours."

"Thanks for everything. Harv."

"That's what you pay me the big bucks for, buddy."

"Yeah, but you went above and beyond for me."

"You wanted the truth, and that's what I gave you. At least you're smart enough to put your loved one's happiness first." Harv offered his hand and Justin clasped it. Their friendship had grown stronger during this ordeal.

Justin followed him out of the study and to the front door and watched as Harv climbed into the rental car. As the vehicle drove away, Justin felt all the tension leave his body. The past couldn't be altered, but their future was in his control, and it was going to be the best he could make it. He had the woman he loved, and he knew she loved him. What more could any man ask for?

He knew the women wouldn't miss him; they were too engrossed with the joy of getting to know each other again. He informed Etta he was running into town on an errand and hurried out to his car. With him gone, his surprise party could get under way.

He was late arriving back home. He had made a stop at a jewelry store to buy two gifts and had to wait to have them engraved. They were all gathered around the dinner table waiting for him. He handed Kathryn and

Sara each a long, gray velvet box. They looked at him inquiringly, then at the boxes. He took his seat at the head of the table and filled his glass with wine.

"All the DNA tests are back. If you'll each open your gifts, you'll have the answer you've been waiting on." Justin said.

Sara opened her box. Inside was a wide gold bracelet with a heart filled with diamonds. Kathryn's gift was a necklace, a locket encrusted with diamonds. Justin stood and raised his glass. "I'd like to purpose a toast. To Kathryn Blanding Crown, my wife, and to Sara Blanding, my most gracious mother-in-law. I love you both with all my heart. I had each gift engraved with your names, and that I love you. This way, you'll never forget who you are, and what you mean to me."

Tears of joy rolled down Sara's face as she rose and rushed to Kathryn. They hugged each other close. Sara said, "My baby, I thought I had lost you forever." She looked at Justin. "Thank you, Justin, for giving me such happiness."

Kathryn turned to meet Justin's gaze.

"This means I am me again." She hesitated and then turned to Sara. "What about my gravestone in St. Petersburg? Should we have it changed?"

Sara patted her hand. "It's up to you, dear. Change it if you want to."

"I have everything I want right here. The name on a tombstone won't change that. Let's not disturb the dead," she said.

Kathryn looked at Justin and ran toward him. As she flew into his arms, the briefest of memories rose up to flit through her mind. She raced past a hallway mirror in

Abby's house and saw her face, as she looked now, reflected back. The memory was too fleeting to retain, so she shoved it back down where all the other memories were dead, buried, and locked away forever.

This was a different day, a new beginning, and she could imagine no other without Justin. Later she would tell him about the baby, later, much later, and they would celebrate together, as they should.

# # # #